THE CORNERS OF THE GLOBE

Also by Robert Goddard

THE CORNERS
OF THE GLOBE

A James Maxted Thriller

Robert Goddard

The Mysterious Press
New York

First published in the United Kingdom in 2014 by Transworld Publishers,
a division of the Random House Group

Printed in the United States of America

ISBN: 978-0-8021-2522-4
eISBN: 978-0-8021-8994-3

The Mysterious Press
An imprint of Grove Atlantic
154 West 14th Street
New York, NY 10011

Distributed by Publishers Group West

groveatlantic.com

16 17 18 19   10 9 8 7 6 5 4 3 2 1

THE CORNERS OF THE GLOBE

MAX COULD ONLY WISH HE HAD MADE THE CROSSING FROM Scotland in such weather: calm, cool and benign, the sea sparkling, the sky blue, with puffs of cloud herded at the horizon like well-behaved sheep. He stepped out of the Ayre Hotel into the peace of early morning, lit a cigarette and gazed around him.

The few locals already up and about would probably have identified him as a visitor even if they had not seen him leave the hotel. Tall, lean and youthfully handsome, dressed in clothes that were just a little too well cut to have been bought from an Orcadian tailor, Max looked what he was: a man out of his element. Yet he also looked relaxed and self-assured: a man as unlikely to attract suspicion as he was condescension.

He turned towards the harbour and started walking. The staff of the Ayre had warned him that Kirkwall Bay did not normally appear as it did now: an anchorage for dozens of US minesweepers and support vessels, most of them stationary at this hour, but some with smoke drifting up from their funnels. They were there to clear the thousands of mines laid around the Orkneys during the war, a task expected to take them many months.

Max knew little of the sea war, sharing the general prejudices of those who had engaged the enemy on the Western Front that the Royal Navy had had a cushy time of it, Jutland notwithstanding. His gale-tossed passage across the Pentland Firth had forced him to reconsider, however. He did not envy anyone who had spent the past four and more years in these waters.

Of all the places in the world where he had never expected to find himself, the Orkneys were high on the list. But he was aware that there were currently a good many people there who wished themselves elsewhere, doubtless including the crews of all those American minesweepers he could see strung out across the bay.

The same was certain to apply to the crews of the interned German High Seas Fleet, under Royal Naval guard in Scapa Flow. Until glancing at an atlas shortly before his journey north, Max had supposed Kirkwall overlooked the Flow and he would there-fore have a good view from the city of the captive ships. But Kirkwall was on the northern side of Mainland, the Orkneys' principal island, albeit at its narrowest part. To the south, enclosed by Hoy, South Ronaldsay and various other smaller islands, lay the vast natural roadstead of Scapa Flow, where seventy-four German warships were corralled at anchor.

Max would see them soon enough, of course. He knew that. They were why he had travelled to Orkney. And they were why he was out so early.

But early or not, he was not proof against unlooked-for encounters. As he passed the Girnel, the old grainstore facing the west pier, he saw a woman he recognized approaching along the harbour front. It was too late to think of avoiding her. She smiled and raised a hand. He smiled too and waved back.

Susan Henty was clearly no local herself, a tall, big-boned young woman with a horsey look about her, dressed in newish tweeds. She had auburn hair and a broad, open smile. Max imagined her as an enthusiastic rider to hounds in the Leicestershire countryside she had already told him she hailed from. She was impossible to dislike, which was half the problem in itself. He could not afford to appear secretive. But neither could he afford to reveal much about himself, least of all the truth.

'An early riser too, I see, Max,' she said as they met.

'I thought I'd take the morning air.'

'Me too. I walked down to the cathedral. Rather a fine structure, actually.'

'Selwyn not up yet, then?'

'Probably still in bed, poring over a map. He's very excited about seeing the Ring of Brodgar. As you are, I trust.'

'Well, I . . .'

'Selwyn's so pleased you agreed to help him.' Most women looked up at Max. Susan Henty engaged him levelly eye to eye. She lowered her voice confidentially. 'I'm not sure he believes I'm completely reliable when it comes to surveying.'

'I'm not sure *I'm* completely reliable.'

'Perhaps not, but you're a man, which makes all the difference.' She smiled. 'This trip's doing Selwyn no end of good, Max. I'm more grateful than I can say for your willingness to indulge him. How's your driving, by the way?'

'My driving?'

'Yes. You know.' She mimed turning a steering wheel.

'Ah, that. Not too hot, I'm afraid. A better pilot than a driver, to be honest.'

'Then I'll do it. One of the few blessings of the war is that it enabled women to take up things like driving without anyone disapproving. And I'm rather good behind the wheel, if I say so myself.'

'I'm sure you are.'

She affected a frown. 'Do I detect a note of sarcasm?'

'Not at all.'

'Mmm. I'll have to be on my guard with you. I can see that. Now, the hotel's recommended a garage where we can hire a car. And it looks like a fine day for it. So, shall we leave around ten?'

'Suits me.'

'Good. See you later, then.'

Max tipped his hat and watched Susan Henty stride on her way, back towards the Ayre. He disliked misleading her. He disliked every aspect of the subterfuge he was obliged to practise. It was a damnable game to have to play.

He lit another cigarette and waited until Susan was out of sight. Then he walked smartly along the street fronting onto the harbour, past the Kirkwall Hotel – of altogether grander appearance than the Ayre – and out along the east pier.

It was considerably longer than the west pier, with an extension added onto the seaward curve where it enclosed the harbour. Max strolled past a warehouse and assorted stacks of cargo and on towards the far end, passing another building that sported a prominently stencilled sign: US NAVAL PERSONNEL ONLY. An American marine of considerable bulk was standing by the door. He stifled a yawn as he returned Max's 'Good morning'.

A US Navy cutter was moored on one side of the pier. Max headed for the other side, propped his foot on a bollard and tossed the butt of his cigarette into the sea as he gazed idly out towards the massed minesweepers. He glanced at his watch and checked the time. Yes. He was neither late nor early. All he had to do was wait.

And not for long.

'GOOD MORNING.'

The man was bulky and bearded, but had a sprightly look about him that owed more than a little to his mischievously twinkling eyes. He was dark-haired, thirtyish, dressed in a US Navy lieutenant's uniform. He was wearing a greatcoat, despite the mildness of the morning, and smoking a cigarette. His accent was indeterminately American. West coast or east or where in between was hard to gauge.

'Good morning,' Max said cautiously.

'I'd take you for an educated man.'

'That's gratifying.'

'And you're English, right?'

'Yes. I am.'

'Maybe you can settle an argument for me. Your prime minister before Lloyd George was Asquith?'

'He was.'

'And before him . . . Balfour?'

'No. Campbell-Bannerman.'

'Ah. I lose the argument, then . . . Max.'

Max nodded in acknowledgement that the preliminaries had been satisfactorily concluded. 'Fontana?'

'Lieutenant Grant Fontana, United States Navy. At your service.'

'What's your role here?'

'Liaison with the local merchant marine. Which is handy for you, considering I know a drifter skipper who likes to make a little

11

money on the black market – including illicit bartering visits to the German ships in Scapa Flow.'

Max paused before responding. 'That does sound handy. Can he be trusted?'

'He can be trusted to do what he has to do to stay out of trouble. And I can land him in a whole load of trouble any time I like, as he well knows. But on the subject of trust . . .'

'Yes?'

'Who was that woman you were talking to?'

'Susan Henty. I met her and her brother on the ferry.'

'You met them?' Fontana suddenly seemed less friendly. 'You should have made it your business to meet no one.'

'They're harmless.'

'So you say. What do they think you're doing here?'

'My brother was killed in the *Vanguard* disaster.'

'Remind me what disaster that was.'

'HMS *Vanguard* blew up while anchored in Scapa Flow on the night of the ninth of July 1917, with the loss of more than seven hundred souls. Probably caused by the spontaneous combustion of cordite in the magazine, though there were rumours of sabotage.'

'And one of those seven hundred was your "brother"?'

'Sub-Lieutenant David Hutton.'

'So, that makes you Max Hutton?'

'As far as the Hentys and everyone here's concerned, yes. I've come to see where it happened – to pay my respects.'

'Touching. Truly touching.' Fontana sucked a last drag out of his cigarette and flicked it away. 'Listen, I don't want to know what you're after on that German ship. I've done what the boss wanted me to do here: make it possible for you to get on board. It's not going to be easy, but Tom Wylie's the man to do it. I'll see him this evening and explain to him what's wanted and brief you on the plan straight after. OK?'

'OK.'

'Meet me in the back bar of the Albert at nine o'clock. Mounthoolie Lane. It's Saturday, so it'll be busy. And noisy. No one will pay us any attention.'

'I'll be there.'

'Any questions?'

'Which ship will Wylie take me to?'

Fontana gave a mirthless little laugh. 'You'll find out when the time comes and not before. I mean to stick to the rules even if you don't. The boss doesn't like deviations.'

'But he isn't here, is he, to worry about how we get the job done?'

'Not here? Well, that depends on exactly what you mean by "here". I often feel he's looking over my shoulder watching what I do.'

'Do you feel that now?'

Fontana lit another cigarette and contemplated Max as he drew on it. 'You should feel that now. It'd be good for you. Stop you taking too many chances. This is your first big job for him, isn't it? If you want to live to do another, you need to be more careful. Guard your tongue and watch your back. That's my advice. I'll see you later.'

Fontana did not wait for a response. He turned and strode away across the pier towards the moored cutter. Max watched him from the corner of his eye as he started down a flight of steps to reach the craft.

The cutter got under way and headed out across the bay towards the minesweepers. Then Max began a slow, measured amble back along the pier.

THE FERRY FROM ABERDEEN TO KIRKWALL HAD TAKEN THE weather as it found it: foul but no fouler than was often the case, according to a member of the crew who seemed to think Max was in need of reassurance, callow Londoner straight off the sleeper from King's Cross that he obviously was. Fresh air was the only cure for seasickness Max knew, so he sat out the voyage on deck, with occasional descents to the saloon to warm himself by the stove.

He was striding back and forth by the rail, muffled up and clapping his arms together, when the ferry docked at Wick to pick up more passengers. That was when he caught his first sight of the Hentys. There was something in their attitude to each other, as well as a slight facial similarity, that told him they were brother and sister rather than husband and wife. And the sister's anxiety about her brother was also apparent, even as they hurried along the pontoon to board. She watched his every step with a worried frown, as if he might fall or stumble – or simply collapse.

The Hentys also shunned the saloon and fell into conversation with Max as the only other passenger who preferred the open deck. Selwyn Henty, big-boned like his sister, but with thinning hair and an altogether less robust appearance, confessed at once that claustrophobia rather than seasickness was the problem in his case. 'I did some tunnelling in the war. Since then I don't seem to be able to tolerate sharing confined spaces with other people.'

The war had left other marks on Selwyn Henty: a gaze that never fixed itself on anything for longer than a few seconds and a tremor of the hands that the motion of the ship disguised until it came to lighting a cigarette or taking a nip from his hip-flask. He spoke with nervous rapidity as well, often jumbling his words.

Jumbled or not, however, his eloquence on the subject of ancient megaliths was undeniable. He was seeking to put the finishing touches to a theory he had devised – 'a mathematical solution', he termed it – concerning the prehistoric stone monuments of Britain. Those of northern Scotland were particularly illuminating, apparently. He and his sister had followed a fortnight in the Outer Hebrides – 'The Callanish circles must be seen to be appreciated, Mr Hutton' – with a tour of the stone rows of Caithness – 'Fascinating, quite fascinating' – and were now heading for the Ring of Brodgar on Orkney. 'You've heard of it, of course?'

Max had not. Nor did he gain any inkling of the nature of Selwyn's 'mathematical solution' from rapid-fire references to azimuths, extinction angles and the rate of decline of the obliquity of the ecliptic. Susan Henty gave him a few sympathetic grimaces during her brother's disquisition, to which she added an apologetic explanation when Selwyn descended to the heads.

'Selwyn's never told me much about his wartime experiences, Mr Hutton, but they've taken their toll on him, as you can see. He wasn't always so intense. This research project is good for him, though. If he can see it through and publish his findings, I think he'll have been able to put some healing distance between himself and all the things that happened to him in France. Of course, he's lucky to be alive when so many of his comrades aren't, but his survival has come at a price.'

'At least he has you to help him through it,' said Max.

'I do what I can. And you? Is there anyone to help you through it?'

'Oh, the RFC was a breeze compared with the Army.'

'I don't believe that for a moment.'

'It was, I assure you. I'm ridiculously unscathed.'

The broad, confident smile Max gave Susan Henty then was much the same as the one he gave both her and Selwyn as they set out in the hired Humber from Kirkwall the following morning. He was

15

a free agent until he met Fontana again that evening. There seemed no reason not to enjoy himself as best he could.

Susan, however, proposed that they take an indirect route to Brodgar along the southern coastal road, so they could have a view of Scapa Flow and the interned German fleet. Since this would also give them a view of the waters in which HMS *Vanguard* had been blown up in 1917, claiming the life of Sub-Lieutenant David Hutton among hundreds of others, Max was in no position to object.

He prepared himself to appear moved by a first sight of the place where his supposed brother had died and was dismayed, when the time came, by how shamelessly he performed the role.

The Flow itself was a bowl of blue sea, enclosed by the mountainous bulk of Hoy and a string of smaller, lower-lying islands. Dotted across it were the grey, recumbent warships of the German High Seas Fleet. They stopped to view the scene from the hill above Houton, where a nearly circular bay was ringed by the jetties, slipways, workshops and hangars of a seaplane base.

A seaplane was taking off as they arrived. Watching it, Max experienced a pang of nostalgia for the days when he had flown virtually daily. As it was, it had been two long years since he had heard the wind in the wires as he piloted a craft into the sky. Fortunately, Susan, looking round at him from the driver's seat, interpreted his doleful shake of the head as a sign of mourning for his late brother.

'Do you know where the *Vanguard* was when it happened, Max?' she asked.

'What?' His reactions snapped into gear. 'Oh yes. She was anchored off Flotta. There.' He pointed to what he judged was the correct island. 'It happened at night. There was no warning.'

'You can be glad of that small mercy,' said Selwyn. 'At least your brother didn't know he was about to die.'

Whether Susan sensed the same meaning as Max did in Selwyn's words – that he had felt certain he was about to die on numerous occasions – was hard to tell.

'There's that, yes,' Max acknowledged.

'Was his body recovered?'

'No.' It seemed safest to deny there was a grave to visit. 'But there's a memorial to all the victims at the Naval Cemetery on Hoy. I plan to go and see it.'

'A frightful thing,' said Susan. 'The death of so many – in an instant.'

'When did you hear of it?' asked Selwyn. 'You said you were a prisoner of war by then.'

'The camp commandant passed on the news. He added his condolences.'

'He did?'

'They were good about things like that.' Max recalled as much from the manner in which other prisoners had received such tidings. The tactics of misrepresentation were beginning to become instinctive, he realized.

'Perhaps you think we're being too hard on them now we've won.'

Max wondered for a moment if Selwyn was trying to pick an argument. If so, he would be disappointed. 'No, I don't. They started it.'

'Yes. And let's not forget it.'

'Well, perhaps we could forget it for the rest of the day,' Susan suggested, her voice tightening slightly.

Selwyn had little choice but to agree. 'You're right, of course. Prehistory awaits us. Drive on, sis.'

The Ring of Brodgar stood on a hill halfway along an isthmus of land separating lochs Stenness and Harray. Only thirty-six of the original sixty stones remained, according to Selwyn, but he reckoned that was enough for his purposes. The site was breathtakingly lovely, with or without the monument. Spring flowers were scattered richly across the turf. The blue waters of the lochs mirrored the sky above. The air was cool and fragrant.

But Selwyn had no interest in the scenery. Ropes, ranging rods and a theodolite were unloaded and the survey work began. Max threw himself into the task, which consisted of measuring as precisely as they could the distances between the stones, their relative heights and the diameter of the circle they formed.

Or was it a circle? Selwyn revealed during a break back in the car for sandwiches and tea from a Thermos that the ring might actually be an ellipse. 'The elliptical form lends itself more readily to the creation of Pythagorean triangles, you see,' he explained, though naturally Max did not see.

'The people who built this were familiar with Pythagoras?'

'No. They pre-date him. That's the wonder of it.'

'But what—'

'We'll know more when I analyse the data.'

With that Selwyn was off, theodolite under arm, striding back towards the stones.

'He doesn't have the patience to explain it properly.' Susan sighed. 'But it's all there in his head. And you've been such a sport. It goes much better with three.'

'What does he think this circle – or ellipse – was for?'

'Observation of the sun and moon for the determination of solstices and the prediction of eclipses. He's detected precise alignments for just those purposes at all the sites we've been to.'

'But building this in its original form must have been a massive undertaking. Think of the man-hours involved in quarrying and transporting the stones, let alone erecting them. It seems incredible.'

'A few thousand years from now it'll seem incredible men spent so much money killing one another on the Western Front for four years.'

Max smiled grimly. 'I don't think it'll take anything like as long as that.'

Susan sighed. 'No, it won't, will it? Now, we'd better report back for duty. Selwyn's beckoning rather petulantly.'

It took longer than Max had anticipated for the survey to be completed to Selwyn's exacting standards. It was late afternoon when they started back to Kirkwall. Half a mile or so along the road they passed four standing stones which Selwyn believed to be all that remained of another, smaller circle. He proposed to return the following day to survey the site as best he could.

'We may be able to establish its relationship with Brodgar. Care to lend a hand, again, Max?'

'Do say you'll come,' Susan urged him.

But Max's availability hinged on what Fontana had arranged for him. He could not afford to make any promises. 'I'll let you know in the morning. I might wake up as stiff as a board after the hard labour you've put me to.' He had, in fact, already experienced several twinges from a month-old bullet wound in his side, but he did not propose to mention it.

'That's the problem with you RFC johnnies,' said Selwyn. 'No stamina.'

Selwyn laughed as he spoke, for the first time Max could recall. Susan's surprised glance at her brother suggested she had not heard him laugh recently either. It seemed Max's company really was good for him. As to whether he would have the advantage of it much longer . . .

'We'll see about that,' Max said softly.

MAX TREATED HIMSELF TO A LARGE SCOTCH AND A SOOTHING bath back at the Ayre, then took himself off to the Kirkwall Hotel for dinner to forestall any invitation from the Hentys to dine with them. A harbourside stroll afterwards filled the time before his appointment with Fontana.

The back bar of the Albert was, as Fontana had predicted, crowded and noisy at that hour on a Saturday evening. A fiddler was adding zest to a bubbling sense of raucousness. Max had to bellow his order to the barman. He had already seen Fontana, installed at a corner table and foot-tapping along to the music like a man with nothing on his mind but gentle enjoyment of the local night life.

Six strapping American sailors were drinking enthusiastically at the bar, but they gave no sign of being acquainted with Fontana. They could, Max realized, have come from any one of the dozens of minesweepers out in the bay.

'Mind if I join you?' Max asked, gesturing to the spare chair as he approached Fontana's table.

'Not at all.' Fontana smiled and slid the newspaper lying by his glass closer to him to make way.

Max sat down. 'Cheers.'

'Your health.' They both took a drink.

'Lively, isn't it?'

'You can say that again.'

'You're with the minesweepers?'

'Yup. But we take it easy on Sundays, so tonight's a chance to relax.'

'Well earned, I'm sure.'

'You're not from round here yourself, are you? Don't I detect an English accent?'

'You do.'

'Well, this is your trusty guide to what happens in these parts – or doesn't.' Fontana nodded to the newspaper between them. 'The *Orcadian*. I've finished with it.' He turned the paper so that it was facing Max. As he did so, he twitched up a corner to reveal an envelope that had been slipped inside. Then he dropped his voice to a level no one near by would be able to hear. 'It's a letter for the captain of the ship you'll be taken to. From the boss.'

'He didn't tell me there'd be a letter.'

'Well, there is. My guess is it contains something to ensure the captain's compliance with whatever you'll be asking of him.'

It sounded a good guess to Max, but he did not say so. 'What have you arranged with—'

'No names,' Fontana interrupted. 'Let's keep it simple. Travel to Stromness on Monday. It's the closest port to the German fleet. Book into a hotel for the night. There's a building contractor's yard north of the harbour. You'll be met at the gate at half past midnight. I've secured you an hour aboard the ship. I was told that should be enough. You'll be back in Stromness around two thirty. On Tuesday morning, you can take the mail steamer to Scrabster and head home, mission accomplished. Does that sound good to you?'

'I suppose so, yes.' Max could not help worrying about the letter. It was the first intimation he had had that Commander Schmidt might not be eager to cooperate. 'How long have—'

'Excuse me.' A figure was standing by their table, holding a glass in one hand and a chair by its back in the other. Looking up, Max saw to his astonishment that it was Selwyn Henty. 'There's room for a third, isn't there?'

'Selwyn? What are you doing here?'

Selwyn twirled the chair round and sat down. He deposited his whisky glass on the table with a heavy clunk. Max's initial impression was that he was more than a little drunk, although his words were not in the least slurred. He extended a hand towards

Fontana. 'Good evening. My name's Selwyn Henty. Has Max mentioned me to you?'

'No,' said Fontana warily. 'But we've, er, only just met.'

'Is that so? Well, now I'm pleased to meet you.' Fontana was more or less obliged to shake Selwyn's hand. 'And you are?'

'Lieutenant Grant Fontana, United States Navy.'

'A long way from home?'

'Quite some way, yuh.'

'Like me and Max. We're all strangers here.'

'I wouldn't have thought this was your kind of place, Selwyn,' said Max, hoping though not necessarily believing that Selwyn's presence in the Albert was just an unfortunate coincidence.

'It isn't. I only came here because you did.'

'Are you saying . . . you followed me?'

'Yes.' Selwyn grinned blithely and Max saw Fontana's face cloud with anger. 'Don't reproach yourself. I did a good many recceing missions behind enemy lines in the war. I'm no slouch when it comes to seeing without being seen.'

'Why would you want to follow him?' Fontana asked, assembling a pseudo-genial smile of his own.

'Let's not be coy, gentlemen. You two are, it pains me to have to say, up to no good.'

'Pardon me?' Fontana looked suitably taken aback.

'What manner of no good I neither know nor care. It's entirely your affair.'

'This is ridiculous, Selwyn,' said Max. 'What the devil are you talking about?'

'Your name isn't Max Hutton, is it . . . Max?' There was absolute certainty in Selwyn's alarmingly round-eyed gaze. He knew.

'What?'

'It's Maxted. James Maxted. We were at Eton together.'

Damn, thought Max. Damn it all to hell.

'I was two years below you, so naturally you don't remember me. Equally naturally, I do remember you. Ironically, most people would think me older than you now. It must be on account of the different wars we had. Mine took rather more out of me than yours

22

evidently did out of you. But then you always did have an enviable quality of effortlessness. I remember watching you score a fifty for the second eleven once. Against Marlborough, if I'm not much mistaken. Lovely timing.'

Denial was futile. Max knew that even if Fontana did not. But what was the alternative? 'You're mistaken, Selwyn. I can—'

'Please don't. We both know it's true.' He was speaking quietly now, almost indulgently. 'I felt sure we'd met before when you introduced yourself on the ferry. It only came to me later, though. James Maxted. Known as Max. Not Max Hutton. From which it followed you had not lost a brother on the *Vanguard*. That was all make-believe. But to what end? Well, as I say, I'm happy to let you keep that to yourselves.'

'What makes you think I have the remotest clue what this is all about?' cut in Fontana.

'You mean what persuades me you are co-conspirators rather than chance acquaintances? Your carefully choreographed meeting at the harbour this morning, Lieutenant Fontana, as observed by me from the Ayre Hotel with my trusty binoculars. That is what persuades me. Max here travelling under an alias, and you patently straying from whatever duties you may have with the minesweeping fleet.'

Selwyn made a sudden grab for the newspaper, but Fontana slammed his hand down across it to stop him. They stared at each other for a moment, fury – at Selwyn, at Max, maybe even at himself – simmering in Fontana's eyes.

'Well, the point is made.' Selwyn sat back in his chair and swallowed most of his whisky. 'Here's the thing, gentlemen. Our parents left Susan and me poorly provided for. My researches have committed me to an extensive – and expensive – programme of travel. I don't expect my findings, when published, to be particularly lucrative. I may need to look to posterity for my greatest reward. But none of us can live on air, can we? And I should like Susan to have a more comfortable existence than she can currently afford. I foresee an offer of marriage, from a lamentable source, which she may feel obliged to accept. I should like to spare her that. I should like to give us both a little freedom

23

in which to consider our futures. Shall we say . . . a thousand pounds?'

'You're out of your god-damn mind,' said Fontana levelly.

'You're not the first to have said that, Lieutenant Fontana. But my sanity really isn't the point. The point is that I shall notify the Kirkwall police and your commanding officer of my suspicions that you are engaged in some form of criminal enterprise unless you agree to buy my silence. I'm sorry the price is a little steep, but, as I've explained, I have my sister to consider as well as myself. On the other hand, I'm not unreasonable. You can pay me in instalments. Why don't we say a hundred pounds as a down-payment? I'll give you until the banks open on Monday to mull it over. But do mull thoroughly. I can't prove a great deal beyond Max's act of imposture. But I suspect all the official attention I can ensure you receive will scupper your plans, or at any rate greatly complicate them. Not that I'm inflexible. Far from it. A counter-offer on your part – a share of the proceeds of whatever you're planning, for instance – will receive my serious attention. Do you see, gentlemen? You have to deal with me, irksome as it may be. Now, I'll leave you to enjoy your drinks – and all the local gossip.' Selwyn pointed airily at the *Orcadian*, still held firmly in place by Fontana. 'Illuminating, I'm sure.' He pushed his chair back and stood up. 'I'll bid you good evening.' He turned towards the door, then turned back again. 'By the way, Max, there's no need to let this stand in the way of your accompanying us tomorrow. Susan will be disappointed if you don't. And so will I.' He essayed a form of salute to them both. 'I'll look forward to hearing from you.'

'YOU DAMN FOOL,' GROWLED FONTANA IN THE DARK DOORWAY along Mounthoolie Lane, where they had retreated from the Albert following Selwyn Henty's departure. Max sensed Fontana wanted to shout at him, even strike him, but the need for secrecy held them both in its grip. The recriminations, bitter as they were, could only be whispered. 'Because you couldn't keep yourself to yourself on the ferry, we've got a blackmailer on our backs.'

'How was I to know I'd meet someone who knew me at school?' Max protested.

'You shouldn't have taken the chance. It looks to me as if that expensive education you had didn't include a short course in common sense.'

'Let's not panic. I'm not travelling light when it comes to cash. We can agree to Henty's terms and pay him a hundred quid on Monday. That'll keep him quiet until I've been out to the ship. After I've got what I'm going there for, he can say what he likes. He can't prove anything. He said so himself.'

'You mean you get clean away and leave me to face the music.'

'What music? There'll be nothing for the police to investigate.'

'We'd better hope that's right. You louse things up Monday night and it could be a different story. If the British guard squadron reports any kind of incident, Henty's allegations will get a lot of attention. And I'll be in it up to my neck.'

'I'm not going to louse things up.'

'Really? Well, excuse me for pointing out that your record to date doesn't inspire confidence.'

'It'll be all right. For God's sake, what else can we do but play for time? The mission's vital. It takes absolute priority. Haven't you been told that?'

'Yeah, I've been told. The mystery to me is why, if it's so vital, a bungler like you was sent to carry it out.'

'The boss trusts me. And he'll expect you to trust me too.'

'Jesus Christ.' Fontana tossed his head and took a few fretful strides along the lane, then stalked back to where Max was waiting. 'All right. We'll keep Henty sweet. Tell him we'll pay up. But negotiate a lower figure. Or at least try to. He might get suspicious if we give in too easily.'

'OK. I'll do that.'

A silence followed, during which Fontana chewed over his anger, evidently long enough to swallow it. Then he said, 'If all goes well, we won't meet again. I'll check with the Ayre that you've booked out on Monday and assume you're proceeding as per my arrangements with Wylie.'

'I'll be proceeding. You can rely on it.'

'I'll have to, won't I?' Fontana pulled up the collar of his greatcoat and headed off without a backward glance. He had no more to say. His opinion of Max was clear. And Max could hardly blame him for holding it.

'Hell and damnation,' he muttered to himself.

Max returned to the Ayre Hotel cursing Fontana for being right. This was all his own fault.

But there was work to be done. 'Have a pot of tea sent up to my room, please,' he instructed the young man behind the reception desk. 'And a jug of hot water. Very hot. I like my tea piping.'

'The kitchen's closed, sir.'

'Just tea and hot water. No milk.' He slipped half a crown into the young man's hand. 'There's a good fellow.'

Max headed straight upstairs, relieved to reach his room without encountering Susan or Selwyn, or, worse still, the pair of them. Once inside, he took the letter out of the copy of the *Orcadian* Fontana had given him.

*

The name was written on the envelope with an italic pen in a neat, brisk hand. *Fregattenkapitän L. Schmidt.* Was it Lemmer's writing? Max had no way of telling. He had seen no examples. But it seemed to him the sort of writing Lemmer might have.

Fritz Lemmer. The boss. The man who had sent him to Orkney. Max remembered him standing with his back to the sunlight flooding through the French windows in the eerily unfurnished chateau near Paris where they had met three weeks before.

A grey-bearded, bespectacled man of dignified bearing, learned, you would have said, expert in some esoteric field, yet light on his feet, square-shouldered, physically as well as mentally alert. The doors were half-open behind him. Birdsong drifted in on the breeze. There was something hypnotic in his tone of voice, something infinitely persuasive. The soundness of his judgement, it implied, was unassailable.

'How gratifying to have your allegiance, Max. I am impressed you grasped the logic of accepting my invitation. Your first task is uncomplicated, though that does not mean there will be no difficulties. There are always difficulties. Do not resent them when they arise. They will harden you. They will expand your capabilities. I want you to travel to Glasgow. Yes, Glasgow. Wait there for further instructions. Nadia will deliver them. Arrange with her how she can contact you. I assume I do not need to tell you not to use your real name. But stay Max. First names stick. Last names are ... flexible. It may be a long time before you hear from Nadia. That will be your first test. To wait – patiently and inconspicuously – until you are needed. If you perform the task well, when the time comes, I will have more interesting work for you. More challenging. More rewarding. The future, Max. That is where we are going. Others falter. Others stand still. We go forward.'

Max was part of Lemmer's team from that day on. The realization was chilling, even though he had chosen to take on the role. His motive was his defence, a motive he could only pray Lemmer had no inkling of. As for Nadia, there too came a chilling realization. She was not merely one among who-knew-how-many operatives

Lemmer deployed for his purposes. She was close to him. She was someone he relied upon, someone who might know more about him than most.

Max had ample time to dwell on such issues while he kicked his heels in Glasgow. He found a gymnasium where he could work off some of his frustration on the punch-bag and dumbbell. He took walking trips around Loch Lomond. He killed innumerable hours lying on the bed in his hotel room reading Sax Rohmer stories. He prowled the city. He lingered in cafés. He waited it out.

Nadia eventually made contact, as agreed, through the personal column of the Glasgow *Evening News*. They met amid the seventeenth-century Dutch masterpieces in Kelvingrove Art Gallery. Nadia, with her glossy dark hair and pale complexion, looked exotically mysterious in an elegant coat and dress. She evidently saw no need to blend with the background. After more than a fortnight of Glaswegian dourness, Max was at once reminded of how powerfully alluring she was. But it was vital never to forget how treacherous she could also be.

They were both working for Lemmer now, though. And Nadia for one was not about to betray him. 'How are you enjoying Scotland, Max?'

'It'll be no hardship to leave it.'

'Ah, but you are not leaving. You are being sent north. To Orkney.'

'Orkney?'

'The German fleet has been held at Scapa Flow since the Armistice. It is uncertain what will happen to the ships under the peace treaty. He cannot wait until then.' She habitually referred to Lemmer by the personal pronoun rather than his name. It reminded Max, as perhaps it was meant to, of the respect she had for him. 'The captain of one of the ships has something he wants. You will collect it.'

'I imagine the Royal Navy's keeping a close eye on those ships. Collection won't be easy.'

'An American officer called Fontana will assist you. He is with a US minesweeping fleet working there. You are to meet him in Kirkwall next Saturday.'

'What am I collecting?'

'A file. Grey. With the letters NBM on the cover. You have that? NBM.'

'I have it.'

'The captain's name is Schmidt. Lothar Schmidt. He will know what you want.'

'Which ship does he command?'

'I do not have that information. Fontana will know.'

'I'm to be drip-fed, am I?'

'You are on trial, Max. Concentrate on doing what you have been told to do.'

'I will.'

She smiled tightly. 'Good.'

They adjourned to the gallery tea-room. Nadia appeared to feel Max needed reminding of the seriousness of what he was about to embark upon.

'Mistakes can be costly in this work, Max. You understand?'

'Oh, yes.'

'He rewards success. He punishes failure.'

'Of course. It's his nature.'

'Yes. It is.'

'When did you first meet him, Nadia?'

She looked at him narrowly. 'You should not ask me that.'

'You know when *I* first met him.'

'Still you should not ask me.'

'If not when, then where? St Petersburg? Berlin?'

'No.'

'Do you want me to go on guessing?'

'No.' She tapped a finely sculpted fingernail against her teacup, pointedly, as if it was a clue.

'China?'

'Almost. Korea. Chosen, as the Japanese call it.'

'What were you doing there?'

'Not all of us who left Russia started by heading west, Max. I went east. I found work with a Japanese businesswoman in Keijo.'

'A Japanese businesswoman in Keijo. That sounds interesting. What sort of business was she in?'

'Many kinds. And one kind involved him.'

'What took him to Korea, I wonder.' Max smiled at Nadia, inviting some further disclosure.

But there was not to be one. 'I have said too much already. I will say nothing more.' And nor did she.

There was a knock at the door. Max took the tea-tray from the young man and sent him away with his thanks. A boiling kettle was what he really needed. But he was confident the steam from the jug and teapot combined would do the trick. There was no time to be lost. He held the envelope above their open lids and began prising gently at the flap.

MOST SECRET   Paris, 27th April 1919

MEMORANDUM – Attention of C only (in cipher) HQ
London

I exercised my discretion by enrolling James Maxted (known
as Max), formerly a lieutenant in the RFC, as a special off-
books operative on 5th April. I considered that logging a
report of the arrangement at the time would risk attracting
hostile attention.

  The extraordinary opportunity Max's engagement
represented was the reason I proceeded on my own initiative.
He first came to my attention following the death of his
father, Sir Henry Maxted, in an unexplained roof-fall in the
Montparnasse district of Paris on 21st March this year. Sir
Henry was attached to our delegation to the peace
conference as an adviser on South American affairs.

  It appeared at first that Sir Henry had committed suicide.
The French police believed he had discovered that his lover,
Corinne Dombreux, who lived in an apartment in the
building from which he fell, had been unfaithful to him with
an Italian artist, Raffaele Spataro. But some of the
circumstances were distinctly suspicious. Mme Dombreux's
status as the widow of a traitor also gave cause for
concern – Pierre Dombreux, a diplomat serving at the
French Embassy in Petrograd, is believed by le Deuxième

Bureau to have acted as a Soviet, and possibly also a German, spy before his death by drowning in March of last year.

The French authorities were happy to record Sir Henry's death as an accident, as was his eldest son, and heir, Sir Ashley. Max, on the other hand, was convinced from the first that his father had been murdered and set about proving it. I tried initially to discourage him, in order to avoid a scandal that might embarrass our delegation. As you know, however, Max's investigations unearthed a possible connection with Fritz Lemmer, whom Sir Henry had met while serving with our embassy in Tokyo in 1889/91.

Max contacted Travis Ireton, an unscrupulous American who peddles titbits of information about the conference. It appeared likely Sir Henry had tried to sell information through Ireton in order to fund a golden future for himself and Mme Dombreux. One of the pieces of information, culled from a list of potential sources of money in Sir Henry's handwriting (I explained the background to this to you and the heads of department at an HQ meeting on 26th March), related to Lemmer's current whereabouts. Max concluded that his father had been murdered to protect Lemmer. I was inclined to agree with him.

Max's attempts to discover who had betrayed Sir Henry revealed the presence of a network of spies maintained by Lemmer within more than one delegation to the conference, including ours, working actively despite the collapse of the Imperial German government whose cause they originally served. Shortly after Max identified one of those spies as Walter Ennis of the American delegation, Ennis was murdered. Spataro was also murdered. In Spataro's case, attempts were made to fasten responsibility on Mme Dombreux. The killings of Sir Henry and Spataro were well managed. They bore Lemmer's hallmark. The killing of Ennis was hasty and public. It smacked of panic. We also lost one of our own men, Lamb, which was another reason I allowed Max to bear most of the risks of the investigation.

32

Max was shot and quite seriously wounded at the time of the Ennis killing. That did not discourage him in the slightest, indicating to my satisfaction that he has what it takes. His war record confirms he is strong-nerved and fearless.

I cannot be sure Max has told me everything he has learnt. He has had dealings with a high-ranking Japanese police officer, Kuroda, who is attached to their delegation. Kuroda evidently knew Sir Henry quite well. He was a senior member of the team that investigated the attempted assassination of the late Tsar (when he was Tsarevich) in Japan in 1891, in which Lemmer was implicated. Ireton, we must assume, knows more than he is telling about Lemmer. His number two, Schools Morahan, is a resourceful fellow. And I am struck by the fact that Ireton's secretary, Malory Hollander, lived in Japan for several years as a young woman.

There is the additional complication that Sir Henry first met Mme Dombreux while serving with our embassy in Petrograd. He and her late husband are said to have been friends. I suspect there is much more to be learnt about Dombreux's activities, in particular who exactly he was working for. It follows there may also be much more to be learnt about Sir Henry.

Max mistakenly believed Lionel Brigham of our delegation to be one of Lemmer's spies. His mistake had the effect, however, of drawing into the open the assassin Tarn, who I now believe murdered both Sir Henry and Spataro. Tarn's killing by Max – the incident in Mayfair on 1st April that Special Branch dealt with for us – removed a probable threat to the lives of other participants at the conference.

The activities of Max's RFC friend, former sergeant Samuel Twentyman, never sanctioned by me, led fortuitously to the unmasking of two members of our delegation who really did work for Lemmer, Herbert Norris and Alfred Dobson. It also forced into the open Lemmer's White Russian henchwoman, Nadia Bukayeva. She killed Norris and Dobson to prevent them revealing any of Lemmer's secrets under interrogation. Twentyman's life was saved by the intervention of Morahan, who appears to be more scrupulous than Ireton.

I know queries have been raised about the role of an Arab youth nicknamed le Singe (real name, we believe, Seddik Yala, a Tunisian) in the killing of Tarn and a spate of burglaries at the hotels and offices of various delegations, including the Japanese. There is a lack of reliable information about le Singe. I am optimistic we may yet be able to benefit from whatever secrets he has succeeded in stealing. There is reason to believe some of those secrets concern Lemmer. He is therefore worthy of our attention.

Tarn worked for whoever paid him. I believe Norris, acting on Lemmer's behalf, hired him to eliminate Sir Henry and to kill Spataro in order to cover his tracks and incriminate Mme Dombreux. Later, it appears, the Japanese hired Tarn to find Lemmer, presumably in order to neutralize a threat Lemmer posed to them.

This threat seems likely to have been something contained in the documents stolen from the luggage of Lou Tseng-Tsiang, head of the Chinese delegation, when he stopped in Tokyo on his way to the conference – referred to on Sir Henry's list as the Chinese box. We originally assumed those documents were stolen by the Japanese, but Kuroda told Max he thought they had actually been stolen by Lemmer. The suggestion is that one of the documents was a letter sent in early 1917 by Japanese prime minister Terauchi to German foreign minister Zimmermann, agreeing terms for Japan to switch to the German side in the war. We know the Americans feared such a development. Their intervention in Mexico at that time confirms they believed a sneak attack by Japan was a genuine possibility. Fortunately, Zimmermann overplayed his hand by making overtures to the Mexicans which we were able to use to push the Americans into declaring war on Germany, at which point the Japanese naturally denied they had ever dreamt of switching sides.

If Lemmer has proof the Japanese were willing to betray their allies in 1917, the threat he poses to them is grave indeed. But the decision to deal with it by sending Tarn after him misfired badly. The question now is what they will do next: move against him again or try to strike terms with him.

As ever, we are in the dark about who within the Japanese government is in the ascendant. Their power struggles, and the outcomes of those struggles, remain opaque. I would conjecture last month's uprising in Korea has strengthened the militarist wing. But how they would propose to deal with Lemmer is hard to judge.

Aside from his entanglements with the Japanese, Lemmer remains a serious and direct threat to us. We know now, as I am on record as suspecting since I first encountered him in Rotterdam in 1915, that he recruited spies in all the Allied countries. What we do not know is who they are and how many they are. The best chance we have of finding out is to plant a spy of our own in Lemmer's camp.

This he has inadvertently enabled us to do by seeking to recruit Max as an agent. Why he is so eager to have Max working for him I do not know. It may be he simply admires his determination and ingenuity. Or it may be there is something only Max is qualified to achieve for him.

There was insufficient time for me to seek sanction for such a step. If he was to take up Lemmer's offer, Max had to make contact with Lemmer's representatives a matter of hours after we first discussed the idea. Otherwise he would not be engaged. I concluded, in view of his willingness and suitability for the task, to give him the Service's blessing.

I have heard nothing from Max since then. But I am confident that if and when he lays his hands on information enabling us to close the net around Lemmer and his organization – the full extent of which we cannot presently gauge – he will do whatever is necessary to bring it to us.

I acted as I did because of the extreme importance I know you attach to pursuing Lemmer. I recommend we await word from Max and respond appropriately when it comes.

If you require further details of any of the actions of mine alluded to above, please advise and I will supply them.

This is a comprehensive summary of the current state of affairs in this matter, subject only to normal operating limitations.

H. Appleby

MAX WISHED HE HAD CONCENTRATED MORE DURING GERMAN lessons at Eton; he also wished he had brushed up his command of the language during his spell as a prisoner of war, although it was true few of the camp guards were what anyone could reasonably call chatty. As it was he gleaned little from the letter to Commander Schmidt, aside from the fact that it was not written by the same person who had addressed the envelope.

It was signed Anna, though what she was to Schmidt was unclear. There were no *mein Lieber*s to suggest she was his wife or lover. But no surname was supplied either and she called him Lothar. They were obviously close in some way.

As to the content of the letter, Max made little progress, thanks in part to the jaggedness of the handwriting. It looked as if it had been written in a hurry. There were several blotches and crossings-out. But one phrase caught his attention: *die graue Akte*. The grey file. And the word *wichtig* was used several times. Something was *sehr wichtig* – very important.

Max made as fair a copy of the letter as he could for later translation, then resealed it in the envelope. The tea was stewed by now. He poured it down the hand basin in the bathroom. Then he turned in.

He woke already irked by the knowledge that he would have to spend the day with the Hentys and maintain a façade of amiability towards Selwyn. The prospect was grisly. But crying off, tempting though it was, might make Selwyn fear he and Fontana planned to defy him.

He headed out for a brisk walk before breakfast, hoping the clear air and sparkling sea views would lift his spirits. They did not.

When he returned to the Ayre, he was surprised to find a burly walrus-moustached police constable talking to the hotel manager. Susan Henty was with them. She looked worried – very worried.

'Max,' she called to him as he entered the reception area. 'Have you seen Selwyn?'

'This morning? No. What's wrong?'

'His bed's not been slept in. It seems as if he went out last night and hasn't come back.'

'I'm sure there's no cause for alarm, miss,' said the constable, casting his eye over the notes he had so far taken. 'We don't know for certain he was absent overnight. Perhaps he, er, likes to make his own bed.'

The manager frowned scornfully at him. 'Willy, my night porter, told me when he went off duty that Mr Henty went out late last night and hadn't returned. His key's on the hook. That much is clear.'

'Is the car still here?' Max asked.

'Yes,' Susan replied, her voice cracking. 'It's where I left it. Besides, the key's in my handbag.'

'So, he's on foot.'

'Not likely to have gone far, then,' remarked the constable, whose counsel of calm was convincing no one, least of all Max, in whose mind an unpleasant suspicion was beginning to form.

'Did he say anything to Willy when he left?'

'We don't know,' said Susan.

'Well, perhaps we should ask him.'

The constable sighed. 'If you let me have his address, sir,' he said to the manager, 'I'll knock him up and see if he can help.'

'I'll get it for you.' The manager scurried off.

'And you are, sir?' The constable turned his reluctant attention to Max.

'Max Hutton.'

The name was noted. 'A friend of Mr Henty's?'

'Of us both,' declared Susan.

'And when did you last see your friend, Mr Hutton?'

A lie could sometimes be calculated and considered. More often, as Max was learning, it was told instinctively, in an instant, for better or worse. 'Late yesterday afternoon.'

'When we got back from our day out,' Susan explained.

'Not during the evening?'

'No. Not during the evening.'

The constable was soon on his way to dig out Willy. Max suggested they have breakfast. Susan agreed, though she hardly ate anything served to her. Max heard himself expressing entirely groundless confidence that all was well. But all was not well. And Susan's fears were not necessarily the worst of it.

'He went out for a walk after dinner, but he was back within an hour. He knocked on my door and wished me goodnight at about half past ten. Why would he have gone out again after that?'

'I don't know. It's odd, certainly.'

'What did you do last night?'

'Oh, I, er, dined at the Kirkwall Hotel. I fancied a change of scene. And then . . . I had a drink in one of the nearby pubs and . . . then I came back here.'

'And you saw nothing of Selwyn?'

'No.' Max was committed to the lie now. 'Nothing.'

'I'm so afraid he's met with some kind of accident, Max.'

'Of course you are. But we shouldn't assume anything. There may be a . . . simple explanation.'

'Such as?'

Max was still trying to devise a convincing answer to that question when the constable returned. He looked altogether less willing to brush the matter off after rousing Willy Gibson from his bed and questioning him.

'It appears there was a telephone call to the hotel at about' – he consulted his notes – 'a quarter to eleven. The caller, a man, asked Mr Gibson to bring Mr Henty to the phone. He said it was a very urgent matter. So, Mr Gibson fetched Mr Henty and left him to talk to the caller while he attended to other duties – taking you some tea, he said, Mr Hutton.'

39

'Ah, yes,' said Max. 'That's true. He did.'

'Well, when he got back to the desk the phone was back on the hook and Mr Henty was nowhere to be seen. About five minutes later, he came down, dressed for outdoors, and left. He said to Mr Gibson that he wouldn't be gone long.'

'Did the caller give a name?' asked Susan.

'He did, miss. And that's a funny coincidence of sorts. He said his name was Maxted.'

'Maxted?'

'And your Christian name's Max, isn't that right, sir?'

'Yes.'

'Heard of anyone called Maxted?'

'No.'

'Miss?'

'Me neither.'

'I was wondering if Mr Henty misheard or misunderstood in some way, you see, and thought it was you, sir.' The constable looked pointedly at Max.

'Well, he'd have realized it wasn't me when he heard the caller's voice, wouldn't he, constable?'

'Yes, sir. He would. And it definitely wasn't you?'

'Of course not. I was in my room. Where Willy Gibson brought me a pot of tea. If you remember.'

'Yes, sir. So he did.'

Thank God for that, thought Max. Otherwise he might be suspected of creeping out of the hotel to make the telephone call. But who *had* made it? There was only one name that came to mind. And it was not one he had any intention of mentioning. As to why that person might have made the call . . .

'I think I'm going to have to interrupt Sergeant Tulloch's Sunday,' the constable continued. 'Which he won't thank me for. But I reckon we'll need to find this Mr Maxted, if we're to get to the bottom of this.' He fingered his moustache thoughtfully. 'I don't know what to make of it, I really don't.'

'What can possibly have happened, Max?' Susan asked him after the constable had left. 'Who is this man Maxted? What did he want? Selwyn's never mentioned anyone of that name to me, yet it seems he knew him. What on earth's going on?'

'I don't know, Susan.'

But that was not true. Max knew – or felt sure he knew. Fontana had made the call, disguising his American accent and using Max's real name to lure Selwyn to the telephone. Then, somehow, he had persuaded Selwyn to meet him, out there in the dark, down by the harbour perhaps, close to the deep water of the bay.

Selwyn was dead. The certainty spread over Max's mind like a stain. Fontana had not been prepared to buy him off. He had solved the problem in the way he much preferred – simple, effective, final. Max had no means of contacting him, of course. That was the beauty of it from Fontana's point of view. There could be no protest, no accusation. It was done.

The moral canker of working for a man like Lemmer was borne in upon Max now. Honour was lost to him. Deceit was inescapable. Susan Henty needed his help. But he could not give it. He could not afford to.

WHILE MAX'S LIFE CONTINUED TO TAKE VIOLENT AND unexpected turns, that of the rest of the Maxted family, to whom he was always known as James, proceeded placidly and predictably at Gresscombe Place, in Surrey.

The ripples that had disturbed it in the wake of Sir Henry Maxted's fatal fall from a Paris rooftop had faded. Sir Ashley, the new baronet, had suppressed the scandal of his father's death as best he could and was determined no more should be heard of it. He was mightily relieved Max had signed away the duties of executor to the family solicitor, Mellish, and regarded the extended absence from England hinted at in Max's letter to Mellish on the subject as a prospect devoutly to be welcomed.

His wife, Lydia, the new Lady Maxted, was at one with him on both points. The problem of her brother-in-law, as she categorized it, had been solved. No cloud now hung over the delivery in due course of a third child to add to her darlings Giles and Henrietta. Spring had arrived to add lustre to the view from the drawing-room windows of Gresscombe Place. All was safely gathered in.

'And there will be no biplanes whining over the countryside like giant mosquitoes,' as she had remarked only recently. 'What a relief.'

She had not visited the London flat since Max had shot dead an intruder there, a man the police still seemed unable to identify conclusively. She was not at all sure she would ever go there again, unless it was to supervise the removal of the furniture after persuading Ashley to sell it. She did not relish the idea of using a

42

bathroom she knew to have been the scene of a shooting. The incident, frightful as it was, especially for the unfortunate Mr Brigham, was so far outside her vision of how life should proceed that she thought on the whole the flat was best disposed of.

But that would wait for another day. The presence as a luncheon guest of the elder Lady Maxted's brother, Uncle George, was the slightest of irritants. There were occasions when he was genuinely amusing, regrettably offset by those on which he descended into vulgarity, usually as a result of drinking too much. Today, however, he had imbibed modestly. And soon he would be gone. All, from Lydia's point of view, was indeed set fair.

George Clissold's relative sobriety had an explanation Lydia could not have guessed at. When inviting her brother to join them, Winifred, the elder Lady Maxted, had emphasized he should keep a clear head with which to consider a matter of some delicacy she wanted his advice on. So it was that a post-luncheon walk down to the orchard was not intended, as she had suggested, 'to aid digestion', but to facilitate confidential conversation.

George's customary levity had never blinded Winifred, as it had others, to his fundamental qualities of honesty and reliability. She knew him as the best of brothers, one who would come to her aid when all others failed her – and never speak of what he did on her behalf.

'Where would I be without you, George?' she asked as they entered the blossom-clouded orchard.

'Better off,' George replied, chewing on his cigar. 'You'd have Papa's money rather than me.'

'I wasn't speaking of money.'

'No? Sorry. It's spending time with Ashley that does it. The boy never stops talking about how much profit he hopes to squeeze out of the estate.'

'Ah . . . you noticed.'

'Hard not to. If you need my help to persuade him to leave well alone, I'm not—'

'This is nothing to do with Ashley, George. Or the estate.'

'What, then?'

'You'll recall the matter of the Sumerian cylinder-seals – one of the assets Henry sold to finance a secure and comfortable future with—'

'Oh, those?' George cut in, sparing his sister the need to refer directly to Henry's Parisian mistress. 'What's the matter? Curator of the county museum been on to you again? You'll just have to tell him Henry sold the seals and there it is.'

'I've already told him that. And he took it in surprisingly good part.'

'Glad to hear it.'

'The blossom's lovely, isn't it?' She paused to run her finger over a soft white petal. 'The pears are even more beautiful than the apples, don't you think?'

'Not sure I can tell the difference, Win.'

'No. It requires an expert eye. As telling the difference between many things does. Genuine Sumerian cylinder-seals, for instance . . . and fakes.'

'Fakes?'

'I've received a letter from a man who claims to have bought them from Henry. He also claims that what he bought . . . are forgeries.'

'Good God.'

'His name is Arnavon. Read the letter for yourself.'

Winifred took the letter out of the pocket of her dress, removed it from its envelope and handed it to George. 'He expresses himself politely but very firmly on the subject.'

George wrestled a pair of glasses from his jacket, perched them on his nose and held the letter at arm's length before him. 'The address is a hotel in Paris,' he said.

'Yes. We can be grateful he hasn't come here to demand restitution, I suppose. Read what he has to say.'

George cleared his throat and adjusted his glasses. '"My dear Lady Maxted, I am informed that you are the widow of Sir Henry Maxted, regrettably deceased. I offer you my condolences on the loss of your husband and apologize for the necessity of writing to you. Prior to his demise, I purchased from a dealer in antiquities named Soutine, acting on Sir Henry's behalf, a small collection of

44

what were represented to me as twenty-third-century BC Sumerian cylinder-seals. I have a receipt for the transaction, dated nineteenth March, in which they are so described. The purchase was concluded the day before I was due to sail to Montréal." – I see he puts an accent on the e in Montreal; he's French Canadian presumably – "I therefore had no opportunity to seek authentication of the articles prior to my departure, but saw no need to do so in view of Sir Henry's unimpeachable credentials as—"'

George broke off for a draw on his cigar. 'He's a wordy blighter, isn't he?'

'Wordy, but insistent, you'll find. Please read on.'

George sighed heavily and resumed. '"The items were destined for the collection of Sir Nathaniel Chevalier, the well-known amateur Assyriologist, whom you may have heard of in his former capacity as chairman of the Continental Pacific Railway Company." – Mmm. Can't say I have. – "I am sorry to have to notify you, however, that the seals, when examined upon my arrival in Montréal, were found to be modern imitations, probably less than a hundred years old. I cabled Monsieur Soutine and Sir Henry in Paris, but received no reply, although my subsequent enquiries established that Sir Henry had died in a tragic accident shortly after my departure."'

George broke off again 'He's rather out of date where the cause of death is concerned, isn't he?'

'He may no longer be. Read on.'

'"The continuing failure of Monsieur Soutine to respond to my cables has obliged me to return to Paris, bearing with me Sir Nathaniel's explicit instructions to reclaim the money paid plus a sum to be agreed by way of compensation. Sir Nathaniel has authorized me to say that he would feel reluctantly obliged to take legal action should no such repayment and compensation be forthcoming. Consideration for your position as a widow has prompted him to stay his hand for the present. I have been unable to contact Monsieur Soutine. His offices are closed and his whereabouts are currently unknown. I have no alternative therefore but to raise the matter with you. I feel sure you do not wish your late husband's reputation to be besmirched—"'

'Besmirched?' George suddenly exploded. 'My God, he's damned high-handed, isn't he? This is surely between him and the dealer, Soutine. And what about caveat emptor?'

Winifred sighed. 'Monsieur Soutine is nowhere to be found, George. Our address, on the other hand, is clearly listed in *Burke's*. I do not wish to be sued by a Canadian railway magnate. I feel he can probably afford to employ better lawyers than we can. Now, please finish reading the letter.'

George harrumphed and peered at the document anew. '"I feel sure you will agree that a private financial settlement of the claim is preferable to litigation. I will await confirmation of this from you or your appointed representative. I can be contacted at the above address until the end of next week. I remain, etcetera, etcetera, S. V. Arnavon, esquire."'

Winifred retrieved the letter before George succumbed to the temptation to screw it up and drop-kick it into one of the trees. She looked at him indulgently. 'I was angry when I first read it myself. Angry with Henry, most of all, I must confess.'

'You surely can't suspect Henry of deliberately selling fake antiquities?'

'We know he was trying to raise money by all means at his disposal, George. Perhaps he hoped to sell the cylinder-seals several times over.'

'I can't believe that of him, Win. He was always too damned . . . honourable.'

'You may be right. He was honourable, of course, in his own fallible way. Besides, I doubt there'd have been enough time between retrieving the seals from the museum in Guildford and selling them in Paris a week later to have convincing copies made. I suppose the greater likelihood is that they were never genuine in the first place. Some enterprising Mesopotamian merchant probably sold them to Henry's father shortly before he came home. I wonder if Sir Charles eventually realized they were fakes. That might explain his willingness to consign them to the county museum.'

'Where nobody ever noticed they had MADE IN BAGHDAD 1870 stamped all over them.'

Winifred smiled weakly. 'I wish I could merely laugh this off, George. I really do. While the pomposity of Mr Arnavon's tone suggests he might be a suitable subject for humour, alas I fear we must take him seriously. I do not think I can bear any more rants by Ashley about his father's failings.'

'You haven't told Ashley about this?'

'No. And I'd prefer not to.'

'You could have Mellish deal with it.'

'He acts for the estate rather than me, George. I suspect he would feel bound to inform Ashley of any potential liability.'

'I notice Arnavon doesn't say how much he paid.'

'No. He doesn't, does he? Within reason, I could recompense him from my own resources, thus resolving the matter without the need for anyone else to become involved. But it would have to be within reason. What I need is someone reliable to travel to Paris on my behalf, to verify what Mr Arnavon has said and to negotiate a private agreement with him if at all possible.'

George puffed at his cigar and grinned at her. 'You mean me?'

'I wouldn't want to interfere with your work, of course.'

'Ha!' George laughed. 'I shouldn't worry about that. No one's likely to begrudge me a spot of leave. They'd probably be grateful not to see me slumped behind a desk for a while. And it'd be no hardship to spend a few days in Paris.'

'Please don't antagonize Mr Arnavon, George. Or Monsieur Soutine, in the event that you locate him. I'd like this settled quickly and quietly.'

'Don't worry, Win.' He looked at her seriously. 'I'll be on my very best behaviour.'

'I know you will.' She reached out her hand and waggled his left ear lobe affectionately. 'Thank you, George. Thank you so much.'

'I could ask after James while I'm there,' George said as they ambled back towards the house. 'I'm sure you'd like some news of him.'

'Don't ask too pointedly, please. James must be allowed to do what he feels he needs to do. I think of him often, of course. Far

47

oftener than Ashley and Lydia suppose. I worry about him. But there's nothing I can do to help him.'

'He's always been a strong-willed boy.'

'Yes.' Winifred smiled wistfully. 'I rather admire that in him.'

'That NCO he was planning to start the flying school with might know something.'

'Mr Twentyman. Yes. James trusts him.'

'I'll have a quiet word with him.'

'I'd like to know that James is safe and well, that's all.'

'I'll see what I can do.' George frowned as he puffed at his cigar, as if considering the scale of the task ahead of him. 'There's no danger I'll bump into Brigham in Paris, is there?'

'None. He's been granted extended recuperative leave by the Foreign Office. I believe he's spending it at his villa in Cannes.'

'He'll invite you down there if you give him the slightest encouragement.'

'I won't be encouraging him, George, however slightly. That door is closed.'

'Glad to hear it.'

'The Secret Service man James and Ashley have both spoken of. Mr Appleby. It might be best to avoid him if at all possible.'

'He'll have no interest in me, Win. I'll just be doing what I'm supposed to do at work: a little quiet brokering.' George laid a protective hand on his sister's shoulder. 'Leave it to me.'

SAM TWENTYMAN ASSUMED WHEN HE TOOK THE JOB OF chief mechanic for the fleet of cars servicing the British Empire Delegation to the Paris Peace Conference that conferring would be suspended on Sundays and peace would therefore reign in the cavernous garage of the Hotel Majestic at least one day a week.

But Sundays, he discovered, though quiet by comparison with Monday to Saturday, were not wholly lacking in demands for transport, although those demands were so unpredictable that the drivers and mechanics on duty were usually either too few or too many.

The latter was the case this Sunday, with the consequence that a couple of drivers' card schools were in session, the players seated on spare crates and boxes. The mechanics were whistling and joking while they checked and retuned some of the engines. And Sam was in his cubby-hole office, sipping treacle-sweetened tea to aid his concentration as he sought to bring order to the chaos of his predecessor's paperwork.

Quite how the small, smiling, morning-suited oriental reached the threshold of his office without anyone noticing him Sam could not afterwards have said, nor how long he was there before coughing delicately to signal his presence. But so it was and so he did.

Sam started with surprise, spilling his tea and cursing as some of it spattered across the garage ledger. 'Blimey O'Reilly, where did you spring from?'

'So sorry.' The man bowed, wringing his hands apologetically as he did so. He gazed at Sam through large, round, steel-framed spectacles and went on, smiling, 'You are Mr Twentyman?'

'Yeah. That's me. Sam Twentyman.'

'My name is Yamanaka. I am with the Japanese delegation.'

'Really? Well, what can I do for you, Mr Yamanaka?'

'I assist Commissioner Kuroda. You have heard of him?'

'Er, yes.' Sam had never met Commissioner Masataka Kuroda, security officer to the Japanese delegation, but knew, because Max had told him, that he was a friend of Sir Henry Maxted. Kuroda had given Max invaluable information about the Japanese government's dealings with Fritz Lemmer and the importance of the so-called Chinese box, a cache of documents stolen from the Chinese delegation on its way to the conference.

'He wishes to speak with you, Mr Twentyman.'

'Me? Why?'

'Only he can tell you. He is waiting for you outside. Will you come?'

'Well, I'm not—'

'It has to be now, Mr Twentyman.' The smile was still in place. But Yamanaka's tone was earnest. 'Delay is not possible.'

Before leaving Paris, Max had asked Sam, as his most trusted friend – in fact, his only trusted friend – to deal with anything affecting his interests that occurred in his absence. He had not been able to say what might arise. But he had upset a lot of people during his time there. And not all of the consequences of that had necessarily worked themselves out.

'Chances are nothing will happen, Sam. But I know I can rely on you to do your best for me.'

'That you can, sir.'

'Don't take any risks on my account, though. I'm not worth it.'

'Right you are, sir.'

A gleaming limousine was parked in the mews. Yamanaka opened a rear door for Sam to climb in, where Kuroda was waiting – a tall, thin, ascetically gaunt old man, morning-suited like his assistant, though there the resemblance ended. Sam had difficulty imagining such an obviously serious man ever actually smiling.

'Mr Twentyman,' Kuroda said, his voice soft and precise. 'Thank you for agreeing to speak to me.'

'Pleasure, I'm sure, sir.'

'Let us hope so.' A closed glass panel sealed them off from Yamanaka and the driver. Kuroda tapped on it with the handle of a tightly furled umbrella. The car started away.

'Where are we going?' Sam asked, faintly alarmed.

'I am going home, to Japan. My journey begins at the Gare de Lyon. We travel there together. Then you will be free to return here, while I board a train for Marseilles.'

'You're going home, in the middle of the conference?'

'I have no choice. I have been summoned. To answer certain . . . accusations.'

'Sorry to hear that, sir.'

'The accusations are groundless. I will be exonerated. That is certain. Unhappily, that is not the point.'

'No?'

'You are Max's friend, Mr Twentyman.' His eyes were sorrowful and far-seeing. 'He spoke of you. And my enquiries confirm what he said.'

'They do?'

'Do you know where he is?'

'No, sir.'

'And even if you did, you would not tell me.'

'Well, I—'

'Please, please.' Kuroda dismissed the matter with a wave of the hand. 'It is so. And it is rightly so. We are both friends of Max. And he is a friend of us both. Listen to me carefully, Mr Twentyman. I must speak to you of secret things. If it became known to my superiors that I had spoken of them to such a person as you, then I would face accusations I could not answer. But my removal from Paris forces me to confide in you. Will you respect my confidence?'

Sam swallowed hard and nodded. 'Yes, sir.'

'Good. You may trust Yamanaka, but no one else. You understand?'

'I'm not at all sure I do, sir, no.'

'No. But you will. There has been a change in the balance of

51

power within my nation's government since the delegation left Tokyo late last year. The Emperor is ill. The court is divided. To remain in office, Prime Minister Hara has had to agree to send Count Tomura to serve as joint deputy of the delegation under Marquess Saionji. He arrived last week. His son is a junior member of the delegation and has caused much trouble. Now his behaviour will go unpunished. Count Tomura represents a political faction that believes the military should control all aspects of government. He is an enemy to my lord Saionji. And me, of course. He is behind my summons to Tokyo.

'I am fearful of what Count Tomura plans to do. Officially, his purpose is to stiffen the delegation's resistance to pressure from the United States to make concessions to China over Shantung. You have read about this, perhaps?'

Sam shook his head. 'No, sir.'

Kuroda raised a single eyebrow to signal his disappointment at Sam's failure to follow the news of Sino–Japanese relations and cast a weary glance out at the Seine as they travelled along the Cours la Reine. The French Foreign Ministry building on the Quai d'Orsay, where, as Sam knew, the business of the conference was painstakingly pursued amid the unrolling of maps and the tabling of demands, appeared ahead of them on the other side of the river.

'The Shantung peninsula was wrested from Chinese control by Germany in 1897. The Japanese army expelled German forces in 1915 and have occupied Shantung since then. Japan's present policy is to insist the occupation continue. The Chinese are naturally opposed to this, as is the United States. Marquess Saionji is suspected by some of sympathizing with the case for restoring Shantung to the Chinese. Count Tomura is here to ensure he does not yield on the issue.'

'Very interesting, sir,' said Sam, feeling he should say something.

'But you do not know Shantung from Southend.' Kuroda surprised Sam by smiling thinly at him.

'You've, er, heard of Southend, have you, sir?'

'I have been there, Mr Twentyman. I strolled along the promenade with a young lady in Southend long ago, when I was also young.'

52

'Blimey.'

'It is true. And what I am about to tell you is also true. Count Tomura is set upon more than Japanese retention of Shantung. He has a greater, darker objective. I do not know what it is. He has arranged for me to be recalled to Tokyo to prevent me finding out. I will speak now of matters I believe you will be aware of because Max has told you of them. Never admit your awareness of these things to anyone else except Yamanaka. To do so would put his life as well as yours at risk.

'The faction Count Tomura represents was responsible for hiring Tarn to find and kill Lemmer. Thanks to Max, he failed. That failure has led to a change of policy. I believe the faction now hopes to neutralize the threat Lemmer poses as a result of his acquisition of the Chinese box by coming to terms with him rather than eliminating him. How that is to be achieved I do not know. Why they should wish to enter into an alliance with him I also do not know, though I may learn the answer to that question in Tokyo.

'There is a fly in the ointment, however: someone who knows too much about Tarn and Lemmer and Count Tomura's fellow travellers to be allowed to live. I sense Count Tomura is particularly concerned about him, perhaps for personal reasons. I speak of le Singe. There is a belief that he entered our delegation's hotel, as well as Marquess Saionji's residence, without being detected, perhaps more than once, and stole – or memorized the contents of – various secret documents. Since his arrival Count Tomura has taken large collections of such documents into his keeping, ostensibly to safeguard them. But he is a tiger who roars so that none will challenge him and discover he is lame. There is a secret touching him, buried deep within all the other secrets. I believe Sir Henry Maxted may have learnt what it is. And I believe he may have learnt it from le Singe.

'If I am correct, le Singe is a threat to Lemmer as well as Count Tomura. He has nowhere to turn for protection. But his wits and his wiles will serve him well. He will not be easy to find. Count Tomura will therefore seek out those he suspects of knowing le Singe. Max is one. But Max has disappeared. So, where will he turn? Who is there close to Max who might also be able to locate le Singe?' Kuroda looked at Sam searchingly.

'You mean—'

'Exactly. You, Mr Twentyman.'

'Oh, my giddy aunt.'

'Quite so.'

Sam clapped a hand to his mouth in dismay. 'You're sure about this, sir?'

'Sure enough to give you this warning. I believe they will come for you eventually.'

'But . . . I don't know where le Singe is.'

'They will not believe you. Nor will they believe you do not know whatever they suspect le Singe knows.'

'You're saying they'll kill me, aren't you?'

'I am sorry to say they will, if it seems to them to serve their purpose.'

'What can I do?'

'You have a little time, Mr Twentyman. I do not think they know yet who you are. And I sense Count Tomura is proceeding at a cautious pace. Other issues will determine how fast he can move. I suspect he wishes to settle the Shantung issue before proceeding with his other objectives, whatever they may be. But they will include le Singe. That is certain. And therefore, sooner or later . . .'

'They'll include me.'

Kuroda nodded solemnly. 'Yes.'

'Bloody hellfire.'

'As to what you can do, only two courses of action commend themselves. The first is flight.'

'Run and hide, you mean?'

'But hiding, I sense, is not your forte. Nor probably your inclination.'

'What's the second course of action?'

'Find le Singe before Count Tomura finds you. Learn the secret that will bring him down. And then . . .'

Sam gulped. 'Bring him down.'

'Yamanaka will help you if he can. There is a laundry in Rue Frédéric-Sauton – la Blanchisserie Orita – where you can leave messages for him and he for you. The owner is a cousin of his and can be trusted. You have that?'

'Rue Frederick Soton. Bloncheesery . . .'

'Orita.'

'Orita,' Sam repeated.

'Max booked out of the Hotel Mazarin on the fifth of this month. Have you heard from him since?'

'No, sir.'

'If you do, please warn him also.'

'Of course.'

'When we last met, he asked me if a certain English surname meant anything to me.'

'Farngold.'

Kuroda nodded. 'That was the name.'

'And it didn't mean anything to you, he said.'

'If you hear it from another, especially le Singe—'

'I've never heard anything from le Singe, sir. Nor has Max. He doesn't seem to speak.'

'Remember the name, Mr Twentyman. It could be crucial.'

'I'll remember, sir.'

'Remember also: the skilful warrior does not rely on the enemy not coming; he relies on his own preparedness. You have a chance.' Kuroda inclined his head towards Sam and fixed him with his soulful gaze. 'Use it.'

Max woke early on Monday morning, well before the
time set on his alarm clock. The dawn was grey and drizzly,
but he did not care. He reviewed the events of Sunday over a stale
cigarette with shame – and relief they had now lapsed into the past.
He only wished he could forget what had happened. But there was
no chance of that.

The arrival on the scene of Sergeant Tulloch had done nothing
to pierce the darkness surrounding Selwyn Henty's whereabouts.
The good sergeant had asked if Selwyn was a drinking man and
had reluctantly suggested he might have fallen into the harbour
and drowned. Privately, Max had little doubt of it, except that he
believed Selwyn had not fallen, but been pushed.

Tulloch had decided to organize a search of the harbour and
inner bay by boat, leaving Susan Henty to her own devices. Unable
to bear the thought of sitting at the Ayre Hotel and waiting for
news, she had resolved to tramp the city, armed with a snapshot of
her brother, asking passers-by if they had seen him. Max had been
obliged to accompany her. The exercise had been in vain.

Clearly clutching at straws, Susan had suggested Selwyn might
have gone back to the Ring of Brodgar to study the alignment of
the stones at sunrise. Why he should have done so without telling
her or how he would have travelled there under his own steam were
questions that had gone unanswered. They had set off in the car to
discover whether he was still there. This journey had also been in
vain.

Max felt a heel and a wretch for his treatment of Susan. He was more or less certain he knew the truth. But he could not speak of it without exposing his stated reasons for being in the Orkneys as a sham.

Late on Sunday, he had set about covering his tracks.

'I forgot with all that's been going on to tell you earlier, Susan, I'm going to Hoy tomorrow to see the *Vanguard* memorial. I had a message from the fleet chaplain saying he'd be happy to show me round the cemetery. I'll be away overnight. I'm so sorry about the timing.'

'Obviously you must go, Max. It's not as if you can do anything here.'

'I only wish that weren't true.'

'But it is. There's nothing I can do either. I greatly fear . . .'

'Don't say it.'

'I'll go on hoping, of course.'

'You should.'

'He was missing once in the war, you know, but he came through.'

'There you are, then.'

'But this is a small island. And there isn't a war being waged on it.'

'Even so . . .'

'Thank you for all you've done, Max. I really am awfully grateful.'

Max winced at the memory of Susan's tearful gaze as he walked out of the Ayre, travelling bag in hand. He headed for the Castle Hotel, where the coach service to Stromness left from, composing in his head as he went the letter he would send Susan before quitting Orkney, explaining that news of a death in his family – a grandmother, perhaps – meant he would have to leave without returning to Kirkwall. Naturally, he would forget to give her any means of contacting him. It was the damnedest business, it really was. But it would have to be done.

Sam was sharp with several mechanics that morning, which he could see by their reactions surprised them. They looked relieved when he withdrew into his office to brood on his problems over a pot of tea and a succession of cigarettes. He had tried to convince himself Kuroda was mistaken. But the truth was he believed the old man's every word. Sitting tight and doing nothing was not the answer. Nor was fleeing, especially since it was far from clear where he could flee to. He was left with only one course of action open to him: find le Singe and learn what he knew.

But how? He would have valued Appleby's advice, but he had promised Kuroda he would tell no one what they had discussed. Where, then, could he turn?

He turned over in his mind everything he knew about le Singe, which was precious little. The boy had to live somewhere. And those who engaged his services had to have some means of contacting him. What could it be? How had Sir Henry managed it?

Then, in a flash, it came to him. Max had voiced the suspicion that Sir Henry had been put on to le Singe by Travis Ireton. Yes, of course. The well-informed Mr Ireton. He would not tell the likes of Sam the time of day, let alone how to find le Singe. But there was someone close to Ireton who might be a little more forthcoming.

Sam picked up the telephone.

The Orkney Motor Express service from Kirkwall to Stromness was thinly patronized that morning. Max watched the spring-tinged fields and hills unfurl around him as the journey proceeded. He wished the day over so he could head out for the rendezvous with Wylie and be on with the urgent business of the night. He recollected Sam's advice whenever he chafed at cancelled missions or groundings on account of bad weather during the war. *There's not a minute that passed quicker for wishing it would, sir.* It was no more helpful now than it was then. But at least the recollection made him smile.

Stromness was a narrow, grey-stone town strung out along the western shore of the deep inlet of Hamnavoe. It looked grim and unwelcoming to Max as the coach drove down into it. He could see the northern hills of Hoy as a dark, blurred mass somewhere ahead, beyond the sound that formed one of the entrances to

Scapa Flow. The Flow itself lay to the east, with the ships he knew to be dotted across it invisible in the murk.

Discharged from the coach by the harbour, Max headed for the main hotel, the Stromness, and booked himself in for the night. The rest of the day and the evening that would follow stretched unenticingly ahead and he had little hope of doing anything but pass the hours stoically.

The only reconnaissance he needed to carry out was swiftly accomplished: a walk round the harbour to the contractor's yard established where Wylie was due to meet him; the men at work there, unloading timber, paid him no attention.

After a cheerless lunch, Max walked out of the town, past a busy boatyard, aiming for the headland overlooking Hoy Sound. An army encampment restricted access, however. It housed a battery to defend the entrance to Scapa Flow and was still manned, though the men he saw had a lethargic, post-war slouch to them. Evidently no one was expecting the Germans to make a run for it.

But there were other precautions against such a possibility nonetheless. Between Stromness and Hoy lay the island of Graemsay. A Royal Navy destroyer was on station in the waters between Graemsay and Mainland. Beyond it, Max could see a line of what appeared to be trestles stretching across the sound from Mainland to Hoy, with a gateway in the middle permitting access to Scapa Flow. And in the distance he could make out the dark smudges of the anchored German ships. They were securely bottled up, no question.

Wylie had privileged access, of course. That was crucial to Fontana's plan. But if anything went wrong, if the Navy suddenly, for whatever reason, cast their beady eye upon them . . .

There would be no way out. There was no question about that either.

Sᴀᴍ ᴡᴀꜱ ᴛᴀᴋɪɴɢ ᴀ ꜰɪɴᴀʟ ᴡᴀɴᴅᴇʀ ʀᴏᴜɴᴅ ᴛʜᴇ Mᴀᴊᴇꜱᴛɪᴄ garage before locking up for the night when a figure stepped in out of the rain drumming down in the mews. He was wearing a long black waterproof with the collar turned up and his face was barely visible beneath the brim of his sodden hat, but Sam recognized Schools Morahan by his mountainous build alone.

'Mr Morahan,' he called. 'Am I glad to see you.'

'I guess the feeling's mutual,' Morahan growled, the lamplight catching the crumpled prow of his nose as he took off his hat and shook it. 'If only because seeing you means I'm in out of the rain.' He shuddered. 'I reckon it's cold enough to snow. So much for spring, huh?'

'I didn't think you'd turn out in this weather.'

'Malory said you sounded worried.'

'Well, I suppose I am, but—'

'Got anything warming to give a feller on a foul night?'

'Whisky?'

Morahan smiled. 'Now you're talking.'

Sam led the way into his office, where he lit the paraffin stove and produced his emergency bottle of Bell's. He poured a generous measure for Morahan into the less chipped of his two enamel mugs and a smaller one for himself. 'Take the weight off,' he said, gesturing to the only chair.

Morahan took his coat off and sat down, leaning forward to warm his hands by the stove. 'You've got yourself a nice job, here, Sam, tuning limousines to ferry the big shots round Paris.'

'Not bad, is it?' Sam sat down on the upturned box he generally used as a chair when anyone above him in the pecking order came calling. He raised his mug. 'Cheers.'

'Your health.' Morahan sighed with pleasure as he swallowed his first mouthful. 'The first drop of the day's always the best.'

'Have you been busy?'

'Not half as busy as you have, I'll wager. There was a plenary session as well as a Council of Four meeting, so there'll have been a deal of coming and going for you to manage. Of course, it's the Council of Three, really, now Italy have walked out. Think they'll be back, Sam? What's the word in the garage?'

'We don't talk about that kind of thing, Mr Morahan. I don't know why the I-ties left, so whether they're likely to come back . . .' Sam shrugged.

Morahan grinned. 'You didn't ask to see me about the conference, then?'

'Not unless they were talking about China and Japan.'

The remark had popped out of Sam's mouth before he could ponder the wisdom of uttering it. And Morahan looked greatly puzzled by it, as well he might. 'China and Japan, Sam? What's your interest in matters oriental?'

'Nothing. That is, I just . . . wondered.'

'Wondered, did you? I call that odd. Especially when you consider they *were* talking about China and Japan. Or rather *not* talking about them.'

Sam frowned. 'You've lost me.'

'The plenary session this afternoon was to approve the League of Nations covenant. Japan raised no objections. There are rumours that means they've struck a deal with the Council of Four over Shantung. Wilson's bought them off, in other words. Probably reckoned he couldn't risk another walk-out after the Italians flounced back to Rome. So, Japan get what they want: a chunk of Chinese territory. Well, that's the rumour, anyway. But why should you care?'

Sam was in no position to answer that question without breaking his promise to Kuroda. He suspected he was looking pretty downcast, though. Events had moved more quickly than Kuroda had led him to expect. If Japan had secured Shantung, Count Tomura was free to turn his attention to the matter of finding le Singe. Sam forced a smile onto his lips. 'You're right, Mr Morahan. Why should I?'

But Morahan was not about to be fooled by a mere smile. 'You tell me.'

Sam only wished he could. He owed Morahan his life. He liked and admired the man. He seemed to be the kind of American Sam wanted to believe in, though his Tom Mix credentials were undermined by his association with Travis Ireton, a man condemned by Max as devious and dishonourable. Morahan was apparently neither. But what exactly he did for Ireton Sam did not know and did not dare to ask. Not directly, anyway. 'Mr Ireton sells information, doesn't he? I mean, that's his business.'

Morahan nodded. 'It is.'

'And you work for him.'

'With. Not for. There's a big difference.'

''Course. Sorry. Thing is . . .'

'Yuh?' Morahan prompted. 'What is the thing?'

Sam took a deep breath. 'I need some information.'

'But surely not the kind Travis deals in. Conference tittle-tattle, Sam. What's your interest in that?'

'I'm in a spot of bother.'

'Oh . . . What kind?'

'I can't say.' Sam gave a heavy sigh and engaged Morahan eye to eye. He needed the American to believe him. 'Honest. I can't go into the details. It would be . . . unfair to someone else. The fact is though . . . certain people . . . are looking for le Singe.'

'Le Singe? What's he to you?'

'Nothing. Except . . . these certain people . . . could easily think I know where he is.'

'Why would they think that?'

'Because le Singe was working with Tarn. And Max killed Tarn. And le Singe . . . did nothing to stop him.'

'Or maybe did something to help him.' Morahan was fully alert now. 'Is that how Max got the drop on Tarn, Sam? Is that why le Singe has gone to ground?'

'All I know is that some nasty pieces of work are after le Singe and if they can't find him they'll come looking for people they think know where he is.'

'Such as Max. And in his absence . . .'

Sam nodded. 'Me.'

'So you figure to track le Singe down before they pay you a visit and . . . what?'

'I just need you to point me in the right direction, Mr Morahan, that's all.'

But Morahan was still turning over in his mind what Sam had already said. 'Are those "nasty pieces of work" Japanese, Sam? Travis told me there was a rumour Tarn was working for them. I can't imagine they'd spend much time chasing a subordinate who'd betrayed him, though. There'd have to be more to it, which, judging by your expression, there is.'

'*You'll never play anyone false, my lad,*' Sam remembered his mother once saying to him. '*What's on your mind is always written on your face, plain as day.*' 'Will you help me, Mr Morahan?'

'By revealing one of Travis's trade secrets? He wouldn't like that.'

'He needn't know.'

'He has a habit of knowing everything in the end. Then where would I be?'

'You saved my life, Mr Morahan. It'd be a terrible waste of effort if I lost it barely a month later for the lack of a word to the wise, wouldn't it?'

Morahan frowned. 'Did Malory put you up to saying that?'

'No. 'Course not. It's just I'm—'

'Only she treated me to some piece of Buddhist philosophy once that says if you save someone's life you go on being responsible for it until the day they die. Or you do.' Morahan smiled and pointed at Sam accusingly. 'I'll be damned if I'm going to spend my declining years nursemaiding *you*.'

'You needn't worry about that, Mr Morahan. I'm not a Buddhist.'

'And neither am I. So don't expect me to ride to the rescue every time you get in a fix.'

'I won't.'

'Mmm.' Morahan glared down at his whisky, then across at Sam. 'Any word from Max?'

'Not a peep.'

'So, I guess you've nowhere else to turn but good ol' me.'

'Sorry.'

'If you get yourself killed, I won't feel guilty, you know, whatever Malory says – or the Buddha himself.'

'I wouldn't expect you to.'

'Interested in antiquities?'

The question took Sam aback. 'Antiquities?'

'Yuh. You know. Statues of Greek gods. Ancient Egyptian amulets. That kind of thing.'

'Well, er, no.'

'Perhaps you should be. There's an antiquarian gallery in Passage Vendôme, off Place de la République, where you could pick up one of Alexander the Great's saddlebags, say, if you had the money and the inclination – and more faith than I could recommend in the proprietor's integrity.'

'I'm not sure I—'

'Laskaris and Soutine, Sam. They're the people for what you want. Well, Soutine, actually. Laskaris is just a name over the door. Soutine's your man.'

'He can lead me to le Singe?'

'He's been a source of valuable information for Travis – the kind of information le Singe is rumoured to have procured on his fishing expeditions round the delegations. But these last few weeks the source has dried up. No one's seen le Singe. Or even had cause to suspect he's paid them a clandestine visit. And Soutine's had nothing to sell but antiquities. As to whether he could lead you to le Singe, I guess the answer is maybe – if he wanted to. But he won't want to. And I don't rightly see how you'd be able to persuade him.'

'I have to try.'

'Good luck, then.'

'You know this man personally, Mr Morahan – Soutine?'

'I've met him a couple of times. Wouldn't trust him further than I could throw him. Maybe not even as far as that, considering he's no heavyweight. He's a dealer, Sam. You'll get nothing from him without paying over the odds for it. And what you want could be very expensive. That's if you get the chance to talk to him in the first place. Last I heard from Travis on the subject, Soutine had left town. Have you thought of doing that yourself?'

'They'd probably come after me wherever I went. Then I'd have chucked in a good job for nothing.'

'You could ask Appleby for help.'

'I can't do that. This has to stay . . . unofficial.'

'Then try Soutine.'

'I will. Thanks.'

'Don't mention it. Literally, I mean.' Morahan looked hard at Sam until he had extracted a nod of understanding. 'My advice is: if the threat's serious, make yourself scarce. I could give you some hints on how to do that without leaving a trail. A job is just a job. You can always get another.'

'I'll think about it.'

'OK.' Morahan drained his mug and stood up. 'But don't think too long, huh?'

DUSK IN STROMNESS: THE GREYNESS OF THE TOWN INTENSIFIED by the greyness of the light. Max trudged through the drizzle back along the main street towards his hotel, dismally aware that he had many hours to wait yet before his rendezvous with Wylie. There was nothing to do and no one to speak to. His experience with the Hentys was a warning against making the acquaintance of strangers. He wondered what Sam was doing at that moment in Paris: downing a bottle of Bass at the Majestic, perhaps, before a meat-and-two-veg dinner rustled up by the imported English chefs. How Max envied him. How he wished he was in Paris himself, taking it easy, like lucky old Sam.

But Sam was not taking it easy in Paris. He had taken the Métro to République, emerging into the square to find Morahan's prediction had been correct: it was snowing hard. He wondered bitterly whether there would be a spring at all this year. One of the mechanics had suggested all the shells fired in the war had poisoned the atmosphere. Sam had pooh-poohed the idea. Now he was not so sure.

Passage Vendôme was an arcade linking Place de la République with the street behind it. Most of the shops and offices were closed and in darkness. He had to pirouette his way round a drunken old soldier to make progress, the man's rantings echoing boomingly in the arcade. '*L'héro de la guerre, c'est moi! L'héro de la merde, c'est moi!*'

There it was. *Laskaris et Soutine, Antiquaires.* Like the other premises, the gallery was in darkness, with a *Fermé* sign on the door. But there was a lamp on in the room above, light from it spilling down a spiral staircase into the gallery itself, illuminating assorted paintings and statuary and objets d'art.

Sam was about to knock on the door, when the light went out, casting the gallery into deep shadow. A few seconds passed, then a figure that was no more than a shadow itself appeared on the stairs. It descended slowly into the gallery and moved towards the door. Sam took a step back, then another into the doorway opposite.

A key was turned in a lock. A latch was slipped. The door opened. A small man in a dark overcoat and homburg emerged, jangling a bunch of keys. He was carrying an umbrella and a bulging Gladstone bag that was heavier than he was used to, to judge by the grunts he gave as he manoeuvred to close the door behind him, casting a wary glance towards the drunkard as he did so.

'Monsieur Soutine?' Sam asked, moving smartly across the arcade.

The man started violently. '*Mon Dieu,*' he gasped. He peered suspiciously at Sam in the thin light of the arcade lamps. '*Qui est-ce?*' He had a flat, loose-skinned face given some distinction by a snowy white Vandyke beard. His small, blue eyes shone like two sapphires dropped in a bowl of porridge.

'*L'héro de la guerre, c'est moi!*' came the slurred bellow.

'Are you Monsieur Soutine?' Sam asked.

'You are English?'

'Yes. But are—'

'I am not Soutine.'

'*L'héro de la merde, c'est moi!*'

'But . . . this is your gallery.'

'Yes, yes. But I am Laskaris, not Soutine. You are looking for my partner?'

'Er, yes. Yes, I am.'

'I am also looking for him.'

'Any idea where he is?'

'No. Of course not. Otherwise—'

'*L'héro de la guerre, c'est moi!*'

'Ach. Come inside.' With an impatient flap in the direction of the drunkard, Laskaris retreated into the gallery, beckoning for Sam to follow. He vanished somewhere amid the shadows, then threw a switch. A lamp standing on a desk in a corner came on, its light a particularly sickly hue of yellow-green.

Laskaris rested the Gladstone bag on a stone sarcophagus bearing faded carvings on its side and sighed wearily. His shoulders dropped and Sam noticed how dusty his clothes were. Laskaris appeared to notice at the same time and started to brush some of the dust off.

'I do not normally come here, Mr . . .'

'Twentyman.'

'Twentyman?' Laskaris gave all three syllables of Sam's name a lot of studious emphasis. His accent was not French, though he was certainly not English. Sam would not have been able to place him on a map of Europe. 'Does Soutine owe you money?'

'No, no. Nothing like that.'

'You surprise me. Most of the customers I have heard from since Soutine' – he pursed his lips and made a plosive noise accompanied by a gesture symbolizing disappearance into thin air – 'have wanted to be paid for something. Or paid back for something they did not receive. I am Soutine's *commanditaire*, you understand. His . . . inactive partner.'

'Sleeping partner?'

'Sleep? I wish I could. Telephone calls. Telegrams. Callers. I am besieged. See that?' Laskaris pointed to an elephant's foot standing by the door. 'Would you believe that belonged to one of the elephants who crossed the Alps with Hannibal?'

'Er, I don't think so, no.'

'Wise of you, Mr Twentyman. It seems others are less wise. Or perhaps my partner is more persuasive than I am. Ach, Alphonse. How could you do this to me? It's too much.'

'How long . . . has Monsieur Soutine been gone?'

'I do not know. It is a week since I began receiving complaints about him. Unpaid bills. Undelivered goods. And I am liable for them. I am an honest man. I have a reputation. I *had* a reputation. Now I have migraines.'

'Where does he live?'

'Here.' Laskaris pointed up the spiral stair. 'In the rooms above. So he told me, anyway. "I do not need a large house, Viktor, when I travel so much to buy antiquities." Ach, another lie. No, no. There is a house somewhere. A chateau, where he reclines on his chaise longue with his mistress. But I do not know where it is. I do not know where *he* is.'

'It's important I find him, Monsieur Laskaris. I, er . . . It's very important.'

'But not because of money?'

'No. Not because of money.'

'Then it cannot be so important.'

'How long have you known him?'

'Alphonse? Ach, too long. We met in Tunis, many years ago. He owned a vineyard then.' Laskaris chuckled at some bittersweet memory. 'Probably he did not own it. Probably he has sold things here that he did not own. It seems to be what he does. And I am left to answer for it.'

'I'm sorry for your predicament, but I do need to find him.'

'Yes, yes. I understand. But you must understand also. I do not know where he has gone. What do you want from him if it is not money, Mr Twentyman?'

'Have you, er, heard of someone called . . . le Singe?'

'Le Singe?' Laskaris frowned. 'You mean the burglar they call le Singe? I read about him at my barber's. I only read newspapers when I visit my barber. It is something to do while I wait. I think perhaps I should find something else to do. The news upsets me.'

'I believe . . . Monsieur Soutine knows le Singe, you see.'

'He knows le Singe? Then it is worse than I thought. Why would he know such a person?'

'I'm not sure. I—'

'I must go to the police. Alphonse has left me no choice. Yes, yes. Tomorrow. No more . . . shilly-shally. Now, I must go home and rest.'

'But how—'

'I cannot help you, Mr Twentyman. I cannot help anyone. Even myself. I am useless, it seems. But here.' Laskaris took something from his pocket, hoisted his Gladstone bag off the sarcophagus and advanced to join Sam by the door. 'My card. Telephone me – or call, if you must – in a few days. I may have news of Soutine. I may not. I think it is unlikely. But . . . you may contact me if you wish.' He gave a heavy, heartfelt, sigh. 'I will do as much as I can.'

Sam headed back to the Majestic in a pessimistic frame of mind. He strongly suspected Laskaris would have no news for him if and when they spoke again. The man was Soutine's dupe, nothing more. They might both end up suffering for what they were wrongly thought to know: where le Singe was hiding. Soutine had decided to drop out of sight and evidently knew how to. Sam would have to try some other way of tracing le Singe. But he had no idea what way that might be.

In Stromness, the evening fused with the night. The town was quiet to the point of eeriness. Max tried to sleep for a couple of hours after dinner, but could not seem to. Then, within minutes of finally dropping off, he was woken by the alarm. It was midnight. The waiting was over.

A FIGURE LOOMED OUT OF AN INKY SLAB OF SHADOW INTO A patch of lamplight as Max reached the gate of the builder's yard. Wylie was a short, wiry fellow in a skipper's cap and pea jacket, with a smell about him of coarse tar and rough tobacco.

'You're early,' was all he said.

'Tom Wylie?'

'Aye.'

'I'm Max Hutton.'

'I know who you are. Ready?'

'Yes.'

'Let's go.'

It was a short, dark walk from the yard to the harbour. The drizzle had seeped into the stillness of the night. The sea was an unseen presence, though audible as it lapped and gently slapped at the quay and the hulls of moored vessels.

'We're here,' said Wylie, leading the way down a short flight of steps to a small fishing boat roped up to the quay. Her engine was turning over, smoke curling up from the funnel. Evidently Wylie was intent on a prompt departure. 'Cast off as you come.'

Max unwound the rope from the bollard and jumped aboard.

'Are you much of a seagoer?' Wylie asked.

'Not really, no.'

'You'll be glad it's such a calm night, then. And there's no moon-light for anyone to see us by. I'll take us out.'

Wylie headed for the wheelhouse. He throttled the engine and, as he steered the drifter away from the quay, lit a lamp fixed to the wheelhouse roof. It shone ahead of them, out through the mouth of the harbour into Hamnavoe.

'There's some sort of barrier across the sound,' said Max, joining Wylie by the wheel. 'I saw it earlier.'

'The hurdles,' Wylie responded. 'There's a gate in the middle. You needn't worry about them.'

'And a Royal Navy patrol ship.'

'You needn't worry about her either. I come and go across the Flow day and night. They all know me.'

'You won't be stopped – or asked to explain why you're out at this hour?'

'I ferry supplies around the shore bases and there are the Yankee minesweepers to see to as well. I'm always on some errand or other. No one will challenge me.'

'Good.' Max understood from Fontana that smuggling was the real key to Wylie's immunity. There were a lot of bored and homesick sailors in these waters to be furnished with alcohol, tobacco and other luxuries. And Wylie was the man to do it. He was thin-lipped and keen-eyed, white hair cropped close to skull and jaw. He looked aptly named.

'I'll thank you to go below when we get out into the sound, even so. No sense tempting fate.'

'Which ship are we heading for?'

'You'll know that when you go aboard.'

'You can tell me now.'

'No, I can't. Fontana's orders. And it's his orders I follow, not yours. So, take yourself down to the cabin. I'll call you when we get there.'

The cabin would have been cramped even if it had not been crammed with battered cardboard boxes, containing, Max discovered when he prised back the lids of a couple, bottles of whisky and schnapps, packs of cigarettes, tins of tobacco, bars of soap and chocolate: Wylie's boat was evidently a floating Fortnum & Mason for the fleets of three nations.

Max sat down on a bench set at the table in the centre of the cabin. He contemplated broaching one of the bottles of whisky and downing a slug from it, but settled for a cigarette instead. He had changed brands recently in search of one he would enjoy, to little avail. Since being shot in Paris, he seemed, bizarrely, to have lost his taste for smoking. He persisted only because he had been unable to think of anything else to do at times when a cigarette would normally have soothed his nerves.

Seasickness was an additional blow to his spirits that soon made its presence felt as the boat headed out into the sound, if anything worse in the gentle swell than it would have been in heavy weather.

A light raked over the vessel at one point, shafting in briefly through the porthole. There was a distant hoot, to which Wylie responded. Max assumed the patrol ship was signalling him through.

Progress slowed soon afterwards. Peering through the porthole Max saw the shadowy fretwork of the hurdle barrier loom up and recede as they passed through the gate.

Then they picked up speed and soon enough other, different, more massive shapes appeared: the German ships.

Another throttling back alerted Max to their imminent arrival. The hull of a ship blacked out the view through the porthole com-pletely. The boat manoeuvred in. Max heard Wylie moving around above him. There was the thud of a rope landing on the deck, then three sharp thumps on the cabin roof. It was Max's cue.

Wylie had extinguished the bow lantern. The only lights were the wheelhouse lantern and a torch Wylie was using to signal to some-one Max could not see, above them on the rail of the ship.

'Make sure the rope doesn't slip while I fetch the stuff,' Wylie said, dodging past Max and descending to the cabin.

He was soon back with a box. 'Make yourself useful and take that up. Look lively.'

The ascent to the deck of the ship was by a rickety accom-modation ladder, with a misstep and a plunge into the icy water of the Flow all too readily imaginable. Max was relieved when he reached the top, the box clutched awkwardly to his chest. It was seized from him so abruptly he nearly fell backwards down the ladder.

'Steady,' said Wylie, bringing up the rear with another, noticeably smaller box. They clambered onto the deck.

Their reception committee was three-strong, dimly lit by a storm-lantern one of them was holding. They clearly knew Wylie, who enquired in a less than genial tone, 'How are you all?'

'What have you?' was the response from a fellow whose peaked cap suggested he was in charge of his two companions.

'The usual, Bosun,' said Wylie. 'And plenty of it. What have you?'

'Who is this?' A finger was pointed at Max.

'He's to see your captain. Special business. Speak up, man.'

'I have a letter for Fregattenkapitän Schmidt,' said Max.

'Who from?'

'I can't discuss it with anyone but Fregattenkapitän Schmidt.'

'*Scheiße*. What is this, Wylie?'

'You heard him.'

'You cannot see the captain.'

'I must. Tell him the letter is from Anna.'

'Anna?'

'Yes. Anna.'

Silence fell on the deck. The only sound was the chug-chug of the drifter's idling engine. Several seconds passed with painful slowness. Then the bosun said, 'Wait here.' And with that he turned and strode away, light flaring briefly from a companionway as he opened a door and went inside.

'Tread carefully,' Wylie whispered. 'The captains of these ships aren't exactly their masters. A lot of the crews mutinied at the end of the war and they still have their own councils to decide which orders to obey and which to disobey. Don't worry about these two, by the by. They don't speak a word of English.' He raised his voice: 'Do you, boys? Bugger the Kaiser, eh? I bet a few men have. What d'you think?'

There was no response.

'See what I mean?' Wylie continued. 'Admiral von Reuter had to change flagships to find a less restive crew, y'know, so you're lucky it's the *Herzog* I've brought you to. This is one of the more orderly ships.'

'Ever met the captain?'

'No. Not sure you will either.'

'Not a natural optimist, are you, Wylie?'

'Oh, but I am. You get sent away with a flea in your ear and I won't have to come back for you an hour from now, will I? That hour, incidentally? It's already ticking away as far as I'm concerned. So, let's hope Commander Schmidt makes up his mind sharpish, eh?'

Another five minutes or so elapsed excruciatingly as they waited with the two mute sailors. Then the bosun returned.

'The captain will see you,' he announced. 'Are you carrying a weapon?'

'No.'

The bosun spoke in German to one of the sailors, who semaphored for Max to spread his arms and legs. He patted him down and found nothing. There was another exchange in German. Then the bosun turned back to Max. 'Go with him. Now.'

THE DESCENT TO THE CAPTAIN'S CABIN WAS THROUGH A WARREN of companionways and narrow corridors. There was a smell of stale cigarette smoke and unwashed flesh in the turbid air. The sailors and petty officers they met along the way were grey-skinned and sloppily dressed. Their cap bands preserved the name of the ship, but a couple of letters were missing in front of it. SMS *Herzog*, it should have read, the German equivalent of HMS. But only a single S remained. They were no longer in the service of the Kaiser.

The captain was waiting for him, pacing up and down in his cabin. Commander Lothar Schmidt was a tall, lean, weary-eyed man. His face was pale, his bearing calm and dignified. He was one of the defeated. But he had not given up. Maybe, it occurred to Max, he at least was still in the service of the Kaiser.

The sailor who had escorted Max gave his captain a desultory salute and a report of few words. He was coolly dismissed. The door closed behind him. And Max was alone with the man he had been sent to meet.

'You are English?' Schmidt asked in a cultured voice, his German accent educatedly subdued.

'Yes. My name is Max Hutton.'

'You have a letter for me, Mr Hutton?'

'Yes.' Max handed it over.

'Do you know what the letter says?'

'No. I'm just the messenger.'

'Are you sure?' Schmidt prised at the part of the envelope flap that had stubbornly resisted Max's attempt to stick it back down properly, but said no more about it, though his iron-grey eyes rested knowingly on Max. 'The man who sent you must want me to read this letter very badly. You know who he is?'

'Yes. Do you?'

'I recognize the writing, Mr Hutton. But you told the bosun the letter is from Anna.'

'That's what *I* was told.'

'I see.' Max had the discomfiting impression Schmidt actually saw rather a lot. 'Thank you.'

The captain sat down at his desk and made a clearance in a drift of documents. He carefully slit the envelope open with an ornate eagle-headed paper knife and moved a lamp closer to read the letter by.

As he did so, Max's gaze drifted round the cabin. There were no personal touches he could see, but the gleam on the brass fittings suggested Schmidt was determined to maintain standards many of his crew no longer aspired to. There was a rectangular mark on one wall where a picture had clearly once hung: a photograph of the Kaiser, perhaps, resplendent in Grand Admiral's uniform. Schmidt's cap hung on the back of the door. If Max stooped slightly he would be able to see if the band still had SMS embroidered on it in full.

But at that moment Schmidt swung round in his chair, the letter in his hand. 'Do you know much German, Mr Hutton?'

'No. Hardly any.'

'Then you will not be able to read the letter.'

'No. But it's for you, not me.'

'Of course.' There was a bitter hint of a smile then on Schmidt's lips. 'I do not approve of the smuggling that goes on here. But internment at sea is unnatural. The men are restless and discontented. So, they trade with Mr Wylie. And now he delivers . . . you.'

'He'll be back for me within the hour, Commander Schmidt. I must have what I came for by then.'

'And if you do not have it?'

'I understood you'd be willing to cooperate.'

77

'Willing? Anna *begs* me to cooperate. She is my wife, though we have not been together for a long time. Since before the war. She believes I still love her. She offers me our marriage – "as it was at the beginning". She offers me everything. Including my son. "I will love you and be loyal." If only I will give up what I took . . . from Lemmer.'

'And will you?'

'He sent you, yes?'

'Yes.'

'With this plea from Anna. My wife. His secretary. But who is she loyal to? Me? Or him?'

'Perhaps she can be loyal to both of you.'

'No. She cannot. What did I take from him, Mr Hutton? What is it that he wants so badly you have to be smuggled aboard to get it?'

'I'll know it when I see it.'

'The Grey File. Yes. Of course. Lemmer expects me to give it up so that I may have Anna again. He thinks I am tired and disillusioned and eager for the comforts of bed and home. And I am. But not tired or disillusioned or eager enough to oblige him in this. Your journey ends in failure, Mr Hutton. You will not be leaving this ship, with the file or without it. I will have you confined. Then I will inform Admiral von Reuter that I have a British spy aboard and he will decide what to do with you.'

Schmidt had spoken in earnest. Max felt his blood chill. But he held his nerve. 'That wouldn't be wise, Captain.'

Schmidt took a box of matches from his pocket, lit one and held it to the letter.

The flame caught. He dropped the sheet of paper into an ash-tray, where it curled and blackened as it burnt. 'I will deny you gave me a letter from my wife. And I will deny knowing Lemmer, if you are foolish enough to mention his name.'

'What about your son?'

'I will not choose between my son and my country. Germany must be free of men such as Lemmer. I will not help him to survive – or to rebuild his empire. I will do what I can to stop him. You are a traitor to your country, Mr Hutton. I will not be a traitor to mine.'

'You must give me the file.'

'Why should I?'

'Because . . .' Max paused and looked Schmidt in the eye, weighing his chances, judging the next move that might avert disaster – or make it certain. 'You don't want to make an enemy of Lemmer, Captain. If you don't accept the deal he's offering you, he won't give up. He'll get the file back eventually. And he'll probably kill you in the process.'

'I'll take the risk.' Schmidt opened the drawer of his desk and pulled out a revolver. 'Enough.' He stood up, pointing the gun at Max as he did so, and stepped across to a telephone mounted on the wall. He lifted the handset and rotated the handle beneath it. 'This conversation is over, Mr Hutton. You are under arrest.'

'Don't do that.'

'I must.'

'*Stop.*'

'It is useless to—'

'I'm not working for Lemmer.' There was nowhere for Max to turn now but the truth.

'What?'

'Let me explain. Please.'

Schmidt frowned thoughtfully and stared hard at Max. He said nothing. Then someone answered his call. Max could hear the garbled words of German from where he was standing. Still Schmidt said nothing. '*Kapitän?*' the man on the other end bellowed.

'*Nichts,*' said Schmidt. '*Macht nichts.*' He pushed the switchhook down and replaced the receiver. But still he said nothing to Max. And he kept the gun trained on him.

'Will you let me explain?'

Schmidt nodded. That was all.

'My name isn't Hutton. It's Maxted. James Maxted. Everyone calls me Max. My father, Sir Henry Maxted, was a diplomat. He met Lemmer in Japan in 1890, when he was at the British Embassy in Tokyo and Lemmer was at the German Embassy there. Something happened between them. I don't know what. But my father knew something that threatened Lemmer – that still does

79

threaten him. Lemmer's been in Paris since the end of the war, rebuilding his network, plotting, I suspect, to influence the outcome of the peace conference. My father was also in Paris, attached to the British legation. He met a woman there and fell in love with her. He tried to secure their future together by offering to trap Lemmer for the highest bidder. He'd seen Lemmer by chance on a tram. He was one of the few people in Paris able to recognize him. There were quite a few bidders for Lemmer's head. But he got wind of what my father was doing and had him killed. It was because of that our paths crossed. He thinks I've gone over to his side because of the money he'll pay me and the excitement he can supply. He thinks I enjoyed flying fighter planes in the war too much to settle for a dull life. And he thinks I've given up the idea of avenging my father.

'But he's wrong. I haven't given up the idea at all. And it's not just about revenge. Lemmer's planning something. Something that will apply the skills and knowledge of the spies he's recruited to some other purpose now the government he worked for has collapsed. It may be the Grey File is crucial to that. Well, I mean to stop him. Give me the file, Captain, and I'll make sure its contents are known to the British Secret Service. Whatever advantage Lemmer will gain by possessing it will be negated. And maybe I'll get what I need to finish him.'

Schmidt went on looking at Max after he had stopped speaking, but said nothing in response. Eventually, he walked back to the desk and sat down. Then he laid the revolver to one side.

'You admit your father tried to profit from his knowledge of Lemmer?'

'Yes. Love blinded him, I'm afraid.'

'And it was late love, of course,' Schmidt said reflectively. 'The worst kind.'

'If you have me arrested, someone else will come for the file. Someone loyal to Lemmer.'

'You are right.'

'Well, then?'

'Do you know what the Grey File contains?'

'No. I'd have said if I did. I'm not keeping anything from you.'

'No. I believe you are not.' Schmidt swivelled his chair round and drew back a curtain beneath a set of shelves stacked with charts and almanacs. Behind the curtain was a safe. He rotated the combination dial several times, then opened the door. He lifted out a grey file fastened with string and dropped it on the desk. 'This is what you came for.'

The letters NBM were stencilled boldly on the cover beneath the eagle insignia of Imperial Germany. It was the Grey File.

'My wife worships Lemmer. It would be easier for me, I think, if she simply loved him. But no. She worships him. She believes he cannot do wrong. He is her emperor. N is the *Nachrichten-Abteilung*, our secret service. BM was the secret department of it Lemmer ran. *Besonderen Massnahmen* – Special Measures. He holds the rank of commodore. He answered only to Tirpitz and the Kaiser himself. Anna worked for him at his office in the Admiralty building in Berlin. He trusted her. Clearly, he still trusts her. For a time, Anna and I trusted each other as well. She told me some of the things Lemmer did and how he did them. She told me about the Grey File: his record of the spies he recruited in other countries. Every country, whether they were allies or enemies of Germany. The spies are all named here. The dates of recruitment. The money paid to them. The information is in code. But I expect the British Secret Service could break the code if they had the chance.'

'I can give them the chance.'

Schmidt nodded solemnly. 'I know.'

'How did you obtain the file, Captain?'

'I stole it. There should never have been a war. It was certain to be a disaster for my country. The Kaiser is to blame, of course. But he was badly advised. Worse, he was encouraged, by people like Lemmer, to believe his dreams of conquest could be made real. So, should I let Lemmer survive to scheme and spy and help to ruin Germany a second time? No. This' – Schmidt tapped the file with his forefinger – 'is my strike against him.

'I believed war was folly. But I believe every sailor in the Kaiser's Navy should do his duty. I was horrified when so many crews mutinied last autumn. There was chaos in Kiel and Wilhelmshaven. I was one of several commanders called to the Admiralty in Berlin to report on what had happened. But by the time I arrived, there was disorder in the capital as well. The Kaiser had fled to Army headquarters at Spa. His government – his empire – was falling apart. There was no one for me to report *to*. I went to see Anna to find out how my son was. Lemmer's office was closed. I found her at home. She said he was well. I pray he still is. Anna said so in her letter, but . . .

'Lemmer was not in Berlin. Anna would not say where he was or how long he had been gone. "He will make everything right," she insisted. I remember her words. And the look in her eyes. Such loyalty. Such certainty. I decided in that moment to do what I could to damage him. And Anna, of course. My motives were not pure. Whose are?

'I knew where Anna kept the keys to Lemmer's office. I stole them before I left the apartment. That was the day the Kaiser's abdication was announced. November the ninth. I heard the news from a stranger running along Königgrätzer Straße towards the Reichstag. "They're going to proclaim a republic," he told me. A vast crowd was gathering. No one paid any attention to me at the Admiralty. Most of the staff had left. I let myself into Lemmer's office. There was simply no one to stop me. I had the key to Lemmer's filing cabinet. I opened it. And I found what I was looking for.' He tapped the Grey File with his forefinger again.

'I took it back with me to Wilhelmshaven and resumed command of my ship. The Armistice was signed two days later. There was drunkenness and desertion in the fleet while we waited to be told how and where to surrender the ships. But Admiral von Reuter pulled us together when the order came. We sailed in good order.

'And now we sit here, waiting for the treaty that will decide what happens to our ships. We have been here five months. We could be here another two or three. It is a long time when there is little to do but think too much about the past and the future. I have thought a lot about what to do with the Grey File. Lemmer knows I have it. He cannot let me keep it. So, you are right. If you fail, he will send someone else.

'I could have handed it over to the British many months ago. I hesitated because it would be an act of treason for me as a serving officer in the German Navy to surrender a secret intelligence document to a foreign power. Perhaps Lemmer realized I would hold back for that reason. Perhaps he judged he could wait until the treaty was signed and I returned to Germany before attempting to retrieve it. If that is true, something has happened to change his plan. His need of the file has become urgent. And he has sent you to get it.' Schmidt smiled faintly.

'What's amusing you, Captain?'

'Lemmer has solved my moral problem for me. You are his representative. And as far as I know he is still the head of NBM. Therefore, in passing the documents to you, I am not guilty of treason. Take it, then. It is time to use it against him.'

Max stepped forward and picked up the file. 'One more question, Captain.'

'Yes?'

'Has your wife ever mentioned someone – or something – called Farngold?'

Schmidt thought for a moment, then said, 'No. I have never heard the name. Maybe it is in the file.'

'Maybe.'

'You will try to trick Lemmer, I suppose. You will copy the contents of the file and deliver the original to him?'

'Yes.'

'He is not an easy man to trick.'

'I know that.'

'As long as you do.' Schmidt held Max's gaze. 'Do you think you are cleverer than he is?'

'No.'

'Then be careful. Be very careful.'

SCHMIDT GAVE MAX A WATERPROOF CHART ENVELOPE TO CARRY the file in. Max concealed it inside his gaberdine coat, buttoned up and tightly belted to hold it fast, then went back on deck to wait for Wylie.

He did not have to wait long. Wylie's drifter chugged out of the darkness on schedule and drew alongside. Max went down the ladder and jumped aboard.

'Got what you came for?' Wylie asked, looking round from the wheel as he drew away again.

'Just take me back to Stromness.'

'Oh, pardon me for breathing.'

'You have your orders, Wylie. I have mine.'

'Aye. But I'm skipper of this boat and I give the orders while we're at sea. I'll thank you to go below. The lamp's lit for you in the cabin.'

The shadowy bulk of the *Herzog* diminished as the drifter picked up speed, the size of it apparent in the drizzle-smeared darkness only because of its bow and stern lights. A few of the boxes Max had to share the confined space in the cabin with were empty now. But most were not. He wondered if Wylie's nocturnal trade had been curtailed by the need to return him to Stromness. Well, there would be many other nights for Wylie to make up the difference. He would just have to tolerate the inconvenience.

Max sat down at the table, loosened his coat and laid the envelope by his elbow. Then he lit a cigarette and steeled himself to

84

ignore the wallow of the vessel as it ploughed on. He would be in Stromness soon enough. And in the morning he would be on his way.

Then a movement on the companionway caught his eye. Looking round, he was astounded to see Fontana standing in the doorway, holding a gun.

'Hello, Max.' Fontana nodded in the direction of the envelope on the table. 'The Grey File, right?'

'Are you mad? You're not supposed to be here.' Max started to stand up.

'*Sit down.*' Fontana motioned with the gun for emphasis. And Max obeyed. 'Is that the Grey File?'

'Yes.'

'Show me.'

'Not until you explain what the hell you think you're doing.' They were brave words. But Max had a horrible suspicion he already knew what Fontana thought he was doing.

'There's been a change of plan, Max. I'll take the file from here.'

'Why has the plan changed?'

'Ours not to reason. Now, open the envelope, please. I need to see it.'

'Does Lemmer know you're doing this?'

'He told me to do it. I'll shoot you if you force me to, Max. You know I will. Look what happened to Selwyn Henty.'

'Did you shoot him?'

'No. That was an old-fashioned sandbagging. Then he went into Kirkwall harbour with a lump of concrete tied round his ankle.'

'Where am I going? The bottom of Scapa Flow?'

'Just open the envelope.' Fontana levelled the gun. The clarity and calmness of his gaze left Max in no doubt that he meant what he said.

Max opened the envelope and slid the file out onto the table.

'Good. That's it, sure enough. How'd you get Schmidt to hand it over?'

'Does it matter?'

'I guess not. The boss said you'd be able to pull it off and he was right. OK. Take your coat off. And your jacket.'

'Why?'

'I need to check if you've pocketed any of the contents of the file.'

'What will I be doing while you're checking?'

'Take them off, Max.'

'OK.' Max raised his hands in a gesture of surrender. He shrugged his coat and jacket off his shoulders. As he pulled them down towards his waist, he reached into the outer coat pocket, where his fingers closed round the handle of Schmidt's revolver.

'*Take it,*' Schmidt had said. '*I think you may need it. I think Lemmer may not trust you as much as you suppose.*' How right he had been. Lemmer could have sent Fontana after the file. But Schmidt would never have surrendered it to such a man. The secret of Max's success was that he was not loyal to Lemmer. And Lemmer must have known that from the outset. In fact, he had been counting on it.

'You can stand up now,' said Fontana.

Fontana intended to shoot him. Probably not here, in the cabin, but up on deck, where the blood could easily be washed away, after Max's body had been thrown over the side with something heavy tied to it. Yes. That was how Fontana meant to arrange it. He was only following orders, after all. It would be nothing personal.

But this would be. Max swung the gun towards Fontana as he jumped to his feet and fired. Fontana jerked back. The bullet missed him, piercing one of the wooden risers on the companion-way behind him.

Then Fontana fired. But the boat lurched to starboard as he did so and the bullet flew wide, sinking harmlessly into the panelling of the rear wall of the cabin. His feet entangled in the bench, Max was thrown across it by the motion of the boat. A second bullet splintered the edge of the table and narrowly missed him.

Wylie must have wrenched the wheel in surprise when he heard the first shot. Now he pulled it back to port to compensate. Max rolled under the table as Fontana stumbled forward into the cabin. He rolled again, onto his stomach, took aim at Fontana's right knee and fired.

The bullet hit. Max heard the fracturing of bone in the instant before Fontana cried out in pain. The leg gave way beneath him. He hit the floor hard, but kept hold of his gun and focused on Max as he squeezed the trigger. Max fired in the same moment, his head still and upright, whereas Fontana was lying on his side, his shoulder twisted under him, pain coursing up from his knee. He missed. Max did not.

He crawled out from beneath the table, watching Fontana's eyes for signs of life. There were none. Max scrambled to his feet and started up the companionway. With a gun to his head, Wylie would cooperate. He owed Fontana nothing. He was a smuggler, not a spy, and a pragmatist to boot.

But the wheelhouse was empty. The boat was chugging forward slowly under its own steam, with the wheel lashed to hold its course.

Max took in the scene for no more than a second. As he started to turn away, something hard struck his wrist, causing him to cry out and drop the gun. It fell to the deck with a thump. He saw a moving shadow reflected in the glass ahead of him and swung round just in time to raise his arms and block the descending blow.

He was driven back against the wheelhouse. Wylie was armed with a gaff, but Max wrestled it to the horizontal, the hook clear of his face. The shaft, though, pressed at his throat as he scrabbled for a hold.

He was grateful for the days he had spent in the gymnasium in Glasgow. He felt the pressure easing as he strained to push the gaff away from him. And in Wylie's eyes he read the realization that Max was marginally the stronger man.

'Listen to me, Wylie,' Max said, forcing out the words. 'I've no quarrel . . . with you. I got . . . what I came for. Fontana's dead . . . but there doesn't have to be any more killing . . . We put him over the side, weighted to make sure he sinks . . . Then you take me back to Stromness, as agreed . . . and we go our separate ways. What d'you say?'

Wylie gave no immediate answer as the gaff wobbled back and forth in their contesting grasps.

'For God's sake, man. See reason . . . Some dangerous people will come looking for what Commander Schmidt gave me . . . if I don't leave with it. They'll kill you without blinking . . . I'm your best chance of surviving this.'

'You'll never make it to shore without me,' Wylie growled.

'Probably not. So, you see? . . . We need each other.'

Suddenly, Wylie broke away. But he did not lower the gaff. 'The two guns, yours and Fontana's, go over the side with him. I don't want you double-crossing me when we reach Stromness.'

'All right.'

'You're tougher than you look, Mr Hutton. You should know Fontana never told me he meant to kill you.' As Wylie spoke, he slowly lowered the gaff to his side.

What, Max wondered, did Wylie imagine Fontana had been intending to do? Offer Max his heartfelt congratulations on a job well done? 'Where did he come aboard?'

'Scapa Bay. It was easy for him to get there from Kirkwall.'

'Was anyone with him at the pier?'

'Not that I saw.'

It had been a futile question. If Fontana had an accomplice, he would not have shown himself. But without an accomplice how had Fontana planned to get the Grey File to Lemmer? His posting with the US minesweeping fleet would have prevented him leaving Orkney – unless the importance of the Grey File meant it was worth him going absent without leave.

In the end, the uncertainties were too many to anticipate. Max was committed to his course. The file stayed with him. And he would do his damnedest to take it where it would damage Lemmer and his spies the most. 'Do we have an agreement, Wylie?'

Wylie nodded. 'Aye. We do.'

WYLIE WAS A PRACTICAL MAN IF HE WAS NOTHING ELSE. HE managed the dumping of Fontana's body with the grim efficiency he would have applied to the disposal of unwanted contraband. He yielded a little on the question of Max's gun, agreeing to let him keep it so long as it was unloaded. The bullets went over the side. An empty gun was not a lot of use, but Max reckoned he might be able to buy some ammunition for it along the way.

He went below during the journey back to Stromness through the hurdles and past the patrol ship. He joined Wylie in the wheel-house as they closed in on the harbour.

'If anyone asks, you've never heard of me, far less met me, OK?' Max said as the frugal lights of the town gleamed ahead.

'I'll thank you to do the same for me, Mr Hutton. I want no reminders of this night's work.'

'You'll get none from me.'

'The Yanks'll look high and low for Fontana. I'll have to keep my head down. You've caused me a pile of problems.'

'You've caused me a few yourself.'

'Who was Fontana working for?'

'All you need to know is that I'm working for the right side.'

'You'd say that anyway.'

'So I would. But it happens to be true.'

Wylie did not linger at the quayside in Stromness. As soon as Max was on dry land, he cast off and pulled away. Max had not asked where he was going and Wylie had not said. The drifter vanished into the night.

Since Fontana had presumably intended to have Wylie take him back to Scapa Bay, no one was likely to be waiting for Max in Stromness. The short walk to his hotel through the silent, empty streets was nonetheless a nervous one.

'Well, well, sir,' the night porter greeted him. 'I'd given up on you.'

'But here I am. Any messages? Any callers?'

'None, sir.'

That was exactly what Max wanted to hear. No messages. No callers. All was well. 'Do you have a *Bradshaw* I could borrow?'

'Certainly, sir.'

'Thanks. I'll drop it back in the morning. Goodnight.'

'Goodnight, sir.'

Max took a look at the contents of the Grey File as soon as he reached his room. There was a page per name, typed on flimsy paper, in German, naturally, and in code, so that the names made no sense. There were lots of uncoded dates, though, stretching back to the turn of the century, and sums of money, paid in marks. Many ran to four figures, a few to five. Running a spy network was evidently not cheap. He could make no more of the documents than that. But the Secret Service had experts who could break the code and unlock every name and every detail of their treachery. All Max had to do was make sure the file reached them intact.

He left the curtains of his room open to ensure the dawn roused him. He would have liked to be on his way at once, but the mail steamer to Scrabster sailed at 10.45. He had no choice but to sit it out in Stromness until then.

He busied himself writing a letter to Susan Henty explaining his sudden departure from Orkney. Then he pored over the timetables in *Bradshaw* for his journey south.

After breakfast, he headed along to the post office, where he posted the letter and dispatched a telegram – to H. Appleby, Hotel Majestic, Paris: *Coming south with precious cargo. Please advise. M.*

90

Wandering back through the town, Max found himself remembering his last meeting with Appleby, in Paris, three weeks before. *'You'll be on your own once you catch that train,'* Appleby had said with some emphasis as they sat in his office at the Hotel Majestic, in the quiet of early morning. *'You shouldn't contact me unless it's absolutely vital.'*

Lemmer's message to Max had instructed him to board the 11.35 Melun train from the Gare de Lyon if he wanted to accept his offer of employment. It was a step into the unknown he had resolved to take. *'What would you deem absolutely vital?'* Max had asked.

'Something that gives us Lemmer or his network of spies. Preferably both.'

'A tall order.'

'That's why I'm not expecting to hear from you.'

'And you won't. Unless I can deliver the goods. But if I can . . .'

'Let me know at once. I'll render all necessary assistance.'

'I may need it.'

Appleby had smiled wryly at that. *'I imagine you may.'*

And now he did.

Though Max was not to know it, Paris was colder than Orkney that morning. Snow was falling from a gun-metal sky, causing Sam all manner of difficulties in arranging for tyre chains to be fitted to several cars at short notice. He welcomed the problems as a distraction from worrying about his failure to track down Soutine – and hence le Singe. He did not know where to turn next. But he had to turn somewhere. The Paris edition of *The Times*, which he had scanned anxiously in the hotel's lobby earlier, carried a small but disturbing mention of Count Tomura, the very man Kuroda had warned him about.

Rumours are rife that the Japanese have persuaded President Wilson not to oppose their retention of the portion of the Shantung peninsula they seized from Germany early in the war. If this is true, it suggests the arrival in Paris of Count Tomura as joint deputy head

91

of the delegation has invigorated their negotiating tactics. There has been some criticism of Marquess Saionji for representing Japanese interests with insufficient assertiveness. It appears Count Tomura may have been dispatched from Tokyo to insert an iron fist into Saionji's velvet glove.

An iron fist? Sam did not like the sound of that. He did not like the sound of that at all.

A more leisurely start to the Parisian day was being enjoyed by George Clissold at the Hotel Mirabeau, in Rue de la Paix. Proximity to the Opéra and the Place Vendôme suited his vision of how life should be led in the city. He enjoyed wandering the *passages* in search of exotic tobacco or whiling half the day away on a café terrace watching the fashionable world go by.

Unfortunately, he was not in Paris to enjoy himself, which he regretted, since it was far too long since he had been. A note from Arnavon had been waiting for him when he arrived at the Mirabeau the previous evening, agreeing to his cabled suggestion of a time and place to meet. Wisely, George had proposed a venue he could easily stroll to, although it was more likely to be a slither in the prevailing weather. He had not been expecting snow. He had hoped for spring sunshine, a nostalgic taste of the Paris of his youth. But his youth, it seemed, had been mislaid.

Despite the fine napery, the flavoursome coffee and the fresh croissant, George did not feel entirely at ease. For that, more than his looming encounter with Arnavon, was to blame. He had just read the same report in *The Times* as Sam had. And the mention of Count Tomura's name had disturbed him as well.

'Tomura, here, in Paris,' he muttered to himself as he sipped his coffee. 'As portents go, George, old boy, that's a hard one to ignore.'

The morning advanced slowly in Stromness. The wind was getting up and, from the window of his room at the Stromness Hotel, Max could see the masts of the mail steamer swaying at its mooring in the harbour. He did not intend to board until the last moment, although he was confident no one was watching out for him. If

Fontana had an accomplice ready to take the Grey File to Lemmer, he would be in Kirkwall, not Stromness.

There lay the danger. From Scrabster, on the north coast of Caithness, it was a short bus ride to the railhead at Thurso, then a twenty-minute train journey to Georgemas, where Max could catch the mainline service from Wick, on the east coast, to Inverness. But the ferry from Kirkwall to Wick would put Fontana's putative accomplice on the very same train.

It was Tuesday morning and he could not reach London before Wednesday evening, Paris before midday on Thursday. He could not bear the thought of prolonging the journey. Laying up in Thurso was therefore out of the question.

He had one advantage to cling to. Fontana's disappearance would be difficult to interpret. It could be seen as evidence of *his* treachery rather than Max's. Hence the importance of the second telegram he had sent that morning, to Miss N. Kislev, Central Station Hotel, Glasgow: *Coming south with precious cargo. Await my arrival tomorrow. M.*

It was the message he was supposed to send if he was still loyally doing Lemmer's bidding, whatever had passed between him and Fontana. Miss Kislev, of course, was Nadia Bukayeva's travelling alias. She would certainly wait for him.

But she would wait in vain.

HORACE APPLEBY SLOWLY AND METICULOUSLY FILLED HIS PIPE as he leant back in his chair in his basement office at the Hotel Majestic. Before him, on the desk, lay the telegram from Max. *Coming south with precious cargo. Please advise. M.*

It had been sent earlier that morning from Stromness post office in the Orkneys. The Orkneys meant Scapa Flow and the interned German fleet. It was hard to resist a connection with Lemmer. And Appleby had been quite specific that he did not want to hear from Max until and unless he had something that would net Lemmer or his spy network or both.

James Maxted never ceased to surprise. He could seem headstrong and reckless. But he had a rare ability to deliver results. He would not have cabled if he did not have exactly what he said: precious cargo.

Yet the fact he had cabled at all suggested he feared Lemmer might have seen through his subterfuge. He might need help to bring home the bacon.

Appleby lit his pipe and considered what he could do. A cable to London would have an agent heading north to meet Max at, say, Edinburgh, to protect him for the remainder of his journey. That was the obvious thing to do. Appleby could travel to London himself and wait for him there.

But that course of action troubled him deep in his cautious soul. Lemmer's reach was unmeasurable. How many spies he had working for him in England Appleby could not say. But there were some. That was certain. And there was no way of telling what position they might occupy. The exposure of the late and unlamented Herbert Norris as one of Lemmer's operatives was a sobering example. And what worried Appleby most of all was the thought that someone within the service might be on Lemmer's payroll. He had not dared raise the possibility with C. But he had been unable to reason the idea out of his mind.

He ground his teeth on the stem of his pipe. Max had presented him with an unexpected conundrum. Precious cargo, indeed. But how precious? And what should he do to secure it? Just how far out on a limb should he go?

George spotted Arnavon as soon as he entered the Café de la Paix. There were several solitary males dotted around the interior. The snow had driven them inside, to huddle over newspapers and warming coffee or *chocolat*. The one George laid a private bet with himself on being Arnavon was a small, goblin-headed fellow with a patchy beard and a querulous expression: half sycophant, half nitpicker. Yes, that was his man.

And George was right. 'However did you recognize me, Mr Clissold?' Arnavon said, once George had introduced himself.

'A lucky guess,' George replied, pleased to have the upper hand from the start.

Arnavon's accent was authentically North American, but he had been reading *Le Figaro*, as befitted a French Canadian. It was folded open at the editorial page.

'What do the French make of the latest shenanigans at the peace conference?' George asked idly.

Arnavon looked at him in mild surprise. 'They think the Belgians are asking for too much.'

'Nothing about the Japanese in there, then?' George pointed at the paper. '*Café crème et l'eau Vichy*,' he added, for the benefit of the hovering waiter.

'Are you particularly interested in the Japanese, Mr Clissold?'

'No. It's just . . .' George smiled and flapped his hand. 'Never mind.'

'I should say at the outset that I'm grateful to you for coming here to meet me.' Arnavon did not look grateful, in George's opinion. Certainly not as grateful as he should be.

'My sister has a highly developed sense of family honour.'

'Well, selling fake antiquities is rather worse than dishonourable, isn't it?'

'Knowingly selling them is, Mr Arnavon, yes. But my brother-in-law was scrupulously honest. He would never have done such a thing.'

'The fact remains that the articles I bought from him are not what I was assured they were. The matter has caused me considerable embarrassment and left Sir Nathaniel Chevalier significantly out of pocket.'

'And significantly out of humour?'

'I beg your pardon?' Arnavon fixed George with his green-eyed gaze. 'I assumed your willingness to travel here meant you were taking my complaint seriously, Mr Clissold. Is that not so?'

'My sister is taking your complaint seriously, Mr Arnavon. Therefore I'm obliged to. I can't help feeling, however, that your argument is with the dealer you bought the cylinder-seals from, Monsieur . . .'

'Soutine.'

'The very fellow.'

'Conveniently absent from his place of business.'

'It's not convenient for me. Nor is it for you, I imagine. But look here. I'm sure the concept is recognized in Canada of caveat emptor.'

'That does not apply to fraudulent misrepresentation.'

'Henry sold what he believed in good faith – as did his father, Sir Charles Maxted, who bought them in the first place – to be genuine Sumerian artefacts. I'd stake my life on that.'

'Well, they're not genuine. I've brought one for you to see.' Arnavon delved in his pocket and took out a velvet bag. From it he slid onto the table a short grey stone rod, with relief carvings on it of human figures dressed in ancient robes and columns of cuneiform symbols.

'May I?' George asked, putting on his glasses to examine the object. 'This is a cylinder-seal, is it?'

'Haven't you ever seen one?'

'Museums aren't really my cup of tea, Mr Arnavon. Henry's

father consigned his collection of seals to the county museum in Guildford years ago.'

'So, they were duped as well.'

'I suspect Sir Charles was also duped, when it comes down to it. If, as you say, this is a fake.'

'The experts Sir Nathaniel referred the seals to at the Royal Toronto Museum pronounced them to be bogus. The cuneiform is no better than gibberish and the clothing on the human figures isn't right either.'

'I suppose they'd know.'

'If you intend to claim they're in fact genuine, I can arrange for the antiquities department at the Louvre to give their opinion. I must warn you it won't come cheap, though.'

'How were these seals originally used?' George asked, in an attempt to lighten the mood.

'They were rolled across clay envelopes containing legal tablets when the clay was still wet to authenticate the contents. The seals represented the personal authority of the owner. They could also be used when sealing sacks or jars.'

George toyed with the seal in his hand. 'Remarkable.'

'But that particular example was used for nothing, of course, except defrauding the unwary.'

'The only fraud was when some devious Mesopotamian merchant sold the seals to Sir Charles, Mr Arnavon.'

'Maybe so. But Sir Nathaniel is still entitled to restitution.'

'In your letter, you mentioned a receipt.'

'You'd like to see it?'

'Yes, please.'

Arnavon retrieved the seal and put it away, then took an envelope from his inside pocket and removed a piece of paper which he laid on the table, flattening it out carefully and keeping his fingers pressed down on the edges so that George could not pick it up.

Suspicious bugger, George thought. But all he said was, 'I see.'

The document was printed with the name of the dealer, *Laskaris et Soutine*, and an address in the 3rd arrondissement. The articles sold were described in French: *6 Sceaux Cylindriques, Sumerien ancien, le XXIIIe siècle av. J.-C.* The price was written next to them and, below that, *Pour acquit*, together with the signature *A. Soutine*.

'This sum in francs must equate to—'

'Approximately three thousand pounds.'

'Good God.'

'Very reasonable, actually, had they been genuine. Sadly, they aren't.'

'I can't help feeling your quarrel is with this fellow Soutine, Mr Arnavon. He sold you the seals.'

'On Sir Henry's behalf.'

'Henry's name isn't mentioned on this document. The liability is Soutine's.'

'But he's nowhere to be found.' Arnavon's mouth tightened tetchily. 'I made it clear in my letter to Lady Maxted that Sir Nathaniel has instructed me to—'

'Yes, yes. I know what you wrote.' George played for time by taking a thoughtful sip of Vichy water, then said, 'My sister would much prefer to avoid litigation.'

'As would Sir Nathaniel.'

'In the first instance, I'll seek to have a word with Soutine.'

'Perhaps you don't quite understand, Mr Clissold. Soutine is gone. Vanished. *Disparu*.'

'I'd like to confirm that to my satisfaction.'

'Very well. The address of his gallery is on the receipt, as you can see. For all the good it'll do you.'

'What sort of a fellow is he?'

'A bad sort, it would seem.'

'I mean what does he look like?'

'You want me to describe him?'

'You've met him, Mr Arnavon. I haven't.'

'No. And you're not about to, as I've already explained. You'll be wasting your time by looking for him.'

'You're probably right.' George smiled at Arnavon, who did not smile back. 'But I believe I'll waste it anyway.'

Appleby had informed his clearly bemused secretary that he would be away for 'a few days' attending to a family emergency. The train schedules had left him no time for prolonged deliberation. He either believed Max had something crucial or he did not. On balance, he believed.

Before boarding the noon train for London at the Gare du Nord, he dispatched two telegrams. One was to the stationmaster at Inverness: *Telegram for passenger Nettles evening arrival from Wick to be delivered into his own hand.* The other was to Max. *You will be met Waverley tomorrow morning. A.*

It was fortunate that rail services in the north of Scotland were sufficiently sparse to leave little doubt as to the trains Max would be travelling on. He was probably using an alias, but Appleby had no way of knowing what it might be, so he had reverted to the one they had settled on before Max left Paris.

According to Appleby's hurried reading of the timetables, he would reach Edinburgh on the sleeper from London an hour before Max arrived on the sleeper from Inverness.

What happened after they met at Waverley station depended on what exactly Max had with him and any steps Lemmer might have taken in the interim. They had both broken cover now. The chase was on.

Morahan entered Chez Georges curious as to why Ireton had summoned him to meet his unidentified luncheon guest at the conclusion of their meal. Malory Hollander, Ireton's indefatigable secretary, had been unable to enlighten him, since her boss had made the appointment without informing her. 'Tell Travis the concept of an office diary relies on its keeper knowing when its principal subject is free and when he isn't,' she had complained. Morahan had assured her he would.

Ireton normally entertained people at Chez Georges when he wanted to persuade them, on account of its genuinely Parisian ambience – banquettes, stucco and gilded mirrors in abundance – that he was at ease with the leisured ways of the city's business classes. The restaurant was not far from the Bourse and always attracted smart-suited men of money.

Morahan was surprised when he recognized Ireton's guest, though only to a degree. The ripples of the peace conference washed many unlikely clients into Ireton's pool.

'Ah, there you are, Schools,' came Ireton's greeting as he approached the table. 'Glad you could join us.'

'Pleased to meet you, Mr Morahan,' said his companion, springing to his feet. He was an athletically built young Asian, expensively dressed, with sleek, dark hair and a lazily arrogant gaze. He was, Morahan happened to know, the son of Count Tomura, the newly arrived joint deputy head of the Japanese delegation to the peace conference.

'The feeling's mutual,' Morahan responded as they exchanged courteous little bows.

'This is—' Ireton began.

'Tomura Noburo,' Morahan cut in. 'An honour, I'm sure.'

'An American who knows the correct rendering of Japanese names,' said Tomura. 'I am impressed.'

'You should take it as an indication of the calibre of the people I employ,' said Ireton as they resumed their seats and a waiter produced a chair for Morahan. He let Ireton's misrepresentation of their relationship pass, as he always did.

'I will, Travis,' said Tomura. 'I will.'

So, they were on first-names terms, a good omen in its way. Morahan ordered coffee.

'I must leave soon,' Tomura continued, toying with a nearly drained brandy glass.

'I've put Noburo in the picture about how we work, Schools. He's aware you'll be handling the practical side of things. That's why I wanted you two to meet.'

'Travis has told me you are a get-doner, Schools,' said Tomura, who grinned with pleasure at his recital of the phrase.

'I do my level best to get done what our clients need to be done,' Morahan responded with a smile. He noticed the shadows beneath the young man's eyes. It looked as if his reputation for dissipation was well deserved.

'I'll run over the details later,' said Ireton.

'Is your father enjoying Paris, Noburo?' Morahan asked.

'Not as much as I am, I think. But I do not have his responsibilities.'

'I guess not.'

'He could not be seen here, with you and Travis, for instance. He could not meet all the . . . *femmes jolies* . . . I do.'

'Paris is the place for them, all right.' Ireton laughed.

'Oh yes. It is a fine city. I like it.'

'Still, your father's not having a bad week, is he?' said Morahan. 'If we're to believe the rumours about Shantung.'

Tomura nodded. 'Believe them.'

'The Chinese won't be happy.'

'We are not here to make the Chinese happy.' There was a flare of venom in Tomura's gaze. 'A nation that is not united deserves to fail.'

'Didn't President Lincoln once say something like that?' Ireton jokingly mused.

'Travis has told me you do not fail, Schools.'

'Not generally, no.'

'I want results. Quickly.'

'And you'll get them,' said Ireton. 'Leave it to us.'

Tomura swallowed the very last of his brandy. He was about to say something when the coffee arrived. He paused, eyeing Morahan with a hint of scepticism. 'Travis has also told me you killed several Spanish soldiers with your bare hands in Cuba, Schools.'

Morahan shrugged. 'It was war.'

'War is a glorious thing.'

'In the history books, maybe.'

'The way of the warrior is to seek death.'

Morahan allowed himself a sidelong glance at Ireton. 'Then I guess I wasn't much of a warrior.'

'I do not believe that.'

'You shouldn't,' said Ireton. 'Don't worry, Noburo. You've come to the professionals. We'll solve your problem.'

'Good. Thank you. I must leave now.' Tomura stood up. Morahan and Ireton followed suit. 'When will I hear, Travis?'

'Soon.'

'Soon, then.'

A farewell bow and he was off, a waiter intercepting him with his hat and coat as he went.

Morahan and Ireton sat down again as the street door closed behind their new client. Ireton sighed. 'He is one haughty sonofabitch, I have to admit.'

'Like father, like son.'

'What was that about the correct rendering of Japanese names?'

'The family name comes first, the personal name second. Malory told me. They never bother to set us right, just wince every time we get it wrong.'

'I'll try to remember that.'

'While you're at it, you'd better remember to tell me what the hell it is we're doing for him.'

Ireton lowered his voice. 'He wants us to find le Singe.'

Morahan turned the implications of that over in his mind for a second, then said simply, 'Why?'

'He wasn't inclined to disclose the reason, just the urgency. I got the impression he was talking to me on behalf of his father, though he never said as much.'

'What interest would Count Tomura have in le Singe?'

'Your guess is as good as mine, Schools. Maybe better. You're the warrior, aren't you? And Count Tomura has as bloodthirsty a reputation as they come. I've heard he sliced off Chinese heads in Port Arthur during the Sino–Jap War of ninety-four/five like my daddy used to harvest cabbages on the farm. And he did much the same to the Russians ten years later.'

'Your father was never a farmer, Travis.'

Ireton chuckled. 'Well, no more he was, it's true. My metaphors tend to run away with themselves. Or was that a simile? I'll have to ask Malory for an adjudication.'

'Which brings us back to why Count Tomura should want to find le Singe.'

'OK. Well, naturally, I don't know. If I was to guess, though, I'd say he's spring-cleaning at the delegation. Rumour has it le Singe lifted information from their hotel and Marquess Saionji's residence on a couple of occasions. Maybe Tomura wants le Singe to tell him exactly *what* information.'

'Or stop him telling anyone else.'

'That's a possibility. He may have hung on to a few choice nuggets.'

'Or Soutine may have.'

'You're way ahead of me, Schools. Tomura's brought a lot of authority with him from Tokyo. He's shaking things up. Kuroda's been sent home in disgrace, you know.'

'He has?'

'Saionji should watch his back.'

'So should we, Travis. You've done a lot of business with

Soutine. Tomura's bound to have considered whether you've handled any of their intelligence.'

'All the more reason to do our best for him. He wants le Singe, not intermediaries.'

'And then there's the fee, of course.'

'You'll get your fair share.'

'Le Singe has gone to ground since Tarn was killed. How do you expect me to find him?'

'I admit it won't be easy. Soutine's become elusive as well. Maybe he knew Tomura would start looking for le Singe. Anyhow, start with Soutine.'

'You normally deal with him.'

'I can't afford to be as active as I'd like, Schools, you know that. Since the Ennis affair, I've been bothered by a draught at the back of my neck. It's Carver breathing down it. Besides, if Soutine's made himself scarce, you'll have to do a little discreet breaking and entering at his gallery. He has a flat over it he stays in. Chances are you'll discover something there on le Singe.'

'And if I don't?'

'He can't live on air. He's hiding somewhere in this city. You'll think of a way to flush him out.'

'He may have left Paris.'

'I doubt it. But, if we can prove he has, Tomura will have to settle for that.'

'How much do you know about the Count – aside from his bloodthirsty reputation?'

'He's wealthy beyond the normal standards of the Japanese aristocracy. He didn't just kill Chinese and Russian soldiers in Korea. He's bought a lot of land over there and invested in a range of businesses, not all of them necessarily legal. And he's on the board of the Oriental Development Company, which virtually runs the place now it's a Japanese colony. I ran a guess past Kuroda once that Tomura also has links with the Dark Ocean Society. They're thought to have been responsible for the assassination of Queen Min and maybe a few other assassinations as well.'

'What did Kuroda say?'

'Nothing. In an eloquent kind of way. But he doesn't trust

Tomura. That was obvious. I surmise the feeling's mutual. It's probably what got him summoned back to Tokyo. The hard men are moving in at the top of Japanese politics, Schools. They're going to be a force to be reckoned with. Do you know how much money Japanese corporations made out of selling morphine and heroin to Britain and France – and Germany, on the sly – to treat the injured during the war? The likes of Count Iwazu Tomura – pardon me, Tomura Iwazu – are rolling in it, let me tell you. And I always believe in looking for my clientele where the money is, which sure isn't war-weary Europe.'

'It seems not all the hard men are in Tokyo.' Morahan gazed frankly at Ireton. 'Pointing Tomura towards le Singe could be as good as signing the boy's death warrant.'

'The boy? You sound almost sentimental about him. He's just some young sneak thief who was lucky to survive the war. If his luck's run out now, it's not our fault. We have to look to the future. This conference won't go on for ever, however much it seems like it might. The Germans are on their way to learn their fate. Their delegation's expected to arrive this evening. And we're told the treaty will be published next week. So, the end's in sight. We have to consider what comes next.'

'What does come next?'

'For you and me?' Ireton smiled confidently at Morahan. 'Something lucrative. You can count on that.'

Max's nausea as the *St. Ola* ploughed across the Pentland Firth was just seasickness. He was satisfied he would not be intercepted before he boarded the Inverness train at Georgemas and maybe, with luck, not even then.

Uncertainty on the point was part of the problem. He wanted to believe he was safe, but he knew he should assume the worst. He and a few other hardy souls waited in the strengthening wind and rain at Georgemas station that afternoon as their train approached. He did not try to hide. He scanned the faces of the passengers aboard the train quite openly as it drew in, prepared for a revealing hint of suspicion or hostility in one of their gazes. He noticed nothing. But that also proved nothing, as he was well aware.

He chose an empty compartment to sit in and hoped he would be left alone. There was no corridor and the bleak, sparsely inhabited countryside was unlikely to yield many travellers.

But, at the very first stop, Halkirk, a young man yanked open the door of Max's compartment and climbed aboard. He was dressed in a black suit and smart overcoat and was wearing a grey fedora. He carried a Gladstone bag, with an umbrella strapped to the side. After removing a newspaper and a file bound with pink legal tape, he heaved the bag up onto the luggage-rack and sat down in the opposite corner to Max.

'Not much of a day,' the newcomer remarked in a soft Scottish burr.

'Indeed not,' Max responded, opening his three-day-old copy of the *Orcadian* to deter conversation.

'Ah! Have you been to the Orkneys?'

'I have.'

'I've never had occasion to myself.'

The young man's auburn hair and rosy-cheeked school-boyishness reminded Max of a pilot in his squadron called Perkins. The real Perkins had gone down in flames over Flanders. But Max found himself thinking involuntarily of his travelling companion by that name. The question was whether this Perkins had been on the train when it arrived at Georgemas and had jumped off at Halkirk in order to join him in his compartment. Max had certainly seen no one waiting on the platform as the train drew in.

'See anything of the German fleet while you were there?'

'Er, yes. That is, well, it's hard to miss it.'

'How much longer will they be kept there, d'you think?'

'I really couldn't say.'

'According to the *Scotsman*' – Perkins flourished his newspaper – 'the German delegation to the peace conference is expected to reach Paris today. Things seem to be moving at last.'

Spared a direct question, Max said nothing and gazed out through the rain-speckled window. Perkins was either a harmless if irritating chatterbox or a wolf in sheep's clothing. Max supposed he would find out which at some point in the coming hours.

'I take it from your accent you're English. Are you heading south of the border, then?'

Max swore silently. 'Er, yes.'

'I'm only going to Inverness myself. But that's far enough, eh? I had to come all the way up here to oblige one of our better clients. A property dispute, d'you see? What took you to the Orkneys?'

'Actually,' said Max, simulating a yawn, 'I'm done in. Would you mind if I tried to get some shut-eye?'

'Not at all. Quite understand. You sleep away.' Perkins' smile was a perfect construction of bland amiability. 'I expect you've earned it.'

As Max stretched out his legs and reclined his head against the cushion, he caught sight of his bag in the rack above him. The Grey

File was inside, with all its secrets. The gun Schmidt had given him was in the bag as well. But it was empty.

It was going to be a long journey.

George treated himself to a good lunch at Au Petit Riche, a restaurant which seemed happily unchanged since he had entertained assorted actresses there – well, that was what they said they were – in his hedonistic youth. Now, after a head-clearing march through the snowy streets, he had arrived at the Passage Vendôme.

It was as Arnavon had said. *Laskaris et Soutine, Antiquaires*, was firmly *fermé*. There was no indication when they might reopen, nor was a telephone number displayed for enquiries.

George tried his luck at the other shops in the arcade. They sang the same song. Monsieur Soutine had not been seen for more than a week. He must have gone away, since he lived above the gallery. Did he have another residence in Paris? They did not know.

George warmed himself with coffee and a brandy at a café in the Place de la République and considered what he should do next. Caving in to Arnavon without a fight did not appeal to him. The fellow had an importunate way with him that nettled George. It was therefore time to discover whether Max had learnt anything about his father's disposal of the Babylonian whim-whams that were causing Winifred – and now him – so many problems.

According to Winifred, Max's RFC chum, Sam Twentyman, had found employment with the British delegation to the peace conference, keeping their fleet of cars on the road. The afternoon was wearing on and the snow had stopped. Twentyman's working day would surely be growing less hectic.

With that thought in mind, George headed out in search of a taxi to take him to the Hotel Majestic.

Morahan was aware he was being followed within minutes of leaving Chez Georges. He and Ireton had gone their separate ways at that point. Ireton had a teatime appointment with a loose-tongued member of the Greek delegation. Morahan was heading back to the office.

His shadow was not incompetent, far from it. Someone less experienced in such matters than Morahan would never have noticed. He made no attempt to shake the fellow off. He was presumably Japanese, trained by poor old Kuroda. There was no sense embarrassing him in the eyes of his new boss, Count Tomura.

Tomura's strategy was clear to Morahan now, though he had not disclosed it to Ireton. Their involvement was merely one part of the Count's effort to find le Singe. The people Sam was frightened of were his people. Kuroda had probably warned Sam to be on his guard before leaving Paris.

Morahan understood the threat, but could not immediately devise a way to counter it. As far as he could see, someone was going to pay for whatever le Singe had stolen from the Japanese, if not le Singe himself.

He needed to enlist Malory's aid. Together, they might map out a path through the thicket. Meanwhile, he would simply have to tolerate the presence of his shadow.

The mechanics were beginning to notice and comment on the number of nobs, as they referred to them, calling by the Majestic garage to see Sam. Telling them to mind their own business was like telling dogs not to sniff lamp-posts. But Sam told them even so.

George Clissold was a nob of a different stripe, however. He engaged Billy Hegg in a discussion of the cornering-at-speed qualities of various models of car before approaching Sam, who had to interrupt the preparation of tea in his office to discover who the well-dressed newcomer was.

'I'm James's uncle,' George explained, grinning as he presented Sam with a card relating to his position at a marine insurance company in London. 'And you're Sam Twentyman?'

'Yes, sir.'

'Any chance of a quiet word, Sam?'

'Well . . .'

'Is that a kettle I can hear boiling?' George's grin broadened. 'I like my tea hot and strong.'

MORAHAN SAT IN THE CHAIR HE HAD PULLED ACROSS TO THE window of Malory's office at Ireton Associates, 33 Rue des Pyramides, and took a sip from the cup of green tea she had just passed him.

'What d'you see in this?' he complained good-naturedly. 'It's got no body.'

'But it does have subtlety,' Malory replied, eyeing Morahan tolerantly over her horn-rimmed glasses. 'Which you appear to be in need of.'

'We could ask my shadow in for a cup.' Morahan nodded down towards the street. 'He'd love it.'

'You're sure you're being followed?'

'I'm disappointed you need to ask me that, Malory.'

'Sorry. You'd know, of course. But what's the problem? You're a past master at losing a tail.'

'I can't afford to lose him. It'd make Tomura suspect I'm up to no good.'

'He wants you to lead him to le Singe?'

'Yup.'

'And then?'

'Not sure. Either he needs to know something le Singe knows or he needs to stop le Singe telling it to anyone else.'

'How could he do that?'

'Oh, by killing him, I reckon.' Morahan took another sip of tea. 'This could use a shot of bourbon in it, y'know.'

With a disapproving frown, Malory fetched a bottle of Jim

Beam down from the shelf behind her, walked across to where Morahan was sitting and poured some into his cup. 'That thing you agreed to do for Sir Henry, Schools . . .'

'Yuh?'

'Was le Singe anything to do with it?'

'I'm not sure. But it would fit with le Singe stealing something from the Japanese delegation: a nugget of intelligence that was pure gold to Henry, maybe.'

'Intelligence concerning Count Tomura?'

'Well, let's ask ourselves why he's here. The official story is Premier Hara wanted to reinforce the delegation as the conference entered its final stages. The unofficial story is he sent Tomura to take over from Saionji in all but name because he thinks the old boy's gone soft. There were riots in Korea at the beginning of March and Hara may have feared Saionji would fail to block Korean representatives getting a hearing at the conference. But what if both stories are wrong? What if Tomura persuaded Hara to send him for reasons of his own? He's been here a week. It's a six-week voyage from Japan. So, he must have set off around March the tenth. Henry was already on the track of his great secret by then.'

'Is that what he called it – his "great secret"?'

'He did.'

'But he never even hinted what it was?'

'Only that he could use my help to get to the bottom of it, but was determined to try even if I turned him down.'

'Which there was no chance you'd do?'

'I owed the man my life, Malory. What d'you think?'

'I think he asked the right guy.'

Morahan took a swig of the reinforced tea. 'That's a whole lot better.'

Malory smiled. 'Have you ever thought you should've told Max about this?'

'"If anything happens to me, Schools, don't breathe a word to my family. Especially my son James." That's what Henry said. Those were his exact words. I reckon he must have said something similar to Ribeiro, his old friend from the Brazilian delegation. So,

111

we've both kept our mouths shut. I figured it was best to let Henry's quest – whatever it was – die with him.'

'But you're afraid it didn't die with him, aren't you?'

'Tomura junior's been here since January. He could've alerted his father to any threat Henry posed to him. And the Count could've decided to come here and nullify the threat in person.'

'Do you think he was behind Sir Henry's murder?'

'No. That was down to Lemmer. At least . . .' Morahan shrugged helplessly and drank some more tea. 'Somehow, I have to find le Singe and learn what he knew before Tomura hears I've found him, then decide how I can use the information to spike Tomura's guns. I can't refuse to look for le Singe because then Tomura will try to squeeze whatever he can out of Sam Twentyman. That'll be nothing, which won't go well for Sam. And I have to do all this while leading Travis to believe I'm obediently trying to track le Singe down via Soutine in order to earn us a fat fee from Tomura via his son.'

'I should say Travis is the least of your problems. He's pre-occupied with the Greeks at the moment. Everyone wants to know how generous a slice of the Turkish pie they're going to end up with.'

'Maybe they should ask you.'

'The Greeks' eyes are bigger than their stomachs. That's all I'll say. Now, what do *you* want to ask me? I mean, I'm happy to listen while you analyse the impossibility of your situation, but . . .'

Morahan laughed. 'Travis has no idea how much smarter you are than he is, Malory. You are aware of that, aren't you?'

Malory arched her eyebrows. 'A good secretary flatters her boss, not herself.'

'He wouldn't be happy to hear about some of the things you do for me.'

'Which is why he won't. Another duty of a good secretary is to spare her boss's feelings. Besides, morally speaking, Travis is a louse. Whereas you, Schools, are a man of honour.' Her gaze was gentle and frank. There were no secrets between them, even concerning what they thought of each other.

'I'm way short of that,' said Morahan softly.

'What d'you want me to do?'

'Look through all the newspaper reports of le Singe's activities. See if there's a pattern to them. I mean a geographical pattern, one that might give me a clue about where I should look for him.'

'If he has any sense, he'll have left Paris.'

'That's the second part of the trawl. Reports of burglaries from other cities that might suggest his . . .'

'Modus operandi?'

Morahan pointed at her over the rim of his teacup. 'You got it.'

Malory gave him a pained smile. '*Un soir à la bibliothèque pour moi, je pense.*'

Morahan grimaced. 'Sorry. You read the lingo much better than I do.'

'Lucky for you I haven't got a date tonight.'

'I *am* sorry.' He smiled. 'On both counts.'

She set down her cup, walked across to where he was sitting and drank from his cup instead. 'What will you be doing while I'm straining my eyes over columns of French newsprint. Schools?'

'Visiting Soutine's gallery.'

'I thought you said he'd gone missing.'

Morahan winked. 'I may have to visit in his absence.'

'I'll keep an eye out for him at the library, then. He could be lurking among the book stacks.'

'Have you ever met him?'

'Once.' She leant back against the desk behind her. 'Travis mentioned him so often I got curious and took Eveline to look at his gallery one Saturday.' Eveline was the Red Cross worker Malory shared an apartment with on the Ile St-Louis. 'He came near to selling her a pair of what he said were Louis Quinze earrings. I talked her out of it.'

'What did you make of him?'

'A charming crook. He'd sell his own mother if the price was right. I should've thought that would apply to le Singe as well.'

'Yep. Which implies Soutine reckons he's in trouble too. The sort he can't bargain his way out of.'

'What kind of reputation does Count Tomura have?'

'Not a peaceable one. He's killed a lot of people. And had a lot

113

more killed on his behalf, I should guess.' Morahan sighed. 'D'you know what his son said to me? "The way of the warrior is to seek death." I mean, Good God Almighty.'

Malory's expression grew serious. 'It's the opening sentence of *Hagakure*, the handbook on the way of the *bushi* – Japan's military aristocracy. They know it by heart.'

'Tomura junior didn't look as if he'd done much in the seeking-death line since hitting Paris.'

'But he'll have wanted to. How old is he?'

'Not sure. Mid to late twenties?'

'He probably didn't see much action. The Japanese army had precious little to do in the war after seizing Shantung. That will have left young Tomura eager to demonstrate his manliness. And I don't mean with cancan girls.'

'His father will keep him under control.'

Malory did not look reassured. 'You could be getting into something very dangerous, Schools. You do realize that?'

He spread his hands. 'It can't be helped.'

'See what I mean?' She shook her head and gazed at him fondly. 'There speaks the man of honour.'

'HIS FRIENDS CALL HIM MAX, SIR,' SAID SAM HESITANTLY AS HE passed George a mug of hot, strong, generously sugared tea.

'Max?' George turned the name over in his mind. 'Well, it's a better nickname than I've ever been landed with. Max it is.'

'I don't know where he is, if that's what you're going to ask me. His mother anxious, is she?'

'Anxiety and my sister are strangers to each other,' George replied with a smile. 'She'd welcome news of . . . Max . . . naturally, but she's confident he knows what he's doing.'

'That's more than I am, sir, to tell you the honest truth. But Max knows his own mind and that's a fact. So, if you haven't come over here to find him . . .'

'I'm here to sort out a . . . potential embarrassment for the family. One involving my late brother-in-law, Sir Henry Maxted.'

'Oh, yes, sir?'

'He sold some Middle Eastern antiquities to a French Canadian called Arnavon who's now challenging their authenticity.'

'That's awkward.'

'Yes. And very possibly expensive for my sister, since the fellow's demanding his money back, plus compensation.'

'See what you mean, sir.'

Sam knew from Max that Sir Henry had been raising money and they both knew from Baltazar Ribeiro what he had been raising it for: a comfortable future with Corinne Dombreux. What Sam did not know was whether Lady Maxted was aware of this. And he did not propose to be the one who enlightened her, via her brother.

'Not sure what I can do for you, though,' he ventured after a painful pause.

'What I want to know is whether Max looked into the matter of these antiquities while he was in Paris.'

'Er . . .'

Something else was troubling Sam now. Laskaris and Soutine dealt in antiquities. And Soutine dealt in information supplied by le Singe. Sir Henry was connected to both strands of Soutine's business. Which, Sam wondered, had come first? And how much could he afford to admit he knew?

'I don't think . . . Max looked into that matter at all, sir.'

'You don't?'

'Er . . . no.'

'That's damned unfortunate. I went to the gallery that handled the sale earlier this afternoon. *Laskaris et Soutine*, Passage Vendôme, off Place de la République. Did Max ever mention them?'

'I don't recall he ever did,' Sam replied, accurately enough.

'No one there. Nor has there been for the past week or so, according to neighbouring shopkeepers. Soutine's evidently disappeared. I need to find him if my sister's not to be sued, Sam. You see how I'm placed? I don't believe for a moment Henry would pass off a fake as the real thing, but I don't want his good name and hence Winifred's dragged through the mud while we try to refute the allegations. Nor do I believe Max would want that to happen either.'

'With you there, sir.'

'Loyalty to a friend's an admirable quality. So's discretion.' George leant closer to Sam and engaged him eye to eye, man to man. 'If Max said anything to you about this in confidence, I perfectly understand your reluctance to let me in on it. But I think he'd want you to help his mother out of a jam of his father's making, don't you? If there was any way you could.'

Sam squirmed inwardly, and to a degree outwardly. Dissimulation was not his strong suit. And what George had said he could not deny. Max would want him to do whatever was in his mother's best interests. But what exactly was that?

'I have the impression,' George went on, 'that there is something you could tell me, Sam. Am I right?'

'Well . . .'

'It'd be strictly between you and me.'

'Bugger it,' said Sam decisively. 'All right. Max spoke to Laskaris.' He could not risk revealing the truth. And the lie was white enough for his conscience to bear. 'He didn't say what about. This antiquities business, I suppose.'

'Laskaris? Not Soutine?'

'No. Like you said, Soutine had gone missing. It was Laskaris. He gave Max his card. And Max left it with me. In case I needed to contact Laskaris, he said, though he never explained why I'd need to. Maybe he foresaw your problem with the buyer.'

George nodded. 'Maybe he did.'

'I've got it here.' Sam fished in the drawer of his desk, took out the card and showed it to George.

'Well, well, well. Viktor Laskaris. Address. Telephone number. Everything. Very useful. Mind if I borrow this?'

'I ought to hang on to it, sir.'

'Yes. Of course.' George produced a notebook and pencil and manoeuvred a pair of glasses onto his nose. ' I'll just . . . jot the details down.'

'Are you going to talk to him, sir?'

'Oh yes.' George snapped his notebook shut. 'As soon as possible.'

Sam extracted two promises from George before he left. One was not to tell Laskaris who had supplied him with his address and telephone number. It was vital he did not, since Laskaris might otherwise point out that Sam too had been looking for Soutine. The second promise was to let Sam know what, if anything, he learnt from Laskaris. The man might be more forthcoming with someone of George's class than he had been with Sam. This way, George might end up doing Sam a bigger favour than Sam had done him. And Sam was in sore need of such a favour.

He did not expect to hear from George before the garage closed for the day. To his surprise, however, he was back within an hour and

117

a half of leaving. Sam saw him in the repair bay, talking to Billy Hegg again. Before he could go and greet him, though, he had left once more, marching out into the mews. And Hegg was heading for Sam's office at a worrying trot.

'What's going on, Billy?' Sam demanded.

'Your friend, Mr Clissold, wants to speak to you, Mr Twentyman. He said he'd wait for you outside.'

'Why didn't he come in here?'

'Search me. He's not as cheerful as he was, though. I'll tell you that for nothin'. Someone's put his nose out of joint, I'd say.'

Sam found George striding up and down in the snow, puffing at a cigar and looking as disgruntled as Hegg had said he was.

'Something wrong, sir?'

'Just a little. I don't suppose you've ever telephoned Laskaris, have you?'

'No.'

'Nor visited his home?'

'No, sir.'

'Thought not. The number doesn't exist, you see. And nor does the address.'

'What?'

'Rue de l'Assomption is a real street. But the odd numbers stop in the nineties. If it went as far as a hundred and forty-one, where Laskaris purports to live, it'd be out in the middle of the bloody Bois de Boulogne.'

'Oh Gawd.'

'Oh Gawd, indeed.'

'I've been had.'

'Is it the lamplight out here or have you gone a funny colour?'

'He fobbed me off with the card.'

'Who fobbed you off?'

'Laskaris.'

George stood directly in front of Sam and clasped him by the shoulder. 'I thought Max gave you the card.'

'Well . . . no. Not exactly. I mean, no, he didn't. What happened was . . . Laskaris gave it to me.'

'You've met him?'

Sam nodded glumly. 'Yes.'

'When?'

'Last night. At the gallery.'

'What took you there? No, never mind that for the moment. Describe Laskaris to me.'

'Pint sized old bloke. White goatee beard. Blue eyes. Face a bit—'

'That's not Laskaris, you booby. That's Soutine. It's how Arnavon described him. To a T, damn it.'

'It was Soutine?'

'Yes.'

'Oh.' Chance had delivered Soutine to Sam. And Sam had let him slip away. He squeezed his eyes shut and grimaced. 'Oh, bloody hell.'

APPLEBY'S TRAIN WAS NEARLY AN HOUR LATE WHEN IT STEAMED and jolted into Victoria station, though the delay, as the guard had defensively reminded him, had been on the French side. 'A flake or two of snow throws them Frogs right out, sir.'

Appleby still had two hours to spare before the sleeper express to Edinburgh left King's Cross. But he did not propose to dally. He strode out through the ticket barrier onto the concourse, sniffing appreciatively the cold, dank, sooty air of the city that was his natural home.

As he headed for the taxi rank at the front of the station, he was surprised – and perturbed – to see a spring-heeled young man he recognized as Davison, a runner at HQ, hurrying across from the arrivals board to intercept him.

'Evening, sir,' said Davison, touching his hat and smiling ingratiatingly.

'What are you doing here?' was Appleby's barely genial response.

'C's orders, sir. He apologizes for the lateness of the hour – even later now, thanks to the rotten old SE and C – but he'd like a word. Straight away.'

'Really?' Appleby was in no position to point out that as far as he knew C was unaware of his departure from Paris. He could have been notified of it, of course, and deduced that Appleby was bound for London. But there were other parties who could have deduced that.

'Yes, sir. Really. There's a car waiting for us outside. Shall we step on it?'

'Did you have C's orders directly from him?'

It was an apparently simple question. But Appleby was more familiar with how C would operate in such circumstances than Davison was, as Davison must have known. He hesitated for a tell-tale fraction of a second before answering. 'Yes, sir. Direct from C.'

'We'd better not keep him waiting any longer, then, had we?'

'No, sir.' Davison smiled. 'Right this way.'

The calculations of risk and probability had whirled to an instinctive conclusion in Appleby's mind. He moved to Davison's side, dropped his bag and grasped him by the shoulder. His over-coat hung open, masking the revolver in his hand. He pressed the barrel against Davison's ribs and felt the young man start in alarm.

'Run or cry out and I'll plug you. Is that clear?'

'For God's sake, sir.' Davison's voice cracked with fear. 'What are you doing?'

'Who really told you to pick me up?'

'C, sir. Like I—'

'One more lie and I'll shoot you here and now. You must know I'm desperate enough to do it.'

'I'm only following orders, sir.'

'Whose?'

It took an extra prod of the gun to extract an answer. 'Political.'

Appleby flinched with dismay. He would never have guessed Lemmer had laid his poison so close to the centre. Political was one of the four section heads in the Service who reported directly to C, known conventionally by their areas of responsibility rather than their names – Military, Naval, Aviation and, standing a little apart and above, Political. 'He personally instructed you to collect me and say you were acting on a direct order from C?'

'Yes, sir.'

'Where did he tell you to take me?'

'An address in Pimlico.'

'Which is?'

'Twenty-four Glamorgan Street.'

'Who's driving the car?'

'Parks.'

'Right. Listen to me carefully.' Appleby glanced behind him at the departures board. 'Go out and tell Parks I wasn't on the train. Ask him what he thinks you should do next. Then do it. Think you can manage that?'

'Yes, sir.'

'Off you go, then.'

Davison started walking.

Appleby pocketed his gun, picked up his bag and headed back across the concourse, watching Davison from the corner of his eye as he went. The police warrant card he carried would get him on the next train out, leaving in a few minutes, without the need to buy a ticket. It stopped, as they almost all did, at Clapham Junction. From there he had a wide enough choice of routes to elude anyone pursuing him. It was the only escape open to him. But it was only escape for the present. He had dodged one trap. But there would be others. And it was doubtful he could dodge them all.

Forced to admit to George Clissold that he too had been looking for Soutine, Sam soon realized he would have to explain why. Over a badly needed beer in a café close to the Majestic but not close enough to be overrun by fellow Brits, he told George much of what he had told Morahan. He was determined to keep his promise to Kuroda, whatever happened. He did not mention Count Tomura by name – or Fritz Lemmer. But what remained was a tale he felt marginally better for telling.

'So,' said George when he had finished, 'in some ways James – I mean Max – has left you in the lurch.'

'He wasn't to know this would happen, sir. And I'm sure he's got a fair few problems of his own to cope with.'

'You'd have a better idea about that than I would, Sam. Care to reveal what you know about his current activities?'

But Sam had a free hand only as far as his own secrets were concerned. 'Sorry, sir. I gave him my word.'

'So you did. Whatever he's up to, though, I assume there's a connection with le Singe.'

'I can't deny that.'

'And it's le Singe these people are after?'

'Yes. And they're not the sort who'll give up easily.'

122

'Which puts you in a tight spot.'

'Too tight for comfort.'

'But it does mean we share an interest in finding Soutine.'

'We do, sir, yes.'

'Then I suggest we set about the task without further ado.'

'How can we? Soutine's not likely to go back to the gallery again. I reckon he had everything he'd gone there for in that bag he was carrying.'

'Very possibly. But he may have left behind some clue to his present whereabouts. We ought to go and look for it.'

Sam frowned suspiciously at George. 'Have you got in mind what I think you've got in mind, sir?'

'You can borrow a few tools from the garage, can't you? We'll need to jemmy the gallery door open. There's probably another door to the flat. But we'll be inside by then, so we can afford to make a bit more noise if we have to.'

'Blimey. You're serious, aren't you?'

'Absolutely. I've always fancied trying my hand at breaking and entering. Like that fellow Raffles.'

'But he's not real, sir. Some writer made him up.'

'Never mind that.' George consulted his watch. 'How about three hours from now?'

Appleby had abandoned all thought of catching the Edinburgh sleeper from King's Cross. Lemmer must have sent Max to the Orkneys, so he could be in little doubt of where Max currently was, or the logical route for Appleby to take to intercept him. They were both in difficulties now.

From Clapham Junction, Appleby took a couple of slow trains north to Willesden Junction. He recalled from pre-war journeys to the north-west that the Liverpool sleeper out of Euston stopped there to pick up passengers. It was a diversion likely to defeat even Lemmer's resources. It would get Appleby to Birmingham in the middle of the night, but from there he could catch a train north to York, where Max's southbound train to London was sure to stop. With luck he would be able to dispatch a telegram to Max from Birmingham to greet him in Edinburgh. By the time they met, he would certainly have devised some kind of stratagem to deliver Max's 'precious cargo' to C.

One thing was certain now. What Max was carrying was pure gold. Lemmer's willingness to expose a highly placed operative in order to wrest it from him proved that.

Standing in the cold and dark on the platform at Willesden Junction, moonlight falling thinly on the rails stretching ahead of him beyond the station, Appleby felt a hard, grim pleasure creep over him. He had been out of the field a long time. But he had not lost his edge. The way he had dealt with Davison had demonstrated that. He had needed to act and he had acted. He was back – where he belonged.

ERKINS BID MAX A CHEERY ADIEU WHEN THE TRAIN REACHED the terminus at Inverness. He bounded away with such alacrity that Max was forced to question his suspicions of the man. Certainly, he had done nothing beyond talk too much to justify them. Maybe he was just the bored young Scottish solicitor he appeared to be.

As he climbed down from the train, travelling bag in hand, Max saw Perkins hurrying on ahead, his figure blurred by the steam of the engine. Then he heard a name he knew being called out. 'Telegram for Mr Nettles! Telegram for Mr Nettles!' A boy in HR uniform came bouncing towards him, envelope held aloft.

Max did not shout to the boy for fear of attracting Perkins' attention, but signalled that he was Nettles. He doled out a small tip as he took the message and moved across to a lamp to read it.

You will be met Waverley tomorrow morning. A.

Well, that was as much as could be expected, he supposed, even though who would meet him was unspecified. It would be good no longer to be operating alone. And the rendezvous was only a night's journey away.

He hurried to the ticket office, sensing as he moved across the station that a tall, overcoated figure had waited for him to appear before heading in the same direction. It could be a mis-apprehension, of course. He was beginning to realize the fear of being followed was apt to create evidence of it everywhere. He paused to light a cigarette. The big fellow overtook him, then diverted to study a timetable board, fingering his moustache thoughtfully as he did so. Or was he studying Max's reflection in a window beyond the board? There was no way to know.

Max walked on to the ticket office and bought a first-class single to Glasgow. The sleeper left in just under two hours. 'I'll need a single berth,' he emphasized.

'You'll have to arrange that with the sleeping-car attendant when you board the train, sir,' the clerk said. 'But there shouldn't be any difficulty. So, it's through to Buchanan Street you'll be wanting?'

'Yes.'

Max paid and turned away, to find the big fellow waiting patiently behind him, still fingering his moustache, apparently giving Max no thought whatsoever. But that failed to supply Max with any degree of reassurance.

He made for the Station Hotel then, in search of a late supper. Quite a few passengers off his train, booked through on the sleeper, had done the same. He felt safe in the half-full dining-room, waiting for his order of beef stew. He sipped a well-watered whisky, aware that he must keep his wits about him. All seemed secure and orderly. But it could change in an instant.

He had bought a ticket to Glasgow. That was what the big fellow would have heard him do. But he was not going to Glasgow. The train split at Perth. He would move to the Edinburgh portion then. That was the moment, if there was to be a moment, when they would know they had to strike.

Sam was if anything more anxious than Max as he and George Clissold emerged from République Métro station. The foul weather had done them a favour in clearing the streets of idlers. But it did little for Sam's confidence. He was never good with tools when his hands were as cold as they currently were and George seemed to expect him to do any jemmying that was required. He was carrying a torch, a tyre lever, a hammer, a screwdriver and a chisel, stowed in a duffel bag he had found behind a cupboard in the garage office. He subscribed to the logic of what they were doing. He needed to find Soutine much more desperately than George did. And there really was nowhere else to start looking for him than the flat above the gallery. But breaking in to do it was risky. And the pessimistic side of his character made him suspect the risk was simply not worth it.

George, emboldened by several more brandies than Sam thought wise, took a different view. Since Soutine was the seller of the fake cylinder-seals, he was fully accountable in George's mind. He had demonstrated his bad faith by posing as his own partner in order to throw Sam off the scent. They were therefore fully entitled to take whatever steps proved necessary to establish his whereabouts, including forcing the lock at his place of business.

They entered the Passage Vendôme from the quieter end, in Rue Béranger. It appeared wholly deserted. There was mercifully no sign of the loquacious drunkard. The lamps in the arcade had been extinguished, though enough were burning in the rooms above the shops to cast dim squares of light down among the shadows.

There was no light in the flat above *Laskaris et Soutine*. The windows were in darkness. Sam switched on the torch and shone it at the door handle.

'There's enough of a gap between the lock and the jamb to apply some leverage,' whispered George. 'Shall we give it a go?'

'All right, sir. But like as not someone will hear us.'

'Before rolling over and going back to sleep. Let's get on with it. Here, I'll hold the torch.'

Sam set down the bag and took out the tyre lever. He slid it gently into the gap George had pointed out, pushing against the snib on the latch.

And the door sprang open.

'Blimey,' said Sam. 'He left it unlocked.'

'An open invitation,' said George. 'I suggest we accept it.'

Sam gathered up the bag and they went in.

George shone the torch beam around the statues and paintings and assembled antiquities. A Roman who could almost have been real, but for the fact that he was only a bust, snarled silently at Sam from atop a fluted column.

'Do people actually buy this stuff?' mused George.

'Shouldn't we go upstairs, sir? Anyone can see us while we're down here.'

'Yes, yes. Quite right. Lead on.'

Sam headed up the spiral stairs, with George following. There was a door at the top. And Sam could see it was ajar. He need not have worried about breaking and entering. Soutine had allowed them to walk straight in.

'Bet you didn't think it would be this easy,' said George from close behind.

Sam certainly had not. What was worrying him now was just how easy it was – altogether too easy, in fact.

He pushed the door of the flat fully open and stepped inside. George followed.

The rooms were small, opening off the cramped lobby in which they stood. There were several crates and boxes stacked on the floor. The air was cold and musty, tomb-like.

George shone the torch through an open doorway ahead of them into a drably furnished sitting-room. There was little sign of luxury. Sam noticed a bureau in one corner. The flap was down, revealing a chaos of papers. The drawers of the bureau had all been pulled open. Two had been pulled out altogether and were lying on the floor.

'Untidy beggar, isn't he?' murmured George, but it did not look like mere untidiness to Sam. He said nothing, though. He felt a keen sense of foreboding, but took some comfort from George's gruff humour and had no wish to puncture it.

'We'll take a closer look at that bureau in a moment, Sam. Let's see what's in the other rooms.'

The next one they looked into was a kitchen. Its door too stood open. But the door on the other side of the lobby was closed. Sam turned the handle and swung it open.

The torch beam moved across a bed, over which some strange, looming shadow was cast. George stepped round Sam and shone it directly into the room. And there was the horror, before them.

'Oh my Gawd.' Sam recoiled from the sight of it.

'Dear Lord,' said George.

A man was hanging upside down from a hook fixed to the ceiling. A chandelier that had once been suspended from it was now lying in pieces on the floor. The torchlight sparkled on its bevelled glass. There was a wide pool of congealed blood below the man's head. His throat had been cut, very nearly from ear to ear.

It was Soutine. Sam could tell that much from his white hair and Vandyke beard, though his face was otherwise a mask of dried blood. His hands were tied behind his back, his ankles bound together. He was wearing black shoes and socks, a white shirt and the trousers and waistcoat of a grey suit, the hems of the trousers held tight around his ankles by the rope fastening them. A gold watch hung upside down by its chain from one of his waistcoat pockets, the watch glass cracked clean across.

How long Soutine had been hanging there Sam could not have guessed, beyond the fact that it was less than twenty-four hours. Some time during those twenty-four hours, Soutine's luck and his lies and his life's blood had run out.

Laskaris et Soutine had lost at least one of its partners.

GEORGE STUMBLED INTO THE KITCHEN, WHERE HE RETCHED into the sink. He had led a sheltered life when it came to the contemplation of violent death. Sam, who had seen more downed pilots crushed or cremated in their own aircraft than he cared to remember, was less sickened than frightened.

He switched on the electric light in the lobby and gazed at the dead man's sightless eyes and blood-clotted mouth. That, he knew, was how someone might find him one day soon. He swallowed hard.

The body swung slightly in the draught created by opening the door, causing the knot around the hook to creak ominously. Sam dropped the duffel bag, stepped into the room and laid his hand gently against Soutine's thigh to arrest the movement, taking care not to tread in the blood as he did so. There was a stench of urine and faeces as well as blood in the closed air. It was obvious Soutine had died in terror as much as pain.

As Sam retreated to the lobby, George emerged from the kitchen, dabbing at his mouth with a towel he had found. 'Sorry,' he said. 'I think it was the smell that did for me.'

'Don't worry, sir,' said Sam softly. 'It's a sickening sight, right enough.'

'What in God's name has happened here?'

'They caught him. Like as not they tortured him. And then they killed him.'

'Why would they torture him?'

'They want le Singe.'

'Who are they?'

'Best you don't know, sir. Best you stay out of it altogether.'

'It'll be the worse for you if I do. We can't leave the poor devil like this. We have to call the police. There's probably a telephone in the sitting-room. But you should ask yourself whether you want to be here when they arrive, Sam. Placed as you are. I have the perfect explanation for my presence: Arnavon and the damned cylinder-seals. They'll be a lot more curious about you.'

'I don't really want to meet the police, sir, it's true.'

'Then leave them to me.'

'Are you sure?'

George smiled grimly. 'There's a condition. I want to know who's behind this. I won't breathe a word of what you tell me to the police. But I do want to know. Henry and le Singe. What exactly is it about?'

'I don't *exactly* know, sir.'

'Then I'll settle for inexactly.'

Sam wrestled with his conscience for a moment. George was offering him an escape from police attention he badly needed to avoid.

'Well?'

'It's a long story, sir. I'd be happier telling it to you somewhere else, if you know what I mean.'

'Not trying to fob me off, are you, Sam?'

'No, sir. You've got my word on that.'

'All right. Tomorrow. After I'm done with the police. The whole thing. Yes?'

Sam nodded. 'Yes.'

'You'd better go, then.'

'Hold on a minute, sir. I'm asking myself why Soutine came back here. He was clearing out when I met him last night. He had every-thing he wanted in his bag, I'm sure of it.'

'Maybe he forgot something.'

'Worth returning for? It would have to have been very important.'

'His killers probably took it.'

'Or missed it. Where's his coat?'

131

'There. On the bed.'

Soutine's overcoat and jacket lay entangled on the coverlet, spotted with his blood. His homburg lay on the floor beside the chandelier. They had been removed there, in the bedroom. There were hooks in the lobby, but he had not even hung his hat on one. It looked to Sam as if he had come to fetch something and leave immediately, then been interrupted. They must have been keeping watch for him. How long had he been dead? How long had passed since the room had been filled with the sounds of his dying?

Sam walked to the bed, pulled the coats towards him and checked their pockets. There were gloves, keys, a handkerchief, a pince-nez in a case, a pen and a wallet, holding only money. There was some loose change as well. Several other coins were lying on the floor by the bed, prompting Sam to kneel down and look beneath it. There was nothing to see there but dust.

He glanced up at Soutine's inverted face as he turned to rise. And something stopped him.

'What is it?' asked George.

'In his mouth,' said Sam. 'There's something in his mouth.'

It was a sharp edge of some kind. A broken tooth was Sam's first thought. But it did not look like a tooth. He edged closer and peered between Soutine's bloodied lips. Something had been wedged at the side of his mouth and now, with the tongue hanging loose, it had become visible.

'What the devil is it?' George crept into the room.

Sam stretched out his hand, delicately grasped the edge and pulled it out.

It was a piece of card, folded in quarters. It had once been white, but was now mostly a dull red. Sam unfolded it and found himself looking at a small, creased, sepia-tinted photograph. He stood up. George shone the torch on the picture and they both stared at it, George fumbling with his glasses to see it properly.

The photograph had been taken inside a pale-walled room, opening onto a balcony. Soutine, some years younger, with darker hair and a leaner face, was reclining amid richly patterned cushions on a divan. He was wearing a gold-braided gown of some kind. Sitting next to him was le Singe, obviously also younger, though his facial appearance was exactly as Sam recalled. He was dressed in a white kaftan and a dark-coloured fez. Soutine's left arm was draped round le Singe's neck. His right hand was resting on le Singe's knee. Both men were smiling broadly.

'Is that who I think it is?' asked George.

'Yes, sir. That's le Singe.'

'More than a servant to Soutine, by the look of it. A lot more. Is there anything on the back?'

Sam turned the photograph over. A few words were written there, in French, hard to read for the intermingling of blood and ink. *Les jours heureux au Tunis.*

'Happy days in Tunis,' murmured George. 'He may have thought of them as he died.'

'He looks happy in the picture.'

'They both do.'

'I reckon this is what he came back for.'

'Yes. I dare say you're right. When he knew they were coming for him . . .'

'He stuffed it in his mouth so they wouldn't have a likeness of le Singe.'

'It looks to me as if he loved the boy dearly.'

'He won't have given him up, then.'

'Probably not, no.'

No. Soutine had died with le Singe's secret intact. They had found Soutine. But they had not found le Singe.

'It doesn't look well for you if they still don't know where he is,' said George. 'If, as you say, they believe you may know where he's hiding.'

'No. It doesn't.'

'Judging by the state of the bureau, they must have searched high and low for a clue. And they'll have taxed Soutine sorely before they killed him.'

'You don't need to tell me that, sir.'

'Sorry. Maybe you should leave Paris.'

'You're not the first person to suggest that, sir.'

'You should certainly leave here. Without further delay. And take that photograph with you. I'll say nothing about it to the police. We should respect any secret a man died to keep. Soutine may have been a rogue, but it seems he wasn't a coward.'

'No, sir.' Sam took a last glance at Soutine's bright blue unblinking eyes. 'Anything but.'

SAM PROWLED AROUND THE JUNCTION OF PLACE DE LA
République waiting to see how long it would be before the
police arrived. Three cigarettes later, a black Citroën with a couple
of motorcycle outriders approached at some speed from the south.
The car and one of the motorcycles turned into Rue Béranger. The
other motorcyclist rode round the square to the opposite end of
Passage Vendôme.

Sam felt he could safely leave now. He had been concerned,
though he had not mentioned it to George, that Soutine's killers
might return before the police arrived, unlikely as that was. But all
had been quiet. And George would be safe with the police. He was
the sort to command their instant respect.

The Métro had stopped running for the night, so Sam was faced
with a long, cold walk back to the Majestic. He shouldered the
duffel bag and set off.

He had only gone a few yards when he heard footsteps behind
him. Suddenly alarmed, he turned round. And was astonished to
find Schools Morahan towering over him, a vast black shadow in
his dark hat and coat.

'Mr Morahan! What are you doing here?'

'I could ask you the same, Sam.'

'Well, I . . .'

'I spotted you as I was crossing the square about ten minutes
ago, though naturally I took care you didn't spot me. I was
planning to pay an out-of-hours visit to Laskaris and Soutine, but
with you loitering in the vicinity I reckoned I'd better wait and see

what was going on. Now the police have shown up and, by the look of it, you were expecting them.'

'Soutine's dead,' said Sam, unable to summon the effort to dissemble. 'Strung up in the flat above the gallery like a pig in a slaughterhouse.'

'They've killed him?'

'Tortured, then killed, it looks like.'

'How did you get in?'

'The door was unlocked.'

'What were you trying to do?'

'Find a clue to his whereabouts. And le Singe's.'

'You called the police? Then left?'

'Mr Clissold's waiting for them. He'll keep my name out of it.'

'*Who?*'

'George Clissold. Max's uncle.'

'What the hell's he doing here?'

'It's a long story.'

'I'll hear it anyway. I've a car near by. And I know somewhere we can get a drink this late. Let's go.' Morahan glanced over his shoulder. 'Before the police start checking the square.'

Max was on the platform at Inverness station well before the sleeper was due to leave. So, worryingly, was the big fellow. They both had business with the sleeping-car attendant, it transpired, as did several others. The attendant was kept busy for some time with requests for berths. Max and the big fellow were accommodated in first-class singles, though not, mercifully, next door to each other. They were half the length of the corridor apart.

Max had no fear of sleeping through the stop at Perth. The separation of the Glasgow and Edinburgh sections would supply enough jolts to rouse him. Not that he expected to sleep much, anyway.

He stowed the envelope containing the Grey File under his NB-monogrammed pillow and lay on the bunk fully clothed, gazing up into the darkness as the train left the station. With every southward mile he covered, he was closer to making an end of Lemmer.

*

'It was Kuroda who warned you of the threat Count Tomura poses, wasn't it?' Morahan asked, when Sam had finished recounting the events of the evening. They were sitting in a booth in the smoky rear of Le Couche-Tard, an obscurely signed basement bar near the Gare St-Lazare, drinking coffee heavily laced with rum.

'I'm naming no names as far as that goes, Mr Morahan,' said Sam. 'I'd tell anyone who asks that Commissioner Kuroda has nothing to do with it.'

'He'd be pleased to hear it, I'm sure. Anyhow, it doesn't matter. Kuroda's gone. Tomura's running the show at the Japanese legation. And he's looking for le Singe. His son, whose acquaintance I wouldn't recommend to my worst enemy, hired Ireton Associates today.' Morahan glanced up at the clock behind the bar. 'Make that yesterday. He engaged our services to find le Singe. That's what took me to Laskaris and Soutine.'

'You mean, it wasn't the Japs who killed Soutine?'

'It might not have been. There could be people we don't know about looking for le Singe. Not to mention people we do know about, such as Lemmer. But I wouldn't rule out Tomura junior. He met with Ireton on his father's behalf. He'd probably like nothing better than to track down le Singe without our assistance. It'd make him look the big man. He wants to be feared and respected. Standard heart's desire for an insecure young bully.'

'What was done to Soutine was butchery plain and simple, Mr Morahan.'

'And having seen that, have you had second thoughts about leaving Paris? Though maybe you won't have to, if Soutine pointed them in le Singe's direction.'

'I don't think he did.'

'Because of the photograph?'

'Because he went back for it. And then stuffed it in his mouth to stop them finding it.'

'You may be right, Sam. Which is bad news for you. If you won't clear out of the city, at least stick to the Majestic, huh? You should be safe there.'

'I won't feel safe.'

'You're sure this guy Clissold will say nothing to the police about le Singe? Or you?'

'He promised not to.'

'And he's an English gent we can take at his word?'

'He is.'

'Well, that leaves you with the Tomura problem. And ironically I'm pleased to help you with that since Tomura's paying Travis – and therefore me – to find le Singe.'

'How can you do that now Soutine's dead?'

'Well, his death will be widely reported. The press love blood. And he was well known in the art and antiquities world. We can assume le Singe will hear of it sooner rather than later. How's he going to react?'

'Run for it?'

'Maybe. Or maybe he'll look to avenge his . . . whatever Soutine was to him.'

'Show himself, you mean?'

'It's a possibility. And about the only way I'm likely to be able to locate him.'

'I can't help hoping he'll stay in hiding. He did all he could to make up for his part in Sir Henry's death. He saved Max's life. He doesn't deserve to end up the way Soutine did.'

'How we deserve to end up doesn't generally have much sway when it comes down to it, Sam. I'd lay my money on le Singe trying to make someone pay for Soutine's murder. But how he'll try, and when, are harder questions than I can answer at this hour of the night.' Morahan rubbed his eyes. 'Drink up. It's time I was taking you back to your home from home.'

THE SLEEPER ROLLED INTO PERTH GENERAL SHORTLY AFTER
five o'clock on the last morning of April. A grey dawn lit the
station beyond the gleam of the platform lamps. Max raised
the blind in his compartment a few inches and peered out. There
were more staff to be seen than passengers, busy loading mail and
preparing to divide the carriages.

Max put on his coat and hat, slid the envelope containing the
Grey File inside his waistcoat, grabbed his bag and make a deft,
silent exit into the corridor. There was no one about. He padded
along, heading for the rear of the train, where the ticket inspector
had previously directed Edinburgh passengers.

Six carriages took him as far as the guard's van. He got out there
and asked a porter how long the train would spend at Perth. The
answer did nothing to soothe his impatience. The Glasgow section
was due to leave at 5.50, the Edinburgh section not until 6.20.

'There's a cafeteria on the other platform, sir. They're open for
breakfast if you've the stomach for it.'

Max was not sure he had, but went anyway. He wanted to be
nowhere in view if the big fellow should look out. He bought a
Scotsman and scanned through it for news from the Orkneys. There
was none, as he had hoped. He drank some tea and forced down
half a bowl of porridge.

He remained in the cafeteria until whistles and the sound of an
engine gathering steam marked the departure of the Glasgow
service. He saw the plume of smoke as it left.

Only then did he deem it safe to return. He found an empty

first-class compartment, pulled down the blinds on the corridor side to discourage company and settled in. It was a two-hour ride to Edinburgh. There was no sign of the big fellow. As far as he could tell, all was well.

The train eventually left nearly ten minutes late. But it left. And that was all that mattered to Max.

The journey proceeded smoothly for the first hour and beyond. The grey dawn became a sunless morning, the sky over the Ochil Hills veiled in flat cloud. The train picked up more passengers at every stop, though none of the few who were travelling first class tried to enter Max's compartment.

The service grew busier still at Dunfermline. Max looked out of the window to check his watch against the station clock. The train was still running late, but it was only forty minutes now to Edinburgh. He was beginning to think Perkins and the big fellow had been innocent wayfarers, the suspiciousness of their behaviour existing only in his overstimulated imagination.

After a couple more stops, the train headed slowly out onto the Forth Bridge, slowing still further as it did so. Peering through the window, Max could see scaffolding up round the arch before the first cantilevered section. Further delay did not worry him unduly. The London express was not due to leave Edinburgh until ten o'clock. He had been promised some kind of reception at Waverley station. It was a surprisingly cheering thought.

The door of the compartment was suddenly wrenched open. Two men entered, one of them the big fellow from Inverness; the other, smaller, leaner and meaner-faced. He was carrying a gun; the big fellow, a flick-knife. Max saw the blade flash out of the handle as the door slammed shut behind them.

Max had hoped he would have to deal with only one man. He had an empty revolver to bluff with and not a lot else. But he had no intention of giving up without a fight.

'Stop where you are or I'll shoot,' he said, whipping out the revolver and taking his stand against the window. They had waited for the bridge so there would be no onlookers, he realized.

They wanted no witnesses to what they planned to do. 'I mean it.'

'We know it's empty, Max,' said the small man, in a slippery, hissing voice. 'There's nowhere you could have bought ammunition since leaving Stromness.'

Damn Wylie, Max thought. *Damn him to hell.*

'We only want the file. Give it up and you can go free.'

'Really? Are those your orders – to let me go on my way rejoicing?' They would try to avoid shooting on the train. That much was true. But the big fellow looked as if he could kill a man quietly with his knife any time he was asked to.

'Just give us the file. Is it in your bag?'

'Where else?'

'Get it down for us.'

'No.'

'What?'

'You heard. I'm not doing anything to help you. Go ahead and shoot me if you like. Plenty of people will hear the shot and come to see what the trouble is. Are you sure you want to risk that?'

The short man appeared momentarily nonplussed. Then the big fellow said, 'I'll do it.'

He heaved the bag down from the luggage-rack onto the seat, opened it and delved inside, while the short man kept the gun trained on Max.'Well?' he snapped, when the search went on a few seconds too many for his liking.

'It's not here.'

'It must be.'

That was the chance Max had been waiting for: the short man's alarmed glance towards his accomplice. Max lashed out with his foot. His kick struck the short man's wrist. The gun went off, a shot shattering the window. Max's gun was empty, but it was a weapon even so. He smashed it butt first into the man's temple. And down he went.

Max went down after him, grabbing for the loaded gun. But the big fellow was already on him, with a boot to Max's jaw that threw him back against the opposite seat. His head bounced against the stiff edge of the cushion and his vision blurred.

The big fellow lifted him by the lapels of his jacket as if he weighed no more than a toddler and slammed him into the corner against the window. He held the knife to Max's throat.

'Where's the file, God damn it?'

'You'll never know . . . if you kill me.'

'It's in this compartment somewhere. We'll find it. You can be sure of that.' The blade pressed into Max's flesh.

Max's vision began to clear. Reflected light gleamed into his eyes. A triangle of glass trembled in the draught of air through the broken window. 'OK, OK,' he gasped, raising his right hand as if in surrender. 'I'll show you where it is.'

The pressure of the blade eased. In that instant, Max grabbed at the loose shard of glass, ignoring the pain as it sliced into his palm, and swung it, point first, into his assailant's neck, striking where he had seen the pulsing of the jugular vein.

The big fellow cried out as blood spouted from the wound. He toppled sideways, dropping the knife as he fell. Max's hand and forearm were soaked in his blood. And more of it was spurting out of him. Max pushed him to the floor and struggled to his feet.

The short man was still unconscious from the blow to his head. The big fellow lay moaning beside him. Max knew it might be wise to finish them both off with the loaded gun, but he was no executioner. And his chances of being hunted as a murderer would only increase if he took the gun with him. He felt the pressure of the Grey File, buttoned inside his shirt, as he paused for one deep calming breath.

He grabbed his coat, struggled into it, jammed his hat on his head, closed the bag, picked it up and stepped past his assailants to the door. His right sleeve was wet with blood and his hand was bleeding. But all he could think about now was escape.

He flung the door open and lunged out into the corridor. 'Was that a gunshot?' came a shout from his left. Max glimpsed a knot of figures towards the far end of the corridor. He ignored them and headed the other way, checking the position of the train through the window as he went.

It was past the last cantilevered section of the bridge. The southern shore of the firth was immediately below Max's carriage. The train would be in Dalmeny station in a few minutes, by which time the people cowering in the corridor would probably have summoned the courage to enter the compartment he had just left. They would alert the guard. The police would be called. And the train would be held at Dalmeny until they arrived.

Max reached the end of the carriage and hurried through to the next. There he pushed down the first window he came to and leant out. Below him was another railway line, curving beneath the bridge as it spanned the shoreward part of the town. Ahead he could see the station platform. The train was slowing as it approached.

Max opened the door and held it ajar, checking over his shoulder for signs or sounds of pursuit. There was nothing yet that he could detect above the rumble of the wheels. The brakes began to squeal as the train drew into the station.

He pushed the door fully open as his carriage reached the platform and jumped out on the run. He jogged on to the foot-bridge and was most of the way over it before any other passengers had got off. At the barrier, he thrust his ticket into the hand of the collector and rushed down the steps towards the exit.

He was five or six miles short of his destination. There was enough time for him to walk to Edinburgh and still catch the London train. But he felt conspicuous on the streets of Dalmeny and knew he would feel even more so tramping along the Edinburgh road. It was odds-on the alarm would soon be raised. Any description of him would be vague to the point of uselessness, but there was blood on his shirt and on the handkerchief he had wrapped round his bleeding hand. Nor could he afford to assume the two men he had left on the train were the only two on his trail.

He reached the shore road and stopped, wondering which way to turn. The wide expanse of the firth stretched ahead of him. Above him to his left loomed the vast stone piers of the bridge. To his right, thirty yards or so along on the opposite side of the road, he could see two people waiting at a bus stop, looking expectantly in his direction.

The bus they were waiting for seemed certain to be bound for Edinburgh. It was the best escape route Max could hope for. He crossed the road and began to hurry towards the stop.

143

'Is he in?' Morahan asked Malory as he strode into the outer office of Ireton Associates that morning.

'Good morning, to you too, Mr Morahan,' Malory said, smiling sweetly.

'Sorry.' Morahan pushed up the brim of his hat far enough to rub his forehead. 'Late night.'

'And no more fruitful, judging by your expression, than my evening in the *bibliothèque*.'

'Soutine's been murdered.'

'Oh my Lord.' Malory stopped typing. 'That's awful.'

'Yuh. Is Travis here?'

'Yes, he is.'

'I'd better report the grisly details toot sweet.'

'Schools—'

'What is it?' He moved closer to her desk.

'Can I speak to you?' Her voice dropped to a whisper. 'Not here. Maybe during my lunch break? La Fontaine, twelve thirty?'

'What's this about – Soutine?'

'No. I'll explain when we meet. Can you make it?'

'Sure.' He smiled uncertainly. 'It's a date.'

Max got off the bus before it reached the centre of Edinburgh. He had buried himself behind his *Scotsman* while he was aboard, but out on the busy streets in broad daylight he became concerned about his bloodied appearance. He strode as confidently as he could into the Royal Hotel in Princes Street and made straight for

144

the toilets. A look in the mirror was reassuring. His jaw was swollen and bruised, but there were few visible bloodstains. He tidied himself up as best he could.

There was nothing to be done about his jacket, though. One sleeve was stiff with blood, which had seeped through to his waistcoat. He went in search of an outfitter's, where he bought replacements, including a new shirt. He put them on in the fitting room and tossed the discarded clothes in the first rubbish bin he came to.

With half an hour still to spare before the London express was due to leave, he found a barber willing to give him a quick shave. Hot towels and eau de Cologne made him feel much better.

He descended the steps into Waverley station apprehensively, even so. Would Appleby be there? Would more pursuers be waiting for him – for both of them – in enough force to ensure there could be only one outcome?

The station was busy, which was to his advantage. Solitude in a first-class compartment had done him little good. He would be travelling third class henceforth, reasoning there was safety in numbers.

He bought his ticket, then checked the departures board. The train was ready. But where was Appleby? If he had sent someone in his place, how would Max know he could trust him? Travellers with bags were milling everywhere. The scene had every appearance of normality. But Max hung back, concealed between a luggage-wagon and the side of a bookstall.

He lit a cigarette and flourished his *Scotsman* as camouflage. There was a later train he could catch and still be in London by early evening. He scanned the crowd before him, looking for some sign, some hint, of something amiss. And he watched the station clock tick down towards the moment when he could delay a decision no longer.

Ireton had received the news of Soutine's demise with more irritability than dismay. 'Damn it, he was a valuable source. It's a real shame we've lost him. It's going to make it a lot tougher for you to track down le Singe, Schools.'

145

'You mean to go on with the hunt?' Morahan frowned. Why he was surprised he did not really know. His long-time partner had never put business second to anything.

'Of course we go on. Tomura's paying top dollar.'

'Only for a result – which his son's just made a damn sight harder to achieve by killing Soutine.'

'You don't know the boy killed him.'

'I can't prove it, no. But I'm certain in my own mind he did. And he's put a tail on me.'

'Someone has, you mean.'

'It's got to be Tomura, Travis. It started right after we met him.'

'There were signs Soutine was tortured, you say?'

'So my informant tells me.'

Morahan's informant, in the version of events he had supplied to Ireton, was not Sam but a pliant police officer. He had said nothing about Sam at all, in fact. Nor about the photograph Sam had shown him.

'Noburo Tomura wants to make himself look cleverer than us in his father's eyes by finding le Singe without our help.'

'Look, if you're right and he got what he wanted out of Soutine before killing him, he will find le Singe before we do. Then our contract with his father will be cancelled in double quick time and you'll be able to tell me I should never have done business with him in the first place. Until that happens, though, we should press on. Soutine may have given nothing away. He was one stubborn sonofabitch, when all's said and done. Or someone else may have killed him. What other leads are you following on le Singe?'

'One or two. No point me detailing them unless they come to something. And I'll certainly be going back to my informant to try and find out if the police came across anything significant in Soutine's flat.'

'Well, don't let me hold you up. I'm going to be pretty busy myself now the Germans have arrived. I gather it was quite a circus out at Versailles last night. I don't envy them the Hôtel des Réservoirs. Gloomy sort of a place.'

'You've got a contact there?'

'The deputy manager. Don't worry. He's reliable. The Germans

146

will pay more or less whatever I ask for advance warning of the peace terms. It's going to be a sweet deal. So, don't stray too far in the days ahead, will you? We may need to be quick on the draw. But it's important for our future that the Japanese regard us as good people to work with. So, don't neglect Tomura whatever you do. OK?'

Morahan nodded. 'OK.'

'Telegram for Mr Nettles!'

The uniformed boy came into Max's view in an eddy of the crowd and he caught the words above the bellowed announcement of his train. '*East Coast Express to London ready to leave.*'

He was about to step forward when he saw two men over by the departures board watching the boy. One of them craned his neck to keep sight of him through the swirl of travellers.

'Telegram for Mr Nettles!'

It was a message from Appleby. It had to be. But accepting the previous telegram at Inverness could easily have been what singled Max out. It was not a mistake he could afford to repeat.

The luggage-wagon began to move, hauled by a beefy porter. Max fell in beside it, obscured from the gaze of the two men watching the boy. They could hardly be sure Max was on the station. They might not yet know what had happened on the train from Perth and had never seen Max before that he was aware of. No description would be enough to distinguish him from dozens of other hatted and overcoated men on the move.

Max broke from the cover of the luggage-wagon as a whistle began to blast on the platform where the London train was standing. He ran to the barrier, flashed his ticket and ran on towards the rear door being held open by the guard, who glared at him before blowing the whistle again.

EORGE ALLOWED HIMSELF A LENGTHY LIE-IN AFTER HIS LATE night with the police. His story had been watertight, of course. Arnavon would confirm Soutine's sale of the fake Sumerian cylinder-seals which had taken George to the gallery in search of answers. Sam's role in events had been easy to suppress. Altogether, the police had been polite and sympathetic, although their ears had pricked up at the mention of Soutine's dealings with George's late brother-in-law, Sir Henry Maxted.

'We may have further questions for you, *monsieur*. You are not planning to leave Paris?'

He had assured them he was not and there it had been left, with George transported back to his hotel with parting expressions of solicitude and regret.

'Our apologies that you should have had such an unpleasant experience in our city, *monsieur*.'

He skipped breakfast, beyond a head-clearing *café noir*, in favour of an early lunch. Later he would visit Sam, reassure him that the police had no inkling of his presence at the gallery and extract the promised explanation of Henry's connection with le Singe.

Most of the snow had melted, but it was still depressingly cold and overcast. George told himself a bracing stroll was nonetheless in order. He aimed for the Tuileries, knowing this would take him in the direction of a fondly remembered bistro near the Gare d'Orsay.

But the gardens proved to be altogether too bracing, so he

abandoned his projected perambulation in favour of a quick march to the Pont Royal.

He was halfway across the bridge, his attention focused principally on the swollen waters of the Seine surging below him, when he became aware that someone was walking very closely behind him. Before he could turn round, something hard and heavy struck him a stunning blow at the back of the head.

Darkness folded round him as he fell. '*Il est malade,*' he heard someone declare. He wanted to protest, but could not find his voice. He was being supported, then lifted and moved. And then . . . nothing.

Max began to relax as the train headed south. He had chosen to sit in a compartment where only one seat remained, which seemed to guarantee the innocence of the other occupants. They paid him no heed whatever. The crossing of the Tweed at Berwick felt momentous to him. He was back in England. The miles were rolling away between him and London. He worried about letting the telegram go unclaimed at Waverley, but knew it had been the right decision. He had been lucky to survive the first brush with his pursuers and had to do everything he could to avoid a second.

Sam was keeping his head down at the Majestic, concentrating as best he could on his work. He expected a visit from George Clissold before the day was out and found himself thinking enviously of Kuroda, who would be most of the way across the Mediterranean by now, bound for Japan. Sam would not have objected to a long ocean voyage himself. Every step he took in his present predicament had to be carefully judged. The bloodstains on the photograph he had taken from Soutine's body reminded him of that whenever he looked at it. '*The skilful warrior does not rely on the enemy not coming,*' Kuroda had advised him. '*He relies on his own preparedness.*' Sam did not doubt the truth of that. He was no warrior. But still he must prepare.

Morahan apologized for keeping Malory waiting when he arrived at La Fontaine ten minutes late. She brushed the matter aside as

149

unimportant, the first sign he detected that what she wanted to discuss with him was itself very far from unimportant.

'If you're worried about me, Malory, I want you to stop. I'll find a way through this business with le Singe, I guarantee. I just need time – and a slice of luck.'

'Well, I didn't turn up anything helpful in the archives, Schools, so luck is what it'll probably take. And you're right: I *am* worried. So should you be, with Soutine dead. Murdered, you said.'

'Yuh. And not prettily. Tomorrow's papers will make quite a splash of it.'

'There won't be any papers tomorrow. A general strike's been called for May Day.'

'It has? Well, that's downright *un*lucky. I was hoping the publicity might smoke le Singe out.'

'Anyhow, he's not who I wanted to talk to you about.'

'No?'

'No.'

Malory broke off at the appearance of the waiter to order a glass of red wine and an *omelette aux fines herbes*. Morahan opted for a steak.

'Good choice. You need the iron.'

'You think so?'

'I do.' She dropped her voice. 'The thing is this. The trading of information between competing delegations is a disreputable way to make money in a lot of people's eyes, Schools, but I've always reckoned it helps ensure fair play. You could argue Ireton Associates performs a public service in that sense.'

'That's a nice way to put it.' Morahan smiled at her. 'I'll be sure to remember it.'

'None of the countries represented at the conference are military enemies of the United States.'

'What point are you leading up to, Malory?'

'The Germans, Schools. They *are* military enemies of our country. The war could resume if they reject the terms offered to them. Travis regards them as just another potential client. But dealing with them – helping them – could be classified as treason. I can't be party to that. Nor should you be.'

150

'What has Travis told you?'

'Nothing. But I know he has a go-between in place at their hotel.'

'You're right. He does.'

'You know who it is?'

Morahan nodded. 'I do.'

'A senior member of the hotel staff, I imagine.'

'You imagine correctly.'

A silence fell while Morahan and Malory looked searchingly at each other, extended by the arrival of their drinks. Then Malory asked, 'Are you really willing to let Travis go ahead with this?'

'It'd be hard to stop him.'

'What if the French authorities were tipped off that the staff member in question represented a security risk?'

'He'd be arrested right away.'

'And it would be difficult, if not impossible, for Travis to replace him at short notice.'

'It would.'

'We'd actually be doing Travis a favour. Saving him from himself.'

'I doubt he'd see it that way.'

'No need for him to see it any way, other than as a stroke of misfortune.'

Morahan sighed and rubbed his eyes. 'Damn it all,' he murmured.

'How should I go about it?'

'You?' He looked at her in surprise. 'No, no. I'll do it.' He sat back in his chair and took a long, slow breath. 'You're right, of course. I've had a fair few other things to think about recently. But there are lines you can't cross and this is one of them. A lot of our boys died in the winning of the war. We can't let them down, can we? And we can't let Travis let them down either.'

'It's a relief to hear you say that, Schools.'

'I'll deal with it as soon as possible. Just leave it to me.'

The train had just left Darlington and several passengers in Max's compartment had begun nibbling at their packed lunches when the door was pulled open and a tubby fellow in NER catering livery looked in. He scanned several faces before fixing on Max.

'Mr Hutton?'

Whatever his use of the name portended, Max knew at once it could not be good. 'Why d'you ask?' he replied coolly.

'There's a lady in the restaurant car, sir, travelling first class, who wonders if you'd like to join her for lunch.'

'What's her name?'

'Miss Kislev.'

It was Nadia. Of course. Who else?

'Bit of a stunner, sir.' The steward winked. 'I'd take her up on the offer if I was you.'

NADIA WAS A PICTURE OF TRAVELLING ELEGANCE IN A GREEN-flecked tweed jacket and skirt and a high-necked blouse. She was smoking a long cigarette and sipping a gin and tonic, while turning the pages of a slim novel. Her dark hair gleamed in the sunlight shafting through the window. There was a lustre to her skin and a depth to her gaze that reminded Max how attractive she was – and how dangerous.

'I am so happy you can join me, Max,' she trilled, rising to kiss him on the cheek.

He said nothing, dumbstruck by her flagrancy. He slid his bag under the table and sat down opposite her.

'It was wise to bring your luggage,' she went on, smiling at him. 'There are thieves everywhere.'

'Are there?' he countered.

'Have you read this?' She showed him the title of the book: *The Thirty-Nine Steps* by John Buchan.

'No.'

'You should. It is very exciting. Though not as exciting as your own adventure.'

'What are you doing here, Nadia?'

'The same as all those people in Paris: trying to make peace.'

'I met some colleagues of yours earlier. They weren't very peaceable.'

'You should have stayed on the train to Glasgow.'

'What difference does it make what route I travel by, as long as I reach the right destination?'

'None. As long as it is the *right* destination.'

'How did you know I'd be on this train?'

'They cabled me from Perth, Max. I left for Edinburgh immediately. This is the quickest way for you to reach London. So, I knew you would be on this train. However late you left it to board.'

'And what d'you want to say to me?'

'You have an agreement with him. You must honour it.'

'Oh, I'm doing the honourable thing. You can rely on that.'

'Will you have a drink with me before we order lunch?' She signalled to the steward. 'It is a long journey.'

'All right.' He ordered a whisky and soda; Nadia, a second gin and tonic.

'I asked,' she said with a smile. 'But they have no vodka.'

'You can't stop me, y'know,' Max declared.

'Where are you carrying it? In the bag or under your shirt? You look a little stouter than I remember.'

'Who says I'm carrying anything? Maybe I stuck a stamp on it and posted it while I was in Edinburgh.'

'No. You did not do that. Precious, you called it. Too precious to post. Besides, who would you post it to? Who can you trust completely?'

'More people than you can, I'm sure.'

'He will get it from you. I think you know that.'

'No. I don't.'

'It is not too late to come back to us. Deliver the file to him. Then what you did to Fontana and what you did to the men on the train will be forgotten. It will be nothing.'

'He's never trusted me, Nadia. Neither have you. D'you think I don't know why I was chosen? He'll get the file over my dead body.'

She looked at him in earnest. 'Then that is how he will get it. Surrender is your only escape, Max. Otherwise . . .' She shook her head. 'You have not a hope.'

'We'll see.'

'There is another reason why you should give it up.'

'Oh? What's that?'

'Farngold.'

Max was at first too amazed to react. He stared at her in silence as their drinks arrived.

'Ready to order?' the steward enquired, nodding to the menus that lay on the table.

'Not yet,' Nadia answered quietly, without taking her eyes off Max.

The steward retreated. Nadia touched her glass against Max's. '*Za vashy zdarovy,*' she said, drinking to her own toast.

'What d'you know about Farngold?' Max asked, as calmly as he could.

'You want the secret, Max. Of course you do. It is natural. You want to know why your father died. Put the file in his hand. And it will be.'

'You expect me to believe that?'

'You will not learn it otherwise.'

'Do you know the secret, Nadia?'

'I know a few things he has said I can tell you. The woman I worked for in Keijo. We called her the Dragonfly. I never knew her real name. He wanted her to help him find a man who had been asking questions about him. An Englishman, called Farngold. Jack Farngold.'

'You met him?'

'Once, yes. The Dragonfly wanted me to talk to him – distract him – while she alerted Lemmer. So, I sat with Jack Farngold in a teahouse and I listened to him and I learnt what had brought him to Korea. He had been chasing a secret for a very long time. He did not look well. He had taken on a burden and slowly, very slowly, he had buckled under it. I never met anyone more tired – or more determined.'

'What did he say had taken him to Korea?'

'I cannot tell you, Max. That *is* the secret. It is worth the Grey File, I think. What do you think?'

'What happened to Farngold?'

'He was arrested. They said he was deranged. He was put in the Governor General's Hospital. I heard he was transferred from there to a hospital in Tokyo. After that, who would know? A mad Englishman, without a family, without friends, locked

155

up in an asylum in Japan. Who would know anything about that?'

'Did he say where he came from in England?'

'Maybe.'

'Did he or didn't he?'

'I cannot tell you any more. It is enough. My reward for helping the Dragonfly trap Farngold was an offer of employment.'

'From Lemmer?'

'Yes. I met him at the Chosen Hotel and we walked out into the garden and he told me what was in his mind for me. And I liked what he told me. I liked it very much.'

'When was this?'

'Not so long ago in some ways. In other ways, as distant as another life.'

'Which year was it? Which season?'

Nadia smiled. 'You want the date they arrested Farngold? You think that will help you find him? You think that will take you to the secret? No. Give up the Grey File. Then you will know the secret. Refuse and it will be taken from your dead hand. That is your choice. I will tell you no more. Hold a gun to my head or a knife to my throat. It will make no difference. I will tell you no more.'

'You sound like Anna Schmidt.'

'You have never met Anna Schmidt, Max.'

'No. But her husband said she worships Lemmer. It seems you do as well.'

'In a world where empires fall, he stands. I stand with him. You can too.'

Max shook his head. 'Never.'

'There is still time for you to reconsider.' She picked up the menu. 'We should order.'

'You propose we sit here together over lunch and watch the countryside roll by and talk about ... what? Your childhood summers at the family *dacha*?'

'If you like.'

'Well, I—'

'James Maxted,' a voice cut in.

Max looked up to see, standing at his shoulder, a stocky man of late middle years, wearing an overcoat and trilby. Beside him was a brawny police constable, eyeing Max as if taking the physical measure of him.

'You are James Maxted, aren't you, sir? You fit your description, so I'd advise against denying it.'

'What's going on?'

'You're under arrest, sir.'

'*What?*'

'I'm Detective Chief Inspector Tunnicliffe, North Riding Constabulary, acting on a request from the Metropolitan Police. We'll be taking you off the train at York, for questioning by an officer from London.'

'What is he charged with?' Nadia asked.

'A possible breach of section one of the Official Secrets Act, miss. Now, we don't want a commotion, do we, sir? There are people here trying to enjoy their lunch. Come along with us, please, there's a good fellow.'

MORAHAN DID NOT STIR FROM THE BENCH WHERE HE WAS sitting when he saw the unmistakable figure of Frank Carver of the US Secret Service descending the stairs to the eastbound platform of Concorde Métro station. The man was square-shouldered and lantern-jawed, conspicuously larger and better nourished than most of the assembled passengers. Someone had told Morahan Carver hailed from Iowa and certainly he had a healthily farm-reared look to him.

They waited at opposite ends of the platform, smoking cigarettes – Morahan, French; Carver, American. Only when the rumble of the approaching train became audible did they move towards each other. They boarded the same carriage and took adjacent seats.

The doors closed and the train set off. Carver finished his cigarette and extinguished the butt beneath the toe of his shoe. 'Busy?' he enquired of Morahan, pitching his voice so that no one near by could have heard what he had said.

'Not idle, that's for sure.'

'Let's get to it, then, shall we? What d'you want?'

'An accommodation.'

'What in hell does that mean?'

'You've been making it hard for Travis to operate, Frank. Obstructing his business. Harassing his clients. He'd like it to stop.'

'Sure. And I'd like Christmas once a month.'

'What would it take for you to lay off?'

'Proof that he isn't undermining American interests at the peace conference. Got any in your back pocket?'

'Proving a negative is a difficult thing to do, Frank.'

'Well, I thought that's what Ireton paid you to do: difficult things.'

'You've got him all wrong, y'know. He's a patriot.'

'Patriot my ass.'

'He fought for his country in Cuba.'

'So did you. Matter of fact, Schools, Ireton's an open book compared with you. I mean, I know how his mind works. Yours is way more complicated. How much of an American are you? You sure weren't born one.'

'My parents left Belfast when I was two years old. My earliest memories are of New York.'

'So, you were one of the huddled masses. But it's not just about birth, is it? Far as I can tell, you haven't spent a straight year in the States your whole adult life.'

'Been studying me, have you, Frank?'

'Best I can. But tracking you's not easy. I get the feeling you've never wanted it to be.'

'I didn't ask to meet you to rehearse my autobiography.'

'I can believe that. Why, then?'

'I thought if I gave you something that showed you Travis draws the line well short of compromising American interests, you might, well, go a little easier on him.'

'You did, did you?'

'Sound reasonable?'

'Tell me what it is and I'll let you know.'

'All right.' Morahan paused to light a cigarette. He held the match for Carver to light one of his own, a small gesture of conciliation, and lowered his voice confidentially. 'The deputy manager of the Hôtel des Réservoirs has offered us his services as a conduit for selling information to the German delegation.'

'The hell he has.'

'We're not proposing to do business with the Germans, Frank. Those consciences you don't credit us with won't let us. But if we just refuse, he'll likely look elsewhere. We don't want that to happen either.'

'It won't now.'

'I imagine you'll want to speak to *le Deuxième Bureau* about him.'

'You can count on it.'

'Good. And as for our future relations . . .'

'Don't push it, Schools. This is a first step on a long road to redemption for you and Ireton. But it's a step in the right direction, I'll say that.'

'You'll bear it in mind to our advantage?'

Carver gave the question some thought during a long draw on his cigarette, then said, 'Maybe.'

Sam's afternoon in the garage was interrupted by an unexpected summons to the office of Shuttleworth, i/c support services for the British delegation. When he arrived, he was surprised to see Shuttleworth had a visitor he recognized: Commissioner Zamaron of the Paris police.

'*Bonjour*, Mr Twentyman,' Zamaron greeted him, a smile forming beneath his luxuriant moustache.

'I gather you know each other, Twentyman,' said Shuttleworth, who looked as if the fact did not sit well with him.

'We've met before, yes,' said Sam cautiously.

'Well, the Commissioner has some questions for you. And there are some problems requiring my attention elsewhere in the hotel, so I'll leave you to it.'

'*Merci beaucoup,*' said Zamaron, bowing faintly as Shuttleworth took his leave of them.

'Er, right, thanks,' murmured Sam.

Shuttleworth closed the door behind him. Zamaron's smile grew broader, but no more reassuring.

'What can I do for you, Commissioner?' Sam spotted a stray smut of oil on his thumb, which he wiped off on the back of his overalls. 'Sorry, about the, er, kit.'

'I am sorry, Mr Twentyman, to interrupt your important work. You are the wheels of the British delegation, no?'

'Sort of.'

'So, I will not delay you more than I have to. Are you acquainted with Mr George Clissold?'

'Er, yes.'

'How so?'

'Well, he's Lieutenant James Maxted's uncle. He came to see me yesterday.'

'Why?'

'Oh, in case I had news of his nephew.'

'And had you?'

Sam shook his head. ''Fraid not.'

'Did he tell you why he had come to Paris?'

'Yes. Something about a dispute with an antique dealer. Name of, er . . .'

'Soutine?'

'Yeah. That's it. Soutine. He was wondering if Max – Lieutenant Maxted – had mentioned him to me.'

'And had he?'

'No.'

'Soutine was found dead in the *appartement* above his gallery last night, Mr Twentyman. By Mr Clissold.'

'Oh lor'. Sorry to hear that. How did Soutine—'

'He was murdered.'

'Murdered? Blimey.'

'Mr Clissold reported his discovery at once. I did not hear of it until this morning. I have not met Mr Clissold. He was not at his hotel when I called there earlier. Have you heard from him today?'

'No, I haven't.'

'Have you a thought about why Soutine was murdered?'

'Me? No. Haven't a clue.'

'You are sure?' Zamaron's gaze had suddenly hardened.

'I don't know anything about it.'

'Did Mr Clissold mention speaking to anyone else about Soutine?'

'Not as I recall.'

'Anyone Chinese . . . or Japanese?'

Sam tried to look suitably baffled, though he was actually more worried now than confused. George was not supposed to have said anything about the people they believed had killed Soutine. 'No. Nothing.'

161

'It is a very serious matter, Mr Twentyman.'

''Course. Murder is.'

'It is not only murder. I received a report after visiting Mr Clissold's hotel that a man fitting his description was attacked while crossing the Pont Royal earlier today. Witnesses saw him dragged into a van and driven away. They described his attackers as *Orientaux*: Chinese or Japanese.'

'Mr Clissold? Kidnapped?'

'It seems so.'

'Oh my Gawd.'

'It is a strange thing, Mr Twentyman.' Zamaron cocked his head suspiciously. 'For the first time this afternoon, I feel I have told you something you did not know already.'

Max had expected another move to be made against him by Lemmer's agents. The attention of the police had caught him unawares. He was still trying to imagine what might lie behind his arrest as he was marched down the train towards the guard's van. Tunnicliffe led the way and the constable brought up the rear, carrying Max's bag. They kept close in the narrow corridors and vestibules, rendering escape impossible.

When they arrived, it was clear the guard had been expecting them. 'Is he dangerous?' he asked, as Max was handcuffed to the bicycle rack.

'Can't be too careful,' Tunnicliffe replied. 'You'll get your van back after York.'

The guard took that as his cue to leave and the constable soon followed, with instructions to stop anyone coming in.

'Cigarette?' Tunnicliffe asked, taking a pack from his pocket once he and Max were alone.

'No, thanks.'

'Suit yourself.' He put the cigarettes away and lit a pipe. 'You got Horace's telegram?'

'What?'

'Horace's telegram. At Edinburgh. Warning you he'd pull some stunt like this to get you off the train.'

Anxiety turned suddenly to optimism. 'Appleby sent you?'

'We're old friends, Horace and me. We go way back. It's not safe to go on to London, apparently. He'll be waiting for you at York. I haven't a clue what this is all about, but, if Horace says special precautions are necessary, they're necessary. We'll take you off under guard for the benefit of anyone tailing you. After that, it'll be up to Horace. Carrying something important, are you?'

'You could say that.'

'You're in the same organization as him? The one that doesn't officially exist?'

'Not exactly.'

Tunnicliffe mulled Max's answer over for a moment, then said, 'I suppose you have to be pretty tight-lipped in your game.'

'It helps.'

'Well, Horace vouches for you, so that's good enough for me. Sorry about the 'cuffs. But we have to make this look like a genuine arrest. Want me to do anything about the young lady you were having lunch with?'

'No. Leave her be.' Max wondered how Nadia would interpret what had happened. With any luck, she would be as baffled as initially he had been. 'Have you seen Appleby?'

'Not seen, no. Spoke to him on the blower earlier.'

'How did he sound?'

'Worried. Which he isn't easily. Should he be?'

'Yes. I rather think he should.'

C AND HIS PRINCIPAL LIEUTENANTS WERE SEATED ROUND THE conference table in his office at Secret Service Headquarters. It was an unscheduled meeting, called at Political's request. The suavest and most obviously cerebral of the Service's section heads, Political looked unusually animated, if not troubled. The absence of his customary languor had tinged his colleagues – Military, Naval and Aviation – with faint but unmistakable anxiety, though there was no sign this had extended to C.

They were all drinking tea, or at any rate the sludgy brown liquid served under its name by the redoubtable Mrs Ferris, who had also supplied some finger-slices of fruit cake no one had so far ventured to sample. Military, Aviation and Political were smoking cigarettes. Naval was puffing at a pipe – 'signalling to the fleet', as Political often described it. And C was watching them.

'Where is Appleby now?' he asked after perusing once again the urgent memo Political had circulated.

'We don't know,' Political replied. 'We assume he left Victoria by train. There are many destinations he could have chosen from.'

'Have we had a full account from Paris yet of the circumstances of his departure?'

'We only know what he told his secretary: that he had to attend to a family emergency and would be away for a few days.'

'Does he have a family?' Military enquired.

'He's a widower,' said C. 'He had a son who was killed in the war.'

There was a brief silence, reflecting the fact that C, as well as

Naval, had also lost sons in the war. Then Political said, 'It seems unlikely in Appleby's personal circumstances that there was any such emergency.'

'Do we know why he left, then?' asked Aviation.

C looked at Political. 'Tell them,' he said quietly.

Political cleared his throat. 'Yesterday morning, shortly before Appleby left his post, I heard from our contact in the German delegation that another member of the delegation staff had named Appleby as a German spy.'

'Good God,' said Naval, putting down his cup of tea so hurriedly he spilt some of it into the saucer.

'Is this to be credited?' asked Military.

'It's certainly to be taken seriously,' Political replied. 'The informant is a secretary accompanying Posts Minister Giesberts, a woman by the name of Anna Schmidt. She previously worked in the special measures department of the Nachrichten-Abteilung as personal secretary to—'

'Lemmer?' Military interrupted.

'Exactly. She is someone in a position to know. I felt obliged to act quickly. I intended to recommend Appleby's immediate recall, but he'd left before I had the chance.'

'Tipped off, you think?' asked Aviation.

'It's the obvious conclusion to draw. He'd received a telegram – we don't know from whom, obviously – shortly before leaving. I arranged for him to be met at Victoria if he headed this way. As indeed he did. But he pulled a gun on our man and got away.'

'Who did you send?' asked Military.

'Davison, with Parks driving.'

Military shook his head contemptuously. 'They'd never have been a match for him. I'm surprised you didn't realize that.'

'My resources aren't infinite,' Political snapped. 'It was by no means certain he'd come to London. And he'd have accompanied my men readily enough if he'd really been attending to a family emergency. His reaction confirms his guilt to my mind.'

'What did you have planned for him?' asked Aviation.

'Questioning at the section house.'

'Questioning?' queried Military. 'Or interrogation?'

'Whichever proved appropriate.'

'Shouldn't we have had warning of this?' asked Naval, with a hint of peevishness.

'There wasn't time.'

'Clearly there wasn't enough time to manage the operation properly,' pronounced C. 'Which is a pity, to put it mildly.'

'No one regrets more than I do that he slipped through our fingers,' said Political. 'I'm taking all the steps I can to find him.'

'I can't believe a fellow like Appleby would be a turncoat,' said Naval, shaking his head incredulously.

'Perhaps he isn't,' said C. 'But his conduct is certainly worrying.'

'How worried should we be?' asked Military. 'I mean, as to the ramifications, if indeed Appleby is one of Lemmer's agents.'

'Very,' said Political firmly. 'He was here barely a month ago, telling us how determined he was to track Lemmer down in Paris and what methods he'd use to go about it. If the information I've received is correct, he was deliberately misleading us, on Lemmer's orders. Consider what happened. There was no trace of Lemmer, but one of our agents and two members of our delegation ended up dead, along with one of the Americans. We've assumed Norris and Dobson were working for Lemmer and that Norris arranged the murder of Sir Henry Maxted. But what if Appleby was behind it all? What if he arranged to dispose of Sir Henry and then covered his tracks by disposing of Norris and the Yank as well? He blamed Dobson's and Norris's killings on a Russian woman for whose very existence we have little evidence beyond his own account.'

'What about Sir Henry's son? Wasn't Appleby working with him?'

'Supposedly. But nothing's been seen or heard of young Maxted since that business in Mayfair.'

'You think his body's waiting to be found somewhere?'

'I can't say. He may have been eliminated. Or he may have thrown in his lot with Appleby.'

'This is awful,' said Aviation pitifully.

'It's not good, I agree,' said Political. 'There may be grave implications for the security of the conference.'

'No one will thank us for sowing alarm unnecessarily,' declared C. 'It's imperative we find Appleby. We can only assess the situation properly once we've been able to establish the truth. Who's his number two in Paris?'

'He doesn't really have one.' Military sighed. 'It's been rather a one-man show.'

'Then we'll have to send someone over.'

'Jefferies?' suggested Political.

'Mmm.' C thought the matter over, then said, 'Yes. Jefferies will do to hold the fort. Have him sent to me for briefing.'

'And as to Appleby?'

'Turn all resources to finding him. Involve Special Branch if you need to. I want Appleby available for questioning within twenty-four hours – forty-eight at the most.'

'It may prove difficult to take him alive.'

'He's no use to us dead. And you're to give him the benefit of the doubt as far as his loyalty's concerned until we've been able to put it to the test. Is that clear?'

Political nodded. 'Completely.'

'Very well. That'll be all for now, gentlemen. One point, though. The Germans have only just arrived in Paris. It'll be another week or so before they're presented with the peace terms. It's a week that could well contain a lot of delicate manoeuvring. We must do nothing to complicate matters unless circumstances force us to. It's our task to ensure they do not. You understand?'

There were mumbled affirmations all round.

'Good.' He gave a nod of satisfaction, then watched as they gathered their papers and rose to leave.

At the last moment, he signalled for Political to remain.

'How reliable would you say your contact in the German delegation is, Nick?' he asked as soon as the others had gone.

'Extremely. His reports on how the SPD would react to the Kaiser's abdication were borne out by events and he alerted us to the trap Ebert set for the radicals in January. I've never had cause to doubt him.'

'So, you believe Appleby is Lemmer's man?'

'I do.'

167

'Then he must be apprehended and interrogated. But the second is just as important as the first. You do appreciate that, don't you?'

'Of course, sir.'

'You'd better get on with it, then.'

After Political had left, C moved from the table to his desk and sat down heavily behind it. He pulled a drawer open and took out Appleby's personal file, which he had ordered up earlier. It was thin and generally unrevealing, though what it did reveal was an improbable background for a traitor.

Appleby and C were of the same generation. Appleby was in fact the older man by two years, born in 1857, the son of a Woolwich Dockyard foreman. He had gone straight from school into the police – first the Surrey Constabulary, then the Met, ending up in Special Branch before he was recruited by the Service at the start of the war. There were no blemishes on his record, unless a hint of truculence towards superiors he considered incompetent ranked as one, which it did not in C's estimation. There was, above all, no suggestion of bribe-taking. He was not, on the evidence, an easily corruptible man. And the memorandum he had recently submitted explaining his recruitment of James Maxted, which C had not seen fit to mention at the meeting, made it easy to believe – as perhaps it was designed to – that he was in fact acting in the Service's best interests.

But the war years had heaped tragedies upon Appleby, as they had upon others. An only son, slain at Loos in 1915. Then his wife, a few months later, by her own hand. He had been stationed in Rotterdam at the time and, for operational reasons, had not come home for the funeral.

Was it there, C wondered, alone and grieving in the neutral Netherlands, that he had succumbed? Was that the opportunity Lemmer had seized upon?

There was no way to know for sure. Political favoured public-school men for senior positions, men such as himself. He did not approve of Appleby and his kind and that may have made him hasty in his judgement. C did not share Political's prejudices. As far as he was concerned, the question of Appleby's guilt was not settled. But soon it would have to be.

THE TRAIN PULLED INTO YORK. DURING THE USUAL BUSTLE OF passengers boarding and disembarking, Max left the guard's van handcuffed to the constable and escorted by Tunnicliffe. They proceeded at a grim-faced plod along the platform, passing the restaurant car en route. Glancing up, Max saw Nadia watching him as he went. He gave her as ambiguous a grimace as he could contrive. She looked perplexed, as he had hoped. Perplexed was how he wanted her – and Lemmer – to remain.

A Black Maria was waiting outside the station. When Tunnicliffe swung the rear door open, Max found himself swapping a smile with the only occupant of the van: Appleby. At a word from Tunnicliffe, the constable released the handcuffs and Max clambered aboard. His bag was handed in after him. He sat down on the bench facing Appleby.

'Good journey?' Appleby enquired, with a crumpled grin.

'Rather fraught, actually, since you ask.'

'Me too.'

Tunnicliffe climbed in behind Max and sat down next to him. The door was slammed shut. The only light they had now was through a grille from the cab.

'We're heading for HQ, if that's all right by you, Horace,' said Tunnicliffe.

'I'll tell you in a moment, Bert,' Appleby replied, as the engine started and the van drew away. 'Once I've heard what Max has for me.'

'He didn't get your telegram, by the way.'

'Things were rather hot at Waverley,' said Max.

'They'd have been even hotter if you'd made it to King's Cross. Now, what's the precious cargo? You can speak freely in front of Bert. We were in the Met together, before he decided to come back to his roots.'

'I'll put my finger in my ears if you want,' said Tunnicliffe.

'It might be safer for him if he didn't know who we're talking about,' Max pointed out.

'Don't name him, then,' said Appleby. 'We discussed why you might contact me before you left Paris. Have you got the goods?'

'Yes.' Max unbuttoned his waistcoat and shirt, pulled out the Grey File and handed it to Appleby. 'A coded list of all his agents.'

Appleby gave a whistle of appreciation. 'How'd you land this?'

'Long story.'

Appleby peered at the file. 'I can't see a thing in this gloom. Here, hold it for me a moment.' He delved in his bag stowed beneath the bench and pulled out a bicycle lamp, which he switched on. 'Right. Let's take a look.'

He retrieved the file, studied the letters NBM and the Imperial eagle on the cover by the light of the lamp, then leafed through the contents.

Several minutes passed with nothing said, then Appleby switched off the lamp and closed the file. He had seen enough.

'Well?' Max prompted.

'Do you have a photographic unit up here, Bert?'

'Photomotography? What's that, then? Some newfangled Lon'on notion? Yes, of course we have a bloody photographic unit.'

'I need them to do something for me. Straight away.'

Sam was chain-smoking and drinking strong tea in his office at the Majestic, shuffling paperwork without the least consciousness of what it comprised, while pummelling his brain in search of a half-decent idea about what he should do next.

It was bad enough that Tomura's men might be on his scent. Worse, they had evidently taken George Clissold captive. Sam had been unable to tell Zamaron what he knew about why George

170

might have been kidnapped, though he was doing precisely nothing to help the poor fellow by staying silent. Zamaron had mentioned that Appleby had left Paris for unknown reasons. He had wondered whether his departure was connected in any way with Soutine's murder and George's kidnapping. Sam found himself wondering as well. Most of all, though, he wondered whether the people who had come for George would come for him next.

The arrival in the doorway of the towering figure of Schools Morahan counted as the only form of good news he might have expected. Sam's relief must have been obvious.

'I expected to hear from you this morning, Sam. We agreed it'd be wise for me to meet George Clissold.'

'I know, Mr Morahan. But you can't meet him. You'd better sit down. And close the door, will you?'

'What's happened?' Morahan closed the door, as requested. But he did not sit down.

The photographic unit at York police headquarters comprised a poky, fume-filled basement room and a staff of one. Since Appleby had no intention of leaving the pages from the Grey File in the photographer's unsupervised possession, he and Max remained there while each page was photographed.

A ban on smoking, due to the flammability of the chemicals, denied Appleby the use of his pipe, other than to chew on, which he did while perusing a *Bradshaw* borrowed from the front desk. Max sat down and promptly fell asleep. The photographer was busy by now in his dark-room.

The arrival of Tunnicliffe woke Max with a start. 'Word on the wire from the Linlithgowshire force,' Tunnicliffe announced. 'A man fatally stabbed on the Inverness to Edinburgh train as it crossed the Forth Bridge. Assailant fled the scene at Dalmeny. Another man involved in the incident also fled before the police arrived. Clues to what happened are scant.'

'Let's hope they stay that way,' said Max warily.

'This isn't going to end up biting me in the arse, is it, Horace?' Tunnicliffe asked.

'Only if it's already bitten our heads clean off.'

171

'High stakes?'

'None higher. We were never here, Bert, all right?'

Tunnicliffe gave Appleby a slight but entirely adequate nod of agreement. 'All right. Someone was. But not you. Or Max. I'll see to that.'

'We need a ride to Sheffield.'

'The Chief Constable's Rover do for you?' Failing to raise a retort from Appleby, he went on: 'I'll arrange something.'

'Also a stout foolscap envelope and stamps to cover a decent weight.'

'Right.'

Tunnicliffe left. Max stood up and stretched. 'Why Sheffield?'

'That man you killed on the train, Max,' Appleby said softly. 'He's unlikely to be the last if we're to get through this.'

'Can't we just go straight to your boss?'

'Getting to him will be half the battle, if not most of it. Lemmer will put all his best men on stopping us.'

'You still haven't explained Sheffield.'

'We can pick up a through train on the Great Central there. It's a sleeper to Penzance.'

'*Penzance?*'

'We'll get off at Oxford.'

'And why Oxford?'

'I want to know what's in the file before I try to deliver it. It'll tell us exactly who we're up against. For that we need someone fluent in German and expert in code-breaking.'

'You have such a person?'

'Yes. And we'll find him in Oxford.'

'Fair enough.'

'We'll take the prints and the originals with us. The prints are for the code-breaker to work on. But I intend to post the negatives to a safe address before we catch our train.'

'In case we don't make it, you mean?'

'The odds are against us, Max. You know that.'

'How heavily against us, would you say?'

'Lemmer has at least one of the Service section heads on his side. That gives him a lot of firepower to draw on. It means he can

172

reinforce his own men with loyal British agents led to believe we're traitors.'

'Every man's hand will be against us,' Max said bleakly.

'Not every one,' Appleby corrected him. 'Just most of them.'

IRETON RETURNED TO 33 RUE DES PYRAMIDES LATE THAT afternoon flushed and clearly intoxicated after a lengthy lunch with three members of the Greek delegation.

'I swear Metaxà is even more potent than tequila,' he complained to Morahan, who was waiting to see him. He slumped down in an armchair in front of the fire.

'We need to talk about Soutine, Travis,' Morahan said, propping himself against the desk.

'Again? Surely we said everything we needed to this morning.' Ireton yawned expansively.

'The man who found Soutine's body has been kidnapped.'

'He has?'

'George Clissold. James Maxted's uncle.'

Ireton frowned. 'You never said the guy was related to Max.'

'I didn't find out until earlier this afternoon. Sam Twentyman told me.'

Ireton's frown deepened. 'Why'd you go and see Twentyman?'

'He met le Singe once. There was a chance he'd know something useful.'

'But he didn't?'

'Not about le Singe. Listen, Travis, it's pretty obvious Noburo Tomura arranged for Clissold to be grabbed, with or without his father's consent. Witnesses say the kidnappers were either Chinese or Japanese. Zamaron's on the case, but he has no idea Tomura's looking for le Singe and could have seen Soutine as a means of getting to him. So, there's not much chance he'll figure out

174

who even took Clissold – far less where they're holding him.'

'And this concerns us how?'

'Considering what happened to Soutine, Clissold's life has to be in danger. We should tell Zamaron Tomura's the obvious suspect.'

Ireton's frown turned to a gawk of amazement. 'You're kidding, right? Why in hell would we do that? Tomura's a client, Schools. We can't rat on him.'

'Clissold's likely to end up dead if we don't.'

'That's not our fault. We've never even met the guy. But we have met Tomura. And I'm trying to establish a business relationship with his father. Our commercial future's at stake here.'

'A man's life is at stake as well, Travis.'

Ireton seemed entirely sober now. He turned deliberately and fixed Morahan with a stare. 'We don't *know* Tomura killed Soutine and we don't *know* he kidnapped Clissold. What we do know for a hard financial fact is that he's paying us to find le Singe. We should concentrate on the job in hand.'

'And to hell with Clissold?'

'We didn't come to Paris to help anyone except ourselves. I get the feeling lately you may have forgotten that.'

'How could I, with you to remind me?'

Ireton stood up, holding his stare. 'Say nothing to Zamaron. Forget Clissold and find le Singe. OK?'

Morahan was still and silent for a moment, his expression unreadable. Then he nodded and said, 'OK.'

Sheffield Victoria station was thronged with locals hurrying home from work. Max and Appleby would have looked to a neutral observer like two unremarkable members of the crowd. And as far as they could tell, neutral observers were the only kind around. No car had followed theirs from York. The driver supplied by Tunnicliffe had taken a few diversions to confirm as much. They had also called on a gunsmith, who had readily supplied ammunition for Max's gun once Appleby had waved a warrant card under his nose.

Max was carrying the Grey File. Appleby had the photographs of its pages in his bag. The negatives were in a stamped envelope

175

addressed to Mrs C. Jeavons, 64 Balcaskie Road, Eltham, London SE9, currently clasped in Appleby's hand. He had written a note to accompany the negatives during the car journey from York: *Cora – Keep these safe until you hear from me. Strictest confidence. Love, H.*

'Who's Cora, Horace?' Max asked as they threaded a path through the commuters towards the station's postbox. He realized with faint surprise that he had taken to calling Appleby by his Christian name.

'My sister.'

'Lucky for you you have a sibling you can trust. What about her husband?'

'Dead and gone. No one will see this but Cora. She's straight and true.'

'And your code-breaking friend in Oxford. Is he straight and true?'

'I think so. I hope so. Bostridge is a mathematical genius as well as a fluent German speaker. There's none better at what he does. We shared him during the war with Admiralty Intelligence. It's largely thanks to Bostridge that we cracked the Zimmerman telegram.'

'It's an obvious question, but how can you be sure his name isn't on the list you'll be asking him to decipher?'

'He insisted on being allowed to go back to Oxford as soon as the war was over. I reckon that's a good sign. But I can't be *sure* of anything. Or anyone.'

'Except Cora.'

'Except Cora. And you, Max.'

For safety's sake, Sam could not leave the Majestic. Morahan had advised him to sit tight and he knew that was the only sensible thing to do in the circumstances. If they could lift George Clissold off the street, they could do the same to him. An evening confined to his room or the designated common room in the basement was an unappetizing prospect, but there was no alternative. He would just have to while away the hours as best he could.

His visit to the front desk to check if there was any mail for him was undertaken with little hope there would be. In the month he had spent in Paris, he had received just one letter of a personal nature: from his mother, telling him his father was 'in a bait' about Sam walking out on his job at the bakery and had declared he would never be allowed to walk back into it; she urged Sam to bide his time before attempting a reconciliation and to 'take care of yourself among all them foreigners'.

When, to Sam's surprise, he was informed there was a letter for him after all, he assumed it must be from his mother, perhaps reporting his father's heart had begun to soften. But no, the letter had a French stamp on it and Sam did not recognize the hand-writing. The smudged postmark indicated it had been sent from Marseilles, but the date was illegible.

Sam moved to a corner of the lobby and opened the envelope. There was a second sealed envelope inside, addressed to Max, together with a covering note. Surprise compounded surprise when Sam saw who the note was from.

Marseilles, 28th April
Mr Twentyman – I must soon board the steamer that will take me to Japan. Therefore I write in haste. Please convey the enclosed letter to Max when you see him next. It contains information I believe he will wish to have. It was not in my possession when we met. I hope you will find a way out of your difficulties. Remember everything I said.
– Kuroda.

Sam went up to his room, where he debated what to do with the letter. There was nowhere he could store it that was absolutely secure, so he decided to carry it with him. He resisted the fleeting temptation to open it. If it contained anything Kuroda thought he ought to know, he would have told him.

Sam turned off the lamp, lit a cigarette and stood by the window, gazing out at the dank, twilit roofs of the city. Le Singe might be somewhere out there, watching him, even at that moment. There was no way to be sure. There was no way to be sure of anything.

He pondered Kuroda's closing words – *Remember everything I said* – and tried to do exactly that. What did Kuroda mean? What had he learnt in Marseilles that Max – but not Sam – needed to know?

THE TRAIN THREADED DOWN THROUGH THE MIDLANDS AS THE evening advanced. Max drifted in and out of sleep. Appleby was wide awake, tending his pipe and staring thoughtfully out through the rain-speckled windows at the deepening darkness.

It was late when they reached Oxford. Few other passengers disembarked and there were fewer still waiting to join. Steady rain was falling, blown on a cold wind.

They took a taxi to Bostridge's college, Appleby reckoning that a walk along thinly peopled streets was a risk they did not need to run. As to whether they would find Bostridge at his college, Appleby did not know. 'I wouldn't know where else to try,' was all he said on that point.

They were in luck. The porter told them *Dr* Bostridge was indeed somewhere about the place. He ventured as far as the quad and peered across it. 'Yes, gentlemen, there you are.' He pointed. 'His light's on.'

'He's always been one to burn the midnight oil,' Appleby remarked.

'I see you know him well, sir,' said the porter.

They crossed the quad and climbed the stairs to Bostridge's room. The outer door was open, indicating he was available. Appleby knocked on the inner.

'Who goes there?' came a shrill-voiced response.

'Horace Appleby, Jeremy, with a friend.'

'Horace?'

179

A few seconds later, the door was yanked open. Dr Jeremy Bostridge looked to Max to be all of about twelve years old, with a pale, unblemished and apparently beardless face, a mop of unruly hair and chestnut-brown eyes twinkling behind thick-framed glasses. The flannel trousers, collarless shirt and cricket sweater he was wearing all appeared to be a couple of sizes too big for him.

'Horace, this is wonderful.' He clasped Appleby by the shoulder. 'A dream fulfilled.'

'If I figure in your dreams, Jeremy, I don't want to know about it, all right? Can we come in?'

'Please do.'

Bostridge stepped back and they entered a large, comfortably furnished room. There was a blackboard on an easel in one corner, covered with scrawled equations, and a broad desk in another, the top barely visible beneath a slew of papers.

'Keeping busy, Jeremy?' Appleby asked.

'Oh, always. But mathematics is infinite, so that's more or less guaranteed. Who, er . . .' Bostridge looked towards Max.

'Sorry. This is James Maxted.'

'Call me Max,' Max said, shaking Bostridge's hand.

'How d'you do, Max? Where have you both travelled from?'

'Different starting points,' Appleby replied as he surveyed the room. 'Same destination.'

'I don't recall you being much of a riddler, Horace. I'm seeing a new side to you. But what's brought you to my door so late at night? I only ask. I'm delighted to see you whatever the reason. Glass of port for either of you?'

'No, thanks,' said Appleby, answering for both of them.

Bostridge looked quizzically at Max. 'Are you the strong, silent type? Horace likes that in his assistants.'

'I'm not his assistant.'

'Heard from anyone in the Service since you came back here, Jeremy?' Appleby asked levelly.

Bostridge frowned. 'No. Clean break and all that. C made it pretty crystal I'd be cut off like an erring nephew. Hence my surprise at your manifestation out of the night.'

'We're in a tight spot.'

'Really?'

'And we need your help.'

'Mine? Well, any time. What can I do for you?'

Appleby sat down on the sofa, wedged his bag between his feet and opened it. 'Events in Paris have led me to suspect Lemmer has spies in our own network.'

'That sounds nasty. You've been in Paris, have you? A cushy berth, I imagine.'

'Far from it.' Appleby pulled from his bag the buff envelope containing the photographs of the contents of the Grey File. 'Max has brought me confirmation of my suspicions.' He handed the envelope to Bostridge.

'What's this?'

'A coded list of Lemmer's foreign operatives.'

Bostridge whistled. 'You're joking.'

'No. It's the real McCoy.'

'Good God.' Bostridge walked over to the desk, sat down and angled the lamp for a clear view of the photographs as he slid them out of the envelope. '*Nachrichten-Abteilung. Besonderen Massnahmen.* It's a top-secret file. From Lemmer's own office.'

'Yes.'

'How did you come by this?'

'Pretend you're still in the Service, Jeremy. Limit your questions to the task in hand.'

'Well, it certainly looks like it's what you said: a list of agents. All non-Germans?'

'Probably.'

'Then Lemmer was busier than most of the Kaiser's generals. There are lots of names here, Horace.'

'And we'll know some of them as loyal friends.'

'Truly?' Bostridge looked pitifully afflicted by the thought.

Appleby nodded. 'I'm afraid so.'

'People within the Service?'

'Oh yes. I'm sure of that.'

'Good Lord. Is that why you've come to me direct?'

'Can you decode the list?'

Bostridge's expression suggested the question was absurd. 'Of course I can decode it. There isn't a German code devised I can't crack.'

'Then we need you to do it. As soon as possible.'

'OK. Yes.' Bostridge looked down at the photographs. 'I'm answering the call of patriotic duty again, am I?'

'You are.'

'Then I'd better jump to it. But I'll need my code log. It's a record I kept of the keys I worked out to various German code systems. Chances are this will have been coded using one of them, though not necessarily straightforwardly. Anyway, it's at the cottage. My little rural hideaway. Do you have a car?'

'No.'

'Then we can all squeeze into mine. Don't worry. The cottage is only a few miles out of Oxford. I can put you up overnight if you like. Unless you want to leave me to it.'

'No. We'll come with you. Thanks for the offer.'

'It's not the Ritz.'

'Never mind. We'll take anything, won't we, Max?'

'We will.' Max looked at Bostridge. 'How long will it take you to decipher the list?'

'Hard to say. Could be an hour. Could be twelve. Could be twenty-four. And I do have my teaching commitments, remember.'

'This takes priority,' said Appleby.

'Even though I'm no longer in the Service?'

'Even though.'

'Good news for you, then: I work at my best in the small hours. Shall we go?'

Morahan had drunk more rum, bourbon and tequila than was good for him in his younger days. In his middle years, he had virtually abandoned drunkenness. That evening had been a rare exception. He had already betrayed Ireton once – as Ireton would see it – over his contact with the German delegation. He could not bring himself to defy him where George Clissold, a man he had never actually met, was concerned. But agreeing not to tell Zamaron what he knew did not sit well with his conscience.

The brandy did not make it sit any better either. But it blunted the edge of his guilt. It blunted just about everything.

Making his way home from the last bar he had visited, aware that Tomura's man was still on his tail but no longer caring, he reflected, almost neutrally, that his partnership with Travis Ireton would soon have to end. How and over what and with what consequences he could not foresee. But it could not endure. He knew that much for certain.

His apartment was on the third floor in one of a row of peeling-stuccoed buildings near Gare St-Lazare. The *gardienne*'s light was out when he let himself into the hall. He made his way slowly and unsteadily up the curving stone stairs, confident he would sleep deeply.

When he entered his apartment, he was surprised to see a note had been slipped under his door. The *gardienne* must have let a visitor in, which suggested the visitor was possessed of a persuasive character.

That was confirmed when he focused clearly enough on the writing to recognize it. The note was from Malory.

Schools: I have learnt something you will want to know as soon as possible concerning le S. Come to my apartment. If you return after ten, leave it until tomorrow morning, as early as you and your hangover like. M

Morahan struggled out of his coat and sat down on the bed, holding the note limply in his hand. It was long after ten and he was in no condition to speak to Malory now, as she seemed, with her infuriating perceptiveness, to have guessed would be the case. He kicked off his shoes and threw his fedora towards the hatstand. It missed. Then he lay down.

Bostridge piloted his Hillman somewhat erratically along the damp, dark lanes of Oxfordshire, asking Appleby a string of questions he seemed disinclined to answer about former Secret Service colleagues. The irony that some of them might be on Lemmer's list appeared to escape him. Suddenly, his

183

butterfly mind alighted on another topic: the file containing the list.

'You have the file with you, Horace?' he asked. 'The original, I mean.'

'It's authentic,' Appleby replied evasively.

'Grey, by any chance?'

'How did you know that?' Max cut in from the cramped rear seat.

'Good question.' Bostridge swivelled round to look at Max, pulling the car to the left, which Appleby corrected to steer them away from the verge. 'How did I know?'

'Well?'

'Take your hand off the wheel, Horace,' Bostridge said tetchily as he turned back to address the road ahead. 'You'll have us in the hedge.'

'The colour of the file, Jeremy?' Max prompted.

'Ah, yes, *Die graue Akte*. Well, it came to me just now. I remember the phrase from a cable we intercepted. From Lemmer, we suspected, in Weihaiwei, though what he was—'

'*Where?*'

'Weihaiwei. Aren't you familiar with that adornment to our Imperial crown, Max?'

'It's a British-leased enclave on the Shantung peninsula,' said Appleby.

'Exactly.' Bostridge went on. 'So, it was worrying – and puzzling – that Lemmer should be there, if he was there, early last year.'

'Who did he cable? And why?'

'His secretary in Berlin. I can't recall—'

'Anna Schmidt?'

'Yes. That's it. Come across her, have you?'

'Max's recent activities ought to stay between him and me, Jeremy,' said Appleby.

'Right. Sorry. Anyway, the cable was to Frau Schmidt. We deciphered it readily enough, but the message was veiled, as we call it. They obviously had a private code within the code. There were other cables around that time, also from Lemmer, we suspected,

184

from Far Eastern locations. We never penetrated their meaning. But the Grey File was certainly mentioned in them, which suggested it was important. And now we know just how important, don't we? Ah. Here we are. Home, sweet home.'

THE COTTAGE WAS AT THE END OF A ROUGH TRACK. MAX HAD subconsciously expected a thatched roof and neatly fenced flower garden, but what he saw in the glare of the headlamps was a slate-roofed labourer's dwelling.

The interior was in surprisingly good order, however, with every sign that someone had taken care over furnishing and decorating the place. Those signs revealed themselves in the soft glow of the oil lamps Bostridge lit. 'No electricity out here,' he explained. 'But no irritating students either.'

'You live here alone?' Appleby queried.

'No, no. I, er, share my country retreat with a friend.'

'Where's your friend now?'

'Visiting relatives. We won't be interrupted. Do you two want anything to eat or drink?'

'We don't want to hold you up, Jeremy. The sooner you start working on that list the better.'

'Of course. But I work better after a bacon sandwich. Any takers?'

It transpired there were. Also for the bottles of Bass he fetched from the pantry. Appleby set about lighting the fire, while Bostridge went into the kitchen. An appetizing aroma of frying bacon was soon wafting through to them. Max sat down in an armchair. He suddenly felt weary to the core of his being.

As the fire caught, the logs began to spit and crack. Max decided he should take his coat off before he fell asleep wearing it, so he pushed himself out of the chair and went to hang it up.

'Max,' Appleby called to him from the hearth.

'Yes?'

Appleby pointed to their bags, one of which – Max's – now had the Grey File stored at the bottom of it. Appleby motioned for Max to bring the bags into the centre of the room. Clearly, he did not want the file to be out of his reach, let alone his sight.

Max stowed them beside the armchair and sat down again. 'Assuming Jeremy can decipher the list, what's our next step?'

'Get it to C. Which won't be easy. But I have a few ideas.'

'You'd better pray C's name isn't listed.'

'That's not funny.'

'Sorry. I tend to imagine the worst when I'm tired.'

'Shut up and drink your beer.'

Max raised the bottle to his mouth and drank. He would have preferred whisky, but beggars could not be choosers. Bass was Sam's favourite, he remembered.

A draught of cold air from the kitchen caused smoke to billow into the room from the chimney. There was the sound of a door closing.

'What was that?' Appleby looked round suspiciously.

'I think Jeremy must have stepped out the back,' suggested Max. 'Maybe he's gone to the privy.'

'Leaving a frying pan on the stove? That'd be typically irresponsible. You'd better check it's all right.'

Max sighed and made to rise.

'Oh, stay where you are. You look all in. I'll go.'

With some relief, Max subsided back into the chair as Appleby moved past him. He closed his eyes and felt sleep flooding over him like a spring tide.

Suddenly, he was awake, roused by the click of a gun being cocked.

There were three men in the room with Appleby, who had a gun to his head. They were hard-faced, muscular characters of military bearing, steely-eyed and serious. One of them was pointing a revolver straight at Max.

'Tell him,' the man said to Appleby.

'Tell him yourself, Grattan.'

'That's smart, Horace. Go on. Introduce us all. Name names. Then there's no going back.'

'Grattan's with MI5, Max. Counter-espionage. So's Hughes.' Appleby nodded to one of the others. 'Their companion is a colleague of mine, Meadows. Former colleague now, I suppose. No doubt they each have their own tale to tell of why they sold out. So does Jeremy, I'm sure.'

Bostridge shambled apologetically into view behind them, absent-mindedly clutching the spatula he had been frying bacon with. 'Sorry,' he said in an uneven voice. 'I hoped you wouldn't walk into the trap.'

'He means he hoped we'd walk into another trap somewhere else to spare his conscience,' said Appleby bitterly.

'Sanctimonious bugger, aren't you, Horace?' said Grattan. 'You ought to know we had to force Bostridge's hand.'

'What have they got on you, Jeremy?'

'Friendship, Horace.' Bostridge looked genuinely sorry. 'There's someone I care about more than you.'

'There's a surprise,' said Grattan. 'Now, stay exactly where you are, Max. They'll be carrying, Len. Check their coats.'

Hughes crossed the room to where Max and Appleby's coats were hanging. He found the guns and returned with them.

'Good. Stand up, Max.'

Max rose reluctantly to his feet. Appleby caught and held his gaze for a second, moving his head by a fraction of an inch to caution against resistance.

'Search them.'

Hughes frisked first Max, then Appleby. He found no more weapons.

'All right. What did they bring you, Jeremy?'

'Photographs . . . of the contents of the Grey File.'

'Show me.'

Bostridge crossed to the table where he had dropped the envelope containing the photographs. He pulled them out. 'It's a coded list . . . of Lemmer's foreign agents.'

'With a record of payments made,' said Appleby. 'Maybe you three should check it tallies with what you received.' He

188

turned to Meadows. 'How much did you hold out for, Stan?'

'You have no bloody idea how I was placed,' Meadows snapped.

'Ignore him,' said Grattan, though the expression on Meadows' face suggested he would not find that easy. 'It's good of you to have lit a fire. Tear up the photographs and burn them, Jeremy.'

Bostridge tore them up, as instructed, and dropped them a couple at a time into the fire.

'Where are the negatives, Horace?'

'Left luggage, York railway station.'

'You should have gone on the stage with your sense of humour, you really should. Search their bags, Len.'

Hughes carried the bags to the table and emptied them an item at a time. He found the envelope with the Grey File in it soon enough. But not the negatives. Grattan seemed well pleased, even so.

'Does it look genuine, Len?'

Hughes nodded. 'It's the Grey File.'

'All right. We'll return to the subject of the negatives later, Horace, after we've taken you and Max on somewhere.'

'Who's waiting for us there?' asked Appleby.

'Never you mind.'

'Lemmer?' Max looked Grattan in the eye. 'I bet it is. He'll want to inspect the file as soon as possible.'

'You'll have to wait and see, Max. Our orders are to deliver both of you alive if possible. It'd be no hardship to any one of us if that didn't prove possible, though. So, consider yourselves warned.'

'I really am sorry,' said Bostridge dolefully.

Max glanced accusingly at him. 'So you should be.'

'You're right there,' said Grattan. Then he turned towards Bostridge, raised the gun and fired.

Bostridge let out no more than a grunt as the bullet entered his head through the bridge of his nose, shattering his glasses. He toppled backwards and crashed to the floor, where he lay motionless – and very obviously dead.

'What in God's name did you do that for?' Appleby asked, his voice hoarse with shock.

'No decipherer; no decipherment.' Grattan swung the gun back towards Max. 'Bostridge's talents are no longer required. But don't worry. His fey little friend is waiting to console him on the other side.'

'Lemmer told you to kill him, didn't he?' Max cut in. 'You want to ask yourself whether he told someone else to kill you.'

Grattan took a step forward and pressed the barrel of his gun against Max's forehead. But Max did not flinch. He had often debated with himself during the war whether his fearlessness was an asset or a liability. Maybe he was about to find out.

'Go ahead and shoot,' he said, staring straight at Grattan. 'You're the big man with the big gun.'

'You've had a soft life, Max. I reckon it's going to have a hard ending.'

'Yours too, I shouldn't wonder.'

'If Lemmer wants us alive,' cautioned Appleby, 'he won't thank you for delivering either of us dead.'

It seemed for a moment that Grattan was seriously tempted to ignore the truth of what Appleby had said. Then something changed in his expression. He could not do as he pleased. He was not his own man. He was Lemmer's.

'All right,' he said, taking a step back. 'Go and get the car, Stan. We're leaving.'

THE THROATY SOUND OF A CAR ENGINE AND THE BEEP OF A HORN was the cue for Grattan to order them out of the cottage. Grattan held a gun to the back of Appleby's neck as they left; Hughes, one to the back of Max's. The darkness beyond the glare of the headlamps was utter, but the odds against fleeing successfully into it without being shot were long. They did as they were told.

The car was a big four-seater. Max and Appleby sat in the rear with Hughes. Grattan took the front passenger seat. A bag at his feet contained the Grey File.

'Try anything and we'll shoot you,' said Grattan, turning to face them over the seat back as Meadows started away.

'We'll be sure not to give you any excuse,' said Appleby. 'Won't we, Max?'

'Oh yes.'

'You should never have let Horace get you involved in this, Max,' said Grattan. 'It was a big mistake.'

'I seem to just go on making them.'

Max hoped his light-hearted tone would deflate some of Grattan's confidence, though Grattan had every reason to be confident. He had them exactly where he wanted them. And his cold-blooded execution of Bostridge stood as a warning of what would happen if they resisted.

When they reached the end of the lane and turned left, Max was momentarily puzzled. Right was surely the route back to Oxford.

Then he remembered they were not necessarily going back to Oxford. There was no telling where Lemmer would be waiting for them.

But it soon became clear left was a wrong turn after all. 'Sod it,' said Meadows when a scatter of lit windows appeared ahead. 'This is the centre of the village.'

'Don't you know where you're bloody going?' Grattan snapped. 'Turn round.'

They came to a halt just before the village green. A short distance along the road was a pub. The headlamps caught its name: the Cross Keys. Three men were standing outside it discussing something which involved gesticulating towards the church on the other side of the green. The tower was a slab of blackness against the moon-paled sky.

Meadows ground the gears noisily and reversed into a gateway they had just passed. But he misjudged the manoeuvre. Suddenly, the back of the car plunged into a hole.

'Sod it,' said Meadows again. He jammed the car back into forward gear and tried to move. But the rear wheels found nothing to grip and the car simply slewed round into an even worse position.

'Get us out of here,' said Grattan. 'We're beginning to attract attention.'

It was true. The men by the pub had lost interest in their conversation and were now looking in their direction. Meadows pressed the accelerator and the car skidded and jolted – but stayed where it was. He grunted, grabbed a torch and clambered out. He was back within a few seconds.

'We're stuck in some kind of drainage ditch. We won't get her out without a tow.'

'Maybe we could all push,' said Max.

'Shut up,' barked Grattan. 'We're not pushing. And we're not getting a tow.'

'What are we doing, then?' asked Meadows.

'You're going to walk back to the cottage and fetch Bostridge's car. We'll go in that.'

'It'll never be big enough for all of us.'

'Well, maybe whoever got us into this mess will have to travel by shanks's pony. Why don't— Oh no.'

The worthies by the pub were now on the scene – three middle-aged villagers, beaming broadly. 'Come a cropper, have you?' asked one.

Grattan had hastily tucked his gun inside his coat, as had Hughes. He opened the window. 'We'll be all right, thanks,' he said airily.

'We'll give you a push.'

'No need.'

'You won't be going nowhere otherwise.'

'There's *really* no need.'

'It'd be easier if you all got out 'cept the driver. Less weight, see. This a Crossley? I drove one in the war. They used 'em as staff cars. Probably still do.'

'We don't want any help.'

'Yes, we do,' said Max. 'Let's get out and do as they suggest.'

'Here you go.' One of the villagers pulled open the rear door. Max almost fell into his arms.

'Very kind of you,' Max said, stepping lightly away from the car.

Appleby remained where he was, with Hughes beside him.

'They're obviously right,' he said. 'What are we waiting for?' With that he slid across the seat and climbed out. And neither Hughes nor Grattan lifted a finger to stop him. But what could they do? Shoot them all?

Grattan and Hughes finally got out too and rounded the bonnet, moving purposefully towards Max and Appleby.

'Lend us your torch,' said one of the villagers to Meadows. 'Then we can see what the trouble is.'

'I've already seen,' snapped Meadows.

'No need to bite my head off.'

'Why don't you leave us to it?' said Grattan, trying to sound reasonable.

'Is the pub still open?' piped Max.

'Nah. But it's the landlord's birthday, so there's a bit of a party going on.'

'Any chance you could smuggle us in? I'd murder for a pint.'

'Me too,' said Appleby.

'Well . . .'

'We don't have time for that,' said Grattan. He pulled Max and Appleby away from the group and lowered his voice. 'They're not going to get you out of this. Tell them to leave us alone or it'll be the worse for you – and them.'

'A gunshot will bring a mob running from the pub,' said Appleby. 'How will that turn out, d'you think?'

'You won't be alive to find out.'

'Maybe not. But if you bungle this and fail to deliver the file to Lemmer . . .'

Before Grattan could fashion a response, the sound came to their ears of another car approaching along the lane. Its headlamps swept over them and the driver braked to a halt.

'Can I help?' he called.

'That you, Mr Varney?' one of the villagers responded.

'Yes, Ern, it's me.'

'You're out late.'

'Troublesome birth at Rosehill Farm. So, what's the bother here?'

'These gentlemen have got their car stuck in the ditch.'

'I've got a tow rope. I dare say it'll be easier pulling them out than it was that calf I've just delivered.'

'What are you going to do, Grattan?' Appleby whispered. 'We've got the local vet here now as well. It's getting out of hand, isn't it?'

'Where's the driver?' Varney asked as he climbed from his car.

'Here,' said Meadows reluctantly.

'Well?' pressed Appleby.

'All right,' Grattan growled back. 'We'll take the file and drive away, but we'll leave you two behind. Not a word out of place and not a shot fired.'

Appleby hesitated for a moment, then said, 'OK. Max?'

There was no other way out. They all knew it. 'Yes,' said Max.

'You're gambling on the negatives, aren't you?' said Grattan.

'We're gambling on your common sense,' Appleby replied.

'You've been lucky. Damned lucky. That's all.'

'It's all we need to be,' said Max. 'And I have a history of it.'

'Why don't you—'

'Shall we get you back on the road or are you going to stand there muttering to each other all night?' Varney called to them, a touch irritably. 'I've a bed to go to even if you haven't.'

'Yes, yes,' Grattan responded, the grinding of his teeth almost audible. 'Kind of you to stop. Let's hitch up the rope.'

'WE HAD NO CHOICE,' SAID APPLEBY DOLEFULLY AS HE AND Max hurried along the lane out of the village. They were heading in the opposite direction to that taken by Grattan, Hughes and Meadows. The signpost on the green had indicated it was five miles to Abingdon. From there, come morning, they could travel by train to London. 'Without the file, Grattan would've had to report to Lemmer empty-handed. He'd never have been willing to do that. If we'd tried to hang onto it, it would've ended badly. Probably for several innocent bystanders as well. As it is, we're lucky to have escaped.'

'Maybe so, but it means all I've accomplished is what Lemmer sent me to the Orkneys to do: retrieve the Grey File for him.' Max looked up at the grey-black sky, where the moon hovered faintly behind drifting clouds. He swore softly.

'We still have a photographic record of the contents, Max. It's not everything. But it's enough.'

'You mean your sister has a photographic record of the contents. Or will have, once the postman's delivered it to her.'

'We'll make for Eltham tomorrow.'

'If we make it to Abingdon tonight. What's to stop Grattan and co coming in search of us?'

'They'll have to report to Lemmer first. He'll decide their next move. I doubt even he's capable of guessing where we're going now.'

'What about Eltham? Does he know you have a sister?'

'I don't think so.'

'That's not quite as categorical as I'd like.'

'It'll have to do. I don't know what he knows. We're going to have to play this by ear to some extent. Was there anything in your bag that could identify you?'

'No. Just clothes and shaving gear.'

'Good.'

'Will you try to find someone else to decode the file?'

'After what happened to Bostridge, I'm not sure. I wouldn't have contacted him if I'd thought it was going to cost him his life.'

'They'd probably have killed him anyway. You heard what Grattan said: "No decipherer; no decipherment". And it could be us next.'

'It could. But I'm hoping news of the negatives will catch Lemmer off balance. It's a complication he mightn't have anticipated. And it may not be the only one.'

'What else is there?'

'Bostridge. He wasn't stupid. He might have foreseen how it was going to turn out. I've been thinking about what he said in the car. That business about Lemmer's cables to Anna Schmidt from the Far East.'

'Weihaiwei.'

'Exactly. Weihaiwei. Why did he make such a point of mentioning it?'

'Because the Grey File was referred to in a cable Lemmer sent from there.'

'Yes. But maybe there was something else.'

'What?'

'Do you remember what he said about "veiled messages" – the code within the code?'

'Yes. Once you'd broken the code, you could still be left with a message only the recipient was equipped to understand. So, what was he really saying?'

'There's a chance – no more than that – Bostridge was trying to point me towards one of his assistants who was an expert in this field. She had a special . . . sensitivity . . . to what she called textual undercurrents.'

'Who is this woman?'

'Veronica Edwards. But she left the Service last year to get married. I can't remember, if I ever knew, what her married name is. Or where she lives.'

'It's hopeless, then.'

'Maybe not. Or . . . I'll dwell on it. Something might come to me. Meanwhile . . .' He stopped and fumbled in his pocket, then thrust a box of matches into Max's palm. 'Light one and hold it, would you? I want to write something down.'

Max struck a match and saw that Appleby was clutching a pencil and a notebook, folded open. He held the match for Appleby to see by as he recorded a short sequence of letters and numbers. 'What's that?'

'The registration number of the Crossley. You never know if it might come in useful.'

Max shook out the match. A worrying thought had occurred to him. 'The police will be after us once Bostridge's body is found, won't they, Horace? That college porter can describe us. So can the villagers.'

'You don't need to worry about them.'

'Why not?'

'Because the villagers can describe Grattan, Hughes and Meadows as well. And Bostridge's spell in the Service means his death will be referred to Special Branch. Political will make sure they quash any serious investigation.'

'What's Political?'

'Who, you mean. He's one of the section heads. They go by their section title. Political's real name is Grieveson. By telling you that, I'm in breach of the Official Secrets Act, so don't spread it around, will you? Political's on Lemmer's payroll. The men who tried to pick me up at Victoria were acting on his orders, apparently in good faith. They were going to take me to a house in Pimlico he's acquired. I don't know what he uses twenty-four Glamorgan Street for, but I doubt it's quiet fireside chats. He'll obligingly cover our tracks as well as his own operatives'.'

'That's some small comfort, I suppose.'

'But smaller than a warm bed would be, eh?' Appleby started moving again. 'We'd better press on.'

*

In the event, they only pressed on for another mile or so. Then Appleby spotted what a shaft of moonlight revealed to be an open-fronted barn a short distance down a track between two fields. They clambered in among the bales of hay and settled down to sleep.

'How many tighter spots than this have you been in in your time, Horace?' Max asked drowsily.

'None.'

'So you can't draw on your vast experience to tell me what our chances are?'

'I can. But you don't want to know the answer. Go to sleep.'

'D'you snore, Horace?'

'That's a secret. One you'll share with my late wife by morning. Goodnight.'

THE *GARDIENNE* OF THE HOUSE WHERE MALORY HOLLANDER lived on the Ile St-Louis was never welcoming to male visitors, perhaps because all her charges were female. Morahan had encountered her a couple of times before, without eliciting much in the way of helpfulness. He supposed he should be grateful she was not on strike, like so many other Parisians. It was May Day, the great day of action for Socialist protesters, who believed they had a lot to protest about, and the gods had decided to add their own complaint in the form of steady rain.

Morahan's attempts to charm the *gardienne* fell predictably flat. He was hung-over and had nicked his chin while shaving. He was not at his best, though he had been equal to the task of losing the tail Tomura had put on him – a necessary precaution in the circumstances.

After apologizing several times, ever more profusely, for calling so early in the day, he was admitted and allowed to ascend the curving stairs to Malory's apartment, though he was kept under surveillance from the hall as he went.

Malory was halfway through applying lipstick as a finishing touch to her toilette when she answered the door. 'You look awful,' she said.

'I had a rough night.' He propped himself against the hall wall while she retreated to her bedroom mirror.

'So I see.'

'Sorry I wasn't in when you called round last night.'

'Never mind. How did you get here?'

'I drove. Métro's out. So are the trams and buses.'

'You can give me a ride to the office, then. We'll talk on the way.' She bustled back out of her bedroom, *maquillage* complete, and handed him her raincoat so he could help her on with it.

'One of the reasons I agreed to come to Paris was to enjoy a spring in the city of light,' she remarked as they tiptoed through the puddles to Morahan's car. 'I could have got weather like this staying in New York.'

'At least it'll dampen down the protests.'

'Talking of which, I may need a ride home as well. Things could turn ugly.'

'You're such an optimist.'

'It pays to look ahead, Schools.'

'It surely does.'

They reached the car and climbed in. Morahan started up and headed for the Pont Marie.

'Your note mentioned le Singe, Malory. That wasn't just a ploy to get me to pick you up this morning, was it?'

'Of course not. I found something out last night from Eveline. You just missed her.'

'You're not going to tell me she's acquainted with le Singe?'

'Obviously not. But she had met Soutine, as you know, so I felt I ought to inform her of his death before she read about it in the newspaper. To my surprise, it emerged she'd seen him once more after our visit to his gallery.'

'She had?'

'Yes. She went to a party in an apartment near La Samaritaine last Saturday. It's Peggy White's place. I know her slightly. She's with the Red Cross too. Anyhow, Eveline arrived quite early, while it was still light. She went into the spare bedroom, where the coats were being left, and saw Soutine through the window.'

'What d'you mean – "through the window"?'

'Well, Peggy's apartment is on the top floor of her building, which is a floor or two higher than most of the surrounding buildings. So, Eveline was looking down at a small top-floor balcony a short distance away. And she saw Soutine standing there.'

'On the balcony?'

'Yes. Large as life, she said. He was smoking a cigarette. Taking the evening air, I suppose.'

'He must have a hideaway there.'

'That's what I thought. And maybe le Singe hides there too.'

'We've got to find the apartment that balcony belongs to, Malory.'

'I know. Eveline's agreed to ask Peggy if we could take a look out of her spare bedroom window this evening and try to figure out exactly where it is.'

'To hell with this evening. We'll go there now. If she hasn't left yet, I'll back you to talk our way in.'

Sam was breakfasting glumly on porridge and strong tea in the basement room of the Majestic set aside for British delegation support staff – the workers, in other words – when one of the specially imported hotel clerks appeared breathlessly at his table.

'Urgent message for you, Mr Twentyman.'

'For me?'

'Do you know a Mr Clissold?'

Sam braced himself. 'Yes.'

'He's laid up at the Hôtel Dieu after some kind of accident. Seems he'd like to see you as soon as possible.'

Peggy White was on the point of leaving when Morahan and Malory reached her apartment in Place de l'Ecole. Malory had to engage in a lot of fast and persuasive talking to get them inside. It was an accomplished performance, just as Morahan had expected it would be.

'Eveline will mention it to you later, Peggy. We'd hoped you'd agree to let us come this evening, but Schools is busy then. This really is awfully kind of you. We won't hold you up long. It's just that we've been trying to locate this particular gentleman for some time. And Eveline is convinced she saw him from here.'

Fortunately, Peggy was intrigued and clearly not worried about delaying her departure for work. She even offered them coffee, which they accepted largely to occupy her in the kitchen while

'Really?'

'And we need your help.'

'Mine? Well, any time. What can I do for you?'

Appleby sat down on the sofa, wedged his bag between his feet and opened it. 'Events in Paris have led me to suspect Lemmer has spies in our own network.'

'That sounds nasty. You've been in Paris, have you? A cushy berth, I imagine.'

'Far from it.' Appleby pulled from his bag the buff envelope containing the photographs of the contents of the Grey File. 'Max has brought me confirmation of my suspicions.' He handed the envelope to Bostridge.

'What's this?'

'A coded list of Lemmer's foreign operatives.'

Bostridge whistled. 'You're joking.'

'No. It's the real McCoy.'

'Good God.' Bostridge walked over to the desk, sat down and angled the lamp for a clear view of the photographs as he slid them out of the envelope. '*Nachrichten-Abteilung. Besonderen Massnahmen*. It's a top-secret file. From Lemmer's own office.'

'Yes.'

'How did you come by this?'

'Pretend you're still in the Service, Jeremy. Limit your questions to the task in hand.'

'Well, it certainly looks like it's what you said: a list of agents. All non-Germans?'

'Probably.'

'Then Lemmer was busier than most of the Kaiser's generals. There are lots of names here, Horace.'

'And we'll know some of them as loyal friends.'

'Truly?' Bostridge looked pitifully afflicted by the thought.

Appleby nodded. 'I'm afraid so.'

'People within the Service?'

'Oh yes. I'm sure of that.'

'Good Lord. Is that why you've come to me direct?'

'Can you decode the list?'

Bostridge's expression suggested the question was absurd. 'Of course I can decode it. There isn't a German code devised I can't crack.'

'Then we need you to do it. As soon as possible.'

'OK. Yes.' Bostridge looked down at the photographs. 'I'm answering the call of patriotic duty again, am I?'

'You are.'

'Then I'd better jump to it. But I'll need my code log. It's a record I kept of the keys I worked out to various German code systems. Chances are this will have been coded using one of them, though not necessarily straightforwardly. Anyway, it's at the cottage. My little rural hideaway. Do you have a car?'

'No.'

'Then we can all squeeze into mine. Don't worry. The cottage is only a few miles out of Oxford. I can put you up overnight if you like. Unless you want to leave me to it.'

'No. We'll come with you. Thanks for the offer.'

'It's not the Ritz.'

'Never mind. We'll take anything, won't we, Max?'

'We will.' Max looked at Bostridge. 'How long will it take you to decipher the list?'

'Hard to say. Could be an hour. Could be twelve. Could be twenty-four. And I do have my teaching commitments, remember.'

'This takes priority,' said Appleby.

'Even though I'm no longer in the Service?'

'Even though.'

'Good news for you, then: I work at my best in the small hours. Shall we go?'

Morahan had drunk more rum, bourbon and tequila than was good for him in his younger days. In his middle years, he had virtually abandoned drunkenness. That evening had been a rare exception. He had already betrayed Ireton once – as Ireton would see it – over his contact with the German delegation. He could not bring himself to defy him where George Clissold, a man he had never actually met, was concerned. But agreeing not to tell Zamaron what he knew did not sit well with his conscience.

The brandy did not make it sit any better either. But it blunted the edge of his guilt. It blunted just about everything.

Making his way home from the last bar he had visited, aware that Tomura's man was still on his tail but no longer caring, he reflected, almost neutrally, that his partnership with Travis Ireton would soon have to end. How and over what and with what consequences he could not foresee. But it could not endure. He knew that much for certain.

His apartment was on the third floor in one of a row of peeling-stuccoed buildings near Gare St-Lazare. The *gardienne*'s light was out when he let himself into the hall. He made his way slowly and unsteadily up the curving stone stairs, confident he would sleep deeply.

When he entered his apartment, he was surprised to see a note had been slipped under his door. The *gardienne* must have let a visitor in, which suggested the visitor was possessed of a persuasive character.

That was confirmed when he focused clearly enough on the writing to recognize it. The note was from Malory.

Schools: I have learnt something you will want to know as soon as possible concerning le S. Come to my apartment. If you return after ten, leave it until tomorrow morning, as early as you and your hangover like. M

Morahan struggled out of his coat and sat down on the bed, holding the note limply in his hand. It was long after ten and he was in no condition to speak to Malory now, as she seemed, with her infuriating perceptiveness, to have guessed would be the case. He kicked off his shoes and threw his fedora towards the hatstand. It missed. Then he lay down.

Bostridge piloted his Hillman somewhat erratically along the damp, dark lanes of Oxfordshire, asking Appleby a string of questions he seemed disinclined to answer about former Secret Service colleagues. The irony that some of them might be on Lemmer's list appeared to escape him. Suddenly, his

183

butterfly mind alighted on another topic: the file containing the list.

'You have the file with you, Horace?' he asked. 'The original, I mean.'

'It's authentic,' Appleby replied evasively.

'Grey, by any chance?'

'How did you know that?' Max cut in from the cramped rear seat.

'Good question.' Bostridge swivelled round to look at Max, pulling the car to the left, which Appleby corrected to steer them away from the verge. 'How did I know?'

'Well?'

'Take your hand off the wheel, Horace,' Bostridge said tetchily as he turned back to address the road ahead. 'You'll have us in the hedge.'

'The colour of the file, Jeremy?' Max prompted.

'Ah, yes, *Die graue Akte*. Well, it came to me just now. I remember the phrase from a cable we intercepted. From Lemmer, we suspected, in Weihaiwei, though what he was—'

'*Where?*'

'Weihaiwei. Aren't you familiar with that adornment to our Imperial crown, Max?'

'It's a British-leased enclave on the Shantung peninsula,' said Appleby.

'Exactly.' Bostridge went on. 'So, it was worrying – and puzzling – that Lemmer should be there, if he was there, early last year.'

'Who did he cable? And why?'

'His secretary in Berlin. I can't recall—'

'Anna Schmidt?'

'Yes. That's it. Come across her, have you?'

'Max's recent activities ought to stay between him and me, Jeremy,' said Appleby.

'Right. Sorry. Anyway, the cable was to Frau Schmidt. We deciphered it readily enough, but the message was veiled, as we call it. They obviously had a private code within the code. There were other cables around that time, also from Lemmer, we suspected,

184

they examined the view from the window of the spare bedroom.

It was a considerable panorama, encompassing the Eiffel Tower, a long stretch of the Seine, the eastern flank of the Louvre and, close by, the Church of St-Germain l'Auxerrois.

Between them and the Louvre was a jumble of chimneys, roofs, walls, windows and courtyards. But there was only one balcony in sight. Perched high and narrow on a building that looked in greater need of repair than most of its neighbours, the balcony was accessible through a set of double doors from a tiny apartment that appeared to have been added as an afterthought above a sloping roof, backing onto a blank wall that supported a high chimney-stack.

'That must be it,' exclaimed Morahan.

'That must be what?' Peggy asked, bustling in to join them rather sooner than they had anticipated.

'The balcony Soutine was standing on.' Malory pointed for her to see. 'Have you ever noticed anyone out there?'

'A dapper little guy with a white goatee beard,' added Morahan.

'Not that I can recall. But you see people at windows watering flowers or leaning out to admire the scenery all the time from here. I wouldn't have thought anything of it.'

'What about a young Arab boy?'

'The same applies.'

'D'you know where that apartment is – what building it's in?'

'I'm not sure. But it's a deal grubbier than the ones either side, so you should be able to find it. The entrance either faces the river or the side of the church.'

'Yes.' Morahan nodded. 'I see.'

'Now, how about that coffee?'

Billy Hegg was cramming a slice of toast into his mouth as if afraid someone might grab any he left on his plate when Sam tapped him on the shoulder.

'Don't worry, Mr Twentyman,' he responded instinctively. 'I'll be in the garage by half eight.'

'Good. 'Cos I want you to drive me to the Hôtel Dieu.'

'Where's that when it's at home?'

203

'Eel de la City. It's the main hospital. I had a stay there myself a while back.'

'Oh yeah. Well, happy to, I'm sure, but you could drive yourself. You've got the pick of the fleet.'

'I can't drive while I'm lying on the back seat.'

'What?'

'I don't want to be seen and followed, Billy. Get it?'

'Not really, Mr Twentyman. Not by a country mile. But, if you want to be chauffeured over there, I'm your man.'

The accumulations of several more decades' worth of soot and grime on the exterior than on those of its neighbours distinguished the apartment building Morahan and Malory were looking for, as Peggy had predicted.

The concierge's bell went unanswered, but fortunately a yawning, scruffily dressed man who seemed not to notice them emerged while they were waiting and they slipped inside before the door swung shut.

The hall was gloomy and none too fragrant. There were numbered mailboxes on one wall, some bearing names, some not. Morahan had to hunt down a distant light switch before they could read them.

'It's apartment seventeen,' Malory announced as he rejoined her by the boxes.

'How d'you know?'

'The name.'

Morahan looked and saw a label bearing in blotchily typed capitals: SOUKARIS.

'Did Laskaris ever really exist, I wonder,' Malory mused.

'Who knows?' said Morahan.

'What now?'

'We go take a look in apartment seventeen.'

'You're going to pick the lock?'

'I'm certainly going to try. So, if that's a little strong for your taste, now's the time to leave.'

Malory did not leave. They passed no one on the stairs and found the door of apartment seventeen round a corner at the end of a corridor. Morahan worked through his assortment of skeleton keys and, within minutes, they were in.

The apartment was a spotlessly clean contrast with the common areas of the building. It comprised three rooms. One, a bed-sitting-room, overlooked the balcony. The walls were white, with several hanging rugs and a couple of mirrors. There were raffia mats, a high-sided, deep-cushioned sofa, a small dining-table and chairs and a double bed. The tiny bathroom and kitchen were windowless, their doors latticed to admit light. Clues to the identity of the occupant were entirely absent, although the rugs had a Persian look to them. Otherwise, there was nothing – no books, no papers, no photographs.

Morahan stepped out onto the balcony and looked around. To either side was a tilted, tangled roofscape. But he had no doubt le Singe could negotiate it when or if he came and went. Drainpipes, windowsills and chimney-stacks were his personal highway. He needed no key. He was a spirit of the air.

'Do you think he comes here?' Malory asked, standing in the doorway.

'Yes. I do.'

'Where is he now?'

'Out there somewhere.'

'How will you communicate with him?'

'The same way he does. Can I borrow your lipstick?'

Suspiciously, Malory handed it over. Morahan walked across to the narrow fireplace. On the mirror above it he wrote in scarlet capitals:

SOUTINE IS DEAD.
TO KNOW WHO KILLED HIM
BE HERE DUSK THIS EVENING
FIRST OF MAY

'D'you think he will be?' Malory asked, protectively retrieving her lipstick as she looked at the message.

'I don't know,' Morahan replied. 'But I will.'

205

BREAKFAST AT GRESSCOMBE PLACE THAT MORNING WAS interrupted by an urgent telephone call from the Deputy Chief Constable of the Surrey Police. More discomposing still for Sir Ashley Maxted was that it was his mother to whom the Deputy Chief Constable wanted to speak.

In Winifred's absence from the room, Ashley and Lydia anxiously pondered what could be the matter. Their greatest fear was that it concerned James in some way. In their view, it was inevitable he would land himself in serious trouble sooner or later.

'You're not to let your mother dispatch you to some corner of the globe to rescue James from a predicament of his own making,' Lydia insisted. 'I need you here.'

'And I want to stay here, Lydia, believe me. But my mother isn't an easy woman to say no to.'

'*I* can say no to her, darling. Leave it to me.'

'What can have happened, d'you think?'

'Whatever it is it'll be James's own fault. He's not a child. He must stand on his own two feet.'

'Ah, but he's never had to, has he? Straight from Cambridge into the RFC. The boy's never needed to knuckle down to anything.'

'That's half the problem. He always wants to—'

Lydia broke off as Winifred returned to the room. She sat down and waited for Fuller, the manservant, to pour her another cup of tea before she said to him: 'Ask Ethel to pack a case for me, Fuller. I'm going away for a few days.'

'Very good, Your Ladyship. Will Ethel be accompanying you?'

'No, no. I'll be travelling alone. And I'll be leaving shortly, so could you see to it straight away?'

'Of course, Your Ladyship.'

Fuller left the room at a smart pace. Winifred sipped her tea. Ashley flushed with irritation. And Lydia said, 'May we be told where you're going?'

'Paris, my dear.'

'*What?*' Ashley exploded.

'Paris,' Winifred repeated more loudly.

'I heard what you said. I just . . . *Why* are you going to Paris, Mother?'

'George is in difficulties.'

'But he isn't in Paris . . . is he?'

'He is. I asked him to go when he was here last Sunday.'

'You *asked* him?'

'Why?' Lydia cut in.

'A Canadian railway magnate, Sir Nathaniel Chevalier, is threatening to sue me because a number of ancient Sumerian cylinder-seals he bought from your father have turned out to be fakes. I asked George to meet Sir Nathaniel's agent in Paris and settle the matter as discreetly and inexpensively as possible.'

Ashley gaped at her in amazement. 'I knew nothing of this.'

'No. We agreed it was best to keep it from you.'

'Ashley is head of this household,' said Lydia affrontedly. 'You had no right to keep it from him.'

Winifred half-turned in her chair and gave Lydia the benefit of her gaze. 'I cede the right to protect my late husband's good name to no one, Lydia. Please be so good as to remember that.'

'You should have told me, Mother,' Ashley fumed.

'Well, I decided not to and there it is. George went, loyal brother that he is to me. Alas, it's not gone well for him.'

'What's happened?'

'According to the Paris police, he's been kidnapped.'

'*Kidnapped? Good God Almighty.*'

'Information is limited. But however bad a fix George is in, it's because he did what I asked of him. So, I shall go to Paris myself and find out exactly what occurred and what can be done.'

'You can't go to Paris.'

'Why not? Haskins can run me up to town in time for the afternoon train from Victoria.'

'You simply can't. A woman of your age, alone in Paris. It's . . . it's . . .'

'Hardly Tangiers, Ashley. I shall be extremely careful. George may well not have been, I admit. He's inclined to be impetuous. But the circumstances are not of his making, so I must do all I can for him. And I cannot do that by staying here.'

'You should've told me about this complaint from Sir Nathaniel, Mother. I'd have asked Mellish to negotiate a settlement. I certainly wouldn't have asked Uncle George to do anything. You know how unreliable he is.'

'I know no such thing.'

'He'll have behaved like a bull in a china shop,' declared Lydia.

'You both seem remarkably unconcerned for his safety, I must say,' said Winifred.

'We're not unconcerned,' Ashley responded. 'But the Paris police are surely the people who should be investigating the matter.'

'You'd happily consign your uncle's fate to them?'

'They're better qualified than we are, Mother. Look at what happened after Pa's death. If James had only been prepared to let the matter rest, we—'

'Would still believe your father killed himself. Really, Ashley, I find your attitude incomprehensible. George has been kidnapped. His life may well be in danger. Do you seriously suppose—'

'Has there been a ransom demand?' Lydia interrupted.

The question drew a stare from her mother-in-law. 'Are you worried I might squander your children's inheritance on buying George's freedom?'

'They're *your* grandchildren.'

'Yes. And George is my brother. But don't worry, my dear. I'm sure you can rely on your husband to prevent a single penny of his father's estate being spent on rescuing George.'

'How did you intend to fund any deal Uncle George struck with Sir Nathaniel, Mother?' Ashley asked pointedly.

'I have resources of my own, Ashley. I wouldn't have expected you to contribute.'

'I don't see why we – or you – should have offered to pay anything,' said Lydia. 'The authenticity of some old museum exhibits is between the buyer and the seller. And since the seller's . . .' Her words petered out.

'Dead?' Winifred offered. 'That is what you mean, isn't it? You're right, of course, more right than you know, in point of fact. Henry sold the cylinder-seals through a dealer called Soutine. Apparently, the poor fellow's been murdered. George found his body. The police believe that may have something to do with his kidnapping.'

'Good God,' said Ashley. 'This is worse than I thought. It's connected with Pa's death, isn't it? James has stirred up a hornets' nest by his confounded meddling and this is the result.'

'There may be some truth in what you say,' Winifred conceded. 'But I have no intention of abandoning George in his hour of need.'

'You're not to go, Mother. I forbid it.'

'Fortunately, Ashley, I am not subject to your forbiddance. So, I shall go whether you want me to or not. I cannot, of course, prevent you accompanying me if you feel I need your protection.'

'It's clearly unsafe for *any* member of this family to go to Paris,' Lydia responded.

'I agree,' growled Ashley.

'I quite understand,' said Winifred, gazing at Ashley not so much in disappointment as in grim satisfaction at having foreseen how he would react.

Fuller came back in at that moment to report that Ethel had embarked on her packing.

'Good. I believe I'll go and make sure she doesn't pack more than I'll actually need.'

With that Winifred rose and left Ashley and Lydia to the remains of their breakfast and the remnants of their conversation.

MAX AND APPLEBY SLEPT SO SOUNDLY IN THE BARN – DESPITE the scurrying of assorted rodents – that they reached Abingdon railway station after the first train of the day had already left. The second had them on their way at eight o'clock, after a rudimentary wash and brush-up in the station toilet.

By then, following a thoughtful few pipefuls of tobacco, Appleby had devised a plan of campaign. 'We need to capitalize on the few advantages we have, Max. At the moment, Lemmer doesn't know where we are, or, more importantly, where the negatives are. We have an opportunity and it won't last long. So, we must make the most of it while it does.'

'How, exactly?'

'Firstly, I'm going to telephone my secretary in Paris. I can rely on Miss Willis's discretion if on no one else's in the delegation. She may well know how we can contact Veronica Edwards. I have a vague recollection of her mentioning she'd gone to the girl's wedding. We'll get off at Reading and I'll prevail on the station-master to let me use his telephone. My warrant card should ensure his cooperation. Now, we can't go to Paddington. Political's bound to have put a watch on all the London terminuses. So, we'll take a stopping train from Reading and get off at Ealing. From there we can travel by Underground.'

'I hate the Underground,' Max objected.

'It's a small price to pay. And a lot of that line's above ground, so stop complaining. Exactly where we go depends on what I learn from Miss Willis, but you may have to continue to Eltham on your own.'

'Why?'

'Because we have to move quickly and to do that we may have to split up. If so, I'll give you a note to hand to my sister, reassuring her she can safely entrust the negatives to you. And I assume you haven't lost your passport?'

'No.'

'Then your photograph will clinch the matter. But let's not get ahead of ourselves. I'll know more when I've spoken to Miss Willis.'

At Reading station, Max waited on the platform while Appleby tackled the stationmaster. He returned after ten minutes or so with the news that agents acting on instructions from London had ransacked his desk and filing cabinet, much to Miss Willis's disgust. She had evidently helped them as little as she could. As for Veronica Edwards . . .

'Miss Willis's memory holds more than my filing cabinet, so we're in luck. Miss Edwards is now Mrs Underwood. She and her husband live in Harrow-on-the-Hill. She's currently employed as a secretary herself, by a local solicitor.'

'Does Miss Willis know which one?'

'No. But I'll visit as many as I need to until I find her. Then it's just a question of persuading her to help us.'

'At the risk of her life.'

'She's a patriotic girl. She'll do it. But only I can talk her into it.' Appleby handed Max a folded sheet of paper. 'The note I mentioned for Cora. Once you've got the negatives, get prints made as quickly as possible. There's a photographer in the high street Cora's on good terms with. Use him. I'll take Mrs Underwood to the British Museum. Meet us there with the prints for her to work on. Let's say three this afternoon. In the tea-room. Earlier if possible. Later if necessary. Just be there waiting.'

They switched to the Underground, as planned, at Ealing Broadway. Appleby got off at the next stop, in order to travel to the northern end of the line, close to Harrow-on-the-Hill.

'Good luck,' was all Appleby contrived by way of a parting remark as he stood up to leave the train at Ealing Common.

'You too,' murmured Max.

A hunch-shouldered, hatted and raincoated figure moving slowly along the platform was Max's last glimpse of Appleby as the train started moving again. Three people had died already for the sake of the Grey File. Max did not delude himself that they would be the last. Nor that he might not be one of those joining them.

Max stayed on the train when it reached Charing Cross, despite the fact that trains to Eltham started from there. Appleby had advised him to travel from London Bridge station instead. 'It's a warren and I'm betting Political's too stretched to cover it. Use the Underground entrance, then go up to the mainline platforms.'

So it was that Max finally emerged from the claustrophobic depths of the Tube at Monument station. The London morning was cool and grey and damp. He walked out onto London Bridge, surveying the murky curve of the Thames to either side. Behind him was the City, to the west the Houses of Parliament. He was close to the twin centres of the Empire's wealth and power. And close to the treachery that had fed Lemmer's plot. Fear and frailty; hatred and ambition: they beat away their rhythms beneath the louder rhythm of London.

Near the middle of the bridge, a one-legged beggar was slumped by the railings, mumbling and grimacing to himself. A crutch lay beside him. His begging bowl was a frayed military forage cap. As Max drew closer, he noticed the poor fellow was wearing a military tunic as well. And then he saw, embroidered at the shoulder, the magical words: ROYAL FLYING CORPS.

Max stopped, his mind drawn back in an instant to the blue skies above Flanders, to the sweet song of the breeze in the rigging, to the perverse beauty of the woolly yellow smoke plumes of anti-aircraft fire, to the joyous intensity of combat in the air. He delved in his pocket for a coin.

'Max?'

The beggar was staring at him in recognition. His voice was slurred. But his eyes were gleaming.

'It's you, isn't it . . . Max?'

'I beg your pardon?'

'It's Wilko. Don't you . . . remember me?'

Wilko? Could the bundle of despair at Max's feet really be Wilkinson? They had trained together at Farnborough and briefly served in the same squadron at Vert Galant.

'Max?'

Max hardened his heart. He could do nothing for Wilkinson beyond the coin he leant forward to drop into his forage cap. On another day, in different circumstances . . . but on this day, in these circumstances, he had to play the stranger. 'I'm sorry. You've got the wrong man.'

'I have?' The light in Wilkinson's eyes went out. 'Yes. I see now. You're not Max. He's dead, isn't he? Like all the others. Max is dead.'

HEGG SUPPLIED THE RECUMBENT SAM WITH A COMMENTARY ON the signs of looming disorder as they drove from the Majestic to the Hôtel Dieu: shuttered shops, a mob gathering on the Place de l'Alma; tin-hatted *poilus* standing by with rifles stacked; the Red Flag fluttering in the damp Parisian air. 'Looks like they're spoiling for a fight, Mr Twentyman. I wouldn't mind getting back before it kicks off.'

Sam gave him no reassurance on the point. He had more to worry about than a riot.

So did George Clissold. He was propped up on several pillows in a room on his own, with a policeman stationed outside.

'Blimey, Mr Clissold,' said Sam upon seeing him. 'You look as if you've gone ten rounds with Jess Willard.'

George had a black eye, a split lip and various other visible bruises. He also had a bulky padded bandage on his left forefinger.

'If it weren't for my good friend morphine, I might feel as if I had too,' George said, in a rasping voice. 'They broke one of my ribs and this . . .' He waggled the bandaged finger. 'They pulled out one of my fingernails, Sam. Confoundedly painful, let me tell you. Though not as painful as I'd make it for the fellow who did it if I caught him with a horsewhip in my hand, I assure you.'

'You'd know them again?'

'Actually, no. They kept me blindfolded. But they were Japanese. I recognized the language from my days out east. They're the people you were warned about, aren't they?'

214

'Yes, sir.' Sam dropped his voice to a level certain to escape the ears of the policeman on the door. 'I was going to tell you yesterday. Count Tomura of the Japanese legation is the man looking for le Singe. And his son's doing his dirty work for him, by all accounts.'

'Such as murdering Soutine when he wouldn't give le Singe up?' asked George in a matching undertone.

'Such as that, sir, yes. You're lucky he didn't kill you.'

'Ah, but I gave him something, you see, Sam. That's why I wanted to speak to you so urgently. I'm sorry to have to tell you I don't withstand torture very well. I named you as the party who could lead him to le Singe.'

Sam blanched. 'You did?'

'My apologies, old chap. Very bad form. I can only say you have to know how it feels to have a Japanese muscleman taking a pair of pliers to your fingernails before—'

'It's all right, Mr Clissold. They'd have found their way to me sooner or later. You should've told them before they did you a mischief.'

George smiled stiffly. 'I would have. But then they might have thought there was more to extract from me. As it was, they gave up and deposited me outside this very hospital before it got light this morning.'

'At least you're alive.'

'Unlike Soutine, yes. Well, he wasn't a close friend of the chairman of Jardine, Matheson and Co., was he? That was his fatal disadvantage.'

'And you are, are you, sir?'

'No. But I convinced them I was. I did work for the company once, so I was able to throw around a few influential names. Happily, it seems even Count Tomura's murderous son can't ignore the imperatives of Anglo–Japanese commercial relations.'

'Have you spoken to the police?'

'Oh yes. Commissioner Zamaron came to see me. He mentioned he'd been to see you too. He suggested there was something you were holding back.'

'What did you say?'

'That I didn't have the first idea what he meant. We can't prove it was Tomura's people who kidnapped me, Sam. Or that it was his serpent-tongued son who interrogated me. So, I prefer to keep my powder dry on that front. The account I gave Zamaron of what took place was accurate as far as it went. But I led him to believe the identity of my kidnappers is a complete mystery to me. Nor did I—' George broke off. 'Hello. Is this another visitor?'

Sam looked up to see Morahan filling the doorway. 'Mr Morahan! What are you doing here?'

'I went to see you at the Majestic, Sam. One of your underlings said you'd come here. The receptionist told me who you were visiting.' He extended his hand. 'Schools Morahan, Mr Clissold. What's the damage?'

'Aside from what you can see, a broken rib and one fingernail fewer than I'm used to.'

Morahan grimaced. 'Nasty.'

'He's just been telling me what happened,' said Sam.

'We'll get to that, Sam. Hold on.'

Morahan left the room. Sam could hear him conversing with the policeman in French. Then he was back, closing the door behind him.

'Money speaks every language. I just bought us some privacy. Which we badly need right now.'

Morahan made it plain Soutine's murder and George's kidnapping freed him of any obligation he might otherwise have felt to protect Noburo Tomura and his father as clients of Ireton Associates. 'Travis is prepared to overlook almost everything,' he said. 'But I'm not.'

George described his own experiences in greater detail than he had to Sam. After being grabbed and bundled into a van on the Pont Royal, he was blindfolded and gagged and his wrists tied together. Then he was driven away. 'We didn't go far; about a mile, I'd say.' He was led down a rickety flight of steps into a cellar and tied to a chair, then left to contemplate his plight for an hour or more before the interrogation began. 'Fellow with a youthful, arrogant voice asked all the questions. Noburo Tomura, I assume.

I'm not sure the others spoke much English. He wanted to know where le Singe was and what my dealings with Soutine were. He didn't ask nicely, as you can see. I knew I'd have to tell him something to escape alive.' He duly explained what that was. 'Pulling out my fingernail seemed to please him mightily. He's a sadistic blighter.' But even Tomura's sadism had its limits. He evidently decided George could tell him no more and, not wishing to draw any fire from the likes of Jardine, Matheson, spared his life.

'I had the impression young Tomura means to do whatever it takes to find le Singe,' George concluded. 'It's as if he's frightened of him. Or his father is. And from what I've read in the papers Count Tomura isn't a man who's likely to scare easily, so le Singe must know something *very* important.'

'We need to learn what that is and use it against him,' said Morahan.

'Good idea,' agreed Sam. 'But how?'

'Well, that's why I came looking for you. I think I've tracked le Singe down.'

'You have?'

Morahan explained about the hideaway. 'I want you to go and wait there with me this evening. The chances are no better than fifty-fifty he'll show up, but, if he does, we've got to convince him we're all on the same side. He's seen you before, so he's more likely to trust you. And he'll want to avenge Soutine, so there's good reason to hope we can persuade him to help us.'

'I'll try anything, Mr Morahan.'

'Reckoned you would. We just have to keep you out of Tomura's clutches in the meantime.'

'The Majestic will be safe, though, won't it?'

'I guess so.' But Morahan looked unconvinced.

'I may be able to set you off in the right direction where le Singe is concerned,' said George. 'While Tomura's people were holding me, there was a lot of discussion between them in Japanese. Well, the language is a closed book to me, so I hadn't a clue what they were actually saying. It was different when young Tomura spoke to me in English, of course. And different on one other occasion. Someone – an outsider, I assume – came to talk to him. They went into an adjoining room, but I could still hear their voices. They conversed in Mandarin Chinese. Well, thanks to my years in Shanghai, I know a smattering of Mandarin, so I was able to follow some of what they said. Tomura and the Chinaman were plotting something. "The details have been delivered," the Chinaman said. "The conditions are right for us to move."'

'When was this?' Morahan asked.

'Last night, although I only know that now, by counting back from the time I was delivered here. Tomura asked the Chinaman if someone called Chen Sen-mao could be relied upon to "do it".'

'Do what?'

'They didn't say. But the Chinaman was anxious about le Singe. "You catch le Singe. Then I give Chen the order." Tomura wanted him to proceed whether he caught le Singe or not. "Act soon," he urged. The Chinaman demurred. I mean, he appeared to agree, but it was dressed up with oriental subtleties. I had the impression he wanted le Singe in the bag before he went ahead.'

'With whatever it is.'

'Exactly. Whatever it is.'

'Where does this get us, Mr Morahan?' Sam asked.

'I'm not sure. But it sounds as if le Singe knows what they're planning – and probably who's planning it. So, we need to find him before Tomura does. We'll go to the apartment this evening and wait. We'll have to be patient.'

'And meanwhile?'

'I'll travel back with you to the Majestic. Say you're sick and take to your room. Stay there until I call for you later.'

'All day in my room?' Sam looked genuinely sick at the prospect.

'You're next on Tomura's list, Sam. Out of sight is out of danger. Shall we go?'

MAX WAS ONE OF A HANDFUL OF PASSENGERS WHO DISEM-barked at Eltham Park station that morning. The residential streets were disquietingly empty and he found himself glancing over his shoulder as he went, though there was no reason whatever to think he had been followed from London Bridge.

Number 64 Balcaskie Road was a substantial semi-detached Edwardian villa, a red-bricked, bay-windowed statement of conformity and rectitude. The woman who answered the door looked like, and soon identified herself as, the housekeeper. Mrs Jeavons, she reported, was not at home.

Max was still debating how to talk his way in to wait for Mrs Jeavons when the housekeeper looked past him and said, 'Oh, here she is now.' Then she called, 'This gentleman's looking for you, Mrs Jeavons.'

Cora Jeavons was a stout woman of sixty or so, smartly turned out in a quiet sort of way. There was a definite facial resemblance to Appleby, though her smile was notably warmer. 'What can I do for you, young man?' she asked.

'I'm a friend of your brother, Mrs Jeavons. My name—'

'You're Max, aren't you?'

'Yes. How did—'

'Never mind. Show him in, Mrs Wise. We'll have tea in the drawing room.'

Mrs Wise pointed the way for Max, took her mistress's coat and then bustled off. Cora followed Max into the drawing-room, a haven of ticking clocks, potted palms and burnished woodwork.

'Horace talked about you when he was last here and you are, I have to say, exactly as he described you. A pilot, he said.'

'I flew in the war.'

'I can see that.'

Max let the strangeness of the remark pass. He took out his passport. 'You should satisfy yourself about my identity, Mrs Jeavons. This is no time to take anyone on trust.'

She glanced at his photograph and nodded. 'It's you.'

'Did you get a letter from Horace this morning?'

'Yes.'

'Were you surprised by the nature of the letter?'

'I know what Horace's work involves, Max. I may call you Max, mayn't I? It's your work too, of course. He said he might recruit you. Actually, he said he might need to.'

'He said that?'

'Yes.'

'I have a note from him for you.' Max handed it over.

While Cora was reading the note, Mrs Wise arrived with the tea.

After she had left, Cora went to the bureau, took out the letter she had received and brought it back with her to the sofa. 'Do sit down, Max.'

Max sat. Cora poured tea for them both. 'Biscuit?' There were shortbreads on a plate. Max swiftly devoured one. 'Have another.'

'Thanks. They're very nice.'

'And you're hungry. I could ask Mrs Wise to prepare something more substantial.'

'I don't have a lot of time, Mrs Jeavons. Neither does Horace. That's why I came without him.'

'"Something's brewing, Cora," he said on his last visit. "I don't know how it's going to turn out." Does he know now?'

'No.'

'But these negatives he sent me are central to it?'

'They're everything to it.'

'Well, there they are.' She handed Max the letter. 'I confess I didn't expect them to be collected so soon.'

'I need prints made as quickly as possible. Horace mentioned a photographer you know.'

'Oh dear. Am I going to have to impose on poor Sydney's good-will? Horace knows full well I don't want to encourage him. His first proposal was embarrassing enough. I don't want to risk a second. But I suppose you're going to say the security of the realm is at stake.'

'As a matter of fact, it is.'

Cora sighed. 'Then I must do my duty, mustn't I?'

The second telephone call of the day to Gresscombe Place from the Deputy Chief Constable came less than an hour after Winifred's departure. Ashley took the call, though Lydia sat close by, trying to infer the meaning of the conversation from his side of it.

'What's happened?' she asked as he rang off. 'Has Uncle George been set free?'

'Yes.' Ashley looked relieved as well as surprised. 'Early this morning. He's in hospital: battered and bruised, evidently, but not seriously injured.'

'Thank God. So, he wasn't kidnapped for ransom?'

'No. The motives of the kidnappers are a little murky, according to the Paris police. But happily ransom didn't come into it.'

'It's a pity we didn't learn this before your mother left. She might have agreed not to go if she'd known Uncle George was safe.'

'I doubt it. She seems to feel responsible for what happened to him. I'll send a telegram to her hotel giving her the good news. There's not much else we can do.'

'What about the threat of legal action from this Canadian?'

'Ah, well, as to that, I shall see Mellish and have him institute some proper negotiations. Lawyer to lawyer. Uncle George has made a predictable hash of the business.' Ashley sighed. 'It will need to be managed more professionally from now on. Let's hope Mother allows it to be.'

'We must do more than hope.' Lydia gave Ashley a spine-stiffening look. 'We must insist.'

The display window of Sydney Heyhoe's photographic studio in Eltham High Street contained the standard assortment of grinning newly-weds and infants fondling baubles. Max's requirements were

221

far from standard, however, and he had the impression Heyhoe – a nervous, fussy little man – might have baulked at them had Cora not been on hand. It was an opportunity to impress her that he was evidently determined not to waste.

'Yes, yes, it can be done immediately, if it's a matter of overriding urgency, Mrs Jeavons.'

'It is, Mr Heyhoe.'

'Then I'll see to it, of course. You know you can rely on me.'

'I do. And I'm very grateful.'

'This is first-rate work.' Heyhoe held one of the negatives up to the light. 'Very sharp. Very distinct. The words are . . . German, aren't they?'

'Can you read German, Mr Heyhoe?' Max asked.

'Er, no.' Seeming to detect a hint of a rebuke in Max's question, Heyhoe moved to the door and turned the sign on it round to CLOSED. 'Well, this won't take long. Please wait here.' With that, he headed for his dark-room.

'Tell me, Max,' said Cora as soon as they were alone, 'why is Horace resorting to these . . . unorthodox arrangements?'

'Are they so unorthodox?'

'Yes. As I'm sure you're aware.'

'Well . . . I can't say.'

'Can't or won't?'

'I'm sure Horace would want me to tell you as little as possible.'

'Yes.' Cora nodded. 'I'm sure of that too. But I do worry about my brother.'

'Naturally.'

'I thought he'd be able to lead a safer life – retire, perhaps – once the war had ended. I put that to him when he was last here.'

'What did he say?'

'That it hadn't really ended.' She smiled fondly. 'And that he was too young to retire.'

Veronica Underwood did not work at the first solicitor's practice Appleby visited in Harrow-on-the Hill. As it happened, however, she was known to them. 'Mrs Underwood? Oh yes. You'll find her at Sanderson's. Just round the corner in West Street.'

Appleby followed the directions he had been given, rehearsing as he went the arguments he would use to persuade the former Miss Edwards to help him.

His confidence that Lemmer could not have anticipated he would turn to her proved his undoing. He spotted a turning ahead signposted West Street as he passed the mouth of a narrow alley. In the same instant, he felt the jab of a gun barrel against his ribs as a man closed in suddenly on his shoulder.

'I've orders to shoot if you resist, Horace,' said Maurice Fairbrother, known to Appleby as one of the safest pairs of hands in this kind of business. 'Don't make me do it.'

'Whose orders are you acting on?'

'Political's.' Fairbrother waved to the driver of a car parked on the other side of the road. As it pulled across to them, Appleby recognized the driver as Parks. Young Davison was sitting beside him.

'How did you find me?' Appleby asked, genuinely baffled.

'Political arranged for someone to be listening in on your secretary's phone line in Paris. We were sent to wait for you here. Veronica doesn't know you're on your way to see her. And she never will now.'

'Political's a traitor to the Service, Maurice. I'm telling you that because it's the God's honest truth.'

The gun was jabbed into his ribs again. 'Get in the car, Horace. You can tell him that yourself. To his face.'

SAM WALKED OUT OF THE HÔTEL DIEU WITH MORAHAN INTO the deceptive tranquillity of the Place du Parvis-Notre-Dame. There were fewer beggars and idlers in front of the cathedral than usual. The threat of riots had lured them elsewhere.

'Billy's waiting for me round the corner,' said Sam.

'Let's go and find him, then,' said Morahan.

They walked along one side of the square and turned left into Rue d'Arcole. The car was parked at the side of the road, directly ahead. Hegg waved to them from the driving seat and gestured with his thumb to a car parked immediately behind him.

Out of it, as Sam and Morahan approached, stepped an elegantly overcoated young man of Asian appearance. He said something to his driver before striding forward to meet them. Sam noticed the other occupants of the car were older, bulkier men of passive but somehow threatening demeanour.

'Noburo Tomura,' murmured Morahan. 'Leave the talking to me.'

Sam was happy to do that. He did his best not to flinch as Tomura cast him a raking, contemptuous glance in which several generations of arrogance had been distilled to a poisonous essence.

'Mr Morahan,' said Tomura. 'I see you have succeeded.'

'Not sure what you mean,' Morahan responded as they came to a halt.

'You have the man I wanted to speak to. Twentyman.'

'What d'you want with him?'

224

'Nothing. If he has already told you what I want to know.'

'He doesn't know where le Singe is, if that's what you mean.'

'Perhaps you have not asked him . . . forcefully enough.'

'You should have waited for Travis and me to find out what we could, Noburo. Killing Soutine and kidnapping Clissold has got you nowhere. And it's made our job much more difficult.'

Tomura smiled faintly. 'I know nothing of killing or kidnapping.'

'Is that so? Why your interest in Sam here, then?'

'He is James Maxted's servant. And James Maxted is close to le Singe. Therefore . . .'

'Well, as I've just told you, he can't help you.'

'I prefer to question him myself.'

'Don't you trust me, Noburo?'

'No, Mr Morahan, I do not.'

'That's a sad thing to hear.'

'I think Mr Ireton will agree with you when I tell him you have obstructed the search for le Singe.'

'Tell him what you like.'

Tomura's gaze narrowed. 'Oh, I will.'

'Now, you'll have to excuse us, I'm afraid.'

Tomura took a sidestep, blocking their path to the car. 'Twentyman comes with me, Mr Morahan,' he said softly.

'No,' said Morahan, looking Tomura in the eye. 'He doesn't.'

'You are outnumbered. I only have to raise my hand and you will *both* come with us.'

'Do that and you'll be dead before your thugs' feet hit the pavement. I have a gun, Noburo, and I'm prepared to use it. I might wind up dead myself, but you won't be around to find out. I promise you that.'

Something changed in Tomura's expression. Sam could see it. Some vital portion of his confidence drained away. He believed Morahan. And so did Sam. 'You have made yourself my enemy, Mr Morahan.'

'It appears I have.'

'You will regret it.'

'Maybe. Maybe you will too.'

Tomura did not move as they walked past him to the car. But he did not raise his hand either.

'Get in the back, Sam,' Morahan said. Then, to Hegg: 'It's Billy, right?'

'Yes, sir.'

'Move over. I'll drive.'

'Well, er . . .'

'Do as he says, Billy,' Sam cut in as he clambered into the rear. 'He's the boss.'

'Right you are, Mr Twentyman.'

Hegg made way. The engine was already idling. Morahan slammed the car into gear and accelerated away.

Looking back, Sam saw Tomura scrambling into his own car. It lurched forward and set off after them. 'They're following us, Mr Morahan.'

'They're allowed to, Sam. We'll soon know if that's all they want to do.'

Morahan swerved round a van turning onto the Pont au Double and they sped across the bridge. Tomura's car stuck with them. Both cars took sharp rights onto the Quai de Montebello.

'We're not losing them,' Sam reported. 'Give her some more juice.'

'It's a straight run along the quays from here, sir,' put in Hegg. 'No need to hold back.'

'Oh, but there is,' said Morahan.

Tomura's car appeared alongside them, in the middle of the road. The driver steered in, crashing into their bonnet and forcing them off course. Sam glimpsed Tomura's scowling face, separated from him by only a few feet of air and some glass.

The car crashed into them again and this time did not veer away. Steel squealed against steel as they were pushed towards the edge of the road. Passers-by looked up in alarm. Place St-Michel, thick with traffic, was approaching fast. Sam braced himself for impact.

Then, suddenly, Morahan slammed on the brakes. The other car tore clear of them, carried forward by its momentum. Sam realized what Morahan had planned in the same second as the Japanese driver. He braked as well, but too late, his instinctive wrench of the wheel inducing a skid that carried the vehicle up onto the pavement and straight into one of the bookstalls lining the riverside wall.

The stall was closed. The shutters gave way as the bonnet of the car struck them. The speed and weight of the vehicle carried it all the way through the stall to the wall behind it. There was a sound of crumpling metal and an explosion of steam from the fractured radiator.

Morahan accelerated and drove past them without a backward glance. But Sam looked back and saw Tomura and his men spilling out of the crashed car.

'Looks like they're all in one piece,' he reported.

'Pity,' said Morahan.

'Bloody hell,' Hegg contributed eloquently.

'Tomura's not going to take this lying down, Mr Morahan,' Sam cautioned.

Morahan nodded. 'No, Sam, he's not.'

Protesters were noisily confronting the gendarmerie and a squad of *poilus* in the Place de l'Alma, obliging Morahan to drive on to the Pont d'Iena before crossing the river and heading for the Majestic. As he sped up an eerily traffic-free Avenue Kléber, he announced a change of plan to Sam.

'After what's happened, they'll lie in wait for you outside the hotel. So, we'll drop Billy and the car off there and find you somewhere else to lie low. You'll have to cope without Mr Twentyman today, Billy, OK?'

'If you say so, sir.'

'Don't mention our run-in with the Japanese to anyone, will you?'

'I'll have your guts for garters if you do,' Sam added, leaning close to Hegg's ear for emphasis.

'Where d'you want me to say you've got to, Mr Twentyman?'

'Say you don't know.'

'But I don't.'

'There you are, then.'

Morahan pulled into the side of the road as the graceful frontage of the Majestic loomed ahead. 'She's all yours, Billy,' he said. 'Come on, Sam. Let's get moving.'

'Where are we going?' Sam asked as he and Morahan set off on foot in the direction of the Arc de Triomphe.

'My apartment. Tomura will assume you're at the Majestic, so you'll be safer at my place. Leave at six and make your way to the church of St-Germain l'Auxerrois. It faces the eastern entrance to the Louvre. Wait there until I pick you up. Soutine's hideaway is close by. Oh, and help yourself to any food you find around the place, but lay off my bourbon, OK? You'll need a clear head.'

'I'm sober as a judge right now, Mr Morahan, and my head doesn't seem very clear. What'll you be doing while I'm holed up in your flat?'

'I've got plenty to keep me busy, Sam. Don't you worry about that.'

MALORY GREETED MORAHAN AT THE OFFICES OF IRETON Associates with a meaningful roll of the eyes and a whispered warning. 'Travis isn't a happy *hombre* this morning, Schools. His plans for trading information with the German delegation have hit a snag. I didn't realize you planned to move so quickly on that front.'

'There was no sense delaying.'

'No. And I'm glad you didn't. But . . .'

'I'll ride out the storm. Don't worry. And remember: you know nothing.'

Malory nodded. 'I'll remember.'

He left her then to her coffee and typewriter and went down the corridor to Ireton's office.

'There you are,' Ireton said as Morahan entered. 'What's kept you?'

'I called in at the Hôtel Dieu to see how Clissold is.'

'Who?'

'I told you about him yesterday, Travis. Max's uncle. He's in hospital recovering from a roughing-up by Noburo Tomura.'

'Any proof of that?'

'Not as such. He was blindfolded, but—'

'So, he could have been held by Barbary pirates for all we know, couldn't he?'

'He was questioned about le Singe.'

'Forget le Singe for a moment. I've lost my contact at the Hôtel des Réservoirs.'

229

'The deputy manager?'

'Yes. Blachette.'

Morahan exerted himself to look surprised. 'What happened?'

'The police tried to arrest him last night.'

'*Tried?*'

'Somehow he gave them the slip. They're still looking for him. But he's no use to me as a fugitive.'

'I can see that.'

'I don't know how they rumbled him. I told him to be careful. I smell Carver in this, Schools. I've had him on my back ever since the Ennis affair and I'm sick to hell of it.'

'It's surely more likely to have been *le Deuxième Bureau*. They're bound to be giving the Germans a lot of attention. Blachette must have given himself away somehow.'

'The damn fool.' Ireton poured himself a drink and waggled the bottle at Morahan. 'Join me?'

'A little early, I reckon.'

'Yeah. But it's May Day. And this sure is an emergency.' Ireton slugged some of the whisky down and slumped despondently into his fireside chair.

'If the police catch Blachette, can he give them anything that incriminates you?'

'Nothing clinching. It'd be his word against mine. And you can alibi me if needs be.'

'Sure.'

'The problem is how to open up another channel of communication with the Krauts. We maybe have another week before they get the terms.'

'It's not worth the risk, Travis.' Morahan sat down and looked seriously at his long-time partner. '*Le Deuxième Bureau* and Carver will be watching every move the Germans make. That goes for the hotel staff now too.'

'But it's a gold-plated opportunity.'

'Find another.'

'I'm trying to, God damn it.' Petulance flashed in Ireton's gaze. 'It'd help if you delivered le Singe to the Japs. Then we'd be able to cement a lucrative relationship with one of the winners of this damn war.'

'As far as that goes, doing someone else's dirty work without knowing just how dirty it is can be a dangerous business.'

'What the hell's that supposed to mean?'

'I got a whisper that our esteemed client, Noburo Tomura, has done some kind of a deal with the Chinese.'

Ireton shook his head. 'Not possible. Wilson's handed the Japs Shantung. That's the only deal that's been done. The Chinese got confirmation yesterday. The Japs have won. Tomura wouldn't have anything to offer the Chinese. Besides, he does what his father tells him to do. And Count Tomura wouldn't give them anything except his boot on their throats.'

'Something's wrong somewhere, Travis. There's something we're missing about why they're so anxious to find le Singe.'

'What *you're* missing is le Singe, Schools. Stop asking yourself why Tomura wants him and—'

Ireton broke off at the sound of a commotion in the outer office. Malory's voice was raised, insisting the visitor wait there. But heavy footfalls in the passage indicated they had paid her no heed.

Noburo Tomura burst into the room, his face flushed with anger. Malory followed him in.

'I'm sorry, Mr Ireton. Mr Tomura insists on seeing you.'

'Send the *furui tori* away, Ireton. We must talk as men.' Tomura curled his lip as he looked at Morahan. 'You are here, then. That is good.'

'It's all right, Malory,' said Ireton, rising to his feet. 'You can leave us.'

Malory withdrew, casting dark looks at Tomura as she went. Ireton walked across and closed the door behind her, then faced Tomura. Morahan stood up as well. The air was close in the room, electric with the tension of the moment.

'What's this about, Noburo?' Ireton asked, smiling cautiously.

'Ask your friend.' Tomura pointed accusingly at Morahan.

'We had a . . . disagreement . . . earlier this morning,' Morahan said neutrally.

'He stopped me questioning Twentyman. I suspect Twentyman knows where le Singe is. I suspect Morahan knows also. I hired you

231

to find le Singe for me, Ireton. Now your man blocks my path. Explain, please.'

'Schools?' Ireton looked dubiously at Morahan.

Morahan shrugged. 'I'm not prepared to be a party to murder and kidnapping. I know who murdered Soutine and I know who kidnapped Clissold. You, Noboru. You and no one else.'

'You accuse *me*?'

'I do,' said Morahan, facing him down. 'If I knew where le Singe was, I wouldn't tell you.'

'Do you know?' asked Ireton.

'We shouldn't do business with this man, Travis. I can't put it any plainer than that.'

'We have a contract,' said Tomura, rounding on Ireton. 'You must honour it.'

Ireton stared at Morahan for a silent moment, then said, 'Tell him everything you know about le Singe, Schools.'

Morahan's only answer was a shake of the head.

'*Tell him.*'

'I occasionally have to explain to people that I work *with* you, Travis, not *for* you. I guess the time's come to explain that to you as well, though I really shouldn't need to.'

'We're finished together if you don't come clean about le Singe right now.'

Morahan took his measure of Ireton for a few seconds, then nodded. 'I reckon we're finished, then.'

'God damn it to hell, Schools. How can you do this to me?'

'I warned you when we struck up our partnership there were lines I wouldn't cross – things I wouldn't do, however fat the fee.'

'There'll be no fees at all if we quibble about the use people make of the information we supply.'

'There's no danger you'll quibble, Travis.'

'Will you let him defy you?' Tomura demanded.

'I'll find le Singe for you, Noboru,' said Ireton. 'You have my word.'

'But Morahan knows already where he is.'

'There's nothing he can do for you about that, Noboru,' said Morahan as he ambled past him to the window and looked out.

'Ah, I see you've got fresh transport. New car, same crew. Sorry about the mess the last vehicle ended up in.'

'You damaged their car?' said Ireton.

'No. I let them wreck it all on their own.' From an underarm holster concealed by his jacket Morahan took a small revolver. He turned and pointed it at Tomura. 'Come over here and signal for them to drive away, Noburo.'

'What?'

'Put the gun down, Schools,' implored Ireton, panic skittering across his face.

'I don't want them waiting down there when I leave, Noburo,' Schools went on calmly. 'Signal for them to drive away.'

'No,' Tomura spat out. 'I will not.'

'I know you like inflicting pain, but I doubt you like experiencing it.' Morahan pointed the gun at Tomura's groin. 'You do want to go on enjoying those *femmes jolies*, don't you?'

'For God's sake, Schools,' said Ireton. 'Think what you're doing.'

'It's for Noburo to think. About what I'm willing to do. And what he is.'

'He's Count Tomura's son.'

'And I'm the son of an Irish pauper. But we're both capable of killing people. And you know that, don't you, Noburo? So, what's it to be?'

'You will pay for this,' said Tomura.

'Just get over here.'

Reluctantly, Tomura walked to the window. Morahan pulled it open and moved back to make way for him, keeping the gun trained on him every step of the way.

Tomura leant out of the window and waved, then gave several violent dismissive gestures with his arm. Morahan stood behind him, watching as the men who had been waiting climbed obediently back in their car and, a moment later, drove away along Avenue de l'Opéra.

'Good,' said Morahan. 'Close the window.'

Tomura closed it and turned to face him. Shame and fury were knotted on his sweat-sheened face. 'You are a dead man,' he blustered.

'We all are, sooner or later. I'll take my chances.' Morahan strode to the door and paused, holstering his gun as he turned the handle. 'Goodbye, Travis,' he said, glancing at Ireton.

'Go to hell.'

Morahan smiled. 'I'll see you there, no doubt.'

MAX WAS EARLY FOR HIS APPOINTMENT WITH APPLEBY AND Veronica Underwood. He prowled the Assyrian and Sumerian halls of the British Museum for a reminiscent half-hour, recalling a visit with his father when he was no more than seven or eight.

The figures on the elaborately decorated Standard of Ur had fascinated him as a child: recognizable humans, young and old, male and female, fat and thin, plucking lyres or drinking wine or carrying wood. 'Imagine, my boy,' his father had said. 'The artist who made this lived about four and a half thousand years ago.'

'What was it like to be alive so long ago, Pa?' Max had asked.

'Oh, much the same as now. Not as comfortable, of course, but otherwise much the same.'

'Who was the Queen of England then?'

'There wasn't one. There wasn't an England to be queen of.'

'Really?'

'Really. And one day there won't be again.'

'Won't England last for ever?'

'No, my boy.' A distant look had come into his father's eyes then. He had patted Max on the head and ruffled his hair affectionately. 'Nothing will.'

Well before three o'clock, Max was in the tea-room waiting impatiently. All he wanted now was to be on and doing. How long it would take Mrs Underwood to decipher the list he did not care to ask himself. He was confident Appleby had been able to secure her cooperation. That was all that mattered for the present.

But the present stretched into an empty hour. Appleby did not arrive, with or without Veronica Underwood. Max fretted, smoking cigarettes and drinking numerous cups of tea. Unable to bear sitting where he was any longer, he left the tea-room and stationed himself in the corridor outside.

Around 4.30 Max realized Appleby was not going to appear. The certainty formed like lead in his stomach. Something had happened. Something had gone wrong. Appleby was not coming.

But certainty was not enough for Max to call off his vigil. He stayed where he was, waiting and hoping – and eventually just waiting.

The day had passed with agonizing slowness for Sam as well, confined to Morahan's apartment. Preparing himself a meal from the meagre ingredients in Morahan's kitchen had not distracted him for long from gloomy contemplation of the fix he was in. They were staking more or less everything on being able to forge some kind of alliance with le Singe. But le Singe was by his very nature unknowable. He might not even come to meet them. Then they would certainly have nothing to use against Tomura.

He was relieved, nonetheless, when the time came to leave. However vulnerable he felt on the streets it was better to be moving than not.

The strike seemed to have ended. There were a few taxis about and some buses were running. He tried to board one heading south, but was rebuffed by a broad-bosomed conductress. *'Complet, monsieur.'*

It was not a long walk and he needed to stretch his legs, though he would have preferred for safety's sake to be squeezed inside a crowded bus. He turned up his collar, kept his head down and marched on with as much nonchalance as he could muster.

Max stood at the bar of the pub opposite the entrance to the British Museum, weighing his choices. He could linger there all evening and those choices would neither change nor improve. Appleby was not coming. His plans had gone awry. He had been waylaid. He might already be dead.

More likely he was alive, though – much more likely. The reason was the board-backed envelope containing photographic prints and negatives Max was carrying with him: the Grey File and its coded secrets. That was what Lemmer wanted above all to secure. And that was what must be denied him.

But what could Max do? Attack, his wartime instincts told him. Engage the enemy. Turn in the sky and swoop.

Appleby had spoken of a house in Pimlico where Political had planned to interrogate him. There was a good chance he had been taken there. Maybe Veronica Underwood too. Number 24 Glamorgan Street. Yes, that was the address Appleby had given. It was possible he had deliberately specified where it was with a contingency such as this in mind.

Max drained his whisky glass. He needed to find somewhere safe to lodge the negatives. It would be crazy to keep them with him. Once he had done that, he would not hesitate. They would not need to come looking for him. He would go looking for them.

Sam was relieved to find Morahan waiting for him in the church porch when he reached St-Germain l'Auxerrois. He had not relished the prospect of a lengthy vigil there. Morahan looked relieved to see Sam as well.

'How do we know le Singe is going to turn up, Mr Morahan?' Sam asked glumly as they set off.

'We don't.'

'Or that he'll be willing to help us if he does?'

'We don't.'

'Or—'

'Shut up, Sam, for God's sake. You don't need to tell me how desperate a throw this is. I quit Ireton Associates today and I've ensured Tomura is after my blood as well as yours. So, there's a lot riding on this for both of us. But it won't help to mention that every step of the way.'

'Sorry,' said Sam dolefully.

'Me too. But sorrow's next to gladness on the barometer dial of life, so they say.'

'They do?'

'Oh yuh. All the time.'

Max gave the porter at the Athenaeum the warmest of smiles as he requested an envelope in which to leave something for one of the club's more senior members. The porter had explained Mr Brigham was abroad at present and offered to post the article on, but Max insisted it should await his return to London. 'Or I'll retrieve it myself first and deliver it in person. My name's Maxted. James Maxted.'

'Right you are, sir. I'll make a note of that.'

L. Brigham, Esq., Max wrote on the envelope. *For collection. Private and confidential.*

'It's rather important,' Max said as he handed it over, accompanied by a generous tip.

'Don't worry, sir. It'll be safe as houses here.'

'I'm counting on it.'

And so, of course, he was.

A GROUND-FLOOR TENANT GROUCHILY ADMITTED SAM AND Morahan to the building after they had despaired of rousing the concierge and rung his bell instead.

'*Pardon, monsieur,*' Morahan said. '*Soukaris est un ami.*' He pointed to Soutine's *nom de résidence* on the mailboxes in the hall.

The man looked mildly surprised, but said nothing and padded back to his apartment in his slippers. Morahan was halfway up the first flight of stairs before his door had closed behind him. Sam hurried to keep up.

Morahan had the skeleton key he had used on his previous visit ready in his hand as they approached the door of apartment 17. But he had no need to use it. The latch was up on the lock. The door opened as he pushed against it.

'We're expected,' he murmured, stepping cautiously inside.

'Looks like it,' Sam whispered, engaging the latch carefully as he followed Morahan in and eased the door shut.

Grainy pearly-grey light filled the bed-sitting-room. Curtains had been partly drawn across the half-open French windows. Sounds of the city – echoing voices, fluttering pigeons, barking dogs – drifted into Soutine's tiny, white-walled haven. A hideaway, Morahan had called it, though to Sam it seemed less that than a retreat from a raucous and uncaring world. He had seen Soutine as a rogue and trickster, but, standing beside Morahan at the foot of the dead man's bed and thinking of the end he had come to, Sam found himself admiring the last-gasp bravery of the devious antiquarian.

239

'The message has gone from the mirror,' Morahan said softly.

Sam looked in the direction he was pointing. The glass in the mirror was clean and clear. Le Singe had read the message and erased it. And he had left the door unlatched. They were there, as he wanted them to be. But where was he?

A movement, reflected in the glass, caught Sam's eye. Morahan's, too. They both turned round.

Le Singe was standing in the doorway leading to the balcony. He was wearing his normal rags and tatters of army uniform, but had put on over them a long, loose white tunic, intricately embroidered around the neck. Sam could not have explained why, but he had the impression the garment was a symbol of mourning. It certainly made him look more Arabian.

Le Singe was not smiling, as he had been when Sam had last encountered him. His expression was calm but sombre. And in his eyes there was the watchfulness a hovering hawk might bestow on its prey – intent, patient, all-perceiving. He flicked back the tunic to reveal a knife, held in a scabbard on a belt around his waist. He was armed and he was cautious. But he was there.

'I left the message for you,' said Morahan slowly, enunciating his words carefully, as if le Singe might be deaf and needed to read his lips. 'And this man you know.'

There came from le Singe the faintest of nods. He was not deaf. But quite possibly he was dumb. Sam found it hard to imagine him speaking.

'We are sorry for your loss,' said Sam. From his pocket he took the photograph inscribed *Les jours heureux au Tunis* and held it up for le Singe to see. 'His killers did not find this.'

Le Singe beckoned for Sam to place the photograph on the dining-table that stood against the wall. Sam stepped forward and laid it down, then stepped back.

Le Singe kept his eyes on them as he moved forward to collect the photograph. He glanced at it and kissed the picture. He slipped it into a pocket of his fatigues and nodded to Sam, as if in thanks, though there was nothing in his expression to indicate gratitude.

'We need your help,' said Morahan. 'And you need our help.'

Le Singe gave that several stationary moments of thought before

240

he bent down and picked up an object that had been propped against the wall behind him.

As he turned it in his hand, they saw it was a square of slate, framed in carved maroon-painted wood. From a pocket le Singe slipped a stick of chalk and wrote on the slate, before turning it for them to read.

WHO YOU?

'My name is Schools Morahan,' said Morahan. 'And this is Sam Twentyman. We're friends of James Maxted, son of Sir Henry Maxted. I think you knew him. I used to work with Travis Ireton, but I work with him no longer. We bought information from Soutine. Information you obtained for us. Something you found out is very dangerous. Maybe you know what it is. We don't. But Soutine's killers think we do. So, you and we are on the same side. We need to help each other.'

Le Singe's searching gaze rested on them as he considered Morahan's reply. Then he plucked a cloth from a fold of his sleeve, rubbed the slate clean and wrote another question on it.

WHO KILLED HIM?

'Noburo Tomura, son of Count Iwazu Tomura of the Japanese delegation to the peace conference.'

Le Singe nodded, as if this answer only confirmed what he already knew.

'The Tomuras are after you because they believe you know something that could damage them – maybe destroy them.'

Le Singe gave another nod. It seemed to be true, then. He did know something.

'Will you tell us what it is? We can help you bring them down. We can help you avenge Soutine.'

Le Singe wrote on the slate again. NO REVENGE.

'No?'

JUSTICE.

'We'll settle for that,' Sam put in.

'So we will,' said Morahan.

More silence and more immobility. They were elements in which le Singe seemed to dwell quite naturally. Eventually, another word appeared on the slate: HOW?

'Tell us what you know,' said Morahan. 'You can trust us.'

More deliberation, then: WHY?

'Because Tomura is our enemy as well as yours.'

Something in le Singe's expression told Sam that was not enough. He required more. Instinctively, Sam said, 'Because *we* trust *you*.'

Le Singe nodded. That was what he wanted to hear. FOLLOW ME, he wrote. Then he pointed to Sam.

'Me?'

Another nod. Le Singe laid the slate on the floor and stepped out onto the balcony.

'Be careful,' murmured Morahan.

'You can count on that,' Sam replied as he started after le Singe.

The boy was waiting for him on the narrow balcony, the still, grey evening air suspended around him in a world of roofs, windows, chimney-stacks, drainpipes and blank, steepling walls.

One drainpipe was several feet from the near end of the balcony. Le Singe kicked off his espadrilles and jumped up onto the balcony rail, then stretched out, grasped the pipe and climbed it with such speed and ease that Sam could not have said exactly how he had done it. But there he was, on the sloping roof above, looking down at him and beckoning. It might have been possible to reach the roof from the balcony using a ladder. But there was no ladder to be seen. And as soon as Sam tried to follow by the route le Singe had used, the full height he might fall into the courtyard below was revealed. The pipe was none too securely fixed to the wall and the rail was slippery. To manage the climb he would have to step into a void and hope to brace himself on the bracket holding the pipe before pulling himself up onto the roof. It was madness to attempt it.

'Don't do it,' said Morahan, looking out at him from the doorway.

Le Singe went on beckoning. 'He won't believe we trust him if I don't,' said Sam tremulously. 'And he won't trust us.'

'We can persuade him some other way.'

'I don't think so. I truly don't.'

Le Singe looked down at Sam, his white tunic bellying in the gentle breeze. And Sam looked down as well, to the distant, cobbled surface of the courtyard below. Yes. It *was* madness. He could not do it. He should not do it. But then . . .

Hoping momentum would carry him where caution would not, Sam lunged forward, reaching for the bracket with his foot and the outward curve of the pipe, where it met the gutter, with his hand.

He reached both. But the crevice le Singe had found with his toes was inaccessible to Sam. His stolidly shod foot slid off the edge of the bracket into thin air, pulling his other foot off the rail behind him. He grasped the pipe, but his feet swung free. 'Oh Christ,' he cried out.

He was going to fall. He did not have the strength to pull himself up and round with his arms alone. He was going to fall. And it would be a fall to his death.

Morahan was on the balcony now, stretching out towards him. But the gap between them was too wide. It suddenly occurred to Sam that he had jumped into a trap – that le Singe was so suspicious of them he had lured him out there precisely so that he would fall. He looked up. And le Singe was smiling.

Then a rope-ladder, released by le Singe, unfurled itself from the roof, falling across Sam's shoulder. He thrust one foot into a rung and clasped the sides, uttering a silent prayer of thanks. He was safe, even if far from secure.

He hauled himself up the ladder, ignoring the ominous creaking of the rope as it sagged and swayed. Le Singe grabbed him by his hand and wrist to help him scramble up over the gutter and onto the roof, where he fell on all fours, heart racing, lungs straining, nerves shredded. 'Bloody hell,' he gasped. 'Bloody sodding hell.'

He looked up then and saw le Singe climbing the slope of the roof to the wall behind it, above which stood a broad stack of chimneys. The rope-ladder was fastened to two hooks fixed to the base of the wall. Le Singe hauled the ladder back in and rolled it up. There were two other hooks sunk in the wall about six feet up, painted cream, like the plaster, so that they would not be noticeable from any distance.

Le Singe jumped and lightly grabbed one of the hooks, found the other with his foot and was suddenly up on the chimney-stack, fully fifteen feet above, grinning down at Sam. The fluidity and seeming weightlessness of the boy's movement reminded Sam of monkeys he had seen at London Zoo. That was not quite it, though. There was a distinctiveness to le Singe's agility that was beyond the simian. It was more like dancing than gymnastics – a celebration of something he could do that no one else could.

Le Singe nodded semi-formally to Sam, arms by his sides, then turned and vanished from view, stepping off and away on some roof-tree road to wherever he wanted to be. Like a bird taking flight, but without the faintest flutter of wings, he was gone.

'Sam?' Morahan called. 'Where in hell are you?'

Sam raised himself uneasily, feeling more afflicted by vertigo now than when he had followed le Singe onto the drainpipe. Morahan's head came into sight as he leant back against the balcony rail and craned his neck.

'I'm here,' said Sam, raising his hand feebly.

'And le Singe?'

'Gone.'

'Gone where?'

'Where we can't follow.' Sam pointed behind him. 'Up there somewhere.'

'But why? Why run away?'

'I don't know. I can't think while I'm stuck up here.'

'Well, crawl along till you're above the balcony and drop down. Don't worry. I'll catch you.'

Climbing out and over the gutter, then letting go and trusting Morahan to break his fall without both of them toppling off the balcony, was terrifying, and Sam was shaking like a leaf by the end of it.

'How can you have been in the Air Force if you're afraid of heights?' Morahan demanded, as they picked themselves up from the foot of the balcony rail, against which they had fallen.

'I was ground crew,' Sam mumbled apologetically.

'And what exactly d'you think this escapade accomplished?'

'I'm hoping it'll make him trust us.'

'He's given us nothing. You realize that, don't you?'

'But maybe he will give us something now.'

'Maybe. I—'

A movement within the apartment caught their attention. A movement and a sound: a click, as of a latch engaging. They rushed into the bed-sitting-room.

Le Singe was not there. But something had changed while they had been on the balcony. 'Look,' said Sam.

A small sheaf of papers had been placed on the table. There were about half a dozen sheets in all, hole-punched in one corner and held together by a tag. They were covered in script – some typed and some handwritten. It was spidery, oriental script arranged in columns. Sam was hardly qualified to judge, but he felt instantly certain it was Japanese.

PARIS WAS EERILY QUIET IN THE AFTERMATH OF THE EARLIER protests and disorders. This did not give Sam any particular sense of safety, however, as he and Morahan hurried across the Pont Neuf and headed east along the Quai des Orfèvres. Proximity to Police Headquarters should have supplied some reassurance and was, he guessed, the reason Morahan had chosen the route. But somehow he was not reassured.

The document le Singe had given them might be all and more they needed to move against Count Tomura and his son, but it was impenetrable to them. They needed to have it translated as quickly as possible and the only way Sam could suggest of achieving that was to enlist the help of Kuroda's assistant, Yamanaka, via his cousin, the *blanchisseur* of Rue Frédéric-Sauton.

'How can we be sure Yamanaka will respond to our message, Sam?' Morahan asked, almost reflectively, as he strode along.

'Kuroda assured me he would,' Sam replied, breaking into a half-jog to keep up with the tall American.

'Well, I guess that's good enough. We'll just have to hope the document gives us something we can use.'

'It will, Mr Morahan: that's why le Singe gave it to us.'

'You're a sight surer of him than I am. That dance he led us . . .' Morahan shook his head. 'I'll bet it's not all he could have given us. He must have a secret stash somewhere on the roof of that building.'

'It wouldn't be easy to find it.'

'No. But he has no need of that rope-ladder, does he? He must have rigged it up for Soutine to use in an emergency. And if Soutine could reach the stash, so can we.'

'We shouldn't try, Mr Morahan. He wouldn't trust us if we did.'

'All right, God damn it. We'll trust him. *If* that document yields something useful.'

The Blanchisserie Orita was plainly not the kind of establishment where a general strike was likely to be observed. The staff were all Asians, though they spoke French. English was incomprehensible to them, so Morahan switched to French to ask after the eponymous Orita.

He appeared through a doorway concealed by a thickly hung row of bagged garments awaiting collection. Bald, spectrally thin and spaniel-eyed, clad in snowy white overalls, he heard their request expressionlessly.

'Twentyman,' he said slowly, stressing each syllable, when Morahan had finished. '*D'accord.*' He looked Sam in the eye. 'A message for my cousin?'

'Yes,' Sam replied.

'What is it?' Orita leant forward, so that Sam had only to whisper to make himself understood.

'We want him to meet us at Gare St-Lazare at eight o'clock tomorrow morning.'

'I will tell him.'

'When?' Morahan pressed.

Orita greeted the question with a frown, perhaps of irritation. 'Before eight o'clock tomorrow morning.'

'Will he be there?'

'I will give him the message.'

'Thank you,' said Sam, pressing his foot against Morahan's. Annoying Orita struck him as a bad idea. 'That's all we needed to know.'

Sam acknowledged he could not return to the Majestic that night in case Tomura did have the hotel under surveillance. But having heard about Morahan's rift with Ireton, he was not convinced Morahan's apartment was a wise choice of bolt-hole either.

'Don't worry,' Morahan reassured him. 'Tomura won't have learnt where I live. I guard the information carefully. But we need cast-iron certainty on the point, I agree. Which is why we're going there via the Ile St-Louis.'

Malory Hollander was drinking light beer and smoking a long, slender cigarette in a café halfway along the Rue St-Louis-en-l'Ile. It was clear to Sam she had been waiting for Morahan. She was reading a book, the title of which – *Of Human Bondage* – made him feel no happier about his situation.

Sam had never met Malory before, but she seemed to know everything there was to know about him. His first impression of her – stiff and starchy, quite possibly hoity-toity – changed rapidly. She was Ireton's secretary, but Morahan's confidante.

'I'd have spat in Travis's eye and resigned on the spot, Schools, if you hadn't said it was vital I remain there in the short term. You will make that the very short term, won't you? Travis has burnt his boats with me by siding with Tomura against you.'

'It's important he doesn't know that, Malory,' said Morahan. 'If Tomura found out you were helping us, you'd be in as much danger as we are. I can't allow that.'

'Travis actually instructed me to give Tomura your address, you know.'

'Which you did?'

'Certainly. Your *old* address, anyhow. Just as well you never settle anywhere.'

'It's my footloose character.'

'I'll be sure to act surprised if Tomura comes complaining you don't live there any more. Now, what happened at the apartment? Did le Singe show up?'

'He did. And we have something that may be useful. But we won't know for certain until tomorrow. It's a document – in Japanese.'

'Let me see.'

'You read Japanese, do you, Miss Hollander?' Sam asked.

'No, Sam, I don't. But I might be able to turn up something useful.' She began scanning the pages Morahan had passed her, squinting through her horn-rimmed glasses. 'And please call me Malory. Also please stop calling Schools Mr Morahan. However you'd choose to describe our little alliance, formal wouldn't be it, I reckon.'

'OK, Malory,' Sam said with an effort. 'How'd you get a name like Schools . . . Schools?'

'I'll tell you some other time,' Morahan growled.

'You're going to get this translated?' asked Malory as she read on.

'Kuroda's assistant will do the honours.'

'It'll be fascinating to find out what it— Ah! My goodness me.'

'What?'

'Here. And here again.' Malory pointed to two blocks of characters on one of the pages. 'This word. I'm pretty sure I recognize it. It's the word Max showed us when he came to the office that last time. The word written on a scrap of wallpaper. It's written vertically here, of course, rather than left to right in the Western style. But it *is* the same.'

Sam peered at the characters. They meant nothing to him as such, of course. They looked familiar, it was true, but he could not have sworn they were the same as those he had seen himself on the scrap of wallpaper Max had brought back from London. It was tempting to believe they were, though, since le Singe was the source of both.

'Farngold,' he said under his breath.

'That's what it means? The name Farngold?'

'It's what le Singe wrote on the wallpaper at the flat in London after he helped Max get the better of Tarn. Yamanaka translated it for him.'

'So this document tells us all about Farngold,' Morahan suggested.

'Maybe,' said Malory. 'Yamanaka will be able to tell you.'

'Does Max know who Farngold is, Sam?' Morahan asked.

'No, he doesn't. But he'd badly like to. Farngold was the name his father held a safe-deposit box under at the Bank Ornal. The box Lemmer emptied.'

'Lemmer and Henry and Farngold and Tomura,' Morahan mused. 'There's the thread.'

'And it leads to Japan, Schools,' said Malory, in a tone that suggested a significance to the point beyond any Sam was equipped to comprehend. 'Japan thirty years ago. And Japan today.'

'What d'you mean, Malory?' Sam asked.

'Tell him, Schools,' she responded. 'You must tell him now it's come to this.'

'Yuh.' Morahan nodded sorrowfully. 'I guess I must.'

MAX FORMULATED A PLAN OF SORTS AS HE WALKED DOWN through Westminster towards Pimlico. He helped himself to a fist-sized chunk of masonry from a building site he passed and bought a pair of thick woollen socks at the next draper's he came to. He stuffed the chunk inside one of the socks, knotted it and reckoned the result was the most serviceable weapon he could hope to come by.

The draper helped him out with directions to Glamorgan Street as well. It ran between Lupus Street and Grosvenor Road, close to Belgrave Dock. The streets around the dock were, he saw as he approached, lined with terraced working-class houses. He decided to approach Glamorgan Street from the river end and walked down past the dock to reach it. The night was closing in and the warehouses were shuttered and silent. The evening was damp and windless.

He turned in to Glamorgan Street and saw a pub sign ahead: the Balmoral Castle. Number 24 was some way beyond it on the same side. It was not quite as dark as he wanted it to be. Patience, he knew, was as important as determination. He went into the pub, where men who looked for the most part as if they worked at the dock were drinking and smoking and playing cribbage and bickering amiably. He ordered a Scotch and sipped it slowly, standing at the bar. He did not know exactly what he was going to do. But he was going to do it

Morahan declined to say any more until he and Sam had reached the privacy of his apartment. There they settled over glasses of bourbon and talked the matter through.

'Going back to the life of an ordinary working Joe after you've fought in a war is no easy thing, Sam,' Morahan began. 'I guess I don't need to tell you that. Well, after Travis and I had served together in Cuba in 'ninety-eight, Travis fixed us up with an assignment in Colombia. There was a civil war brewing and the US government had a hand in it. Travis knew more than he told me and that was fine by me. I did more drinking than thinking back then. Anyhow, the plan was to foment a revolution in Panama, which was still Colombian territory, in order to set up a US-friendly government that would cede the US a strip of land to push the Panama Canal through.

'That all worked out well if you were sitting in Washington with a map spread out on your desk, but it was dirty business down on the ground. We were paid well, though, I can't deny it. We moved on to Peru afterwards. "American interests" – that was how Travis always described our anonymous paymasters – wanted to secure control of some copper deposits, by fair means or foul. They were mostly foul. I split with Travis because I didn't like what he was turning me into and we went our separate ways, though it seems I hadn't learnt my lesson, because I partnered up with him again later. Before leaving Peru, I did a few stupid things. Sabotage of US corporation assets, they called it. I never thought they'd come after me. But they did. I went to Brazil and found work – the semi-respectable kind in Rio de Janeiro. Then I was arrested. The Brazilian government was pro-American and the authorities would've been happy to send me back to Peru, where I'd have been tried on exaggerated charges and likely executed.'

'Cripes,' said Sam.

'Yuh. Annoying the wrong people can be costly in Latin America. I claimed I was British because it was the only way I could think of to stop them dispatching me in chains to Lima. It was true up to a point. I was born in Belfast. The British Embassy sent someone to interview me. It was Sir Henry Maxted. I told him my whole sad story. I didn't think he was going to help me. All I had to offer was the place of birth written in my US passport. But he wasn't the stuffed-shirt type I was expecting. He was ...

sympathetic. For some reason I never properly understood, he seemed to like me. He said he'd see what he could do.'

'And he got you out?'

'He did. On the technicality that I was British-born and had never renounced British citizenship. "But I wouldn't linger in Brazil if I were you, my boy," he said. "London might countermand me if anyone cares to take it that far." So, I vamoosed. I haven't been south of the Rio Grande since, though there have been enough military coups and changes of government in Peru over the years to bury the charges against me.

'I hooked up with Travis again a few years ago in New York. I'm not proud of all the things we've done together, but there's been nothing like what we fell out over in Peru – until now. We came to Paris to make money the way Travis likes to make money – by brokering information. "Clean hands, full pockets" is how he describes it. With so many politicians and diplomats in the city, it occurred to me Henry might be among them. I checked with the British delegation and they confirmed he was part of their team, so naturally I looked him up. It was good to see him again.

'It was around the end of February that he asked to meet me to discuss something important. I didn't know what to expect, but it surely wasn't what it turned out to be. He needed my help – and my advice. He wanted to launch a rescue mission, as he called it. Someone was being held in conditions of close captivity in Japan. He never said who they were or who was holding them or where exactly they were being held. But getting them out would be, well, challenging was how he put it. Impossible, in fact, without a team comprising hardened professionals in that kind of game. Did I know any such people? Could I put such a team together? And would I be willing to lead it?'

'What did you say?'

'I said yes, Sam. Ordinarily, to anyone else, I'd have said no. But I owed Henry my life. It's not the kind of debt you walk away from. So, I agreed to help him. But I warned him it wouldn't be quick or easy and it certainly wouldn't be cheap. From the little he said I judged I'd have to recruit at least half a dozen good men. None of them were in Paris. I'd have to go back to New York to arrange it. Henry admitted we'd be up against some powerful people in Japan. I asked him if he really wanted to go through with it. He said he had to. "Now I know, I have no choice." Again, what he knew and how he'd come to know it he wouldn't reveal. He said he'd supply the details when our plans were further advanced. He didn't have the money I told him would be needed, for one thing. But he meant to set about raising it right away. As we know he did.'

'Hold on, Mr— Schools, I mean,' said Sam. 'Senhor Ribeiro told Max and me Sir Henry was raising money to keep Madame Dombreux in comfort.'

'Ribeiro was an old friend, Sam. He told you what Henry asked him to tell you. Henry realized he was playing a dangerous game that could cost him his life. He didn't want Max trying to finish what he'd started. So, he had Ribeiro ready with an alternate explanation for his money-raising efforts.'

'You think this person he was trying to rescue . . . is Farngold?'

'Maybe. The name means something. That's for sure.'

'And you think whoever it is is being held . . . by Tomura?'

'It would explain why he's so anxious to lay hands on le Singe. Henry may have hired le Singe through Soutine to steal that document from the Japanese. With any luck, we'll soon know why Henry might have wanted it. But it never reached him, did it? Soutine may have realized how valuable it was and tried to play both sides against the middle, ultimately with fatal results. As for Count Tomura, he left Japan around the second week of March. His son could have cabled him to say Henry was onto them. And he got here just as quickly as he could.'

'We really do need to know what's in the document, don't we?'

'Yes, Sam, we do. Let's hope Yamanaka plays ball.'

'He will. I'm sure of it.'

'Good. One other thing, though. Henry swore me to silence about this. I'm only telling you because your neck's on the line now along with mine. As far as Max goes, we'll have to tread carefully. "If anything happens to me, Schools, don't breathe a word to my family. *Especially my son James.*" That's what Henry said. Telling Max what we find out won't necessarily be the right thing to do.'

'Doesn't that depend on *what* we find out?'

'Yuh.' Morahan sighed. 'It does.'

Max stepped out of the Balmoral Castle into the full darkness of night. Glamorgan Street boasted only a paltry ration of gas lamps. Max crossed to the opposite side of the road and walked nonchalantly along, neither hurrying nor dawdling, checking the house numbers he saw and calculating how far he was from number 24.

There were a couple of commercial vans and a cart standing by the roadside. And one car, just about where Max reckoned 24 was. As he drew alongside the vehicle, he saw to his relief there was no one sitting behind the wheel. The door closest to the car was actually that of 22, but the entrance to 24 was only a few yards further on. The lights were on inside the house – on both floors.

Seeing his chance, Max crossed the road and headed along one of the narrow, covered alleys that he presumed led to the back lane between the yards of the houses in Glamorgan Street and those of the next street. He was committed now. He was going in.

IT WAS AS DARK AS THE INSIDE OF A COAL BAG IN THE LANE AND the ground was uneven, but Max worked his way along to number 24 by counting the gates serving the yards. He reckoned 24's gate was certain to be bolted and he could not afford to make any noise trying to open it. Someone had considerately thrown out an old slatted box into the lane from 22, however. Max stood gingerly on it and peered over the wall into the yard of 24.

There were lamps on in the rear windows of the house, upstairs as well as down. The curtains were closed, but enough light escaped into the yard to show Max the lie of the land. To his right, on the other side of the gate, was the privy. Below him, its upper leaves brushing against him, was a bay hedge. And straight ahead, standing by the wash-house door, was a man smoking a cigarette, its end glowing at intervals as he drew on it.

There was no way Max could scale the wall without the man seeing or hearing him. If he raised the alarm the game would be up. Max stood where he was, wondering what he should do next.

The decision was made for him. The man finished his cigarette, tossed it away and started across the yard towards the privy. He went inside, not bothering to close the door behind him, hawked and spat, then began to urinate.

Max cast caution to the winds, scrambled up onto the wall and half-jumped, half-fell into the yard. There was a suspicious grunt from the privy. The man stepped back out, still buttoning himself up. Max struck him with the socked lump of masonry somewhere

256

around the back of the neck. He grunted again and collapsed, Max lowering him gently to the ground.

The gun he found in the man's raincoat pocket reassured him he had not knocked out an innocent householder. Max took the weapon and headed for the house.

He opened the wash-house door and stepped inside. The door to the passage was open and in the lamplight he could see the first few treads of the stairs. He could hear voices in one of the bedrooms and someone moving around in the kitchen.

Then he heard another sound, that of a car drawing up outside, directly outside, given the sudden glare of the headlamps through the fanlight above the front door. The man in the kitchen stepped out into the passage. A second man started to descend the stairs. Max moved out of sight, deeper into the wash-house.

'It's all right, Fairbrother,' said the man on the stairs in a cultured tone. 'I've decided to move Appleby.'

So, Max was right. Appleby was there. But apparently he would not be there for much longer.

'I had no warning of this, sir,' said Fairbrother, who sounded aggrieved.

'Unusual times dictate unusual arrangements. It's been necessary to coordinate our response with our sister organization.'

'Thought you liked to keep them at arm's length, sir.'

'Ordinarily, yes. But there's nothing ordinary about this, is there? Let them in, would you?'

Max heard Fairbrother move down the passage and open the door. The engine of the car outside was still running. There were heavy, entering footsteps. And another voice – one Max recognized.

'We're here for Appleby,' said Grattan. 'You'll have orders from Political. Ah, there he is. Evening, sir.'

Max realized then that the man who had come downstairs was Grieveson, otherwise known as Political, Lemmer's most highly placed spy within the Secret Service and Appleby's captor.

'Good evening,' said Political. 'Let's get on with it, shall we? Appleby's upstairs. Follow me.'

'Where are we taking him, sir?' asked Fairbrother.

257

'You're taking him nowhere. Leave it to Grattan. You're to stay here until you hear from me again. Is that clear?'

'Yes, sir. But—'

'That'll be all, thank you. Chop chop, gentlemen. Time waits, etcetera.'

Heavy footsteps on the stairs told Max that Grattan and a companion – probably Hughes, the other MI5 man who had turned up at Bostridge's cottage – were following Political up the stairs. The moment to strike, Max calculated, was when they brought Appleby down. He stayed where he was.

But Fairbrother was restless. Maybe he decided to consult his colleague, last seen exiting into the yard. He marched into the wash-house.

And straight into Max, who pressed the barrel of the revolver against his temple and cocked it. 'Move or cry out and you're dead. OK?'

Fairbrother nodded. 'OK,' he murmured. He was a bluff, burly, middle-aged man who looked as if he had seen a lot of action. He was surprised but not frightened. It was beginning to become clear to Max that for such men guns being held to their heads was all in a day's work.

'I'm James Maxted. I've come for Appleby.'

'You won't get him.'

'Listen carefully. Whatever you've been told, this is the truth. Political's sold out to Lemmer. So have Grattan and his friend. So have quite a few others Appleby and I are determined to expose. You have to decide whose side you're on.'

'What have you done with Parks?'

'If you mean the chap I met coming in, he's nursing a headache out by the privy. He'll live. The only killers in this house are the men who've just walked through the front door. I saw Grattan shoot Jeremy Bostridge in cold blood.'

'Political said Appleby did that.'

'And you believed him? Who do you really trust? Appleby or Political? A lot hinges on your answer. You know there's something wrong about handing Appleby over to Grattan. Political's behaving oddly, isn't he? He's not sure of you, so you're to stay behind.

You know there's a plot afoot. You just don't want to believe it.'

'Say I do believe it . . .'

'Help me stop them taking Appleby.'

They were coming back down the stairs now, moving more slowly than when they had gone up. Max heard Appleby say, 'You won't get away with this. None of you will. Your names will be on the list.'

'Shut up,' said Grattan.

'Lower your gun and I'll do what I can,' whispered Fairbrother.

Max had no time to weigh the odds that Fairbrother could be trusted. He lowered the gun.

Fairbrother strode into the passage quickly enough to block the path of Appleby's escort.

'Get out of the way,' said Grattan.

'We need to talk this through,' said Fairbrother. 'I can't let you remove Appleby without a direct order from C.'

'*I'm* giving you a direct order,' barked Political.

'Not good enough, sir. I'm afraid—'

There was a loud crack and a moan from Fairbrother. He had been shot.

Max burst out of the wash-house. He saw the gun in Grattan's hand; Fairbrother sliding slowly down the wall of the passage; Appleby, hands trussed behind his back, glancing towards Max in surprise; Grattan swinging towards him.

Max fired at Grattan's chest. The bullet hit. He went down with a groan. Hughes, who was holding Appleby, struggled to free his gun. But Appleby thrust his weight back against the man, felling him on the stairs. Max jumped forward and fired twice, hitting him in the throat.

Then he trained his gun on Political, who was standing a few treads higher on the stairs. 'Give up or I'll shoot you where you stand.'

Political was pale and trembling, much of his self-assurance stripped away. A lean, aquiline Englishman of the mandarin class, Max guessed he was not accustomed to witnessing sudden, violent death.

A man, younger than the others, was watching from the landing.

Hughes was twitching and gurgling, choking on his own blood. Grattan and Fairbrother were dead. The smell of cordite was thick around them. 'Stay where you are, Davison,' said Political nervously.

'Untie me,' growled Appleby, looking over his shoulder at Political. 'Now.'

Max kept his gun trained on Political as he moved down to where Appleby was standing. He had to step over Hughes to reach him. There was blood pooling on the stairs and dripping down from tread to tread.

Max risked a glance at Appleby as Political fumbled with the rope fastening his wrists. There was a cut and bruising over his left eye. He did no more than nod in acknowledgement of what Max had done. Political seemed to take an age to untie the rope. But at last Appleby shook his hands free and stepped clear of Hughes's crumpled form. He slowly stooped and picked up Grattan's gun.

'Are you all right, Davison?' he called up to the young man on the landing. 'You saw Grattan shoot Fairbrother?'

'Yes, sir,' Davison mumbled.

'What?'

'*Yes, sir.*'

'So, you know now what I told you was true, don't you?'

'Yes, sir.'

'Political's in my custody.' Appleby looked at Political. 'Aren't you . . . sir?'

Political cleared his throat. 'What do you intend to do?' he asked, his voice recovering some of its steadiness.

'I'm going to telephone C on the direct line only people at your level know the number for and give him a report of what's happened. And he'll decide what to do. You have the photographs, Max?'

'Yes.'

'And the negatives?'

'Safely stored elsewhere.'

'Good. I imagine C will want to put deciphering in hand as soon as possible. So, the number, Political, if you please. There's no time to lose.'

Political looked Appleby in the eye. 'Are you sure that's how you want to play it, Horace? I was going to take you to Lemmer. If I don't turn up, he'll know something's gone wrong. He'll leave the rendezvous immediately and drop out of sight. But if we go there now, he'll be waiting. You'll never have a better chance to catch him. Do you really want to throw it away?'

Appleby hesitated, assessing the prospect being dangled in front of him.

'Well, do you?'

APPLEBY THOUGHT HARD FOR ABOUT HALF A MINUTE BEFORE accepting Political's offer. Max did not feel the need to point out it might be a trap. They both knew that. But the prize was too great to resist.

'I want consideration for this, Horace. I want a guarantee I won't face criminal charges. Immediate retirement with no loss of pension in return for full cooperation. How does that sound?'

'Like more than you deserve or are likely to get. But helping us catch Lemmer will count for something. It'll be for C to decide.'

'We don't have time to consult him.'

'I agree. Shall we go?'

They went, leaving Davison to telephone HQ and report what had happened. They took the car Grattan and Hughes had arrived in, though Appleby fetched something from the other car before they set off. Political seemed incurious, dazed, somehow, by the disaster that had overtaken him. He mumbled directions as Appleby drove through the London night. They were heading west through Chelsea. His answers to Appleby's questions were grudging and unrevealing.

'Where are we going?'

'You'll see.'

'Why did you betray your country?'

'You wouldn't understand.'

'Tell me anyway.'

'I'm not about to unburden myself to you.'

'You'll be made to unburden yourself in due course.'

'Then I'll wait until I am.'

'How long have you worked for Lemmer?'

'Long enough.'

'And now you're willing to betray him as well?'

'It's a question of self-preservation.'

'No principles to call your own?'

'None worth dying for.'

'So, where *are* we going?'

'Cross the river at Putney Bridge.'

'And then?'

'And then you'll see.'

The house was one of several gated and gabled villas in a leafy close. They stopped some way short of the entrance and looked at it through the trees. There were lights burning in most of the ground-floor windows and the gates to the drive stood open. There was no sign of caution or watchfulness.

'Who normally lives here?' Appleby asked in the silence that followed the dying of the engine.

'I do,' said Political quietly.

'This is your home?'

'Be it e'er so humble. My wife and I like to have a lot of space in which to avoid each other.'

'Where is she?'

'I sent her away. And her maid with her.'

'And where's Lemmer?'

'Inside.' Political pointed to the lights. 'Waiting.'

'How many people will he have with him?'

'Nadia may be there. Otherwise . . . nobody.'

'You're sure?'

'I'm *sure* of nothing.'

'Give me the keys.'

Political handed them over. 'You want me to lead the way?'

'No. I want you to wait here.' Appleby took a pair of handcuffs out of his coat pocket. He snapped one round Political's wrist and the other round the steering wheel.

263

'You'd have a better chance of outwitting him if I came with you.'

'I doubt that. Come on, Max.'

They trod carefully as they approached the house, communicating in whispers. It was agreed Max would enter from the rear, Appleby from the front. Beyond that their intentions would be determined by what happened. They were both carrying guns.

'It's hard to believe Lemmer will just be sitting by the fire waiting for me to be delivered to him,' murmured Appleby.

'Maybe he's certain Political will do what's been asked of him.'

'Maybe. But even so . . .'

They came to the open gates and went in. A gravel drive led between shrubs and trees towards the house. They walked on the grassy verge, the undergrowth brushing damply against them.

The drive curved ahead, slowly revealing the frontage of the house as they proceeded. As Max's line of sight altered, he saw that the front door was wide open. Much of the length of the parqueted hall within was clearly visible.

'Something's wrong,' Appleby whispered from close behind.

'What, d'you think?'

'I don't know. But there's only one way to find out. I'll go in. Forget cutting round the back. Stay here and watch out for me.'

'No, Horace. You stay here. I'll go in. I'm faster on my feet.'

'I suppose I can't argue with that. But for God's sake be careful.'

'I will be.'

Max started towards the house, keeping to the shadows. The open door and the blazing lights were either an invitation or a declaration. There was no way to tell which.

Max was holding his gun in both hands to steady his grasp as he crossed the drive, his shoes crunching on the gravel. He stepped into the porch, then the hall.

No one sprang out to meet him. He heard no movements in nearby rooms, though he could hear the crackle of a fire some-where. He paused by the first doorway he reached, then strode through it, gun raised.

He found himself in an empty drawing-room. A fire was

warming the hearth and the surrounding sofa and chairs. But no one was there.

As he moved back out into the hall, a telephone began ringing. He followed the sound to a book-lined study, empty, like the drawing-room. The telephone stood on the desk. He walked across to it and hesitated before picking up the receiver. But not for long.

He said nothing. And for a moment neither did the caller. Then: 'Is that you, Max?' The voice was Lemmer's.

Max swallowed hard. 'Where are you?' he asked, hardening his tone to suppress any note of surprise.

'In a safe place. Is Appleby with you?'

'Maybe.'

'Of course he is. And Political too. I knew what he would do as soon as I heard matters had miscarried at Glamorgan Street. He is very predictable. As are you, Max, I have to say.'

'How did you hear what had happened?'

'Nadia had the house under observation. She came to warn me the operation had been bungled. I considered waiting for you, but the judgement of risk is a fine art. It must always be done dispassionately.'

'You've lost, Lemmer. We have the Grey File.'

'No. You have photographs of the contents. That is regrettable. I would have preferred to obtain them as well as the original. But you have been resourceful, as ever. I cannot complain. It was because of your resourcefulness that you succeeded in Orkney where others would have failed.'

'We have your list of spies.'

'You do, yes. But it is double-encoded. I decided to take extra precautions after the fiasco of the Zimmermann cable. You would need a genius to decipher it. A genius such as Bostridge. And Bostridge is dead. Without him, British Intelligence does not have the capability to unlock my secrets. Political will not be able to tell you much of value. I seal my operatives in watertight compartments. The ship itself cannot sink.'

'You *hope* they don't have the capability.'

'I *know* they don't, Max. And time will prove me right. Time in which I can make use of the document you have so kindly returned to me.'

'What are you going to do with it?' Appleby appeared in the doorway as Max asked the question. Max mouthed 'Lemmer' silently to him. And Appleby gave a rueful half-smile, acknowledging it had always been unlikely Lemmer would expose himself to capture.

'The file is an asset to be traded, Max. Don't you understand? Those who have been bought can be sold. I told you before. This is about the future, not the past. It is the future I offered you. And you can still have it. I can give you Farngold in return for your services. You want to know about Farngold, don't you? You want to know what your father died for. I can tell you.'

'Nadia's already put that to me. I told her to go to hell. I tell you the same.'

'You will not learn the truth any other way.'

'We'll see about that.'

'Think about it. The offer remains open.'

'I don't—'

Max broke off. He had half-heard something that sounded like a gunshot. And it was obvious from Appleby's reaction he had heard it too.

'What was that?' he asked, pulling away from the telephone.

'I'm not sure,' said Appleby. 'We'd better check Political.'

Appleby set off. Max heard the burr of a dead line in the earpiece of the telephone. Lemmer had hung up. He headed after Appleby.

A dog was barking in one of the neighbouring houses, roused by the noise. Max and Appleby hurried towards the car. The was no sign of movement inside the vehicle.

The reason soon became clear. Political was dead, sprawled across the front seat of the car, his right wrist still handcuffed to the steering wheel, a splatter of blood and brain haloed around his head. A revolver lay close to the curled fingers of his left hand.

'Damn,' said Appleby. 'I should've searched the car. The gun must've been hidden under the dashboard.'

'You think he killed himself?'

'What else?'

'Lemmer mentioned Nadia. This could be her handiwork.'

As if to confirm Max's conjecture, a noise reached them through the darkness of a car driving away from somewhere not far off.

'It makes no difference.' Appleby sighed. 'He's dead either way.'

'There's worse,' said Max. 'Lemmer asserts that without Bostridge you'll never decode the contents of the file.'

'And you believe him?'

'He sounded as if he believed it.'

'And he's always right, isn't he?' Appleby slapped his hand down in frustration on the bonnet of the car. 'Damn it all to hell.'

GLANCING THROUGH THE WINDOWS OF C'S OFFICE AT SECRET Service Headquarters, Max noticed dawn was already lighting the London sky. It had been a sleepless night for many besides him and it did not promise to be a restful day. The shootings at 24 Glamorgan Street, the death of Political and the failure to apprehend Lemmer cast shadows that would stretch a long way into the future.

C had reproached neither Max nor Appleby for what they had done. He seemed relieved to be able to discuss the events with two men whose loyalty he could rely on. But those events gave him no cheer. His sombreness was that of someone who knew more questions were going to be asked of him than he could satisfactorily answer during the official deliberations that were bound to follow. 'This,' he had gloomily confided at one point, 'could finish us.'

By 'us' he meant the Secret Service he had more or less single-handedly created. Lemmer had nibbled away at it like a mouse presented with a cheese. How many holes there were only Lemmer knew. The answer was in their hands.

'D'you think he's right about Bostridge, Appleby?' C asked after a brief, mournful silence. 'Uniquely gifted and therefore irreplaceable?'

'Quite possibly, sir, yes.'

'What about Mrs Underwood?'

'I'm sure she'll do her best.'

'But it probably won't be good enough. Is that what you're saying?'

Appleby shrugged helplessly 'I don't know, sir.'

'And we have to worry one of Lemmer's people will be looking over her shoulder all the time, monitoring her progress?'

'We do, sir, yes.'

C emitted something between a groan and a sigh. 'I always took Political's air of knowing more than I did for natural super-ciliousness. Now I realize he was probably chuckling to himself at the knowledge that he was serving a different master. He and God knows who else. The Foreign Office will at least be relieved MI5 is compromised as well, so there'll be no crowing at the War Office. There'll be no crowing anywhere.'

C looked at Max with weary benignancy. 'You've done well, young man. Don't think because I'm downcast I don't appreciate the risks you've taken to open our eyes to the ugly truth. Appleby will try to persuade you to take some further risks on our behalf, if only because men we can trust absolutely – men such as you – are presently in short supply. But I want you to understand you're not obliged to agree. You've earned the right to leave us to clear up our own mess.'

'I mean to nail Lemmer, sir,' said Max, as clear as a blue sky in his own mind on the point.

C nodded gratefully. 'I'm glad to hear it.'

'The question is how,' said Appleby.

'Indeed,' said C. 'The hunt for traitors will threaten to consume the Service in the days and weeks ahead. I anticipate a summons from Lord Curzon as soon as he receives reports of what's occurred. Assuming he leaves me in post – and I'm not counting on that in the circumstances – I shall need you as my right-hand man, Appleby, in rooting out the truth. Naturally, we'll put the best decipherers we can find onto the job of cracking Lemmer's code, but we have to assume they won't achieve early success. While they rack their brains, we'll have to subject every member of this Service to scrutiny, beginning with Political's own department. And we'll have to share information with MI5 and Admiralty Intelligence. There'll be no room for inter-service rivalry. I suspect Special Branch will become involved as well. It won't be agreeable work. But it has to be done. Can I rely on you?'

269

Appleby, whose expression suggested he was under no illusions about the scale of the tasks ahead, nodded grimly. 'Yes, sir.'

'Now, as to Lemmer, what do we think he's up to? Why did he want the Grey File so badly? It's disturbing to suppose he had so many people working for him that he'd forgotten who some of them were.'

'It would've been risky to let Commander Schmidt hold onto it,' said Appleby. 'Sooner or later, he'll leave Scapa Flow. Lemmer couldn't afford to wait until then.'

'It was more than that,' put in Max. 'It's about what he does next. "Those who have been bought can be sold." That's what he said.'

'But what exactly does that mean?'

'Maybe he plans to turn freelance,' said Appleby. 'Sell the information his agents obtain for him to whoever's willing to pay for it.'

'Or maybe he plans to sell his agents as a job lot,' Max suggested, suddenly realizing how such a scheme could easily commend itself to a man such as Lemmer: a cynic, a manipulator, a grand puppeteer. 'That would explain why he needed the Grey File so urgently. To show it to a prospective buyer. To display the goods on offer.'

'Yes,' said C thoughtfully. 'I believe you may have it, young man.'

'Sell it to who?' asked Appleby.

'One of the powers represented in Paris,' C answered, still in a thoughtful vein.

'But everyone's represented in Paris, except Germany and their allies.'

'Even Germany's represented now, Appleby.'

'Then we need someone there to find out who the prospective buyer might be, sir.'

'Agreed. Which you're no doubt about to say brings us to our young friend here.'

Appleby leant forward intently in his chair and stabbed the air with the stem of his pipe. 'Political based his trumped-up case against me on information from inside the German delegation attributed to Anna Schmidt. She's obviously still working for Lemmer. The letter she wrote to her husband proves it. Bostridge

270

referred to cables Lemmer sent her from China early last year. He said the pair had . . . what was it?'

'A private code within the code,' said Max.

'Exactly. And some of the cables mentioned the Grey File. Just a phrase to us at the time, of course. But Lemmer told you, didn't he, Max, that he'd double-coded the contents?'

'Yes.'

'Who'd process new material for the file – who'd encode it – while he was in the Far East?'

'Anna Schmidt.'

'So, she knows the code. And she's waiting for Lemmer in Paris, to play her part in this . . . auction.'

'I'll go,' said Max, answering the question that had not yet been put to him.

'You can't go *officially*, Max,' said C. 'You'd be answerable to Jefferies. Political nominated him to replace Appleby, so he's inherently suspect. He'll be recalled for questioning, of course, but as things stand I can't be entirely confident of anyone I send in his place. You'll have to operate alone.'

Max shrugged. 'It's how I prefer it.'

'And you'll have to operate *quickly*,' said Appleby 'Lemmer's not likely to let the grass grow under his feet.'

'I can leave straight away.'

'It might be best if you did,' said C. 'Inquiries may be launched that I can't control. There may be attempts to detain you here if you linger.'

'The German delegation is housed at the Hôtel des Réservoirs in Versailles,' said Appleby. 'How you're to gain access to Frau Schmidt I don't know. Political's contact within the delegation is almost certainly working for Lemmer.'

C flipped open a file on his desk. 'Otto Krenz. Private secretary to their finance specialist, Theodor Melchior. I agree with Appleby, Max. Krenz is tainted by association with Political.'

'That doesn't matter,' said Max boldly. 'I don't intend to hide from Lemmer. He claims he still wants me to work for him. My best chance of getting close to Anna Schmidt is to let him think I'm willing to consider it.'

'That'll be a dangerous game,' said Appleby in a tone suggesting he knew his warning would be in vain.

'But there's no other game to play, is there?'

Appleby looked at Max and shook his head. 'No. But watch out for Nadia Bukayeva. There's nothing she's not capable of.'

'You believe Miss Bukayeva killed Political rather than that he shot himself?' asked C.

'I do, sir, yes. And there's Meadows to worry about as well. He's on the loose somewhere.'

'It seems we can give you little in the way of encouragement, Max,' said C, smiling wanly. 'Fortunately, you don't appear to need much.'

'I'll give it my best, sir.'

'We can have you on a nine-fifteen express to Paris,' said Appleby.

'That suits me.'

'You'll escort him to the station, Appleby?' asked C.

'Yes, sir. We'll go via the Athenaeum so I can retrieve the negatives.'

'Yes. We must have them. Though without the code . . .' C cast Max an impenetrable glance. It bestowed no great confidence. But any scepticism he felt was buried deep. 'I can offer you a hearty breakfast before you go, Max. We have a Scottish cook. Breakfast is really the only meal she has any talent for. Shall we go and have some?'

NORMAL LIFE HAD RESUMED IN PARIS NOW MAY DAY HAD passed. The concourse of the Gare St-Lazare was bustling with commuters, some of whom had time to sit at one of the tables outside the station café and peruse newspaper reports of the previous day's disorders over coffee and a croissant. Among them were Sam Twentyman and Schools Morahan, whose newspapers served mostly to camouflage their frequent scans of the crowds in search of a Japanese face: that of the indispensable Mr Yamanaka.

He contrived to appear in the end from a corner of the station they could not see, shortly after Morahan had complained he was late, though by no more than five minutes.

He too was clutching a newspaper, along with an umbrella and a briefcase. He was wearing an overcoat that appeared to be a couple of sizes too big for him and an expression of suppressed apprehensiveness.

'Mr Twentyman,' he greeted Sam, joining them at their table. 'Who is this gentleman?'

'Schools Morahan,' said Morahan, offering his hand.

Yamanaka gave a formal little half-bow as he shook Morahan's hand. 'You are Travis Ireton's partner,' he said with a frown.

'Ex-partner.'

'I see.'

'Schools and I are working together, Mr Yamanaka,' said Sam. 'We need your help.'

'Then you will have it. Mr Twentyman has explained that Commissioner Kuroda is my master, Mr Morahan?'

'He has. You don't dance to Count Tomura's tune, then?'

'Ah. He is my superior. I dance, as you say, if he tells me to. But he is not my master.'

'He mustn't hear anything of this.'

'He will not.'

'How are things between your delegation and the Chinese right now, Mr Yamanaka?'

'Ah. You have heard there is . . . friction . . . over Shantung?'

'A little more than that is what I've heard.'

'Yes. The Chinese are angry. They do not believe the assurance they have been given that Shantung will eventually be restored to them. They blame President Wilson for the bargain he struck with my lord Saionji. I hear the President has been given extra body-guards in case there is an attempt on his life. There are many Chinese students in Paris. Some of them are very . . . hot-headed.'

'What about Saionji? Has he been given extra bodyguards?'

'No, no. My lord Saionji is not a fearful man.'

'Maybe he should be.'

'Maybe so. But . . .' Yamanaka glanced at Sam. 'We should not sit here too long in public view like this, Mr Twentyman. What help do you need from me?'

'We've got a Japanese document we need you to translate.'

'It may have been stolen from your delegation's hotel, Mr Yamanaka,' said Morahan. 'Or from Saionji's residence.'

'Stolen by whom?'

'Le Singe,' said Sam in an undertone.

Yamanaka looked alarmed.

'Is he thought to have stolen anything?' asked Morahan.

Yamanaka dropped his voice. 'Yes.'

'It's vital we know what it says.'

'I understand.'

'My apartment's near by. You can look at it there.'

'I do not have long. I have duties to perform. If I am missed . . .'

'How long?'

Yamanaka consulted his watch. 'I must be at the Hotel Bristol in one hour and a quarter.'

Morahan nodded. 'Let's step on it, then.'

As Sam and Morahan were hurrying out of the Gare St-Lazare with Yamanaka, Max and Appleby were boarding a taxi outside the Athenaeum in London. In his hand Appleby held the package Max had deposited with the club's porter the previous evening.

'Two, Whitehall Court, then Victoria station,' Appleby said to the driver.

'Right you are, sir.'

'We'll drop this off first,' Appleby said to Max as the taxi drew away. He closed the glass between them and the driver. 'There's time enough.'

'You don't have to come to the station with me, Horace,' said Max. 'I'm not a schoolboy being sent back after the holidays.'

'I'll come and there's an end of it.'

'Very well.'

'I've been thinking about what Lemmer said to you on the telephone.'

'Have you?'

'Would you have guessed he might be planning to sell his operation if he hadn't said, "Those who've been bought can be sold"?'

'Probably not.'

'I think he only said it to lure you back to Paris.'

'So do I.'

'You do?'

'Certainly.' Max craned his neck for a view of Nelson as they headed across Trafalgar Square. 'I decided to turn a blind eye to the possibility.'

'Why?'

'Because I have to go, whatever Lemmer has in mind for me.'

'He's well aware you'll never become his loyal lieutenant, Max. He wants you in Paris because it suits his purpose.'

'I know.'

'Yet still you're willing to go?'

'I have to go. And you have to send me.' Max looked around and smiled at Appleby. 'It really is as simple as that.'

The doings of Max's family had not crossed his mind in many days. If asked, he would have said they were doubtless pursuing their humdrum existences, his brother, sister-in-law and mother in Surrey, his uncle George in London, his nephew and niece at their places of genteel education.

He would have been well wide of the mark, of course, where his mother and uncle were concerned. George Clissold was just then being roused at the Hôtel Dieu in Paris by a nurse bearing a cup of coffee, for which he was grateful, though even more so on account of her radiant smile.

''Zere 'as been a telephone call, Monsieur Clissold,' the nurse announced. 'From 'ze 'Otel Mirabeau.'

'Tell them to hold my room,' George said, surprised by how hoarse his voice had become overnight.

''Zey did not call about your room. Your sister is 'zere.'

'She is?'

'And soon she will be 'ere. So, we must make you . . . *beaucoup arrangé, non?*'

'Win will soon be here,' George murmured to himself, staring dolefully into his coffee. He looked up at the nurse. 'Any chance of some whisky in this?'

'Veesky?' Judging by her horrified expression, the chance was slim.

'I'll settle for brandy.'

YAMANAKA WAS NOT A FAST READER, BUT HIS CONCENTRATION suggested he was a thorough one. Sam smoked his way through numerous cigarettes while he and Morahan waited for their translator to speak. Morahan spent most of the vigil standing by the window, gazing down at the street. Sam wondered if he feared they might be under observation, but was not disposed to ask. Dangers he could not avert were in his view best not dwelt upon.

Yamanaka marked the end of his reading with a pensive sip of tea. 'What time is it?' he asked.

'Half an hour before you're due at the Bristol,' said Morahan, perching himself on the edge of the armchair facing Yamanaka.

'What's it say, Mr Yamanaka?' asked Sam.

'Ah, what does it say?' Yamanaka drew breath. He looked nervous – intimidated by what he had read. 'I wish Commissioner Kuroda was here to advise me.'

'And I wish I read Japanese,' said Morahan. 'Just give us the gist.'

'Yes,' said Yamanaka. 'Of course. This document has come from the most secret files of Marquess Saionji, Mr Morahan, Mr Twentyman. It includes reports made to him by several people and notes in his own hand. Some of the reports are by Commissioner Kuroda. I have never seen any of this before. It is extremely sensitive. I am not authorized to have access to such material. Telling you what it contains is not allowed by my oath of loyalty to the Emperor.'

'But Kuroda said you'd give me any help I needed,' said Sam in alarm.

'Yes. He told me also. And I revere Commissioner Kuroda almost as a son reveres his father. So, I will tell you. It is not easy for me. But I *will* tell you.

'The document concerns Count Tomura Iwazu. Marquess Saionji appears to regard him as a threat to the harmony of the state, perhaps to the Emperor himself. He has assembled information about Count Tomura's life in order to assess the threat he may represent.

'Count Tomura is an unusual man. He was born into a princely family, like Marquess Saionji. But he has not followed a princely life. He has fought in wars and entered court service. That is as it should be. But he has also done business in the wider empire, some of it not respectable, according to this document – some not even legal.'

'Such as?' asked Morahan.

'It begins in Taiwan, colonized after the war against China. He seems to have been close to Goto Shinpei, Chief of Civil Affairs on the island at that time. Through the Bureau of Opium, he acquired large tracts of poppy-growing land. Then, after the war against Russia, he moved into Manshu–Manchuria. He has been a director of the South Manchurian Railway Company since its foundation. Its first president was Goto Shinpei. The SMR owns coal-mines as well as railways. Its reputation is for profit above everything else. It works its coolies hard – often to death. But it makes much money for men such as Count Tomura.

'He is active in Chosen also – Korea, as you would know it. He has been a director of the Oriental Development Company since its foundation.'

'Travis mentioned that to me,' said Morahan. 'And a lot more about the heroin and morphine trade – a real money-spinner for Tomura, apparently.'

'Oh yes. He is very wealthy. And ruthless. Marquess Saionji comments here on the strategy Count Tomura has proposed to Prime Minister Hara for dealing with unrest in Chosen following the March first riots in Keijo. His idea, according to this document, is to suppress opium selling in the colony and encourage the sale and consumption of morphine. You see what he means to do? Literally to drug the Koreans into submission. It is a horrible idea. But it is also very clever, since it will help the Japanese morphine-producing companies whose market has declined now the war is over and there are no more wounded soldiers to treat. Count Tomura is believed to be a large shareholder in Taisho Seiyaku, one of our biggest drug companies. Marquess Saionji calls this in his notes "unprincipled self-interest".

'But that is not the worst. Marquess Saionji also believes Count Tomura has a secret business partnership with Muraoka Iheiji, who is suspected of trafficking kidnapped Japanese women to brothels in Chosen, Taiwan and China. He has no proof, but there is a reference in his notes to a woman kidnapped from her home near Nagasaki and forced to work as a prostitute in Keijo who says she saw Muraoka with Count Tomura on several occasions.'

'Drugs, prostitution and sweated labour,' growled Morahan. 'He'd fit right in in Chicago.'

'If he is a gangster, Mr Morahan, he knows how to hide it. Maybe his political connections are the answer. It is clear from this document that Marquess Saionji believes they are. My lord Saionji is sometimes criticized for treating younger courtiers disdainfully – for not understanding them. When he was born, Japan was still a closed country. Now it is open to the world and the world is open to it. Count Tomura is of the same generation. But some would say he has moved more readily with the times. He has made allegiances with younger politicians. Konoe Fumimaro, who is a junior member of our delegation, is a contemporary and friend of Count Tomura's son, Noburo. Konoe is from a princely family and is spoken of as a future national leader. Count Tomura is also a close ally of Prime Minister Hara. Marquess Saionji notes that in his opinion the Prime Minister is unwise to trust Count Tomura. Clearly, Marquess Saionji does not.

'His reasons involve Commissioner Kuroda, who has long believed Count Tomura was involved in the 1891 assassination attempt against the Tsarevich. I know that because he has told me so. It is not directly mentioned in this document. But

Count Tomura's connections with the Dark Ocean Society are.'

'Travis told me Dark Ocean were responsible for the assassination of Queen Min,' said Morahan.

'Queen who?' asked Sam in bewilderment. The conspiratorial intricacies of oriental politics were beyond him.

'Empress Myongsong of Korea, Mr Twentyman,' Yamanaka explained. 'Assassinated in the Korean Royal Palace in October 1895. Both Commissioner Kuroda and Marquess Saionji fear Dark Ocean remains committed to the murder of its political enemies. But the society does not act openly. It works through intermediaries. That is why it is so difficult to deal with the organization. Some do not even believe it exists.'

'But it does, doesn't it?' asked Morahan.

'Yes.' Yamanaka nodded solemnly. 'Assuredly it does.'

'And Tomura's a member?'

'A *senior* member, according to this document. That is why these . . . pieces of paper . . . are so dangerous. They commit Marquess Saionji to the contention that Count Tomura is a criminal and a terrorist – a traitor to his country. There is no proof. There are only rumours and allegations and suggestive reports and interesting coincidences. But it is hard to read them and not to believe he is those things.'

'No wonder he's desperate to get hold of it.'

'Somehow he has learnt the document exists and that le Singe has stolen it. He will want to know how far my lord Saionji has taken this investigation – what he has discovered and what he suspects. And he will want to prevent anyone else finding out.'

'The question—'

'There is something else.' Yamanaka sat forward in his chair, wringing his hands together, as if trying to rub something off them. 'You should know this. Before he left Paris, Mr Maxted showed me a name on a piece of paper written in Japanese.'

'Farngold,' said Sam.

'Yes. Farngold. The name is mentioned here.'

'In what connection?' asked Morahan.

'In 1889, Baron Tomura, as he was then, married an Englishwoman called Matilda Farngold. Her father, Claude

280

Farngold, was a tea merchant in Yokohama. According to Commissioner Kuroda's report—'

'Hang on,' Sam cut in. 'Your boss told Max he'd never heard the name Farngold.'

'I cannot explain that,' said Yamanaka, who grimaced in embarrassment. 'Perhaps an order from Marquess Saionji compelled him to keep silent. In his report, he says it was rumoured Mr Farngold gave his daughter to Tomura for the sake of business advantages. But he died in a warehouse fire soon afterwards, so there was no advantage. And Matilda died two years later of complications after giving birth to Tomura's son.'

'Noburo Tomura is half-English?' exclaimed Morahan.

Yamanaka nodded. 'Evidently.'

'It's a sad story,' said Sam. 'But why should it matter now?'

'Because Matilda had a brother – John Farngold, known as Jack. Marquess Saionji asked Commissioner Kuroda to find for him as much information as he could about Jack Farngold following an incident in Keijo in December 1917.'

'What kind of incident?' asked Morahan.

'Farngold made trouble of some kind at Count Tomura's place of business in the city. There was a complaint to the police about him from the vice-president of the ODC. Farngold also made accusations against Count Tomura in an interview he gave to the *Keijo Shinpo* newspaper.'

'What accusations?'

'It is not clear. The interview was never published. Farngold was arrested shortly afterwards on the orders of Governor General Hasegawa and confined as a lunatic. He was later transferred to an asylum in Tokyo. Presumably, he is still there, though Commissioner Kuroda reports it is impossible to confirm his current whereabouts. He suggests Farngold may believe Count Tomura murdered his father. There was evidence of arson as the cause of the warehouse fire in which Claude Farngold died.'

'He waited a hell of a time to do something about it, didn't he?'

'Yes. Nearly thirty years. Commissioner Kuroda comments on the strangeness of that. There is altogether much mystery about Mr Jack Farngold. Marquess Saionji suggests in his notes it is a mystery that may undo Count Tomura. "We should find out what it is," he says.'

'He doesn't say how to, does he?' asked Sam.

Yamanaka shook his head. 'No. But Commissioner Kuroda may—'

He broke off, glancing apprehensively towards the hall. Someone had begun knocking at the door of the apartment.

Sam glanced anxiously at Morahan, who signalled them to keep silent and headed hurriedly out of the room.

'*Qui est-ce?*' they heard him call.

The muffled answer seemed to satisfy him. He opened the door. Craning his neck for a view, Sam saw the bobbing, bird-like figure of the concierge out on the landing.

She and Morahan conducted a whispered, urgent conversation in French, during which Morahan appeared to grow steadily more perturbed. Then, leaving her outside, he returned to the room, with a troubled look on his face.

'Bad news, gentlemen,' he announced. 'Madame Berton reports half a dozen Japanese men are waiting for us out in the street. We can't see them from this side of the building. One of them questioned her when she came back from shopping. Judging by her description, I'd say it was Noburo Tomura.'

Yamanaka was visibly shocked. 'Tomura Noburo? Here?'

'Seems so.'

'But . . . how?'

'I'd guess you were followed. They must've been keeping an eye on you as Kuroda's right-hand man. Whoever did the following would have to be an expert, though. I spotted nothing. The other possibility is they somehow learnt my address and had a lookout posted who alerted them to our arrival. It doesn't much matter which, does it? They're here.'

'What did Madame Berton tell them?' asked Sam.

'Nothing. But that won't have fooled them. I reckon Tomura's capable of working out why we'd need the services of a Japanese speaker. If he suspects we have the document, he won't let us leave with it.'

'Then what do we do?'

'You two wait here. I'm going downstairs with Madame Berton. She'll let me use her telephone.'

'Who are you going to call?'

Morahan smiled tightly. 'The cavalry.'

WINIFRED, LADY MAXTED, WAS SO RELIEVED TO FIND HER brother alive and reasonably well she forgot at first to be angry with him. George was reminded of her bedside attention when he had contracted diphtheria as a young man. The danger of infection had not deterred her in the least. Indomitability had been part of her character since childhood.

She expected – and he supplied – a detailed account of what had happened to him, but he held back the nationality and name of the man responsible for his kidnapping because he knew she would be horrified and sparing his sister's feelings had always figured highly among the principles George chose to live by.

'The cylinder-seals probably are fakes, Win,' he explained. 'But that wasn't why Soutine proved so elusive. He was in the secrets-selling game and the people who killed him badly want a secret back that he had his boy steal from them.'

'This Arab youth, le Singe?'

'He's the one.'

'And your friends, Mr Morahan and Mr Twentyman, are look-ing for him?'

'They may already have found him. I expect they'll do their best to keep me out of it from now on. I'm not safe on the streets of Paris, it seems.'

'Your poor finger,' said Winifred, caressing the wad of bandaging around the forefinger from which the nail had been pulled. 'I'd never have asked you to come to Paris if I'd had the least idea such a thing would occur.'

'Of course you wouldn't. I wouldn't have agreed to come if I had either!'

'Oh, I suspect you would. You're over-protective of me, George, and you always have been.'

'Rubbish.'

'Now, these kidnappers. Are the police hopeful of catching them?'

'I don't know. I told Commissioner Zamaron as much about them as I could.'

'Well, I trust that's more than you've told me. Were they French?'

'Er, no.'

'What, then?'

George grimaced. The conversation had reached the delicate stage where he had known it was bound to arrive sooner or later. He had to tell her, of course. He had to tell her, however painful she would find it to hear.

But pain, ironically, was what Winifred at once thought he was suffering from. 'Are your ribs aching very badly, George?'

'No, no. They're fine as long as I don't laugh or cough, so no jokes or cigars, there's a good girl. You're going to have to take this on the chin, I'm afraid, Win. I think Henry had other business with Soutine besides selling the cylinder-seals. I think he wanted to buy the information that ultimately got Soutine killed. Maybe Henry too. The people who did for Soutine and kidnapped me, you see . . . are Japanese.'

'Japanese?'

'Count Tomura, Win. He's a member of the Japanese delegation to the peace conference. His son Noburo led the gang I was held by.'

'*Tomura?*'

Winifred looked shocked and dismayed. And somewhere beneath that outward reaction, George sensed, she was also deeply saddened. He had led her into a shadow she believed she had long ago stepped out of for ever. 'I'm sorry.'

'Count Tomura is here? In Paris? His son too?'

'Yes.'

'And Henry engaged this man Soutine to . . . to enquire into their affairs?'

'I believe so, yes.'

'But why? Why would he do that?'

'I don't know. But I suspect, well . . .' George shrugged help-lessly. 'It has something to do with the Farngolds.'

'No.' Winifred shook her head. 'That can't be.'

'I wish it couldn't, Win, but Noburo Tomura asked me while I was being held if the name meant anything to me. I didn't mention it to Morahan or Sam Twentyman or Commissioner Zamaron. No one knows about it. But he did ask me. I denied it, of course. That's actually what cost me my fingernail. Young Tomura wanted to be absolutely certain of my ignorance. I made sure he was.'

'Oh, George, I'm sorry.' Winifred frowned pityingly at him. 'You shouldn't have been dragged into this.'

'It can't be helped. And don't think holding my tongue was an act of bravery. It was clear to me he'd have killed me if I'd admitted knowing anything on that front.'

'What can there be to know – or for Count Tomura to be afraid of – after all this time?'

'It could have something to do with Jack Farngold.'

'Who?'

'Matilda Farngold had a brother, Win.' George gave his sister an apologetic look. 'I came across him while I was working for Jardine's.'

'Why didn't you tell me this sooner?'

'There seemed no cause to trouble you with it. And no reason why you should ever need to worry about him. He worked for Jardine's too, as a captain in their Far East merchant fleet. In the ordinary way of things, I'd never have known he existed. But during my last tour of duty in Shanghai before I left the company – 1912, it would have been – I was sent to Weihaiwei to sort out a problem.'

'Where?'

'A British enclave on the Shantung peninsula. Jardine's did a lot of business there. A Jardine's employee – Captain Farngold – had been arrested after a break-in at the offices of the Oriental Development Bank. The bank was Japanese-owned. No cash was stolen, but documents belonging to them were found in Farngold's possession. The story given to me by the police was confusing. They didn't know what was in the documents, which had already been returned to the bank. Farngold refused to explain himself. The police rather half-heartedly suggested he'd drunk too much in one of the bars by the port and broken in as some kind of lark. It was an absurd idea, really, but there you are. They were prepared to drop charges, as was the bank, if Jardine's guaranteed Farngold would leave Weihaiwei and never come back. Head Office had already made it clear I was to put a stop to any scandal and get him off the company's books. So, that's what I did.

'I had one stilted conversation with him before he was released. He had no idea who I was, of course. The name Clissold would have meant nothing to him. I was just the pen-pusher who'd been sent to salvage Jardine's good name. He'd worked for them longer than I had. Twenty or thirty years. According to our records, he was in his late forties, I think, though he looked older. A life at sea can have that effect. But I had the impression some other trouble had worn him down as well: the trouble that had caused him to break into the bank.'

'Are you sure he was Matilda's brother?' Winifred asked suddenly, grasping at a straw. 'The name might have been a coincidence.'

'The police showed me what they'd found in his pockets. He was carrying a photograph of two children in his wallet. A boy and a girl. The boy looked about nine, the girl about seven. She was carrying a doll, I remember. He was dressed in a sailor-suit. Someone had written on the back, *Jack and Tiddy 1874.* The ages were right. The names were right. He was her brother, Win, no question about it.'

'What happened to him after he was released?' Winifred asked hollowly.

'I don't know. There were plenty of other shipping lines who'd have taken him on. I put him on a ferry to Port Arthur and that was the last I saw of him.'

'You asked him why he'd broken into the bank's offices?'

'Of course.'

'And what the document was he'd stolen?'

'Yes. But he told me nothing. "I had my reasons." That was all he'd say. After he'd left, though . . .'

'What?'

'I made a few discreet enquiries. One of the directors of the Oriental Development Bank turned out to be Count Tomura. It was plain to me that's why Farngold had stolen whatever the document was.'

'But it was in Japanese, surely. How would he know what it said?'

'A good question. And there's an answer. I had a word with the first officer of Farngold's ship before it left port without him. He said Farngold was fluent in Japanese. He'd taught himself the language, apparently. This fellow had seen him reading local newspapers when they called at Japanese ports. Self-taught Japanese? That's close to impossible, unless you dedicate yourself to the task over many years.'

'Why would he do that?'

'There's only one explanation, isn't there? Know thine enemy. He had – maybe he still has – Count Tomura in his sights.'

'Revenge?'

'His father and his sister. He might blame Tomura for both their deaths.'

'But what has this to do with Henry? How would he even know who Jack Farngold was?'

'It's not so unlikely Henry would know Matilda Farngold had a brother, is it?'

'No,' Winifred admitted.

'As for how he'd know the brother was pursuing Tomura, I've no idea. But there must have been vital information in the material le Singe stole from the Japanese delegation – vital enough to bring Tomura all the way here. If James ever makes this connection . . .'

'Where *is* James?'

'No one knows. Not in Paris, though, which is some kind of blessing. But he may return at any time.'

Winifred drew a deep breath and braced herself. The shock had passed already, George judged. She had accommodated the news. She had done what she always did: accepted reality. 'We must do our best to prevent this harming anyone else, George. Henry is dead and Jack Farngold is beyond our help. I will not allow James to waste his life on a crusade against Count Tomura.'

'You won't tell him the truth, then?'

Winifred looked her brother in the eye. 'Absolutely not.'

'He may find it out for himself.'

'Not if I can prevent it.' She nodded solemnly to herself. 'And I believe I can.'

MADAME BERTON'S TELEPHONE WAS IN THE TINY ROOM – scarcely larger than a sentry box – from which she supervised arrivals and deliveries to the building. Morahan squeezed the door shut behind him and stood while he made the call.

He was mightily relieved when he heard Commissioner Zamaron was in his office, since there was no one else at the Préfecture likely to help him. He was put straight through.

'Léon?' Morahan had been on first-name terms with Zamaron since helping him conclude a clutch of murder inquiries in one night a month earlier. The assistance he had rendered should, he calculated, guarantee him a helping hand now, when he so badly needed one.

'Schools.' Zamaron sounded oddly stiff, his normal jauntiness of tone noticeably absent. 'Are you in difficulties, *mon ami*?'

'What makes you ask?'

'*L'intuition. Aussi . . .*' Zamaron's voice dropped to a whisper. '*Le Deuxième Bureau.* They have been to see *le Préfet.*'

'About me?'

'*Oui.* Count Tomura, joint deputy head of the Japanese delegation, has spoken to the *Ministre des Affaires Etrangères.* You must understand. This is all above my head. It is said you have stolen documents belonging to the delegation. *Le Ministre* has ordered full cooperation with the Japanese in order to retrieve the documents and to place you under arrest. Monsieur Twentyman also. Is he with you?'

'Better I don't say.'

290

'*C'est vrai.* I told them there were reasons to believe people close to the Japanese delegation – and therefore close to Count Tomura – murdered Soutine and kidnapped Monsieur Clissold. But they did not listen, Schools. They did not want to. There has been a *marché*. How would you say? A deal.'

'I guess I shouldn't be surprised.'

'What is it you want me to do?'

'It doesn't matter.' If there was to be a rescue party, it would not be coming from the police. That was graphically clear. They would merely serve as reinforcements for Noburo Tomura. Zamaron had his orders. And they were the sort of orders he would have to obey if called upon. 'Thanks for putting me in the picture, Léon.'

'I am sorry, Schools.'

Morahan did not doubt he was. But in sorrow there was no salvation. He hung up.

Lady Maxted was well aware that her arrival at the Hotel Bristol had caused something close to consternation among the members of the Japanese delegation she had so far encountered. They were evidently unused to visitations from unaccompanied English-women, especially those of Lady Maxted's age and pedigree. Her request to see Count Tomura Iwazu, which had carried a finely judged element of peremptoriness, had thrown them into confusion. Should they brush her off? Or should they ascertain Count Tomura's wishes in the matter? His ogreish reputation made the decision a difficult one. But in the end they did what Lady Maxted had relied on them doing. They undertook to inform their master of her presence.

Whether Count Tomura was actually on the premises was not made clear to her. She was escorted to a first-floor room over-looking Place Vendôme and asked to wait there. It was furnished as a writing-room, thickly curtained, austerely decorated and cold at that hour of the morning.

She took it as a sign that her wait might be lengthy when a grey-waistcoated young man came in, lit the fire for her and asked if she would like some coffee. She accepted.

Tomura was coming. She did not doubt it. He knew all that had occurred and would understand what had brought her to Paris. She imagined he was no keener than she was to have the past disinterred. He had doubtless kept as much from his son as she had from hers. If a line was to be drawn, it was for them to draw it.

Oh yes. Tomura was coming.

'What d'you want, Morahan?' Carver growled down the telephone line.

'A favour.'

'I'm out of stock.'

'I did you a good turn with the name of our contact at the Hôtel des Réservoirs. That must have won you a lot of credit with *le Deuxième Bureau*.'

'For which your reward was me going easy on you and Ireton. Well, I'm going easy. Though if the *flics* catch Blachette and he squeals . . .'

Morahan could almost see Carver smirking and shrugging.

'I'm in a hole, Frank. I need a hand to get out of it.'

'What kinda hole?'

'Noburo Tomura and a bunch of ex-sumos have my apartment staked out. I'm here now. I need a safe passage.'

'I'll bet you do. *Le Deuxième Bureau* have already been on to me. Stolen documents, Schools. That's the story. And Count Tomura kicking up a storm. Twentyman was mentioned. With you, is he?'

'Yes. Along with a junior member of the Japanese delegation.'

'Right. Plus the documents?'

'I just need to get us out of here in one piece. You could arrange that. If you wanted to.'

'What's in the documents?'

'I can't discuss that on the telephone.'

'But you could discuss it? Later?'

'Maybe.'

'OK.' There was a pause. Then: 'Here's what I can do for you, Schools. You and the documents, under my escort. Twentyman and your tame Jap will have to fend for themselves, though. I can bale out a fellow American. That's as far as it goes.'

'It's not far enough.'

292

'Are you sure about that? The Brits will look after Twentyman. And the Jap's not your problem, is he? You could come out of this set up nice and sweet if you play your cards right.'

'You reckon so?'

'I do.' Carver gave Morahan a chance to mull his offer over before adding, 'What d'you say?'

Morahan said nothing, beyond a weary sigh. He hung up.

'Schools Morahan will work something out,' said Sam in an effort to calm his companion's nerves. Yamanaka was pacing the room, rubbing his hands together and taking in ever shallower breaths. 'He outwitted Tomura before. He can do it again.'

'It does not matter ... whether he can or not,' Yamanaka stammered. 'If Count Tomura believes I have acted against him, I am ... finished.'

'It can't be as bad as that.'

Yamanaka looked despairingly at Sam. 'You do not understand. I have read the file. He will know I have read it. He will kill me, Mr Twentyman. Today. Tomorrow. One day soon. He will *kill* me.'

Sam could think of nothing to say to that. He lit a cigarette and offered Yamanaka one. It was eagerly accepted. The pair stood together by the window. The street below was empty. But round the corner, at the front of the building, it was, they knew, a different matter.

'I have thought about the document,' murmured Yamanaka.

'And what have you thought?' Sam prompted.

'That my lord Saionji is not a careless man. If le Singe was able to steal it from his residence, which is where it must have been kept, it was because Marquess Saionji allowed him to steal it – wanted him to steal it.'

'That doesn't make any sense.'

'But it does, Mr Twentyman. Oh, it docs.'

'Call me Sam.'

'Very well. I am Eisaku.'

They shook hands in a gesture of solidarity Sam found faintly disquieting. It was the kind of solidarity bred by the contemplation of extinction.

'I believe Marquess Saionji anticipates Count Tomura may try to remove him from his path to power.'

'Remove him how?"

'By killing him.' Yamanaka dragged fretfully on his cigarette. 'Dark Ocean has a history of killing its enemies. And Count Tomura is Dark Ocean. Marquess Saionji stands for the old ways Tomura and his kind wish to sweep away. And he is respected. The Emperor listens to what he says. His assassination – blamed on someone else: the Koreans, the Chinese – would advance Tomura's cause. It may be Tomura knows Marquess Saionji has a file detailing his dirty secrets. With the authority granted him by Prime Minister Hara, he could have hoped to secure the file and destroy it. Then he would be free to strike at my lord Saionji. But with the file missing, in unknown hands . . .'

'He couldn't strike in case the contents of the file ended up in the newspapers.'

'Exactly so . . . Sam. And if that is so . . .'

'We've done Tomura a big favour by finding it.'

'Yes.' Yamanaka took the longest drag yet on his cigarette. 'We have done more than he could have hoped. And for our reward . . . he will kill us. Before he kills my lord Saionji.'

'Schools?' said Malory. "Where are you?'

'My apartment. Sam and Yamanaka are with me.'

'Did Yamanaka translate the document for you?'

'He did. Now I know why Tomura *père et fils* are so desperate to get hold of it. And Tomura junior has the building staked out. It looks like Yamanaka was followed. Or else Travis gave them my address.'

'He's angry enough with you to have done that. But how are you going to get out?'

'Is Travis there?'

'No. I'm expecting him within the hour.'

'Then I'll have to ask you to pass on a message for me, Malory. And it's not one Travis will enjoy hearing.'

'What is it?'

'The short version? If I go down, he goes down with me.'

'What exactly does that mean, Schools?'

'It means he'll have to save me to save himself. And he won't have long to think about it.'

COUNT TOMURA IWAZU ENTERED THE ROOM WITH A SOFT-footed hint of stealth. He was a bullishly built man of sixty, straight-backed and square-shouldered. He wore his morning-suit as if it were a military uniform: every crease precise, every button just so. He had once been handsome, but age had dragged at his features and one of his ears was disfigured. A stray bullet or an errant blade had robbed him of half of it. His eyes blazed with the pride his bearing confirmed. Except it was not pride so much as hauteur. Winifred clearly saw that as she looked at him. Count Tomura Iwazu almost quivered with the force of his own certainty – in himself and the justness of his wishes.

'Lady Maxted,' he said, his voice gruff, his accent a curious hybrid of Japanese and aristocratic English. He bowed faintly to her.

'Thank you for agreeing to see me, Count Tomura,' she responded. 'You must be very busy.'

'You are right. I have many duties to perform.'

'But you have found time for me. I am grateful.'

Tomura took a curving route towards her, delaying a direct confrontation. 'What has brought you to Paris, Lady Maxted?'

'Complications arising from my husband's death.'

'I heard of that. My condolences to you.'

'Thank you.'

He reached the mantelpiece and glanced at the painting above it: a dark oil of a hunting scene, with dogs ravening a fallen stag. Winifred saw bared teeth and rent flesh, but heard only the crackle of the fire and the deep, powerful breaths of her companion.

'Do you remember when we first met, Count? It was at an Imperial garden party, was it not?'

Tomura looked at her, but did not reply. He had never been a loquacious man and Winifred did not propose to attempt anything amounting to a conversation with him. Much of what needed to be established between them did not need to be spoken.

'Don't worry. I haven't asked to see you in order to reminisce about Tokyo society thirty years ago.'

'It has changed little.'

'As have you.'

'You also, Lady Maxted. I saw the steel in you then. And I see it now.'

'Not long after that garden party, there was an attempt on the life of the Foreign Minister. Do you remember? A dreadful business. What was his name?'

'Okuma.'

'A bomb was thrown at his carriage. He lost a leg, didn't he?'

'Yes.'

'The would-be assassin committed suicide. His name was . . .'

'Kurushima.'

'Your memory is excellent, Count. Henry told me Kurushima was a member of a secret organization called . . . I can't recall. But no doubt you can.'

'*Genyosha*.'

'What would that be in English?'

'Dark Ocean.'

'Ah. Yes. That was it. Were they connected with the subsequent assassination attempt against the Tsarevich?'

Tomura said nothing. He stared at her expressionlessly for fully half a minute. Then: 'No.'

'No. Of course they weren't. Nor you with them.'

Another silence followed, an altogether tenser one. Then: 'What did you say, Lady Maxted?'

'When will you be returning to Japan?'

'When will you be returning to England?'

Winifred smiled. 'I believe I asked first.'

297

Tomura did not smile. 'What do you want with me, Lady Maxted?'

'An assurance that you and your son will go back to Japan on the next available ship.'

Tomura gave a short, barking, derisive laugh. 'I think your husband's death must have affected your judgement, Lady Maxted.'

'It has. It has greatly sharpened it. You were not in Paris when Henry died, of course. But I understand your son was. Then *my* son, James, came here to find out why his father was murdered.'

'Was he murdered?'

'He was enquiring into your affairs, Count. This is known to both of us, as is the reason.'

'The reason?' Tomura puffed out his considerable chest and glared at her. He looked as if he wanted to snarl. But he did not. 'You should be careful what you say, Lady Maxted.'

'I will be. I want to protect my son, as I feel sure you want to protect your son. On that at least we can agree, as parents, can we not?'

Tomura went on glaring. 'Yes.'

'I shall tell you something I have told no one else. Henry was in St Petersburg at the time. I was alone at home in Surrey. This was a couple of years before the war. I received a visit from a Mr Jack Farngold.'

Tomura visibly flinched. 'Farngold?'

'Yes, Count. Jack Farngold. You know who he is, of course.'

'I do not believe you.'

'He told me many disturbing things. He could not prove they were all true. He said he needed to carry out further investigations before he could be sure.' She paused for a moment, then continued. 'You're not going to ask sure of what?'

'He never visited you.'

'It was a few months before he stole some documents relating to you from the offices of the Oriental Development Bank in Weihaiwei.'

Tomura was rattled now. Winifred felt sure of it, well though he hid it. As a seasoned warrior, he knew better than to let an

298

adversary see what was in his mind. 'I know nothing of this,' he growled.

'I believe the information Henry was seeking here in Paris concerned the matters Jack Farngold discussed with me. I never passed on what he said to Henry. I did not believe it was in his best interests – or those of my sons – for such matters to be raked over . . . or exposed to public scrutiny.'

'Public scrutiny?' Tomura took a step towards her. 'Are you threatening me, Lady Maxted?'

'Threatening you would be foolhardy, Count, in view of what tends to happen to those who do. I am explaining to you that our interests coincide – that neither of us has any wish to revisit the past or to make it possible for others to do so. The dead should stay buried and their secrets with them.'

'Your son, James . . .'

'Will seek to avenge his father's murder if he is pointed towards those who were responsible for it.'

'I was not responsible. Neither was my son.'

'Yet James could easily come to suspect otherwise, considering the lengths people close to you have gone to in order to find le Singe and a document he stole from the Japanese delegation.'

'You should go home to England, Lady Maxted.'

'Before I meet with a fatal accident? Where is Jack Farngold now, Count? Is he even still alive?'

'*Go home.*'

'Gladly. As soon as you've arranged to leave Paris yourself, with your son. You can't intimidate me, Count, and you'd be unwise to do me any harm. It would look far too suspicious for the authorities to ignore, in light of what happened to Henry. No doubt the Emperor would afford you his protection. But you'd certainly be recalled to Japan. And then . . .'

Tomura said nothing. His breathing was deep and audible.

'I gather you've succeeded in negotiating the Japanese retention of Shantung, or at any rate in obliging Marquess Saionji to negotiate it. Perhaps you think he is an inconvenient relic of the Meiji regime you and the current Emperor would be well rid of.'

'You speak of things of which you are ignorant.'

299

'I met Marquess Saionji once, a long time ago. Not in Tokyo. I believe he was out of the country during Henry's posting there. Certainly we never encountered him. But some years earlier he was the Emperor's Minister Extraordinary in Vienna. Henry was only a humble third secretary then and I was a humble third secretary's wife. Still, I was introduced to Marquess Saionji at an embassy reception. A charming man. Quite charming.'

'You were never humble, Lady Maxted.'

'Then I apologize, Count. For I know how highly you value humility in a woman.'

'If you were Japanese . . .'

'You would strike me dead and suffer no ill consequences. But I am not Japanese. I am an Englishwoman well capable of lodging a statement with her solicitor for publication in the event of her unexpected death. Such a statement might include speculation that an interested party could see Chinese unrest at Japan's retention of Shantung as perfect camouflage for the murder of the statesman who negotiated that retention. It might name that party. And it might detail much else known to her about him.'

Tomura's glare had softened. He looked surprised now – surprised and impressed. 'Are you familiar with the writings of Sun-Tzu, Lady Maxted?'

'I'm afraid not.'

Tomura gave her a tight, grim little smile. 'In many that would be a loss. But it seems you do not require the advice of Master Sun. "Weakness comes from preparing against attack," he wrote. "Strength comes from obliging your enemy to prepare against attack."'

Winifred allowed herself to smile too. 'It sounds eminently sensible advice.'

'We understand each other?'

'I believe we do.'

'Then we can part. And we will not need to meet again.'

'I'm glad to hear it.'

'Of course.' He bowed to her then, turned and stalked towards the door.

MORAHAN INSPECTED NOBURO TOMURA'S CREW THROUGH THE window of Madame Berton's ground-floor parlour. There were more of them than had been lying in wait for him and Sam outside the Hôtel Dieu. Tomura had brought an extra carload. They were hefty, watchful customers: the patient kind. Morahan rated his chances of getting past them without outside help as poor. If he was forced to try it, he would wait until dark.

But waiting was inevitable however the issue was to be forced. If Ireton came to their assistance, it would not be for some time. During that time Morahan would have to decide whether calling in the police, even though they would arrest him and his companions and seize the documents, was better than making a break for it.

It was certainly safer. And he had the welfare of Sam and Yamanaka to consider. He turned away from the window and spoke to Madame Berton in his best French, telling her to admit no visitors without consulting him first. Unless Ireton came, on his own. '*Ireton,*' she repeated carefully. '*Je comprends tout à fait, Monsieur Morahan.*'

He hoped she did understand. He truly did.

Malory was scarcely less anxious, though under no personal threat, as she waited for Ireton to arrive at 33 Rue des Pyramides. He had no diaried engagements, but his comings and goings were always erratic.

The newspapers were back in print, however, which supplied her with interesting reading matter. *Le Figaro* made much of the previous day's disturbances – *"les affrontements"*, as a headline termed them – but Malory was interested in less prominently reported events. It was reliably believed, according to *le Figaro*, that Japan had secured what it wanted in Shantung. An outraged reaction in China was predicted. There had already been an outraged reaction in Paris, with a protest meeting of Chinese students at which some speakers had demanded a violent response.

Malory wondered if Chen Sen-mao, the person George Clissold had heard Noburo Tomura discussing, was one of those students. Marquess Saionji, as head of the Japanese delegation, took the blame as well as the credit for the Shantung settlement. And Noburo's father hated Saionji and his kind: the old guard, the traditionalists, the men of peace. He wanted them all – but Saionji in particular – out of his way.

According to *le Figaro*, security for President Wilson, who stood accused of betraying the Chinese, had been tightened. There was no mention of security for Marquess Saionji.

Footsteps on the stairs suddenly captured Malory's attention. She laid aside the newspaper and pricked her ears. But no, it was not Ireton. She did not recognize the tread. A visitor, then, apt to be disappointed.

And a visitor it was, though not one Malory would ever have expected. She had never seen Tomura Iwazu in the flesh till now, but she knew him at once. He closely resembled the photographs of him that had appeared in the press at the time of the Russo–Japanese War and the intervening fifteen years had only weathered him to a more rugged version of his indomitable self. The Butcher of Port Arthur stood in the doorway, grasping a silver-topped cane and surveying her haughtily.

'Ireton,' he said, in a simple statement of his requirement. His voice carried the tone of a muffled cannon.

'He's not here,' she responded.

'When will he be here?'

'Soon . . . I think.'

'You think?' He stepped into the office and looked at her more closely. 'You are Malory Hollander,' he stated plainly.

'You know my name?'

'As well as you know mine.'

'I don't believe we've ever met, Count. I can't imagine how we might have.'

'We might have, very easily, Miss Hollander. We both know this.'

'I'm sure I don't.'

'Would you like me to tell you how Shimizu Junzaburo is?'

Malory was on the point of asking 'Who?' in a puzzled manner. But the pretence turned to ashes in her mouth. Denial would somehow, she felt certain, weigh heavily on her conscience. So she said nothing.

'He is not well. Here.' Tomura tapped his temple. 'You made him dream, Miss Hollander. And then you stole the dream from him.'

'I stole nothing.' Memories Malory had striven to suppress flooded into her mind. For some reason, the clearest of them was eating riceballs with Junzaburo at Yudanaka hot springs. She could see the expression on his face as if the sunlight of that day was still shining on them. She swallowed hard. 'It was ... a misunderstanding.'

'You mean he did not understand you. That is certain. But you understood him, I think.'

'I don't wish to discuss this with you, Count. Forgive me, but it's none of your business. There are questions I could ask you that you wouldn't want to answer.'

'Is it true I drank blood from a Russian officer's skull after we took 203 Metre Hill in December of '04? You mean that kind of question, Miss Hollander?'

'No,' she replied coolly. 'Not that kind.'

'You know why Western men are so weak? It is because their women are so strong.'

'Do you wish to leave a message for Mr Ireton?'

'No. I wish to speak to him. And therefore I will wait for him. In his office.' He moved towards the door into the corridor that led to Ireton's office.

'You can't go in there.'

'Would you prefer me to wait with you?' He cast an oddly sympathetic glance at her. 'No? I thought not. He will not blame you, Miss Hollander. He would not expect you to defy me. Only

303

you and I will know that you could. Bring me coffee. Strong. Black.' He bowed faintly. 'Please.'

Sam took Morahan's announcement of his tactics rather better than Yamanaka, who sank into the gloom of one convinced a catastrophe was imminent. Sam, who would have conceded, if pressed, that it might well be, saw no merit in lamenting their situation. Morahan's argument for waiting – till nightfall if necessary – was unanswerable. And his ground-crew experience during the war made Sam an expert in the waiting department. Tomura and his men could not force their way into a Paris apartment building without the police being called. So, they would stay where they were. Which left Sam, Morahan and Yamanaka with little choice but to do the same.

'What can Mr Ireton do for us, Schools?' he asked mildly, once Yamanaka had calmed himself.

'Get us off the hook with Tomura senior.'

'But we have what Tomura senior wants.'

'Then we may have to give it up to save our necks. Marquess Saionji's a wily old bird. This won't be the only copy.'

'But we know all Tomura's dirty secrets now. He won't be happy about that, will he?'

'No,' put in Yamanaka.

'We can't *un*know them,' said Morahan. 'And I doubt they're *all* his secrets. There's going to have to be a compromise.'

'Tomura does not compromise,' said Yamanaka glumly.

'Everyone does if they're forced to,' Morahan asserted. 'Believe me.'

Sam for one was willing to believe him, however doubtful Yamanaka looked. The alternative was best not dwelt upon. 'Shall I brew some tea?' he suggested.

'Sure,' said Morahan. 'Let's all have some tea.'

MALORY SERVED TOMURA HIS COFFEE AND LEFT HIM TO IT, sitting by the fireplace in Ireton's office. It was as easy to disregard him as it was a large spider in the bath, but Malory did her best. She carried on with what little work she had to do for a distracted half-hour, trying to still her multiple anxieties. In this she was only partly successful.

Relief eventually arrived in the form of the long-awaited Travis Ireton. Malory had never before been so pleased to see her employer, to the extent that she paid little attention to his distracted state. He crossed immediately to the window and peered down suspiciously into the street. 'Now you see him, now you don't,' he murmured under his breath.

'Count Tomura is here to see you, Travis,' Malory announced. She had decided conveying Morahan's message to Ireton, urgent though it was, would have to be delayed until Tomura had left.

'*Count* Tomura?' Ireton rounded on her. 'Not the son?'

'No. Count Tomura Iwazu. He's in your office.'

'You let him into my office?'

'He's not an easy man to turn down.'

'God Almighty.' Ireton glared angrily at Malory, then appeared to decide reprimanding her was not as important as appeasing Tomura. He strode towards the door.

'I need to speak to you in private as soon as possible, Travis,' Malory called after him.

'First things first,' Ireton fired back as he left.

*

305

They were closeted in Ireton's office for the next twenty minutes or so. Malory made a couple of forays into the corridor to try to hear what they might be saying, but their voices were only audible as a low murmur. She did not feel she could leave her typewriter for long without running the risk of making Ireton wonder if she was eavesdropping. It had become apparent to her that he doubted her loyalty following Morahan's defection. And he was right to, of course.

Eventually, the door of Ireton's office opened. 'You're the boss,' she heard him say. He strode along the corridor and into her office, flourishing a piece of paper in his hand, which he slapped down on her desk. 'Bank this right away, Malory,' he said.

It was a cheque in the sum of $10,000, a much larger figure than Ireton Associates normally received from a client. Small wonder Ireton wanted it paid into his dollar account at the bank as soon as possible. Malory stared at it – and in particular Count Tomura's fluent English signature – in some surprise.

'Right away would mean now,' said Ireton sharply.

'Of course.'

She gathered herself together, fetched the paying-in book, slipped the cheque inside and stowed it in her purse.

Ireton was ready by then to help her on with her coat. 'I'll come out with you.'

Where he was going he did not explain. Nor did Malory feel able to ask, as Tomura chose that moment to join them.

'For my son,' he said, handing a letter with Japanese writing on the envelope to Ireton. 'It explains what he is to do.'

'I'll be sure to have him read it,' said Ireton, pocketing the letter.

'He will not act without my authority, Mr Ireton. You are nothing to him.' And nothing, Tomura's tone implied, to him either.

Ireton displayed no reaction to the slight. This did not surprise Malory. She knew her employer would tolerate being slighted all day for $10,000.

'Miss Hollander does not ask where you will find my son,' Tomura continued.

'She knows better than to ask,' said Ireton.

'Or perhaps she knows already.'

Ireton frowned suspiciously at Malory, uncertain what to make of Tomura's remark. But now was not the moment to pursue the point. 'We should be going,' he said.

And Tomura concurred. 'We should.'

They left the office, Malory locking up after them, and started down the stairs. Etiquette dictated she should lead the way. Nothing was said. The decisive rap of the ferrule of Tomura's cane on every other tread kept time with their footsteps, while Malory's mind raced to deduce what Tomura had instructed Ireton to do. She wanted to ask Ireton, but could not do so in Count Tomura's presence. It remained to be seen whether she would get the chance.

As she neared the street door, Count Tomura slipped past to open it for her. Who he was mocking – her, himself, Ireton – with this small display of chivalry was unclear. She smiled weakly at him in acknowledgement.

Then she stepped out through the doorway. And a man – small, gaunt-faced and grey-suited, flat cap worn low over his eyes – appeared suddenly in front of her.

'*Traître!*' he shouted, raising his arm.

In that instant she realized he was holding a gun and had thrown the accusation of treachery at one of her companions. 'Blachette,' she heard Ireton say. Of course. The man was Ireton's go-between at the Hôtel des Réservoirs, on the run from the police. 'For God's—'

The gun went off so close to Malory she felt the heat of the discharge and was at once deafened, her head ringing like a klaxon. She shrank back instinctively and ducked aside. The gun went off three more times, registering with her as dull thumps.

She looked round and saw Ireton toppling backwards through the doorway, clutching at his stomach, his face creased with pain. Count Tomura had been hit as well. He was grimacing and holding his left shoulder.

Blachette stepped forward, shouted something inaudible and fired twice more at Ireton. Everything was happening very quickly, it seemed to Malory, and very slowly at the same time. She saw

Count Tomura's expression harden, erasing the grimace of pain. He moved his right hand to his cane. It was a swordstick, she realized. He drew out the sword in one sweeping movement. The blade was a flash of cold light.

Blachette never saw it coming. The sword struck his wrist. The gun fell from his fingers. And his hand fell too, severed from the arm in a spurt of blood and snap of bone. He watched it with frozen incredulity. Then Tomura drove the sword into his side, deep and hard.

Malory could not breathe, could not think. The Butcher of Port Arthur. Yes, she saw now what that meant. Blood was oozing through the shoulder of Tomura's coat, but he paid it no heed. He wrenched the blade out and watched Blachette drop to his knees. Then he swung the sword back. Malory believed for a second that he meant to decapitate the man, like the Russian whose skull he had drunk from. But his glance shifted to Malory and he held off long enough for Blachette to slump face down on the pavement, blood flooding out beneath him. The *coup de grâce* never came.

Malory's head was still ringing as she stumbled past Blachette to where Ireton was lying in the doorway. He was not bleeding heavily, but one look at his face told her he was dying. His eyes engaged woozily with hers. His lips moved. But, if there were words to hear, she could not hear them. She knelt beside him and clasped his hand. His grip was feeble. And it weakened still further. The light behind his eyes flickered and went out.

She released his hand. And noticed then the tide of Blachette's blood seeping through the fabric of her skirt. She felt Count Tomura's hands at her elbows, urging her to rise. But she resisted long enough to stretch forward and press Ireton's eyelids shut.

'I'm sorry, Travis,' she murmured.

TEA HAD DONE LITTLE TO SOOTHE YAMANAKA'S NERVES AS HE waited for news with Sam and Morahan. He was worried for his future, both in the short and the long term. And rightly so. There was nothing Sam could say to reassure him. They were all in peril. But Yamanaka's position was worse than theirs by far. And it was Sam, by contacting him, who had put him in such a position.

'I'm sorry I dragged you into this, Eisaku,' he ventured as he poured a cup from the second pot of tea he had brewed. 'It hasn't exactly turned out as I'd expected.'

'I chose to be loyal to Commissioner Kuroda. This is the result,' said Yamanaka dolefully. 'To lament the consequences is futile. So, I shall not.'

'How much longer d'you think it'll be before we hear from Mr Ireton, Schools?' Sam asked, striving to brighten his tone.

Morahan smiled grimly, as if preparing a discouraging response. But he was spared the need to deliver it by a knock at the door. 'Talk of the Devil,' he said, jumping up and striding out to answer it.

Sam followed, eager to know what Madame Berton had to report. A phone call from Ireton was his guess. But it was not Madame Berton at the door.

'Malory,' declared Morahan in surprise as he opened it. 'I never meant you to come here.'

Malory looked pale to Sam's eye, her normal composure fractured in some way. Then he saw the bloodstains on her coat and the hem of her skirt beneath it. 'Are you all right?' he asked.

'Oh yes.' She stepped inside and Morahan closed the door behind her. Then he too saw the bloodstains.

'What's happened?'

'Travis is dead, Schools.'

'*What?*'

'Blachette shot him as he was leaving the office with me and Count Tomura. Blachette's dead too. Count Tomura ran him through with his swordstick.'

'Good God.' Morahan put a hand to the wall to support himself. 'The blood?'

'Mostly Blachette's. Some may be Travis's. There was . . . a lot of it.'

'You'd better come and sit down.'

They ushered Malory into the room where Yamanaka was waiting. She acknowledged his presence with the faintest of nods.

'Count Tomura is injured as well,' said Malory. 'Not seriously, though.'

'What . . . was he doing there?' asked Morahan haltingly. He seemed to be finding it difficult to concentrate.

'He came to pay Travis off. I still have the cheque in my purse. Travis was so . . .' She shook her head. 'He was so anxious I should bank it at once.'

'I don't understand,' said Morahan. And it was clear from his expression that he did not. 'Pay him off?'

'Count Tomura plans to return to Japan as soon as possible, Schools, taking his son with him. He's abandoned the search for le Singe.'

'Why?'

'He didn't say. Travis was to have come here and told Noburo to withdraw. I had to come instead. The Count gave me a letter to deliver to his son. Whether it explained his decision to back down I don't know. Noburo was alarmed to hear his father had been wounded, obviously. He left at once. There's no one outside now.'

'Did Count Tomura mention the documents?' asked Yamanaka.

'Yes. He said they should be returned to Marquess Saionji.'

'Sounds like he's giving in,' said Sam. He could see how shocked Morahan was by the news of Ireton's death and how upset Malory was. But he had never met Ireton himself. And he knew nothing good of him. What he did know was that, for some reason, Count Tomura had decided to back down.

'I don't know why he's done this,' said Malory. 'You're right, Sam. In effect, he is giving in.'

'Where's he now?' asked Morahan.

'His suite at the Bristol. He refused to go to hospital. He treated his injury lightly, though it looked quite nasty to me. He said the delegation's doctor would be able to patch him up.'

'Ever the warrior,' Morahan murmured.

'I didn't wait for the police, though I should have. They'll have lots of questions for me. And for you, Schools.'

'But not for the Tomuras?'

'I guess not. Marquess Saionji will shield them as members of his delegation. The Count asked me to tell you something, though. Just before he was driven away.'

'What?'

'If you leave him alone, he'll leave you alone.'

'He said that?'

'His actual words were: "If the tiger ceases to hunt you, do not hunt the tiger."'

'Count Tomura is not a merciful man,' said Yamanaka. 'He gives way only to superior force.'

'Who would that be?' asked Sam.

'Whoever it is,' said Malory, 'they've done us a big favour.'

'How much was that pay-off?' Morahan asked thoughtfully.

'Ten thousand dollars.'

Sam whistled. 'What's that in pounds?'

'Two or three thousand,' said Morahan.

'Blimey O'Reilly.'

'Yuh. Blimey O'Reilly. Tomura really is in retreat. And he doesn't want us to know why.'

'Perhaps it'd be best not to know,' said Malory, grasping Morahan's arm to command his attention. 'This lets you off the hook. Sam too. And Mr Yamanaka.'

Morahan sighed. 'But not Travis. Blachette must have thought he'd betrayed him. But he hadn't.' He looked Malory in the eye. 'We had.'

'You can't betray a traitor, Schools. We did the right thing. We weren't to know what it would lead to.'

'No regrets, then?'

A moment of silence passed. Then Malory said softly, 'More than I can express.'

'Me too.'

Morahan hugged her. And Sam heard a sob muffled by the big man's chest. Then they broke apart. Malory moved to the window and gazed out, dabbing at her eyes with a handkerchief.

'OK,' said Morahan decisively. 'You can return the documents to Marquess Saionji, Yamanaka?'

Yamanaka nodded. 'Certainly.'

'And make up some story about how they came into your hands?'

'An anonymous source.'

'Good enough. You'd better get back to the Majestic, Sam. It'll be business as usual for you.'

'Where are you going?' asked Sam.

'To face the music.'

'Yes,' said Malory, turning round from the window. 'It's time we did that.'

It WAS LATE AFTERNOON WHEN MAX'S TRAIN REACHED PARIS, TOO late, he felt, for an immediate attempt to see Otto Krenz. Members of the German delegation were unlikely to enjoy complete freedom of movement. A meeting with Krenz required careful arranging.

Max booked into a dowdily functional travellers' hotel opposite the Gare du Nord, paying extra for a room with a telephone. After a badly needed bath, he put a call through to the Hôtel des Réservoirs in Versailles. He asked to speak to 'Herr Krenz' on a matter of urgency, using the codename supplied by Appleby that he knew Krenz would recognize: Kahr, which could just as easily be Carr; it was neatly Anglo-Germanic.

Krenz took the call on an extension, after some delay. He sounded breathless – and suspicious. '*Herr Kahr?*'

'I was pleased to hear you're in town,' said Max. 'We must meet.'

'Difficult,' said Krenz. 'I am very busy.'

'We *must* meet.'

'You sound . . . a little odd.'

'Only anxious to see you, Otto. You name a time and place. I'll be there.'

Max thought he heard Krenz groan. Then: 'I will have to buy some . . . *Schreibwaren* . . . tomorrow morning. We have not brought enough pencils and paper-clips. Absurd, no?'

'Where will you buy them?'

'There is a *papeterie* in Rue de la Chancellerie. I shall go there at nine.'

313

'Be sure you do.'
'I will. Now I must go. I am wanted.'

His appointment with Krenz secured, Max contemplated an idle evening in Paris. It would be wise, he knew, to lie low. The fewer people who knew he had returned to the city the better. But the past few days had stretched him to breaking point, both physically and mentally. He craved friendly company as keenly as he did food and drink. It would be good to see Sam, on whose discretion he knew he could rely utterly. A quiet drink somewhere could surely do no harm. Sam would probably be as glad to see Max as Max would be to see him. The decision was made.

'Garage.' Sam sounded as game as ever when he answered his extension at the Majestic.
'It's me, Sam.'
There was a moment's hesitation before Sam recognized Max's voice. Or perhaps he simply could not believe his own ears. 'Sir? Is that really you?'
''Fraid so.'
'Where are you?'
'In the same city as you.'
'You're back?'
'For a little while. For tonight, anyway. Can I buy you a drink?'
'Listen, sir.' Sam's voice dropped to a hoarse whisper. He sounded serious. 'A lot's happened I need to tell you about. And it's not the sort of thing we can risk being overheard. Why don't you come here – to the garage? I'll have to stay late anyway, to make up for missing yesterday and most of today. The mechanics will all be gone by eight. Come at half past. We can slide out for a jar afterwards.'
'Is everything all right?'
'To tell the truth, sir, I'm not sure. But it's a lot better than it was. And better still for hearing your voice again.'

The mews behind the Majestic was in darkness when Max arrived and nightfall was well advanced. He approached with caution,

314

wondering if some other rendezvous might not have been safer.

The garage doors were closed. He tapped at the wicket door, reluctant to announce himself too noisily. It was opened promptly. Sam beamed at him and ushered him inside, snapping the latch down on the lock behind him.

'You're a sight for sore eyes and no mistake, sir,' said Sam as they shook hands warmly.

'So are you, Sam. It really is good to see you again. There have been times of late when I thought I never would.'

'Me too.'

'I have the feeling it hasn't all been plain sailing for you here.'

'Anything but. Come into the office and I'll put you in the picture.'

So it was that Max learnt of all that had occurred in his absence. There was much to relate and much also to understand.

If Max had ever doubted Farngold was the key to the mystery that had claimed his father's life – and come close to claiming his and Sam's too – he doubted it no longer after hearing what Sam had to tell him. Jack Farngold and his dead sister, Matilda, once married to Count Tomura, were links in a chain that led from the past – the past of Sir Henry Maxted and Fritz Lemmer as well as Count Tomura – to the present: from Tokyo, thirty years before, to Paris, on the second night of May, 1919. The chain could not be seen. The hands that had forged it were unknown. But it was there, as real and hard as iron.

For his own part, Max disclosed little of what he had done in the month since he had last been in Paris and Sam did not press him for details. He knew without Max having to tell him that Max had done everything he could to draw Lemmer's sting – so far with only limited success. 'I'm looking for his secretary, Sam. She's with the German delegation. Appleby agrees with me she may have the information we need to round up all the spies Lemmer's recruited over the years.'

'Good luck with that, sir. Anything I can do to help . . .'

'You've done enough, I should say.'

'But not enough to get the better of Count Tomura and his sewer-rat of a son. Someone else did that.'

'Yes. But who? And how?'

'Your guess is as good as mine.'

'Well, for what my guess is worth, I suspect Count Tomura backed down because of his involvement with the Farngolds. Lemmer knows all about it, as far as I can gather. It's possible he forced Tomura's hand to ensure the Count's problems didn't complicate his grand strategy.'

'And what is his grand strategy, sir?'

'He has a spy network for sale. Maybe the Japanese are the buyers. My aim is to see he soon has no network left to sell.'

'What about le Singe, sir? He gave us the documents to punish Tomura for letting his son kill Soutine. But the documents are back with the Japanese now and Tomura's taking himself off home. That isn't going to satisfy le Singe, is it?'

'I can't worry about him, Sam. I have too many other things to worry about.'

''Course you do. Such as your uncle. Are you going to see him? I phoned the hospital earlier. They said he'd left – gone back to his hotel. The Mirabeau, in Rue de la Pay.'

Max pondered the question. Why he should be reluctant to visit George he was not sure, but reluctant he was. The old boy would encourage him to contact his mother. And that he did not want to do. To succeed he required insulation from sentiment. His instinct was to stay away.

But instinct could not rule. The Farngold secret amounted to far more than had been revealed by the documents le Singe had supplied. It had to. And Sir Henry had known what it was. There was a chance Lady Maxted knew as well, whether she was aware of it or not. And what she knew George was likely to know also, as her closest confidant by far.

'I should see him, Sam, yes. I'm sorry. We may have to postpone that drink.'

En route to the Mirabeau, Max passed close to the Plaza-Athénée and thought of his father's old friend Baltazar Ribeiro. It was clear from what Morahan had told Sam about his dealings with Sir Henry that Ribeiro had lied to them. He and Sir Henry had cooked up the fable of buying land in Amazonia for a rubber plantation to explain away Sir Henry's money-raising efforts if the need arose, as later it did. Ribeiro had stuck loyally to the story, as agreed. He had probably hated doing it, but he had done it nonetheless.

What would he say now if Max confronted him? It was doubtful Sir Henry had entrusted him with the Farngold secret, if only to spare him the possession of dangerous information. Even if Ribeiro did know the truth, he would deny it. Max would gain nothing from the encounter, except confirmation that his father had chosen his friends wisely. Morahan's behaviour underlined the point. He had kept silent out of loyalty to Sir Henry – until it was no longer feasible to do so.

'What's it all about, Pa?' Max murmured to himself as he walked on. 'Who is Tomura holding? And why didn't you want anyone else going after them?'

At the Mirabeau, a surprise awaited Max, though one he realized at once he should have anticipated. Asking after George Clissold without volunteering he was his nephew, Max was informed Monsieur Clissold was in the restaurant – with his sister.

'His sister? Lady Maxted's here?'

'*Oui, monsieur*. You know 'er also?'

'Yes. But, er, I won't interrupt their dinner.'

'May I give them your name?'

Max smiled blithely. 'That won't be necessary.'

News of his mother's presence had taken Max aback. A suspicion had formed instantly in his mind at the mention of her name. Travelling to Paris after learning George had run into trouble was natural enough. That was not the issue. The issue was Farngold. Sam and Morahan had learnt all they knew of the Farngolds from the documents le Singe had supplied to them. George had said nothing about them. During his interrogation by Noburo Tomura, the Farngolds had evidently never been mentioned. But was that really true? In view of the importance of the subject to Count

317

Tomura, it seemed unlikely – it seemed unbelievable, in fact – that his son, who was also Matilda Farngold's son, had failed to ask George if he had heard of the name. It was the question that mattered above all others. Yet, according to George, it had not been asked.

Suddenly, Max experienced a jolt of certainty. The question had been asked. Oh yes. It had been asked.

He headed nonchalantly along the hallway past the restaurant and lingered by the door, where a menu was displayed for perusal. The restaurant was no more than half full. From where he stood he could see most of the tables.

There they were. His mother and Uncle George. They looked much like other pairs of diners, conversing quietly as they ate. George was holding himself stiffly, as a man with a broken rib was apt to. His left forefinger was heavily bandaged. He had been through it, no question. Max felt sorry for him. George was too loyal to his sister for his own good.

He saw his mother shake her head then at something George said. Max recognized the gesture in all its subtlety. It was not meant to convey disagreement or impatience. The purse-lipped smile that accompanied it told all. It meant: *There is nothing to worry about.* It meant: *I have settled the matter.*

In that moment, Max knew for certain. He knew it as he studied the glance that passed between his mother and her brother. They were each other's oldest ally. But Max understood them too well to be deceived. They were not worried. They were not worried in the slightest. They already knew Count Tomura was leaving Paris. And they knew why.

Farngold was the reason. Lady Maxted was privy to Tomura's secret. So was George. It was the threat that had seen him off. They *knew*. But they would never tell.

Lady Maxted had settled the matter. In her own particular way. But it was not settled. Max would be damned if it was.

He turned then and walked away.

WHETHER THE HOTEL CLERK WOULD ALERT GEORGE TO Max's visit to the Mirabeau, or describe him well enough for George to realize who he was, was out of Max's hands. He did not propose to force his uncle and mother to lie to him, confident as he was that they would if they felt they had to. Sir Henry had been aware of the risks he was running and had engaged Ribeiro's services to cover his tracks because he wanted to ensure Max did not try to finish what he had started. Lady Maxted wanted the same. She would never admit there was a secret, held captive, perhaps with Jack Farngold in Japan, for Max to pursue. She would do everything she could to save him from that.

But Max did not want to be saved. The cards he held he would play. Lemmer had to be stopped. In stopping him, Max hoped to uncover the truth about the Farngolds. And then . . .

But he could not look so far ahead. The war had taught him to study only the sky he flew through. All he knew for a fact was that he had come this far. And he was not about to turn back.

The reception desk at Max's hotel was unattended. But the lobby was not empty. Sam was waiting for him.

'There you are, sir. Thought I'd have to hang around a good bit longer. Short and sweet with your uncle, was it? He was probably—'

'I didn't speak to him, Sam.'

'You didn't? Too tired, was he?'

'I thought better of it. Now, what are you doing here?'

'Something I forgot to tell you earlier. I didn't reckon it could wait.'

'Let's discuss it over that drink I promised you, then. There are plenty of bars around here.'

Plenty of bars there were, most of them insalubrious. But insalubrity promised anonymity. And Max was in need of that. He was also in need of confirmation that George knew more than he was telling about the Farngolds, so no sooner did they have glasses in their hands at the murky counter of the first establishment they came to than Max asked Sam if he would do something for him.

'I want you to speak to my uncle before he goes back to London.'

'Well, I was intending to, anyway, sir. Thought I should tell him how it all ended.'

'My mother's staying at the Mirabeau as well.'

'She is?'

'Yes. And I don't want to have her fussing over me. That's why I've decided to . . . steer clear.'

'Is she the fussing kind, sir?'

'I'd just prefer to avoid having to explain myself to her, that's all.'

'Understood.'

'I'd like you to ask Uncle George if he knows anything about the Farngolds.'

'Righto, sir. But it's not likely, is it?'

'Even so.'

'I'll ask.'

'Take careful note of what he says and how he says it, won't you?'

'I'll be sure to, sir.'

'Thanks.'

'Are you going to see Schools and Malory while you're here?'

'You've got to know them quite well, haven't you, Sam? Yes. I intend to see them. I want a full account from Schools of what he agreed to do for my father.'

'He took Mr Ireton's death hard. It was as if he blamed himself.'

'Why would he do that?'

320

'Dunno. But—' Sam slapped his forehead. 'I still haven't told you about the letter. It's why I came to your hotel.'

'What letter?'

'Commissioner Kuroda wrote to me from Marseilles before catching the boat to Japan. He enclosed a letter he wanted me to pass on to you. I got it on Wednesday, but so much happened yesterday and today I forgot all about it. Anyway, here it is.'

Sam fished the letter out of his pocket and handed it over. It was addressed simply to *Max*.

Max tore the crumpled envelope open and squinted at the letter inside. 'I'll never be able to read it in this light. Let's go back to the hotel.'

'That's all right by me, sir.' Sam glanced around the bar. 'To be honest, this place is starting to give me the willies.'

They went to Max's room. Max sat down to read the letter at the desk. Sam took the armchair – and promptly fell asleep while Max read what Kuroda had written to him.

Marseilles, 28th April 1919

My dear Max,

The habits of caution my long years of police work have imbued in me cause me to doubt the wisdom of sending this letter to you. The sailing schedule of the NYK line does not permit me much time in which to decide the point, however. Nor can I be sure you will receive the letter even if I send it. The matter is hedged about by many uncertainties.

I must begin by expressing my regret for withholding from you certain information concerning your late father. I held him in the highest regard. I gave him a solemn promise that I would not tell you all I knew of his activities and his motives and in conscience I must abide by that.

My impression is that you have inherited his sense of honour and his determination to settle moral debts. I suspect you will come to learn more of him than he would have wished and will therefore realize at some point that I have not been completely open with you.

I am not alone among your father's confidants in keeping secrets for him. I assume he swore them to silence in terms similar to those by which I undertook to be bound. Loyalty to a dead friend is not something of which any of us should be ashamed. So, I do not apologize to you. But I do wish I had been free to speak more candidly to you.

You will undoubtedly have been told by Mr Twentyman of the circumstances of my departure from Paris. I do not exaggerate when I say that my continued well-being is by no means guaranteed. I am considered to be a threat by certain powerful interests within my nation's government. Previous experience shows them to be capable of extreme action. It is possible they may decide to put an end to me. My ability to resist them is limited. My position is acutely vulnerable.

Though your father implored me to discourage you from seeking to uncover his secrets, I no longer feel it is right for me to do so. I cannot speak of things I assured him I would not speak of. But I can say this. Follow him, Max. Beware Count Tomura. Fear Lemmer. Suspect everyone you cannot trust absolutely. But do not abandon your quest, for whatever else it may be, it is not ignoble. It is, I venture to suggest, the gauge of your life. It is what you were born to do.

Truly yours,

Masataka

Max replaced the letter in the envelope. *Follow him, Max.* Such was Kuroda's urging. Such was the urging of his own instincts. He found a scrap of paper and scrawled a note on it: *Stay here if you want. I have gone to see Schools. I may be some time. M.* He propped the note on the bed, where Sam could not fail to see it when he woke. Then he slipped out of the room.

'**H**ELLO, MAX,' MORAHAN CALLED FROM THE DOORWAY OF HIS apartment as Max reached the top of the stairs.

Morahan did not wait for Max to reach the door. He left it open and moved unsteadily back into the sitting-room. The slight slur in his voice and the heavy smell of bourbon that met Max as he entered the apartment told him his host had been drinking heavily.

'Join me?' Morahan asked, flourishing a bottle of Jim Beam.

'All right.'

Morahan poured a generous measure and handed him the glass.

'You don't seem surprised to see me,' said Max.

'Nothing much surprises me. But I am relieved to see you. I wouldn't want another death on my conscience.'

'Sam told me about Ireton. I'm sorry.'

'No reason for you to be. Travis was a snake at heart. He did you no favours.'

'But he was your friend, snake or not.'

Morahan nodded and stared into his glass. 'He was.' He slumped down into a chair.

Max sat opposite him. 'Sam said you blame yourself for what happened.'

'I tipped off Carver that Travis was doing business with the German delegation through their hotel's deputy manager, Blachette. The police bungled Blachette's arrest. He went on the run. And he assumed Travis had betrayed him. So, I can't deny being responsible.'

'That was merely cause and effect, Schools. Travis was

323

responsible for deciding to deal with the Germans. And for the consequences.'

'You think so?' Morahan gazed blearily at Max. 'Well, maybe you're right. I just can't seem to persuade myself to believe it.'

'You said you wouldn't want another death on your conscience. Why would you ever feel responsible for mine?'

'Not sure. It's been a rough day. I've had to answer a lot of questions, some of them pretty damn cagily. And you'll have guessed I'm not exactly sober. So, maybe I'm not seeing everything as it truly is.'

'I wondered if it might be because you didn't tell me the full extent of your dealings with my father.'

'Ah.' Morahan lit a cigarette. 'Sam filled you in about that, did he?'

'You must've known he would.'

'Sure. Even though I advised him not to. But Sam isn't the keeping-things-to-himself type, is he?'

'Not where I am concerned.'

'He explained how Henry and I first met?'

'He did.'

'Then you'll understand I owed Henry my life. I promised him I'd say nothing to you. I kept my promise as long as I could.'

'So did Ribeiro. And Kuroda. My father seems to have sworn quite a few people to secrecy.'

'It's a measure of his character that they could be sworn.'

'According to Sam, you agreed to recruit a team to help my father rescue someone from captivity in Japan.'

'I did.'

'Jack Farngold?'

'Very possibly. Henry never gave me the particulars.'

'How can I be sure of that?'

Morahan sighed. 'You'll have to answer that question yourself.'

'What was Jack Farngold to my father?'

'Dunno. Like I said, Henry never gave me the particulars.'

'And you're baffled by Count Tomura's decision to leave Paris and abandon his attempts to lay hands on the documents le Singe stole?'

324

'I am.'

'I think my mother's responsible.'

'Your *mother*?'

'She's here. In Paris. Staying at the Mirabeau with Uncle George. I suspect they both know what this is about. I think my mother threatened to reveal something she knows damaging to Tomura if he didn't retreat.'

Morahan considered the point. 'I see.'

'During the account he gave you of his interrogation by Tomura junior, George never mentioned being questioned about Farngold, did he?'

'No. He didn't.'

'But he would've been questioned about Farngold. That's certain. He just didn't want to tell you.'

'Because he knew how important it was.' Morahan reached for his glass, then thought better of it. Suddenly, drunkenness had lost its appeal. 'You may be right.'

'Oh, I'm right.'

'Why don't you just ask your mother what it's all about, then?'

'Because she wouldn't tell me. She'll have promised Tomura she'll keep quiet whatever happens. But it's what she means to do anyway.'

'Why?'

'I don't know. If she was ever going to tell me, she already would have. And Uncle George backs her up loyally, so asking him is pointless. They'll say whatever they judge will dissuade me from going on with this.'

'How can you go on?'

'We don't know if it was Jack Farngold my father meant to rescue, but we do know Jack Farngold is held captive. Agreed?'

Morahan shrugged. 'It seems so.'

'On Count Tomura's orders?'

'Probably.'

'You had some people in mind for this mission?'

'Yuh.'

'You just needed enough money to secure their services.'

'I needed enough to stand a *chance* of securing their services.'

'Then go ahead and try. I have the money my father raised, Schools. Lemmer sent it back to me after emptying the safe-deposit box at the Banque Ornal of the things he really wanted. It was his idea of a peace offering, I think. Appleby banked the money for me. It's accessible whenever I want it. I'll make it available to you if you're willing to have a crack at this.'

Morahan stared at Max in some amazement. 'You mean to go through with what Henry planned?"

'Yes.'

'Even though you can't be sure it was Jack Farngold he meant to rescue?'

'I'm certain Jack Farngold will lead us to the truth.'

'Us?'

'You and me and your hand-picked team, Schools. How about it?'

'Can I remind you Tomura's given me an explicit warning not to go after him?'

'To hell with his warning.'

'You don't believe in doing things by halves, do you?'

'Do you?'

Morahan sat back in his chair and looked long and hard at Max. 'It'd be hard to overestimate how risky such an operation would be.'

'You were willing to do it for my father.'

'I'd have been relying on the information he assured me he had about exactly what was involved. We don't have that information. We'd be . . . flying in the dark.'

'I've done that. It can be quite exhilarating.'

'Exhilarating?' Morahan smiled at Max. 'Well, that's one word for it.'

'How long would you need to recruit a team?'

'A week in New York. Maybe two to assemble them ready to go. I might have to go to Chicago as well. It'd be six weeks at the very least before I could have them on the ground in Japan. More likely a couple of months.'

'So be it.'

'What would you be doing in the meantime?'

'I have something to finish for Appleby.'

'Concerning Lemmer?'

'Yes. But I'm not free to talk about it.'

'Even though it may have a bearing on this mission you want me to undertake?'

'If we both make it as far as Japan, Schools, I'll tell you everything there is to tell.'

'And if I make it but you don't?'

'Pay off your team and forget the whole damn thing.'

'Forget? I should say that'd be next to impossible, Max. You and your father are part of my life now, whether I like it or not.'

'Does that mean you'll do it?'

'It means I'll think about it when I'm sober. Henry was adamant you shouldn't be allowed to involve yourself. He wouldn't want me to help you.'

'But I am involved now. And I'm not going to drop it. You have my word on that. So I suppose the question is: would my father want you to help me if I was set on doing this come what may?'

'Yuh. That's the question.' Morahan stubbed out his cigarette. 'I'll sleep on it. Come to the office tomorrow morning. I'll have an answer for you then.'

'I can't promise to be there much before noon.'

'Busy on Appleby's account, arc you?' Morahan smiled when no immediate answer was forthcoming. 'OK. Noon it is.'

S AM HAD GONE BY THE TIME MAX RETURNED TO HIS HOTEL. He had left a note on the desk: *Let me know if you need anything, sir. S.* The *sir* was a habit Max wished but very much doubted he could cure Sam of.

Max headed out early the following morning and took a taxi from the Gare du Nord to the Gare des Invalides. The driver was in good spirits because of the arrival of warmer weather. '*Le printemps, monsieur,*' he said, chuckling. '*Le printemps enfin.*' Spring at last? Well, maybe it was. Max hardly cared.

It was a forty-minute train ride from Invalides to Versailles and a short walk from Rive Gauche station to the stationer's in Rue de la Chancellerie. Finding himself early, Max treated himself to a light breakfast at a café near the station.

The taxi-driver was right about the weather. It was genuinely balmy. Max sat on the pavement terrace, sipping coffee as a gentle breeze stirred the trees in the centre of the avenue and the town slowly woke around him.

'May I join you for a moment?'

The question took Max by surprise. He looked up to be met by the lambent gaze of a thin, middle-aged man clad in a morning-suit and bowler hat. He had a clipped moustache and a sharp-featured face and was trailing a cigarette in his right hand. The arm of a pair of metal-framed glasses was visible over the top of his breast pocket.

'Mr Carr?' the man added as he sat down.

'Yes,' Max replied cautiously. He was virtually certain he recognized Otto Krenz's voice and accent, but he could hardly afford to assume anything.

'I believe I've seen you at the *papeterie* in Rue de la Chancellerie.'

'I sometimes go there, yes.'

'An excellent shop.'

'Indeed it is.'

'Is that what brings you here this morning?'

'No. I'm, er, hoping to speak to someone who's presently staying in Versailles.'

'A tourist?'

'Not exactly.'

'Someone here on business?'

'Yes. State business.'

'Perhaps I can help you.'

'Perhaps you can.'

'What is the name of the person?'

'Schmidt,' Max said quietly. 'Anna Schmidt.'

'I see.' Krenz waved the waiter away. 'If you've finished, would you care to walk with me to the *papeterie*?'

'Certainly.' Max drained his coffee, doled some coins onto the table and stood up.

They set off at an ambling pace. Krenz finished his cigarette and paused to light another. Then, as they moved on, he said, 'Who sent you to me, Mr Carr?'

'You know the answer to that question. How about an answer to mine?'

'Frau Schmidt?'

'I want to see her.'

'What business do you have with her?'

'Are you being deliberately obtuse, Krenz?' Max hardened his tone. 'You're a bought man. We tell you what we want. You supply it.'

'If possible.'

'And is it possible?'

'No. It is not.'

329

'I suggest you—'

'She's no longer here, Mr Carr. She left yesterday.'

'*What?*'

'Gone. A few hours before you called.'

'Gone where?"

'Officially, Berlin. Due to the illness of a close relative. But she has not gone to Berlin. I have paid her careful attention since the delegation left Germany. I do not need to tell you who she serves.'

He did not. Nor did Max propose to mention that Appleby had warned him Krenz might well serve the same person. Max could place little confidence in what Krenz told him. He intended to telephone the delegation later to confirm Frau Schmidt had actually left. Meanwhile . . . 'Where has she gone *un*officially?'

'Marseilles.'

'*Marseilles?* How d'you know?'

'The telephone system at our hotel offers many opportunities to overhear conversations. A woman called and spoke to Frau Schmidt yesterday afternoon. I listened to what they said. The caller did not give her name. They spoke in French. Frau Schmidt was instructed to proceed to Marseilles as soon as possible and lodge at the Pension Marguerite in Rue du Baignoir.'

'What is Frau Schmidt required to do in Marseilles?'

'Wait until called for.'

'Called for by whom?'

'No name was given. But it was obvious to me who had summoned her. She was not surprised. It seemed to be something she had expected. She has a French passport as well as her German papers and speaks the language quite well. She can travel freely.'

'What name's on her French passport?'

'Camille Strauss.'

'There was no objection to her sudden departure?'

'It is known who her master is, Mr Carr. No one would be so foolish as to obstruct him.'

'But he no longer has any standing with the German government.'

'Nevertheless he is widely feared by those who know what he is

330

capable of. I detected only relief at her going. It means there is one less spy in the camp.'

'Are the delegation's loyalties divided, then, Krenz?'

'Divided, no. Shattered, yes.'

'What do you know about Blachette?'

'Deputy manager of our hotel. Suspected by *le Deuxième Bureau* of acting as an intermediary between our delegation and an American intelligence broker, Travis Ireton. Both men were killed yesterday. As I feel certain you are aware.'

'How's that gone down with your bosses?'

'Count Brockdorff-Rantzau has personally assured the French Foreign Ministry that we had no improper dealings with Blachette – or Ireton.'

'A lie, of course.'

'No, no. The Count believed what he said. Others do what needs to be done without informing our leader. As it is, with no means of predicting the demands likely to be made of us ... we are chickens in a coop, waiting to be plucked. There is consequently unspoken admiration for Frau Schmidt's master. And occasionally it is not unspoken.'

'Is he your master too, Krenz?'

'Such a question.' Krenz took a last drag on his cigarette and tossed it away. 'You said it yourself. I am a bought man. And you represent those who bought me. What else is there to say?'

They had reached the Place d'Armes. Before them, beyond the gilded entrance gate, stood the vast and imposing Palace of Versailles. Its frontage glowed like honey in the morning sun.

'Look there, Mr Carr.' Krenz pointed to the centre of the building, the pillared and pedimented section within the inner courtyard. 'On some day to be determined by our conquerors, we shall be led in there to sign a treaty of shame and humiliation. Count Brockdorff-Rantzau will protest. He may even resign. But his resignation will be as useless as his protests. We will sign. We will have no choice. Unless . . .'

'What?'

'Unless the last of our generals left in the field can win against the odds.'

'Lemmer?'

'He has not given up, Mr Carr. He has not surrendered.'

'Why has he sent Anna Schmidt to Marseilles?'

'You ask me to guess?'

'I do.'

'It is a port. Perhaps a journey is planned. A voyage.'

'A voyage to where?'

'From Marseilles, it must be eastwards, I think, don't you?'

'Eastwards?'

Krenz shrugged. 'I can only guess.' He paused and looked at Max curiously. Then he asked, 'Will you go after Frau Schmidt?'

'If I do, and if I find you've lied to me, I'll come back for you, Krenz. I hope that's clear. I'll come back. Without warning. And without mercy.'

Krenz nodded fatalistically. 'I would expect nothing else.'

MAX ARRIVED AT 33 RUE DES PYRAMIDES TO FIND MALORY tearing up letters and other papers and feeding them into the fire in her office. The warmth of the morning made it obvious the fire had been lit for one reason only. Malory was flushed and more flustered than Max could ever recall.

'Schools said you'd be here at noon,' she said, breaking away from the blaze to greet him.

'Isn't he here?'

'I'm here,' Morahan announced, appearing from the direction of Ireton's office. 'We have two fires going.'

'Destroying the evidence?'

'Travis kept a smart French lawyer on a retainer. He'll hold the police off for a few days at least. But we need to use the time wisely.'

'Are you worried about Travis's reputation?'

'We're more worried we might face charges if they have the opportunity to go through Travis's files with a fine-toothed comb,' said Malory. 'There are heaps of handwritten notes about deals he kept to himself. I had no idea quite how unscrupulous he was.' She lit a cigarette and handed it almost unconsciously to Morahan, then lit another for herself, before sitting down behind her desk.

'I've told Malory it might be best if we left Paris,' said Morahan, propping himself against the desk.

'You're probably right,' said Max.

'He's told me what you want him to do,' said Malory.

'Were you shocked?'

333

'Lord, no.'

'I came here for your decision, Schools.' Max looked directly at Morahan.

'He'll do it,' said Malory.

'She knows me better than I know myself,' Morahan grumbled good-naturedly. 'I gave myself until noon to make my mind up. But I won't make you wait.' He drew thoughtfully on his cigarette. 'If you really want to push this boulder up the hill, I'll put my shoulder to it.'

Max walked across and shook Morahan's hand. 'Thank you.'

'Don't thank me. I'll take every cent you've got. And I can't guarantee success. Failure's much the likeliest outcome, though exactly what failure would mean . . .' Morahan fixed Max with his gaze. He was determined to communicate the seriousness of what they had resolved to embark upon. 'There are so many ways this could go badly wrong, Max. More than I can count or anticipate. Travis would have turned you down flat.'

'I would never have asked Travis.'

'There's a condition,' said Malory.

'I'll have the money my father put by deposited in the bank of Schools' choice first thing Monday morning.'

'It's not a financial condition,' said Morahan. 'It's Malory.'

'What d'you mean?'

'I go too,' said Malory, studying Max to take full measure of his reaction.

'You?'

'I speak some Japanese. I know the country. I have to be with you.'

'It's out of the question.' Max looked at Morahan. 'Surely you agree, Schools?'

'Oh, I do. But apparently it's non-negotiable.'

'You have a better chance with me than without me,' said Malory, in a tone suggesting this was a self-evident truth. 'If my friends are determined to risk their lives, I have to do what I can to save them. It's really very simple.'

'Not to me,' protested Max.

'Besides, my life will be boring and lonely if I don't go with you.

Like Schools says, I can't stay here. Maybe I'd have to go home. But I couldn't bear to do that. Wilmington and I . . . just don't suit each other any more.'

'Not to mention that family you don't spend much time in the bosom of,' remarked Morahan.

'Can't you talk her out of this, Schools?' pleaded Max.

Morahan shook his head. 'I stopped trying to talk Malory out of things a long time ago.'

'You gave him a free hand where assembling his team's concerned,' Malory pointed out.

'Yuh,' said Morahan. 'You did.'

'All right.' Max had too many other preoccupations to argue with them any longer. And the question of what they would do if and when they reached Japan was so difficult to address he was in no position to deny Malory might well prove valuable. 'Have it your way.'

'Will you take Sam?' Malory asked.

'Absolutely not. Let the poor fellow stay where he is. He has a good job that might lead on to a better one. He's done more than enough on my account. I want Sam kept out of this.'

'I'll leave for New York straight after Travis's funeral,' said Morahan.

'Wednesday, we think,' said Malory. 'Will you still be here then, Max?'

'I'm leaving Paris tonight. I don't know when I'll be back.'

'Care to tell us where you're going?' asked Morahan.

'Marseilles.'

'You're not thinking of travelling to Japan on the same ship as the Tomuras, are you?'

'Why would I be?'

'The next service to the Far East from Marseilles sails Tuesday,' Malory explained. 'It seems likely Count Tomura and his son will be aboard.'

'I'm not going to Marseilles because of the Tomuras.'

'Are you sure about that, Max?' Morahan looked sceptical. 'Everything in this affair seems to be connected with everything else.'

335

'I don't plan to get in their way. Not yet, at any rate. What I need to know is when you expect to reach Japan.'

'Late June or early July's about as accurate as I can be.'

Max nodded. 'I'll make sure I'm there by then.'

'We'll arrive by steamer from San Francisco,' said Malory, who had evidently already considered the practicalities. 'We'll disembark at Yokohama.'

'We'll meet there, then.'

'All being well,' said Morahan, in a tone implying he was far from confident all would be well.

'There's something else I want your help with,' said Max, ignoring the note of pessimism. 'According to Sam, you and he both suspect le Singe has more documents beyond those he gave you.'

'Maybe,' admitted Morahan.

'Hidden somewhere on the roof above Soutine's flat.'

'That's an even bigger maybe.'

'But if such documents exist they could be crucial.'

'You want to go looking for them, Max, is that it?'

'Yes. But your French is a great deal better than mine. And I imagine we'll have to do a lot of smooth talking to gain access to the roof. So . . .'

'All right.' Morahan pushed himself upright. 'Let's go.'

'Leave it till this afternoon if you want to finish here first.'

'We *should* finish this, Schools,' said Malory.

'Yuh.' Morahan glanced at the crackling fire. 'I guess we should. When's your train, Max?'

'I'll take the sleeper. It leaves at eight.'

'OK. I'll meet you by St-Germain l'Auxerrois church at three o'clock. Good enough?'

'Good enough.'

'Now I'd better get back to work.'

Wearily, Morahan lumbered off towards Ireton's office. Malory smiled wistfully after him as he went. Then she looked up at Max and said, quietly but firmly, 'This is the fusing of several impulses, none of them particularly rational. You do realize that, don't you, Max?'

'Just because something's dangerous it isn't necessarily irrational.'

'You want to avenge your father. On some level, Schools wants to atone for his role in Travis's death. Neither of you has any clear idea of what we'll unearth in Japan. It's all crazily risky.'

'Why are you coming along, then?'

'Oh, I have irrational reasons all of my own.'

'It's strange,' Max mused. 'It's only just over a month ago I stood here in this room and you predicted that one day you'd return to Japan – and so would I. Did you really believe it? I didn't.'

'Some things that aren't believable are true nonetheless.'

Max smiled at her hint of mysticism. 'If you say so.'

'How many men have you killed in your life, Max?'

'Does it matter?'

'It would to some.'

'Not to me.'

'They don't weigh on your conscience?'

'No.'

'What would?'

'This.' He looked at her frankly. 'If I didn't do it.'

GEORGE CLISSOLD SMILED WARMLY AS HE AMBLED INTO Sam's office in the Majestic garage. Sam had laid aside his ham sandwich when he saw George approaching across the repair bay, though he was left with a strand of something sinewy lodged uncomfortably between two molars to remind him that French ham was not to be trusted.

'Good to see you up and about, Mr Clissold,' Sam greeted his visitor. 'The hospital told me you'd been discharged.'

'Yes, yes,' said George. 'Fit to resume service.'

'Take a pew.' Sam vacated his chair and plonked himself on the box he kept for such purposes.

'Thanks.' George sank gratefully into the chair. 'The rib's still giving me gyp.'

'And the finger?' Sam nodded at the prominently bandaged digit.

'Less trouble than a gouty toe, so I can't complain. Neither of us can, really, considering how neatly our difficulties with the Tomuras have been wrapped up.'

'You're right there, sir. Though it's a mystery why Count Tomura threw in the towel.'

'Indeed. Nothing Commissioner Zamaron said when he informed me of the development shed any light on the matter. But the Orient's full of mysteries. Just be grateful when one of them turns out to your advantage.'

'Oh, I am. Grateful and no mistake. I thought I was for the high jump.'

338

George grinned. 'Me too while I was in the clutches of Tomura's loathsome son.'

'Did he ask you about the Farngolds at all?'

'The who?'

Sam felt secretly pleased with himself. The question Max had wanted him to put to George had been delivered in as natural and deadpan a manner as Sam could have hoped to manage. And the answer, accompanied though it was by a puzzled frown, was in some indefinable respect unconvincing. 'The Farngolds. The name cropped up in the documents we got hold of. I wondered if . . . Noburo Tomura asked you about them.'

'No. He didn't. Who are they?'

'Count Tomura's late wife was an Englishwoman. Matilda Farngold. She died in childbirth, delivering Noburo. Her brother, Jack Farngold, has had it in for Tomura ever since . . . apparently.'

'Extraordinary. I had no idea.'

No idea? Well, that was a bold assertion. Sam would have believed it but for Max's doubts on the subject. 'Maybe Sir Henry met Matilda Farngold's father while he was in Tokyo,' Sam ventured. 'Claude Farngold was a tea merchant with a business there. He died in a fire.'

'Well, well,' said George. 'It's possible, I suppose. I don't recall Henry ever mentioning a Claude Farngold. I'll ask my sister. She came over when she heard I'd come a cropper. We'll be travelling back together tomorrow.'

'You're leaving Paris, Mr Clissold?'

'No reason to stay, Sam. Arnavon's taken fright at all the police attention he received after Soutine's murder and scuttled back to Canada. Further dealings with Sir Nathaniel Chevalier will be handled by the lawyers. I'm retiring from the field. That's principally why I called by, actually. To say goodbye.'

'I should thank you, Mr Clissold, for keeping my name out of the Soutine murder. Not sure my boss, Mr Shuttleworth, would've taken too kindly to me being caught up in that.'

'Well, you and Schools Morahan saw off the Tomuras a damn sight more effectively than I could ever have done. And with the stolen documents restored to the Japanese delegation, I take it le

Singe will be left alone. So, honours are even, I should say. By the way, Zamaron told me Schools Morahan reported you found the documents in some garret Soutine used, but there was no sign of le Singe there. Is that strictly true, Sam, or was he protecting le Singe?'

Sam hesitated, unsure of what to say. Then George took pity on him.

'On second thoughts, don't bother to answer that. The less I know the less I have to keep quiet about.' George struggled to his feet. 'I'd better be going.' Sam jumped up and they shook hands. 'Thanks again, Sam. Go carefully, eh?'

Sam nodded. 'You too, Mr Clissold.'

'Oh, I will. This past week's held more excitement than I'll need for many a long day. I'll be going *very* carefully.'

While George was taking his leave of Sam at the Majestic, a sky-light was opening in a chimney-stack-screened corner of roof between the Quai du Louvre and the church of St-Germain l'Auxerrois.

Max eased himself out through the gap and lowered the window back into place with one hand, while grasping with the other the bottom rung of a steel ladder fixed to the sheer wall above him that led to the top of the stack.

Cajolery and judicious bribery by Morahan of the *gardienne*'s handyman husband had gained them access to a loft and then via the skylight to what the husband had eye-rollingly referred to as '*le toit haut*' as if speaking of some remote and unknown landscape. The police, he reported, had searched the apartment rented by Soutine, under the name of Soukaris, without catching sight or sound of le Singe, while making only a desultory foray onto the roof – and certainly not the vertiginous section Max was now out on. Both husband and wife denied all knowledge of le Singe and almost all knowledge of Soukaris. That was the tale they had spun to the police and they were determined to stick to it. But if '*les messieurs*' wished to risk their necks and insisted on offering generous compensation for the inconvenience . . . '*soit*' – so be it.

It was actually only Max who was risking his neck. He insisted

340

Morahan wait in the loft while he climbed up to the stand of chimneys and surveyed the scene.

Paris stretched around him, benign and sparkling in the afternoon sun. He could see Notre-Dame and the Hôtel Dieu, the Eiffel Tower and the Quai d'Orsay. Somewhere, in the mosaic of rooftops to the south, he could even imagine he saw the roof of 8 Rue du Verger, from which his father had plunged to his death.

Up here, in the clear, wide-horizoned air, falling was far from unthinkable. It seemed almost natural. The pathways his eye detected along lead-ridged apexes were tempting but treacherous. Ahead, along one such route, stood, by his calculation, the chimney-stack immediately above Soutine's apartment. But where, if it was anywhere in this aerial world, was le Singe's cache of documents?

Max dropped down onto the apex he had spied out and headed boldly along it. He was immune to vertigo and there was only the slightest of breezes. There was so much open air around him he could almost imagine he was flying again, which only reminded him how much he missed being a pilot.

He reached the base of the next stack. There was no way up it, although he was aware le Singe might know a way. The clodhopping Paris police never stood a chance of seeing the boy, of course, far less apprehending him. And Max acknowledged to himself that he did not stand much more of a chance of finding anything le Singe had hidden up there.

He looked to his right, down one of the slopes of the roof. There was a drop beyond to another roof, sloping away at right angles, with a belly-fronted chimney-stack at its top, below which was a sheer drop into a courtyard. At the base of the stack, bolted to it, was a wooden, louvre-fronted cabinet of some kind. It did not look like a normal feature of a roof. It had been fixed there by someone, for some specific purpose.

Max edged his way down the roof, aware of a hazardous amount of void opening around him. The only way down to the next roof was to jump. Considering the steepness of the slope he was jumping onto, it was a risky undertaking, but he had no intention of agonizing about it. He reached the edge, judged the height and the surface he was landing on as best he could, and launched himself.

He skidded as he hit the roof and started an alarming slide, which he only managed to arrest by grabbing a projecting flue. Risk, he remembered remarking to Sam in a philosophical moment during the war when bad weather had grounded their squadron, began as terror before becoming habit – ultimately an unremarked-upon feature of life. It was the life he had returned to in recent weeks. It was the life he was destined for.

He scrabbled back up the roof to the chimney and moved round it to inspect the cabinet. The door was fitted with a hasp, but there was no padlock. Max opened it.

There was nothing inside, except dust. But Max could see a roughly rectangular patch round which the dust was noticeably thicker. The cabinet was empty, but until recently it had not been.

He had found le Singe's secret cache. But whatever le Singe had hidden there was gone.

As Max began to clamber his way back towards the skylight high among the Paris rooftops, Horace Appleby settled behind his desk at Secret Service Headquarters in London with the telegram he had just received and considered the message Max had sent him.

CLIENT LEFT PARIS. FOLLOWING TO
MARSEILLES. WILL REPORT FURTHER. PLEASE
TRANSFER BALANCE MY PRIVATE ACCOUNT TO
T J MORAHAN BANQUE WITTVEIN DELAMERE
RUE DE RICHELIEU NINETY THREE BIS PARIS
SOONEST.

There was no divining the full import of such a message. The client, of course, was Anna Schmidt. Her sudden flight to Marseilles implied Lemmer had ordered her there. But why? Marseilles was a place of arrivals and departures, France's principal Mediterranean port. What was Lemmer up to? Where might he be going, taking his faithful secretary with him?

Appleby knew he could rely on Max to do everything in his power to find out and to extract from Anna Schmidt the key to

Lemmer's code. How Max's request to have his father's money handed over to Schools Morahan chimed with that Appleby could only guess, though it was interesting to see an oblique reference in the cable to Morahan's real name, the one he had been born with in Belfast in 1872. Thomas James Morahan was a man who had swum in dark waters all his life.

Appleby discarded the telegram and picked up a typed report that lay beside it. This concerned the murder of Travis Ireton the previous day in Paris. Its source, Jefferies, Appleby's successor in Paris, was presently under suspicion, along with many others, but there was no reason to doubt the factual accuracy of his report.

Ireton's killer had also injured Count Iwazu Tomura, a senior member of the Japanese delegation. Tomura, it was given out, would soon be returning to Japan, along with his son, Noburo Tomura. Max made no reference to any of this, which was understandable in the circumstances. But he must certainly be aware of it.

Tomura was heading home, doubtless via Marseilles, where Anna Schmidt was also bound. Tomura had done business of some kind with Ireton. With Ireton dead, Morahan was presumably in charge of Ireton Associates. Max was intent on paying Morahan a lot of money as soon as possible. The money had originally belonged to his father. Sir Henry had first met Lemmer in Tokyo *circa* 1890. Both men might well have met Tomura around the same time. Everything was connected. Everything was converging. But connected by what? Converging on what?

There was no way to tell. Appleby could only put his trust in Max – and await events.

A TELEPHONE MESSAGE HAD INVITED SAM TO LE LAPIN Nonchalant, a bar-café at the Gare de Lyon end of the Rue de Lyon. It was seven o'clock when he arrived, golden evening light etching the time on the station clock in sharp shadows. He went in and found Max waiting for him towards the rear, drink in hand.

'It's warm enough to sit outside, sir,' said Sam as he ordered a beer.

'Better not, Sam. It'd be best for you not to be seen with me.'

'Heading south?'

'Marseilles.'

'On the trail of you know who?'

'I'll tell you everything when I get back.'

'When's that likely to be?'

'Hard to say. Days. Weeks. Months. It's . . . unpredictable.'

'You'll watch yourself, sir?'

'Oh yes. Don't worry, Sam. I won't take any unnecessary risks.'

'None *you* consider unnecessary, you mean. Cheers.' Sam's beer having arrived, he took a swig of it. 'I asked your uncle that question,' he said, lowering his voice.

'Ah, right. What sort of answer did you get?'

'He swore blind he'd never heard of the Farngolds.'

'Did you believe him?'

Another swig of beer. Then: 'Nope. Not for a minute.'

'It's as I expected, then. I'll have to find out despite them.'

'If you want some help . . .'

'I'll look elsewhere for it. It'll be a comfort for me to know you're

344

safe and sound here.' Max finished his whisky and signalled to the waiter for another. 'That really is the biggest favour you can do for me.'

'Doesn't sound like much of a favour.'

'Regard it as an order, then.'

Sam nodded reluctantly. 'Right you are, sir.'

While Max and Sam were sharing a farewell drink at Le Lapin Nonchalant, George was dressing for dinner at the Hôtel Mirabeau. His bandaged left forefinger was complicating the task of tying his bow-tie enormously and he was grateful for the knock at his door, when it came. His visitor could assist him with the task.

'*Entrez.*'

Winifred entered briskly, as she always did. 'Not ready, George?'

'It's this damned bandage.'

'You poor dear. Let me.'

Winifred twisted him round to face the light and came to grips with the tie.

'Have you thought any more about what Sam said to me, Win?' George asked quietly as he stretched his neck and studied the ceiling-rose.

'I have.'

'And?'

'There's nothing to be done. The Tomuras are going home. Commissioner Kuroda has already gone home. There'll soon be no one left in Paris who knows anything about the Farngolds. When James returns, Mr Twentyman will tell him as much as he can, of course. But it won't be enough, not nearly enough. And James will have no reason to pursue the matter.'

'You're sure about that?'

'As sure as I can be. There.' She patted the fastened tie with satisfaction. 'It's done.'

'Thanks, Win.'

'There's no need to thank me, considering what you've been through on my account, not to mention the humble pie we'll both have to eat when we face Ashley and Lydia.' She smiled at him. 'You have my full permission to drink immoderately this evening, George.'

345

While George and Winifred were preparing for dinner at the Mirabeau, Schools Morahan was standing in the kitchen of Malory Hollander's apartment on the Ile St-Louis, watching her prepare a modest supper for them to share. Eveline, Malory's co-tenant, was absent attending a party being thrown by one of her Red Cross colleagues.

'You should have gone too,' Morahan chided. 'It might've done you good.'

'Then you'd have had no one to talk to,' said Malory as she sampled the sauce. 'And we all know what a talkative soul you are.'

'There's not a lot more to be said for the present.' Morahan leant against the cabinet beside him. 'We are where we are.'

'Watertight logic, Schools. That's always good.' She banged the drips off her mixing spoon on the rim of the saucepan and laid it down. 'This'll look after itself for ten minutes. Fix me a drink, would you?'

The raw materials for a gin and it were to hand. Morahan mixed one for her and topped up his bourbon.

'Should we drink to Travis?' Malory asked as she took her glass.

'If you want.'

'Max was right, you know. You're not responsible for what Blachette did. Neither am I. Though thanks to your gallantry, of course, Max has no idea I talked you into sabotaging Travis's deal with the Germans.'

'I talked myself into it.'

'It was the right thing to do.'

Morahan frowned. 'I guess so.'

'Agreeing to help Max go after Tomura, on the other hand, might have been a monumental misjudgement.'

'You can back out if you want to, Malory. Max will understand. So will I. You never needed to volunteer in the first place.'

'It's a venture into the unknown. By any rational analysis, it's madness.'

'It doesn't feel like madness.'

'At some point, it will, believe me.'

He looked at her solemnly. 'I do.'

'There's something I ought to tell you. About the time I spent in Japan. There were . . . complications . . . I've never mentioned.'

'Are those complications likely to help or hinder us?'

'They might do either. Or both.'

'You want to tell me about them now?'

'Not really. I don't unburden myself easily. These are matters I never expected to speak of to anyone.'

'Then don't speak of them. Unless you're certain you have to.'

'Most people are eager to be told a secret, Schools. Why are you different?'

'Maybe I already know too many.'

'I'm not going to back out.'

Morahan nodded. 'I know.'

He drank some more bourbon, then added, 'Neither am I.'

'We're truly going to do this?'

'It seems we are.'

'Then let's drink to that.'

Max settled into his seat in the restaurant car of the Mediterranean Express as it drew out of the Gare de Lyon at the start of its overnight journey to Marseilles. There was something to be said for skulking in his sleeping compartment, where no one could see him. But skulking was not in his nature and he was damnably hungry. If he was being followed, he would have been followed onto the train, so hiding himself away would be futile.

Scanning the crowd on the concourse before boarding, Max had caught sight of a figure who might have been Meadows, sole survivor of the group he and Appleby had locked horns with in Oxfordshire. But his memory of Meadows was not clear enough for him to be certain on the point. A fully trained spy would have taken more careful note of Meadows' features when he had the chance, of course. Max was still in essence an amateur. That, he conceded to himself, probably explained his presence in the restaurant car.

'*Un apéritif, monsieur?*'

'Champagne,' said Max.

Amateur or not, Max had no illusion about the hazardousness

of his situation. Anna Schmidt's abrupt departure for Marseilles and Otto Krenz's ready provision of the address where she might be found were likely to be pawn-movements in Lemmer's chesslike handling of his resources. Max was probably going exactly where Lemmer wanted him to go.

But Max was also going where he wanted to go. He had out-manoeuvred Lemmer before and he backed himself to do so again. As a pilot, he had never been one to pay much heed to tactical planning. No dogfight he had ever been involved in had gone better for chalking optimistic trajectories on a blackboard before-hand. A good meal and sound sleep were all he needed to be ready for whatever Lemmer had prepared for him.

'*Merci beaucoup,*' he said as his champagne was delivered.

He held the glass before him for a moment, watching the bubbles rise to the surface. They rose and they burst, as bubbles were bound to, for they, like him, were governed by their nature.

MAX EMERGED FROM THE GARE ST-CHARLES INTO THE stridently bright light of Sunday morning in Marseilles. In the course of one night, he had moved from a grudging spring into early summer.

Walking out onto the esplanade in front of the station, he gazed out across the slowly stirring city. Bells were summoning the faithful to the basilica of Notre-Dame on the hilltop ahead of him. A few small boats were moving in the Vieux Port. And a smudge on the horizon, out to sea, he reckoned must be the Château d'If. Max's knowledge of Marseilles was almost entirely confined to his adolescent reading of *The Count of Monte Cristo*. But he was well aware Dumas would be of little help to him now.

Of more immediate use was the street map he had bought in the station. The Rue du Baignoir was not far away. He could walk along it on his way to the hotel he had booked by cable from Paris.

The city was still quiet. He threaded his way through a labyrinth of narrow streets, passing from respectability to squalor and back again before he reached the Rue du Baignoir, where there was a bare hint of poverty behind the genteelness.

The Pension Marguerite occupied a handsome terraced building gone faintly to seed. Max took it in at a glance as he passed by. The simple course of going in and asking to speak to Camille Strauss did not commend itself. He had to find a way of manipulating those who were trying to manipulate him. He pressed on.

A few more minutes brought him to the Canebière, the city's main thoroughfare. He walked up it, heading back in

349

the direction of the station, until he came to his hotel: the Grand.

It was the city's finest, which he had been pleased to have a good reason to choose. It was a pound to a penny the Tomuras would stay there before sailing for Japan and the chance to observe them was not to be missed. They did not know what he looked like and he would naturally be using an assumed name. According to Malory, the next sailing to the Far East was on Tuesday, so by Monday evening the Tomuras should be there.

Max's next requirement, second to a bath, was assistance with his enquiries about Anna Schmidt alias Camille Strauss. Gaspard, the young porter who showed him to his room, spoke serviceable English and had a promising pliability about his manner.

'Very kind, Monsieur Morris,' he said, acknowledging Max's generous tip.

'Do they pay you well here, Gaspard?'

'Not as well as I would like, *monsieur.*'

'Well, if you want to earn a bit more, I could put some work your way.'

The work was to visit the Pension Marguerite, sweet-talk the staff and find out as much as he could about the recently arrived Camille Strauss and any visitors, letters, cables or telephone calls she might have received. For the promise of five francs Gaspard was happy to take on the task, although it would have to await the end of his shift at the Grand at four o'clock.

The delay could not be helped. Max needed as much local intelligence as he could obtain and Gaspard's twinkle-eyed exchanges with a chambermaid suggested he was the man to gather it.

After his bath, Max explored the city. '*The better you know a place the likelier you are to be able to get out of it alive,*' Appleby had advised him at the outset of Max's highly irregular attachment to the British Secret Service.

He walked down to the Vieux Port and watched from a café terrace the comings and goings of the boats and the wanderings of the people. France's imperial reach was more evident in Marseilles

350

than it had been in Paris, with many Arabs and Africans to be seen.

He ambled round the headland separating the old harbour from the docks at Joliette. A ship just arrived from Algiers was unloading cargo and crew. He watched the operation for a while before returning to the Vieux Port. There he crossed the harbour on *le pont à transbordeur*, as a helpful fellow passenger told him it was called. A wide-planked nacelle suspended from a high bridge between towers either side of the harbour was winched across the gap, with nothing but a frayed rope-barrier to prevent anyone unsteady on their feet falling off it into the sea.

It was while he was aboard the transporter bridge that Max first suspected he was being followed, by a shifty, flat-capped fellow in a leather jacket he had noticed out at the docks.

His suspicions turned into virtual certainty when the man took the same route as his after leaving the bridge. Max was annoyed rather than alarmed. Lemmer could easily have deduced he would pursue Anna Schmidt to Marseilles. But why, in that case, show his hand so obviously? Leather-Jacket did not exhibit much subtlety. He dogged Max's footsteps along the Rive-Neuve canal that led away from the Vieux Port and then back to it, a wholly unnecessary diversion, stopping and starting in obvious unison with Max as he went.

Max reached the Quai de la Fraternité at the head of the harbour. The Restaurant Basso, directly ahead of him, looked a good place for lunch and rather too smart for Leather-Jacket to follow him into. Max's judgement proved right on both counts. He enjoyed a peaceful lunch, at the conclusion of which he used the size of the tip to buy a discreet and, so far as he could tell, unobserved rear exit.

Gaspard reported back to him at six o'clock, as agreed.

'There is a Madame Camille Strauss staying at the Marguerite, Monsieur Morris, but she did not arrive yesterday. She 'as been there more than a week.'

'Impossible.'

'*Mais non, c'est vrai.* I spoke to the daughter of the *patronne*. She is very pretty, very friendly. She is not trying to deceive me.'

'Then she's mistaken.'

'*Non, non.* Madame Strauss 'as been staying at the Marguerite for nine days. Thérèse showed me the entry in the register when I said it could not be so.'

'She was in Paris until last Friday, Gaspard.'

Gaspard shrugged helplessly 'I cannot explain it, *monsieur*. Madame Strauss 'as been there the time I 'ave said. Thérèse 'as seen 'er every day. She 'as no visitors, no letters, no messages, *rien*, though often she asks if there 'ave been any messages, as if she expects there to be. Would you like to know what she does?'

'From day to day, you mean?'

'Thérèse 'as a young brother, Luc. He is like me when I was his age: curious. Madame Strauss goes out every afternoon at the same time and does not return until the evening. There was no school for Luc on Thursday. So, he was at 'ome when she left. 'E and 'is friend, who was there with 'im, decided to follow 'er: to see where she went.'

'And where did she go?'

'Up to the Basilica Notre-Dame de la Garde. She went, in, er, *l'ascenseur* up to the bridge across to the basilica. She stopped at a bench 'alfway over the bridge and sat down. And she stayed there for . . . a long time. Luc and 'is friend became bored. They went for a walk. There is much exploring for boys to do there. Later they climbed up to the basilica from the other side and looked along the bridge. She was still there, nearly two hours later. A neighbour told Thérèse she also 'as seen Madame Strauss waiting on the bridge.'

'Waiting for what?'

'*Les paris sont ouverts, monsieur.* No one knows. Unless . . . you do.'

'Hardly.'

'But . . . you know 'er. No one else does.'

'What time does she usually return to the *pension*?'

'Around eight.'

'So, she could still be up at the basilica now.'

'*Oui.*' Gaspard winked at Max conspiratorially. 'She could.' And then he rubbed his fingers together in a transparent gesture. It was time for him to be paid.

Max took a taxi from the Grand to the foot of *l'ascenseur* in Boulevard Notre-Dame. It was a funicular, designed to spare worshippers a stiff climb up to the basilica set high above Marseilles on a limestone outcrop. By the time Max arrived there were many more people coming down than going up. A mellow evening was advancing, the lowering sun casting a honey-hued light across the city.

It was a short ride to the top. Max stepped out onto the bridge that led across to the bare, rocky setting of Notre-Dame de la Garde, a huge golden statue of the Virgin Mary glistening atop its high belfry. Halfway along the bridge was the bench Gaspard had mentioned. A woman was sitting on it, her features obscured by a parasol. She was wearing a pale dress beneath a light grey coat.

She might well be Camille Strauss. But logically she could not be Anna Schmidt. That was clear to Max, though little else was. Why had he been brought here? What purpose was the deception designed to serve?

He set off along the bridge, wondering what he would do if she did not look up when he reached the bench.

The distance closed between them. As it did so, a strange sensation of familiarity crept over him. Surely he knew the woman sitting on the bench. Surely . . .

She looked up. And he knew.

She was Corinne Dombreux.

AT FIRST THEY WERE BOTH SPEECHLESS. IT SEEMED CORINNE could no better comprehend Max's presence in Marseilles than he could hers. She stared at him in open-mouthed amazement, as he did at her.

Then she stood up and spoke. 'What ... are you doing here?'

She had dropped her parasol behind her as she rose. The breeze caught it and carried it over the railings behind the bench. Max jumped forward to catch it, but too late: it floated away, then down, slowly, like a petal falling from a flower, towards the sloping ground beneath the bridge.

'It doesn't matter,' Corinne murmured.

Max stepped back, surprised by how close he was to her. They looked searchingly at each other, Corinne's eyes partially hidden from him by the shade of her straw-brimmed hat.

'I don't understand,' she said.

'Neither do I.'

'Why are you here?'

'I came looking for Camille Strauss.'

'What?' She frowned. 'That was just . . . a name I invented.'

'I was told – I was led to believe – that it was the pseudonym of Lemmer's former secretary, Anna Schmidt.'

'Lemmer's secretary? You're here because of Lemmer?'

'He was ultimately responsible for my father's death. And he's a threat to the peace of Europe, if not the world. I'm determined to bring him to justice.'

'But how can you have thought – how can anyone – that I was . . .' She seemed to have forgotten the secretary's name already.

'Anna Schmidt.'

'It makes no sense.'

'You can be sure it makes sense to Lemmer.' Max looked around. Their position was not overlooked, other than from the basilica, but it was exposed. A sniper in a window of one of the houses below would have a clear shot at both of them. 'It's dangerous here. We should leave.'

'I can't leave.'

'Why not? What brought you here?'

'I . . .' She looked away. 'I can't say.'

'You must.'

She gazed at him oddly, as if she still could not believe he was truly there. 'When I wrote that letter to you in Paris, I did not think I would ever see you again.'

'It was a hard letter to read.'

'But what I said in it was right.'

'That I should stop looking for answers?'

'The irony is . . . I did not take my own advice.'

'Why are you here, Corinne?'

She sat down. Reluctantly, he sat down beside her. He could not force her to leave the bridge, short of physically manhandling her. And he could not simply leave without her. The longer they stayed there together the less likely it seemed that they were in immediate danger. He could think of no reason why Lemmer would want to kill them in such a public place. But he could think of no reason why he should want them to meet again at all. He looked at her, the breeze stirring her hair beneath her hat as she stared ahead. At last she said, 'I don't understand what's happened.'

'Just tell me.'

'Do you have a cigarette?'

He gave her one and proffered his lighter. Her hand trembled as she held the cigarette to the flame. She looked at him, aware that he had noticed.

'I went to Nantes, as I said I would. I didn't stay long with my sister. I found lodgings in the city and work as a seamstress. Then, two weeks ago, I received a letter via my sister. The letter instructed me to come to Marseilles.'

'Who gave you this instruction? Why did you act on it?'

'Because the letter was from my husband. Pierre.'

'*Pierre?* He's dead.'

'No. He isn't. It was his handwriting, Max, I recognized it at once. I couldn't believe it. I didn't want to believe it. But there was no doubt. It was from him.'

'You told me he died in Petrograd.'

'So the embassy informed me. His body was identified by a former colleague. But it can't have been him. In the letter, Pierre said it was safer for him – and for me – if he was thought to be dead. He implored me not to alert the authorities. He wanted to explain everything that had occurred after he sent me home from Petrograd. He asked me to come to Marseilles and meet him here, in this spot. I was to wait for him, every afternoon, until he showed himself.'

'You've been here more than a week. You can't seriously believe he's really going to turn up.'

'He said he could not say when he would be able to come. He had to be very very careful. But he would come eventually.'

'This is absurd, Corinne.' Max's protest was heartfelt. But he knew there was something much worse than absurdity at play. They had both been put in this position for a reason. And only Lemmer knew what it was. 'You told me how badly Pierre treated you. You don't still love him, do you?'

'No. I don't.'

'Then why is it so important you see him again – even if he truly is still alive?'

'Because . . . he said there were things he needed to tell me about Henry and . . . and you.'

'Me?'

'He seemed to know a lot about what had happened in Paris. He'd read of Henry's death. Henry had talked about you to him, apparently. They were actually good friends until Pierre discovered how close I was to Henry. But they were reconciled after I left Petrograd. According to the letter, they even discussed the future:

356

what should happen if either of them died, which was quite possible considering how dangerous the city became under the Bolsheviks. Pierre claims he went so far as to give Henry his blessing to marry me.'

'Did Pa ever tell you that?'

'No. But I don't think he would have, even if it's true.'

'Which it almost certainly isn't. My guess is the letter's a forgery. Lemmer has the resources to manage such things with ease.'

'A good enough forgery to fool a man's wife? No, Max. It was from Pierre. He mentioned things only he could possibly know.'

'Unless he was forced to disclose them to others.'

'And to write the letter? It was his hand, Max. I have other letters, from before we were married, to compare it with. I recognized his turns of phrase. He wrote it.'

'You still haven't explained why you think it's so important to take the chance that he's alive – to come here and wait all this time for a man you no longer love.'

'I told you. It concerns your father and you. Pierre said he was arrested by the Soviet authorities just before Christmas, 1917. He did not explain why they'd arrested him, or why they later released him. The French Ambassador must have secured his freedom by some means or other. I was told nothing of it at the time. He said Henry came to visit him in the Peter and Paul Fortress, where he was held. It was their last meeting. Henry had already left Petrograd by the time Pierre was released. Pierre feared he would be put to death. For that reason, he told Henry something – a great secret, he called it.'

'What was it?'

'He said it was too dangerous to entrust to a letter. He would tell me when we met. But it was something we needed to know.'

'We?'

'You and I, Max. He named you. He said he would leave it to me to judge whether to tell you when I'd heard what it was. But he believed he owed it to Henry to make a clean breast of it. And he trusted me to decide what to do with the information.'

'Did Pa ever mention visiting Pierre in prison?'

'No.'

'And he never breathed a word about any "great secret"?'

'No. Pierre said—'

'Wait a moment.' Max held up a cautionary hand as a group of people approached from the direction of the basilica: a man with two women and a couple of children, and another man, a little way behind, who might have been with them, or might simply have been following closely after them. As they dawdled towards them, Max saw to his horror that the second man was Leather-Jacket.

'God damn it.'

'What's the matter?'

'Stay quiet while they go by.'

Corinne looked at Max in dismay, but said no more. The straggling group slowly reached and passed them and moved on towards the lift.

'Have you seen that man before?' Max asked in a whisper.

'Which man?'

'The one in the leather jacket tagging along behind.'

'I don't think so.'

'I have. Once too often for comfort.'

'You think he's following you?'

'Yes. I do.'

'Why would he be?'

'Lemmer's orders, I imagine. Except . . .'

'Except what?'

'He's not as good at it as you'd expect an agent of Lemmer's to be. Finish what you were going to say.'

'Pierre said he didn't think Henry believed him at the time – or at any rate didn't want to believe him. "It was a terrible thing to have to believe," he said. But something must have happened later, in Paris, to convince Henry that what Pierre had told him was true. Pierre was sure that was why Henry had been murdered: because he'd taken it further. He knew I loved Henry. He wanted me to know the truth as well. "There may still be something that can be done," he said.'

'Done about what?'

Corinne shook her head at Max's intransigence. 'We'll only have an answer if we meet Pierre face to face.'

'Can you rely on anything he says, Corinne? He was – is, if he's truly still alive – a spy, a traitor to his country.'

'I'm not sure that's fair. I don't really know what he did in Russia.'

'You know he was unfaithful to you.'

'Infidelity is a long way from treason. Besides . . .'

'Yes?'

'Maybe he wanted me to leave Petrograd for my own safety and drove me away from him in order to achieve it.'

'You can't seriously believe that.'

'When I look back on our life there . . . I don't know what to believe.'

'Well, believe this. Lemmer orchestrated the events that led you and me here. That means he knows what Pierre wrote to you. Either because the letter was forged on his instructions or because he compelled Pierre to write it.'

'It isn't a forgery. And Pierre is here, in Marseilles. I brought a photograph of him with me. I showed it to the lift conductor. He said he thought he'd seen Pierre riding the lift several times.'

'But not once since you arrived?'

'I have to be patient, Max.'

'For how long?'

'A few more days at least.'

'Can I see the letter?'

'I destroyed it.'

'You did *what*?'

'He asked me to, Max. If it fell into the hands of the authorities it could lead to his arrest. He stands accused of treason, as you just pointed out. That means the guillotine. By writing to me, he was putting his trust in me. He was putting his life in my hands.'

'Or our lives in Lemmer's.'

'If Lemmer's as powerful as you say, he could kill us whenever he pleases. Why bring us here? Why involve Pierre at all?'

'I don't know.' Max shook his head helplessly 'I simply don't know.' He stood up and, turning, gazed towards the purple-blue horizon where sea and sky met, out in the Marseilles roads. 'Can I see Pierre's photograph?' he murmured.

Corinne took it from her reticule and passed it to him.

Pierre Dombreux looked younger than Max had expected, although the picture had probably been taken several years previously, of course. And he was smiling. That too was quite illogically unexpected. The man in the photograph was clear-browed and smooth-skinned, almost cherubic, an effect only partly detracted from by a vigorous moustache. He had dark, glossy hair and a soft, amenable gaze. Only Max's knowledge of his previous deviousness – in whatever cause he truly served – tainted the charming nature his appearance implied.

'I believe he may not be as bad a man as I once supposed,' Corinne said softly.

Max looked both ways along the bridge. 'He's not coming. You know that, don't you?'

'I have to give him the chance.'

'You should leave with me.' He returned the photograph to her. 'Now.'

'I'll stay a little longer.'

'And return tomorrow?'

'The truth is . . .' She raised her head and looked at Max directly. 'I don't know what else to do.'

'Go back to Nantes.'

'I'm not ready to give up yet.'

He dropped to his haunches in front of her and held her by the wrists. He wanted her to understand him plainly – to acknowledge what to him was an obvious truth: that the longer she remained in Marseilles the more danger she was in. 'You must leave this city, Corinne. As soon as possible. Whatever Lemmer has in mind for us, it won't be good.'

'Are you leaving?'

'I can't. But *you* can.'

'And that's what you want me to do?'

'You were free when you left Paris. Don't throw that freedom away.'

'I can lead a poor kind of life somewhere, Max. Yes. I can do that. And maybe I will.'

'Think about it, Corinne. Think seriously. For both our sakes.'

She gazed at him for a long time. He could not guess what was in her mind. 'It isn't easy,' was all she said in the end.

He let go of her and stood up. 'I'm staying at the Grand under the name Morris. You can contact me there at any time.'

'Can you let the chance slip through your fingers of finding out what the "great secret" is that your father was pursuing, Max? Can you really do that?'

'I'll find out without endangering you, Corinne. I promise. I'll find out. And when I do I'll tell you everything I've learnt.'

'You don't believe Pierre's alive, do you?'

'If he is, he's doing Lemmer's bidding. Which means you should turn your back on him. And walk away.'

'You may be right.'

'I am.'

'I will think about it.'

'Good. But don't think too long. Because I don't know how long we've got before Lemmer shows his hand.' Max gazed around, wondering if they had been under observation the whole time they had been there. 'I only know he will.'

CORINNE'S REAPPEARANCE IN HIS LIFE LEFT MAX CONFUSED and apprehensive. His only certainty was that Lemmer had lured them both to Marseilles for sinister reasons of his own. For the moment, Max could think of no obvious response beyond trying to persuade Corinne to leave. He was supposed to be seeking out Anna Schmidt, but how he was to do that now he had no idea.

He descended in the lift and headed back towards his hotel on foot through the deepening dusk. An echoing of footsteps behind him as he passed under the railway bridge on Boulevard Notre-Dame alerted him to the fact that Leather-Jacket was once again on his tail. Frustrated by his inability to outwit Lemmer, Max became angry that such a bungler had been assigned the task of following him. Impulsively, he decided to do something about it.

The streets became narrower and denser as he neared the Vieux Port. Max saw the quay of the Rive-Neuve canal ahead, brightened by a ray of the setting sun. The shadows were deep in the street he was walking along, however, and deepening all the time. He turned abruptly into a side alley, then dodged into a doorway.

Within a couple of minutes Leather-Jacket made a cautious entrance into the alley, before abruptly picking up his pace, presumably anxious not to lose Max.

There was no danger of that. Max stepped out just as the man hurried blindly past the doorway, grabbed him by the shoulders, pulled him back and slammed him against the door.

'Please,' Leather-Jacket cried out as dislodged cement dust pattered down around him. 'Don't hurt me.'

The first surprise was that the man spoke English, and in a native Scottish accent. The second was his timidity. He was paunchy and short of breath, his sparsely bearded jowl quivering as he spoke. There was fear clear to read in his glassy, skittering gaze. His voice was a high-pitched wheeze. One of Lemmer's hardened killers he patently was not.

'Who the hell are you?' Max demanded.

'MacGregor. William MacGregor.'

'What d'you want with me?'

'I'm here on behalf of Miss Susan Henty.'

For a second, Max's blood ran cold. He thought he had left his entanglement with the Henty siblings safely behind him in the Orkneys. 'Who?' he countered.

'Miss Susan Henty. She sent me to look for you . . . Mr Hutton.'

'My name's not Hutton.'

'Maybe not. But it's the name you used while you were in the Orkneys.'

'I don't know what you're talking about.'

'I recognized you from your photograph.'

'What photograph?'

'It was taken by Miss Henty at the Ring of Brodgar . . . on Saturday the twenty-sixth of April. It shows you with her late brother, Selwyn.'

A photograph? Damn it all to hell. Susan Henty had taken pictures of the stones at Brodgar, to supplement Selwyn's surveying work. Max had done his best to ensure he was not in any of them. But she must have taken one while he was not paying attention. 'I've never heard of Susan Henty. Or Selwyn Henty. He's dead, you say?'

'His body was found in Kirkwall harbour by a police diver five days ago. He'd been murdered.'

'Sorry to hear that. But it's nothing to do with me.'

'You left Kirkwall without warning last Monday, following Mr Henty's disappearance.'

'I keep telling you, MacGregor. I know nothing about any of this. You've got the wrong man.'

'Miss Henty received a letter from you, blaming your sudden

departure on a family emergency. But you supplied no address where you could be contacted. The Orkney police would very much like to talk to you about what happened to Mr Henty.'

'You mean they'd like to talk to this fellow Hutton. What you don't seem to be able to grasp is that I'm not Hutton.'

'I think you are.'

Max tightened his grip on MacGregor's collar. But the man had conquered some of his fear. Perhaps he had concluded Max was not about to beat him to a pulp.

'Miss Henty received another letter, two days after yours. It said you could be found here, in Marseilles. The police dragged their feet about following it up, so Miss Henty hired me to investigate.'

'What are you – a private detective?'

'When there's call for me to be, aye.'

'And this letter. Who was it from?'

'Oh, it was anonymous. But accurate, as it turns out.'

'Accurate be damned. I'm not Hutton.'

'I say you are. And I'll say it to the police here unless . . .'

'Unless what?'

MacGregor licked his lips nervously, apparently debating what he should demand. Then: 'I'll require a signed notarial statement detailing everything you know about Mr Henty's death.'

'That's easy. I know nothing.'

'You were seen with Mr Henty and a third person, thought to be a US naval officer, in the bar of the Albert Hotel, Kirkwall, late in the evening of Saturday the twenty-sixth. Your statement will need to be specific about what the three of you discussed. It may be that the American wrote the anonymous letter to Miss Henty in order to divert suspicion from himself. So, what can you tell me about him?'

'Not a damn thing. I wasn't there.'

'I believe I can cause you a great many difficulties with the French authorities, Mr . . . whatever your real name is. You could leave the country before the Procurator Fiscal of Orkney submitted an extradition request, I don't doubt. But maybe you don't want to leave. Maybe your business with that young lady you met up by the cathedral obliges you to remain here, at least for the time being. In which case, a statement of the kind I've described really isn't too much to ask.'

Max began to suspect MacGregor's primary objective was not the pursuit of Selwyn Henty's murderer, but the acquisition of a document he could take back to Susan Henty that would encourage her to pay the fee he had it in mind to charge. He was a long way from home and poorly placed to extract much more from Max. What he did not know was that he was still asking too much. The last thing Max could afford to do was put his name to any kind of account of his dealings with Selwyn Henty and Lieutenant Grant Fontana of the US Navy.

'What d'you say? I could arrange for us to meet a *notaire* tomorrow.'

Max held MacGregor in his grip a moment longer, then released him. Time was his best friend in extracting himself from the dilemma. He smiled.

'What's funny?'

'You're a lucky man, Mr MacGregor.'

'In what way?'

'If I'd had a hand in Selwyn Henty's murder, I probably wouldn't scruple to kill you as well.'

'But you didn't?'

'No. I did not.'

'Then you'll favour me with that statement?'

'Where are you staying?'

'The Continental, Rue Beauvau.'

'Give me forty-eight hours to consider my position.'

'I'll give you twenty-four.'

MacGregor seemed to fancy himself a hard bargainer. Max decided to indulge him. 'Twenty-four it is.'

'I'll expect to hear from you no later than this time tomorrow evening.'

'And I'll expect to be spared the sight of you dogging my footsteps in the meantime.'

MacGregor nodded. 'I believe we have an understanding,' he said.

'Yes,' Max agreed. 'I believe we do.'

DESPITE ALL THE MANY REASONS WHY HE MIGHT HAVE SLEPT poorly, Max in fact slept well and long that night, although the problems he was beset by were waiting stubbornly to confront him the following morning.

He breakfasted in his room. Gaspard brought the tray – and the latest news. 'The Japanese party you asked about, *monsieur*: they will arrive this evening. We expect them to be 'ere by eight.'

'Where will their rooms be?' Max asked gruffly as he sipped his coffee.

'Count Tomura is staying in the front corner suite on the third floor. That would be the second to you, *monsieur*: the floor below this one. 'Is son will be in the room next to it, over Boulevard Garibaldi. There is . . . *une porte de communication* – an inside door . . . that connects the two rooms.'

Max digested the information as he munched a slice of toast, then said, 'How much for the loan of a pass-key?'

'*Un passe?*' Gaspard feigned horror. 'You ask too much.'

'Maybe. But that means you can do the same. Who knows? I might agree to your terms.'

Gaspard frowned dubiously at Max, who went on munching his toast. Half a minute or so elapsed. Then Gaspard said, 'When do you want it?'

After breakfast, Max took himself off to the offices of Nippon Yusen Kaisha to confirm the departure of the *Miyachi-maru* at noon on Tuesday, bound for Port Said, Colombo, Singapore, Hong

Kong, Shanghai, Kobe and Yokohama. She was coming from Antwerp and was expected to dock that evening. Berths were still available, moderately priced. Max resisted the temptation to book one. Travelling to Japan on the same ship as the Tomuras would be madness. Besides, he had come to Marseilles in pursuit of Anna Schmidt and so far had accomplished nothing on that front.

When he returned to the hotel, he was surprised to find a visitor waiting for him: Corinne. She looked depressed and careworn, as if her faith in her errant husband had evaporated overnight. Max had not expected her to see the folly of trusting Pierre so soon, but was happy to think it possible.

And it was possible, as she rapidly confirmed. 'I've decided to leave Marseilles, Max,' she announced. 'Can we go somewhere and talk?'

They found a café a short distance away in the Cours St-Louis and sat out on the terrace. Corinne ordered cognac with her coffee and readily accepted a succession of Max's cigarettes, for which he seemed to have less and less use himself. In the dappled sunlight, with the perfume from a pavement flower stall wafting over them and a hopeful violinist sawing away near by, Corinne's anxiety was even more palpable.

'Has something happened?' Max asked. He could hardly believe her sudden change of heart was solely attributable to the force of his argument.

'You haven't heard, have you?'

'Heard?'

'It was in this morning's paper.'

'What was?'

'I thought about what you said and I saw the sense of it. I knew you were right. Still, I doubt I'd have talked myself into acting on it straight away but for this.' She took out of her reticule a half-page torn from a newspaper and passed it to him. 'There.' She pointed to an article headlined *UNE MORT EN MER* – a death at sea.

Max's first scan took in only a few salient words: *Port Said, May 3; NYK Kazama Maru; Une noyade; Un citoyen japonais; Kuroda Masataka.*

'Kuroda's dead, Max,' said Corinne softly.

'Drowned?'

'The report says he was lost overboard on Friday in unexplained circumstances. His body was picked up by a fishing boat later that day.'

The half-page slipped from Max's grasp. He slumped back in his chair. 'I can't believe it.' But he could, of course. He remembered what Kuroda had said in his letter: '*My continued well-being is by no means guaranteed . . . My position is acutely vulnerable.*' How right he had been.

'It's being treated as an accident, Max. But it wasn't an accident, was it?'

'Assuredly not.'

'He was a good friend of Henry's.'

'I know.'

'Why had he left Paris?'

'Recalled to Tokyo to face trumped-up charges. It was Count Tomura's doing. As was his drowning, I don't doubt.'

'Another accidental death.'

'Good God.' Max put his head in his hands. 'He wrote to me just before sailing. He virtually predicted this.'

'There's a dangerous secret buried somewhere in Japan, isn't there? A secret Henry and Kuroda both knew too much about to be allowed to live.'

'Yes. There is.'

'Pierre's mixed up in it somehow, isn't he?'

'He is, yes.' Max looked up at her. 'Which means you're in danger, Corinne. I think you understand that now, don't you?'

'You're in danger too.'

'Let me worry about that. It's vital you leave Marseilles as soon as possible.'

'I know. Though still it troubles me that Pierre may be a better, nobler man than I ever gave him credit for and is relying on me to stay.'

'If that was true, he'd already have contacted you. You've waited more than long enough for him.'

'I know, I know.' She swallowed some of her cognac. 'I should go.'

'You said you *were* going.'

She drew a deep breath and slowly released it. 'I am.'

'When?'

'There's a sleeper to Bordeaux at eight. I can travel on to Nantes from there tomorrow.'

'You shouldn't wait until this evening.'

'What else can I do?'

'Take a local train to somewhere en route this afternoon. Catch the sleeper there later.'

She frowned at him, more deeply worried than ever by being urged to take such precautions.

'We can go to the station straight away, Corinne, find out the times and buy you a ticket.'

She looked intently at him, measuring his seriousness, then nodded. She had accepted the need to do as he said. 'Very well,' she murmured.

The practicalities of arranging Corinne's departure distracted Max from the dismay he felt at the news of Kuroda's death. Somewhere, he knew, the motor of Lemmer's master-plan was continuing to run. Kuroda's demise was merely further evidence of this, following hard on the heels of MacGregor's unwelcome arrival on the scene.

Max wanted Corinne to leave before the evening, not just because the sooner she left the better but because he knew he would then be able to concentrate on the task in hand. The Tomuras were coming. And he had to be ready for them.

When they reached the Gare St-Charles, enquiries revealed there was a 3.30 train to Montpellier, where the Bordeaux sleeper would call later. The booking was made.

'I'll see you off,' said Max as they walked back out of the station.

'So you can be sure I've gone?'

'We must stop doing what Lemmer wants us to do, Corinne. For some reason, he wants you here. Don't let him have his way.'

'I don't intend to.'

'Good. Because neither do I.'

They were brave words. But what they amounted to was an open question. Anna Schmidt's whereabouts were still unknown to Max. As far as breaking the code used in the Grey File went he had achieved less than nothing. And now Kuroda was dead. Max felt the sights of an invisible rifle were trained on him. Only Lemmer's whim would determine when the fatal shot was fired. Until then, Max had a chance to cheat the bullet. He had to find a way to make the most of it.

After walking Corinne back to the Pension Marguerite, where she had packing to attend to, Max returned to the Grand.

A letter had been delivered for him in his absence. By hand. The deliverer had contrived to leave the letter at the reception desk without being noticed. Max did not recognize the handwriting on the envelope. But the writer knew the pseudonym he was using. That was worrying in its own right.

Max took the letter into the reading-room, sat down and opened it. His eye moved straight to the signature at the bottom. *Pierre Dombreux*. There it was, though whether authentic he had no immediate way to tell.

My dear Max
We have never met, though I feel I know you well. Your
father spoke of you often. I saw you with Corinne near the
basilica yesterday evening. I regret contacting her. It was a
mistake – a surrender to sentiment. I should not have done
it. She should leave Marseilles. As for you, I would have said
the same until I heard the news from Port Said. They have
crossed a boundary with this murder. It cannot go
unpunished. That means I cannot stay in hiding. I must
show myself. I will need help to defeat them – your help,
Max. Meet me tomorrow morning at the Villa Orseis. I have
the use of the place. It is on the Corniche, near
Malmousque. Be there by nine. I will not wait long. I can tell
you everything. I mean to tell you everything. The truth is
terrible. But the truth is also freedom. Do not turn away

from it, I beg you. And do not tell Corinne, I also beg you.
Pierre Dombreux

Do not turn away. No. Max would not do that. He would never do that.

He took out his lighter, set the flame to the letter and watched it burn in the ashtray before him. The only person who could confirm the letter was from Dombreux was the only person he could not ask: Corinne. Therefore it was safer to destroy it.

Tomorrow morning, if Dombreux was to be believed, Max would know the truth. And if he was not to be believed . . .

That too was truth of a kind.

Max sat with Corinne in the buffet at the Gare St-Charles. Warm sunshine burnt sallowly through the grimy windows. The whistles and shouts and engine snorts and general hubbub of the concourse drifted in among the rattling crockery and the low burble of intermingled conversations. Corinne looked at Max, then up at the clock, then back at Max.

'Do you think Pierre ever intended to contact me?' she asked through a plume of nervously exhaled cigarette smoke.

'I don't know, Corinne,' Max replied, which he reckoned was not altogether untrue.

'If not, bringing me here was just a cruel hoax.'

'No. It wasn't that. I suspect Lemmer wanted you here to divert me from tracking down Anna Schmidt.'

'Have you any way of finding her?'

'Not yet.'

'Promise me I won't read in the newspaper that you've met with a fatal accident.'

He smiled gamely at her. 'I promise.'

'But you can't, of course. I know that.'

Max said nothing, there being nothing to say. Farewells had often been thus in his experience: much left unspoken, though not unthought. In this case, there was an additional reason for reticence: the letter he had received from Corinne's errant husband.

She looked at the clock again.

This time, so did he. 'We should be going,' he announced.

'Yes.' In her gaze was an unplumbed depth of soulfulness. 'Of course.'

Max walked out onto the platform with Corinne, carrying her bag. Before boarding the train, she handed him a piece of paper with her address in Nantes written on it, along with her sister's. 'In case I move,' she explained. She had tried to break off their acquaintance conclusively when leaving Paris, but seemed no longer to believe that was possible. 'I'll write or cable,' he assured her, worthless though such an assurance was. The sun was warm on his back as he held a door open for her. The paintwork of the carriage was peeling. There was verdigris on the door handle. These details he felt he would remember. And tied to them would be either relief or regret that he had not told her about Dombreux's letter. A decision was always a guess. And a guess was always a hope.

She kissed him once on the cheek and began to say something, then stifled the words, turned away and climbed hurriedly aboard. He passed the bag up to her and closed the door. She leant out through the window. Other doors were slamming the length of the train. A whistle blew. The engine gathered steam.

'Don't worry,' he said, smiling at her. It seemed she could not speak. She grasped his hand, then released it. There was another blast on the whistle. The train clanked into motion. And she stepped back. She did not propose to watch as his figure receded on the platform. The parting was done.

But not for Max. He watched the train all the way out of the station, until it curved out of sight. Silence fell. In the emptiness of the afternoon, he turned and walked away.

Max had experienced a surge of anger on hearing of Kuroda's death. His first instinct was to await the Tomuras' arrival, then burst in on them and shoot them both dead. The idea held a strong appeal: to make an end of these people who had somehow ruined his father's life and Corinne's and the lives of numerous others he did not even know.

But though the death of Count Tomura might obstruct Lemmer,

it would not defeat him, far less destroy him. And it would not give Max what he craved now above all else: the truth. Pierre Dombreux claimed he could give him that. Max had to take the chance Dombreux was in earnest. Until tomorrow morning, at least, he had to stay his hand.

It followed he had to keep MacGregor at bay by seeming to give him what he wanted. Close to the expiry of the twenty-four hours MacGregor had allowed him to consider his position, Max would indicate his willingness to make a sworn statement. It would not be possible to arrange a visit to a *notaire* until the following day. And by then . . .

As Max neared the Grand, a woman emerged from the hotel and stepped into a waiting car, which immediately drove away. It was such a fleeting and distant glimpse that he could not be sure, but his first impression was that the woman was Nadia Bukayeva. He hurried ahead, but the car was already lost to sight in the tangle of traffic on the Canebière.

Judicious questioning of the reception clerk established that a woman had just left after confirming Count Tomura and his son would be arriving that evening. She had not volunteered her name.

It was Nadia, of course. It had to be. She was Lemmer's intermediary for communications with Count Tomura. The pieces were moving on the board. And she was one of them.

Max waited until six o'clock before heading for MacGregor's hotel. Ideally, he would have waited until later, but he needed to be back at the Grand before the Tomuras arrived. Besides, it was already too late for MacGregor to act immediately on any agreement by Max to cooperate.

As it transpired, it was too late for another reason. MacGregor was out. Max left a note for him proposing he call again at nine the following morning. He couched the suggestion meekly enough to delude MacGregor into supposing he had the better of Max, who would actually be elsewhere at nine the following morning – elsewhere and, with luck, more profitably engaged.

*

374

Returning to the Grand, Max caught Gaspard's eye as he crossed the foyer. A few minutes after he had reached his room, there was a knock at the door.

'I must 'ave this back by tomorrow morning,' Gaspard said, slipping the pass-key into Max's hand.

'You will,' said Max.

'You worry me, *monsieur*.'

'Just as well I don't worry myself, then, isn't it?'

From the balconette of his room, Max had a good if oblique view of the hotel's main entrance. He kept it under discreet surveillance as the estimated time of the Tomuras' arrival drew near.

They arrived when expected, transported from the station in the hotel's limousine. Porters scurried out to receive them. Count Tomura's party comprised himself, his son and a hulking, wasp-waistcoated factotum. The Count had his left arm in a sling, causing him to wear his overcoat with one sleeve empty. That and his baleful, imperious expression gave him the appearance of a wounded general. Noburo Tomura looked a softer, over-indulged product of the line – and just a little insecure in his show of arrogance towards the porters. Max suspected recent events might have shaken him rather more than they had his father. He had never seen either of them before. Yet with all he knew about them he felt he had their measure.

Max kept up his vigil by the window long after the Tomuras had gone in. He was waiting to see if Nadia would return to confer with them. That would be his chance to learn enough to give him some slender advantage. Whether the chance would amount to anything in reality he could not predict. Action – and reaction – would govern the outcome. When the time came.

THE ONLY FLYING MAX HAD EVER DISLIKED WAS IN FOG. Aside from the danger of misreading the altimeter, it was the opacity of the world the plane moved through that unnerved him. Enemy aircraft were less of a threat than an unanticipated hillock or an avenue of trees. He could see nothing. He could counter nothing. Hard-learnt skills of evasive manoeuvring did not matter a damn. His opponent was invisibility itself.

To Max, stiff-limbed in his seat by the window of his room, Nadia's eventual arrival felt very much like the sudden lifting of a fog bank. Suddenly, the challenge was clear before him.

A car drew up and Nadia stepped out onto the pavement. Max could see nothing of the driver beyond a coated elbow. It hardly mattered which one of Lemmer's minions he was. He drove on as Nadia entered the hotel.

Max sprang into action. He checked the pass-key in his pocket and the gun in his shoulder-holster, shrugged on his jacket and headed for the door.

He assumed Nadia had come to brief the Tomuras on Lemmer's behalf. He further assumed they would communicate in English. The only other possibility was French and he could hope to learn something even from that. But he reckoned English was likelier.

They would probably meet in Count Tomura's suite. Noburo would walk through from his adjoining room. That would place them some distance from the door of Noburo's room, which Max proposed to enter by. To what extent he could eavesdrop on their conversation remained to be seen. As did what he would gain from it. But it was an opportunity he was determined to press to the limit.

He descended the stairs to the second floor cautiously, in case Nadia came up by the staircase, although he expected her to use the lift. He heard the whirring of its mechanism as he came to the landing and hung back, shielded by a wall. It seemed he had read her right.

The lift doors rattled open. The attendant said something. The doors closed. There were soft footsteps on carpet, like the padding of a panther; a knock; a faint creak as another door opened. No words were spoken.

Max risked a glance along the wide corridor. The door to the corner suite at the far end was closing. Nadia had entered.

Max waited a few moments, then started along the corridor, taking the pass-key out of his pocket as he went.

The whereabouts of the factotum were unknown to him, of course. He hoped the fellow had been sent up to his attic room for the duration of Nadia's visit. Count Tomura would probably not want a servant to witness their meeting.

He reached the door of Noburo's room. There was no sound from within. But the hotel's doors were solid, its walls thick. Max would learn little by straining his ears out in the corridor. He tentatively inserted the key in the lock and turned it. There was resistance. He grasped the handle and pulled the door towards him. The key turned, with the faintest of clicks. He depressed the handle. The door opened.

He stepped inside and eased the door shut behind him. Nobody called out. There was no reaction to his entry.

He was in a shadowy vestibule, with a half-open door before him. He crept through it into the main part of the room. It was larger and more lavishly decorated than his own. And it was, as he had hoped, empty.

He heard voices then, carrying from rooms beyond, through the open door he could see diagonally opposite him. He could not distinguish any words, but it sounded as if English was being spoken.

He crossed the room as lightly as he could, wary of creaking floorboards. None betrayed him. Two vast gilt-framed mirrors on facing walls constructed a tunnel out of reflected and re-reflected images of Max that he did his best to ignore as he proceeded.

The voices grew steadily louder and more distinct as he neared the door. Beyond it he could see the window of a further room. A shadow moved somewhere within. A man coughed. The shadow moved again.

'You must excuse me.' The voice was low and gravelly, the accent well-bred English tinged with Japanese. 'I do not take instructions readily from a woman.'

There was a drift of cigar smoke in the air. Through the crack of the door, Max saw, beyond the communicating doorway, Count Tomura standing by the window, gazing out, smoking with his right hand, while his left was cradled in the sling.

'They are not my instructions, but his.' It was Nadia's voice. She was as calm and self-possessed as ever. The haughtiness she could never quite suppress was bound to annoy Count Tomura. But perhaps she did not care. 'And he would want you to regard them as . . . recommendations.'

Tomura laughed mirthlessly. 'He should remember what I am doing for him.'

'I am sure he has not forgotten.'

'And you, Nadia Mikhailovna? What have you not forgotten?'

'Oh, many things.'

'Do they include the tasks you performed for the Dragonfly in Keijo?'

'Many of those tasks I would prefer to forget.'

Another laugh. 'No doubt you would.'

'But of course some matters . . . stick in my memory.'

Another voice cut in, younger and sharper, clearly that of Noburo Tomura. 'Are you threatening us?'

'We are all threatened by our past,' his father said, turning round from the window. 'You will learn that in time, *musuko*.'

'Nothing that has happened since you arrived in Paris will cause difficulty for us in Tokyo, will it, my lord?' asked Nadia, her tone unaffected by Noburo's intervention.

'No,' Count Tomura replied emphatically. 'Saionji has been luckier than he knows. But it is only a postponement of the reckoning. I hold Hara and most of his ministers in the palm of my hand. And what we bring will enable me to close my fingers around them.' Max saw the fingers of Tomura's left hand curl inwards as he spoke. 'So, how many will you be?'

'Three,' said Nadia.

'Who is the third?'

'His secretary.'

'Ah, so there is someone closer to him than you?'

'I am as close to him as he needs me to be.'

'There is an assurance my father is due,' Noburo said suddenly. 'Why do you not give it?'

'Your father knows it will be done,' came Nadia's unflustered reply.

'Indeed,' said Count Tomura. 'But I will require proof that it has been done.'

'You will—'

Nadia broke off. Someone had entered the suite. Max heard a door close. Words were spoken in Japanese between the newcomer and Noburo.

To Max's horror, a figure appeared in his restricted view, moving past Count Tomura, bowing slightly as he did so. It was the burly factotum, carrying what looked like a suit or overcoat in a cover, complete with hanger.

He walked through the communicating doorway into Noburo's room. Max shrank back, concealing himself in the angle between the door and the bed. The factotum padded across to another door, which he opened. Max heard clothes being parted on a wardrobe rail. He wondered if he should make a run for it, but decided against it. There was still a good chance he could slip out without anyone knowing he had ever been there.

'It is a pity you had to leave Paris earlier than expected,' said Nadia, almost conversationally, stalling, Max assumed, until the factotum had left.

'I am a soldier,' said Count Tomura. 'I adapt to changing circumstances. As does my son.'

'How wise of you.'

'It is also wise of me to employ trustworthy servants. You may speak freely in Ishibashi's presence.'

'I believe I have said all that needs to be said.'

The factotum – Ishibashi – started padding back across the room. Then he stopped. Something had caught his eye. Max saw at once what it was: the coverlet of the bed was ruckled at one corner. Max must have brushed against it on his way to where he was now hiding.

'There must be nothing that can connect me – or my son – to this,' said Tomura. 'I will not provide the necessary introductions unless I am convinced it has been dealt with in a manner that cannot touch us. Is that clear?'

'It is,' said Nadia. 'And it will be so.'

Ishibashi moved into Max's sight. His broad, flat-featured face, in which the eyes were barely visible between folds of flesh, wore a faint frown of dissatisfaction. He bent over the end of the bed and smoothed the coverlet.

'It will be the first and most important test of our alliance,' said Tomura. 'I will not tolerate failure.'

'Nor will he,' said Nadia. 'He never does.'

Ishibashi stood upright. In that instant, he saw Max. And Max knew the game was up. He drew his gun, pushed the door away from him and strode forward, expecting Ishibashi to give ground. Instead, the factotum launched himself bodily at Max, with a bellow of aggression.

They fell onto the bed, Ishibashi grappling for a hold that would enable him to pin Max down. But Max dodged free and clubbed him across the head with the gun. The blow stunned him. With a shove from Max, he slid off the bed onto the floor.

Noboru Tomura ran into the room, followed by his father. Noboru had a gun in his hand. Max lunged across the bed, leapt to his feet on the other side and turned to face them. The Count was armed as well, he saw. Nadia had hurried in behind them.

Max trained his gun on Noboru, but spoke for the Count's benefit. 'I'm not going to take my eyes off your son until I leave this room, Count. One hostile move and I'll kill him.'

'You are outnumbered, Lieutenant Maxted,' stated Count Tomura calmly, levelling his gun at him.

'Noburo will be the first to die. That's certain. For the rest, I'll take my chances.'

The conviction in Max's voice seemed to affect Noburo. Max saw the barrel of the young man's gun trembling.

'Let him go,' said Nadia. 'This should not be settled here.'

'Very well.' Count Tomura's tone was scornful. 'You may go, Lieutenant Maxted.'

'Whatever you're planning, I'll stop you.'

'Will you? Will you really?'

'Where's Lemmer?'

'We will tell you nothing, Max,' said Nadia.

'Won't you?'

'You know we will not.'

And he did. The knowledge angered him. The gun gave him the power to take a life. But it could not help him prise a secret from these people.

No. Not from *these* people. But perhaps from others. An idea had come to him. He said no more, but keeping his gun trained on Noburo he backed slowly out of the room.

He shut the vestibule door behind him, flung open the outer door, holstered his gun and began jogging towards the stairs.

OUT ON THE STREET, THERE WAS NO SIGN OF THE CAR NADIA had arrived in. But Max guessed it was circling and would soon be back. He mingled with a group of people waiting for a taxi, wondering what Nadia and the Tomuras were doing. The situation was riddled with uncertainty. He needed hard information and he needed it now.

A minute or so passed with agonizing slowness. Then the car nosed round the corner from Boulevard Garibaldi, slowing as it approached the hotel's entrance. Max recognized the driver as Meadows.

The car slowed still further as Meadows checked to see if Nadia was waiting to be collected. That was Max's cue. He raced round in front of the car while Meadows' attention was fixed on the hotel entrance, yanked open the rear door and jumped in behind him.

He pressed the barrel of the gun against the back of Meadows' neck. 'Drive straight ahead,' he stated plainly. 'Or I'll do to you what I did to Grattan and Hughes.'

Meadows did not argue. They started away.

'Turn left at the next intersection.'

'Where are we going?'

'Just do as I say.' Max applied a little more pressure to Meadows' neck. 'And speak only when I ask you a question.'

They turned onto Rue de Rome, the main route out of Marseilles to the south-east. Max had no particular destination in mind, but quitting the city appealed to his instincts. Meanwhile, there was information to be extracted from Meadows.

382

'What did Nadia want with Count Tomura?'

'I don't know. I just drove her to the hotel, as instructed.'

'You're going to have to do better than that. Where's Lemmer?'

'I don't know that either. He's not in Marseilles, though. Nadia said he and Anna Schmidt would be arriving tomorrow morning.'

'Are they leaving for Japan with the Tomuras?'

'I haven't been told.'

'*Guess.*'

'Then, yes, I think they are.'

'Why?'

'It'd have to be another guess.'

'Fine.'

'Lemmer's going to sell his network to the Japanese. He tried to make some kind of deal with them during the war. Now he's trying again. Spies in every Western capital? It should be too good for them to refuse.'

'How do you feel about it?'

'Resigned. It's a new world now the war's over. We have to live by its rules.'

'Or die by them.'

'That's you, Max, not me. You won't kill me as long as I do whatever you tell me to do.'

'What makes you so sure?'

'You're too much of a gentleman to be an executioner. You shot down all those German pilots in fair combat, didn't you? And you did for Grattan and Hughes on the same terms. I'm a prisoner of war. The Geneva Convention applies.'

'Not to traitors.'

'You still won't kill me in cold blood. I'm going to outlive you, Max, I guarantee it.'

'We'll see about that.'

'No. *I'll* see. Dead men are blind. And that's what you are: dead. You just don't know it yet.'

Max could not have said whether his contempt for Meadows was greater than Meadows' contempt for him. The wretched man was right in one fundamental: Max had killed a lot of people. But

383

he had never murdered anyone. And he was not about to start.

Still, the gun gave him the upper hand. Meadows had more or less admitted he would not resist. They drove on out of the city, climbing into hilly country through scattered hamlets as the sun sank behind them and the air cooled.

Eventually, Max ordered Meadows to pull off the road. They came to a halt on a stony verge beneath a steep shoulder of wooded land.

'Keep the engine running,' said Max. 'Empty your gun and drop it on the floor. Then empty your pockets as well.'

Meadows obeyed without venturing any comment.

'Get out of the car and walk away from it.'

They emerged together. Meadows took half a dozen slow paces away from the car along the verge. At a word from Max, he stopped.

'Turn round.'

Meadows turned. Max was already pointing the gun at him. 'Tell me, how does a man like you live with himself?'

Meadows shrugged. 'I manage somehow.'

'Your treachery will catch up with you sooner or later.'

'I'm sure it will.'

'What does Lemmer have in mind for me?'

'I don't have conversations with him, Max. He doesn't confide in me. But if you want my opinion, you pose a serious threat to Count Tomura. I don't know why. Maybe you know. I reckon Tomura wants Lemmer to neutralize that threat. It's probably a precondition for Tomura brokering Lemmer's deal with his friends in high places in Japan. You're got rid of. And Tomura has no part in it. His hands stay clean.'

Max had suspected as much from the conversation he had overheard. *'There must be nothing that can connect me – or my son – to this,'* Tomura had said. *'It will be so,'* Nadia had assured him. That was why she had said, *'This should not be settled here.'* Because it was vital Count Tomura and Noburo Tomura should both be able to deny involvement in Max's demise.

'You want my advice as well as my opinion?'

'No. But I'll hear it anyway.'

384

'Run. Get the hell away from here. Lemmer will be banking on you trying to defeat him. That's a fool's game. See sense. Run and hide. It's your only hope.'

'It's a sure way to lose a fight.'

'In the air, maybe. Not down here on the ground. Not this kind of fight.'

'Lemmer didn't corrupt you, did he, Meadows? He just recognized your corruption.'

'Sticks and stones, old boy.'

Max raised the gun and trained it at Meadows' chest.

'You won't do it. You're just not cut out for it.'

'No?'

Meadows shook his head. 'No.'

'You're right. I can't kill a defenceless opponent. But I can slow him down.'

Max lowered the gun, took aim and fired a bullet into Meadows' right foot.

MAX LEFT MEADOWS NURSING A MANGLED FOOT BY THE roadside and drove on through the hills to the fishing village of Cassis, where he found a room for the night and contemplated his situation over *bouillabaisse* and rough red wine.

Meadows' advice was sound enough. He was a marked man. Flight *was* the sane recourse. But his appointment with Dombreux, though it might well be a trap set for him by Lemmer, might also be a heaven-sent opportunity to arm himself against Lemmer. The '*great secret*' could be his grand chance.

Besides, sane or not, flight was ruled out by the pledge he had given Appleby and C. Lemmer had to be stopped. And Max was going to stop him. Or die in the attempt.

He headed out before dawn the following morning. Daylight stole after him on the road back to Marseilles. The country was clear before him. The sky was unbroken blue. It was the day.

He reached the sea again at the racecourse by Prado beach and drove along the shore road past empty bathing stations and deserted promenades. The Corniche led him towards Malmousque, with the Iles du Frioul basking in pale gold early sunlight out in the bay. The Château d'If looked improbably small from where he was, almost a toy castle compared with the vast fortress he had imagined as a boy. Experience had altered the scale of things. It made what he was about to do seem both rational and reasonable. The war had returned to him.

*

The entrance to the Villa Orseis was on the Corniche as Dombreux had said, but the building itself was shielded from view by a high boundary wall, tall trees and another villa closer to the road.

The gate was closed and padlocked. Through its bars, Max could see only parts of the villa's terracotta-tiled roof and cream-washed walls. He scaled the gate, using one of the orb-topped side pillars as a foothold, before clambering down on the other side.

An avenue of plane trees led to the house through a forest of shrubs and bushes long left to run riot. There was no clue as to whether anyone was at home or not. The drive was free of wheel ruts. Birds were singing, but he could hear no human voices. No doors slammed as he approached. No stoutly shod feet crunched on gravel.

The villa was vast, though cramped somehow by its overgrown setting. The roof rose in three tiers, with tall, idiosyncratically shaped chimneys. Beside the pillared porch, a wisteria-swagged pergola ran the length of a lower-storeyed wing. Most of the windows were high and arched, though some on the top floor were square or circular. Max neither saw nor sensed any movement within. An air of melancholy and desertion possessed the place.

He walked up the steps to the front door. He heard the inner latch rise as he turned the handle. The door opened. He went in.

A galleried landing ran round the wide, marble-floored entrance hall. The roof high above was beamed. From it, on a rope thick enough to hold a liner at her mooring, hung an enormous chandelier, shrouded in muslin. The furniture was dust-sheeted. Whatever lives had been led there were now suspended.

Max moved through open double doors into some kind of music-room. Beneath more dust-sheets stood a grand piano and a harp. Fine curtains reduced the light from the vast windows to a grey suffusion. The stillness was tangible.

Then, at last, came a sound that told him he was not alone. A door opened. Footsteps rang on marble. He drew his gun. Another door opened, into the room where he was standing.

'Don't shoot,' said Pierre Dombreux. He walked slowly in, his hands theatrically raised. 'I'm unarmed.'

Any doubt that Dombreux was still alive vanished. Max recognized him at once from the photograph Corinne carried with her, though his appearance was no longer as healthy and carefree. He looked haggard and wary, slightly stooped, his dark hair flecked with grey at the sides. The suit he was wearing had also seen better days. It was rumpled and threadbare.

'Hello, Max.' Dombreux advanced across the room, his hand outstretched. 'It is good to meet you at last.'

Max lowered the gun, but made no move to shake Dombreux's hand. They eyed each other, suspiciously on Max's part, ironically on Dombreux's, to judge by his lopsided smile.

'Thank you for coming.'

'You must have known I would.'

'There is no certainty in the prediction of other people's actions.'

'What's your connection with this house?'

'A good friend of mine inherited it. But he was killed during the last weeks of the war. I believe his cousins are disputing ownership. Meanwhile, I have a set of keys – and my late friend's consent to make use of it.'

'If the authorities knew you were alive . . .'

'They would ensure I did not remain so. But you will not give me up, Max, will you? And nor will Corinne. Where is she?'

'On her way back to Nantes.'

'Good. I am glad. I should have left her in peace. I will now.'

Dombreux threw back a dust-sheet from one end of a low sofa and sat down. He gestured for Max to take one of the nearby arm-chairs. Max did so cautiously, without removing the covering sheet.

'Won't you put your gun down? You're not in danger here.'

'How can I be sure of that?'

'You can't, of course. But I am unarmed.' Dombreux took off the jacket of his suit with a flourish and tossed it down beside him. It was hard to see how any weapon could be concealed about him. Max laid his gun on the shrouded arm of the chair. 'There is no one else here. You have my word. Though I do understand you may not think I can reasonably expect to be taken at my word.'

'Who died in your place in Petrograd?'

'I don't know. There are few luxuries in Russia under the

Bolsheviks. But at least unidentified corpses are readily available.'

'Who do you work for?'

'Myself, of course. From time to time, I've hired out my talents to the Russians and the Germans. Even to the Japanese. And to *la belle France, naturellement*. But none of them owns me.'

'That's a fancy way of admitting you're a traitor to your country.'

'Perhaps I am. But I am not a traitor to your father's memory.'

'Pa never mentioned you to me.'

'Ah, but then there were many things he never mentioned to you, no?' Dombreux flapped his hand apologetically. 'I am sorry. I did not mean to offend you. Your father was a fine man. From what I hear, you are a credit to him.'

'Who have you heard that from?'

'Do the details of how I have survived – who has helped me, who has not – really matter? We are here because of Lemmer and Tomura, Max. We are here because they killed your father and now they have killed Kuroda. Next it will be you. Unless you strike at them first. Unless I give you the *means* to strike at them first.'

'You promised in your letter you'd tell me everything.'

Dombreux nodded. 'I will.'

'According to Corinne you imparted a great secret to Pa while you were in prison in Petrograd.'

'Yes. I did. He did not believe me. He did not want to believe me. I do not blame him. I would not have wanted to in his place. When he learnt in Paris that what I had said was true, he acted as I would have expected him to act: the only way a man of honour could act.'

'What is the secret?'

'I have a letter you should see. Read that first. Then I will tell you the rest. It is from Jack Farngold, sent to your father in Petrograd a year and a half ago. Your father never received it. Lemmer ordered me to intercept it. At that time, I took his orders. That is, I took some of them. I made sure he never obtained the letter himself. Though he knew what it contained, of course. That is certain. Come. Let me show you.'

Dombreux rose and led the way back out through the door he had entered by. Max stood up and followed him.

They crossed a corridor and entered a study. There was a book-case along one wall, draped with a dust-sheet, but a broad desk with a buttoned-leather chair behind it were uncovered. There were several cardboard boxes stacked beside the desk, beyond which French windows gave onto a terrace, where the flagstones were sharply divided between sunlight and shadow. In front of the windows was a dust-sheeted object on a triangular stand. Max did not know what it was: a telescope, perhaps.

'The letter is in the file.' Dombreux pointed to a folder lying in the middle of the desk. 'Please sit down and read it.' He stood back to let Max pass.

Max rounded the desk and flipped the folder open as he lowered himself into the chair. The first thing he saw inside was a frayed manila envelope, addressed to *Sir Henry Maxted, British Embassy, Dvortsovaya Naberezhnaya, Petrograd, Soviet Russia.* It bore a muddy green stamp, illegibly franked, and jottings in different hands in both Japanese and Russian, as well as a single word in Russian rubber-stamped in red.

Beneath the envelope, still folded to fit into it, was the letter itself. Max opened it out. There was no address at the top, though there was a scrawled date: *6.X.17.*

Sir Henry, it began, *you and I have never met, although I have—*

Max felt a sudden stabbing pain in the back of his neck just above his collar. In the fraction of a second it took him to realize Dombreux had moved out of his sight while he was concentrating on the letter and was now behind him, all his energy seemed to drain from him like water from an emptying basin. He managed a half-turn, sufficient for him to glimpse the syringe in Dombreux's hand. Then he slumped back in the chair and began to slide help-lessly out of it.

Dombreux discarded the syringe and gently lowered Max to the floor. He lifted the chair clear and looked down at him. Max could neither move nor speak. He lay where he was, his left shoulder propped against one leg of the desk. He was aware of a twitching in his limbs, but he could not stop it. His mouth had sagged open, but he could not close it.

Dombreux knelt beside him. 'Can you follow my movements,

Max?' he asked, pulling open one of the desk drawers. Max watched as he reached inside and took out a gun. 'Good. You're conscious and the muscles of your eyes are still working. Most of your other muscles are paralysed. Nadia is a good chemist, isn't she? Now, the paralysis will not last very long, so I regret I cannot delay.'

Dombreux sat back on his heels, stretched out his free hand and pulled the dust-sheet off what Max had thought was a telescope. He saw now that it was a camera on a tripod.

'I am sorry, Max. I have personally nothing against you. But I am tired of running and hiding. Lemmer will give me a new identity and a new, wealthy life a long way from here in return for what I am going to do. Your death has to be arranged so that it cannot be traced to him or Tomura, you see. There can be nothing that would make your family – particularly your mother – think you were murdered. It must have an explanation that is . . . complete. And it will. Under one of the dust-sheets in the drawing-room the police will find the body of William MacGregor, shot through the head with a bullet from the gun I am holding. This villa is rented in your name. The name you used in Orkney, that is: Hutton. MacGregor tracked you here and accused you of the murder of Selwyn Henty. You killed him. But you realized you would not get away with it. And you were distraught because Corinne had rejected you. There are unframed canvases from Raffaele Spataro's studio here as well. Nude drawings of Corinne. It does not matter whether he drew them from life or his imagination. They will make you seem . . . *dérangé*, as we say. Good, no? Thorough, I think. Altogether . . . convincing.'

Dombreux leant closer. 'No one will believe Corinne if she says I am still alive. They will think she is mad. They will think you were mad too. Your suicide will confirm it. Lemmer needs proof you are dead, though. Proof he can show Tomura before they sail today. That is what the camera is for. I will take photographs of you after you have shot yourself through the head. Now . . .'

Dombreux folded Max's limp right hand round the gun and lifted it, carefully bending Max's elbow. 'You see how easy this is, Max? It will be fast. And with the drug inside you, it will be nearly painless. The letter from Jack Farngold *is* genuine. But you will never read it.'

Max felt the barrel of the gun pressing into his temple and his index finger being folded round the trigger.

He had always feared dying in a flying accident, as too many RFC pilots had, rather than in combat. It would have been both stupid and futile, a waste of his life as well as a good aeroplane. What was about to happen to him was similar in its unfittingness – and in the shame he felt on account of it. He had failed. He had fallen short. He had made a fatal mistake.

It could not be helped. At least, as when things went disastrously wrong in the air, it would end quickly. There was that to be said for it at any rate.

'We are ready, yes?' Dombreux nodded in evident satisfaction with his handiwork, then drew back and grimaced as he began to squeeze Max's finger against the trigger. '*Adieu,*' he murmured.

A click sounded in Max's ear. Then . . .

TO BE CONCLUDED

AUTHOR'S NOTE

As in the first volume in this trilogy, *The Ways of the World*, I have altered none of the recorded history of the Paris Peace Conference of 1919. Real people, places and events have been depicted as accurately as possible. In the writing of *The Corners of the Globe*, I have benefited greatly from the researches of Geoffrey Stell into Orkney's military past, published as *Orkney at War: Defending Scapa Flow*, and from the material held at the Orkney Library & Archive in Kirkwall. I have also been greatly aided in imagining Marseilles as it was in 1919 by the many wonderful photographs taken of the city around that time by Fernand and Albert Detaille.